Praise for
ELIZABETH LOWELL
and

DIE IN
PLAIN
SIGHT

"Romantic suspense is her true forte."
Minneapolis Star-Tribune

"An artful tale of . . . romance and suspense . . .
[with] likable characters blessed with Lowell's
knack for witty and enjoyable dialogue."
Grand Forks Herald

"Lowell's keen ear for dialogue and
intuitive characterizations consistently
set her a cut above most writers in this genre."
Charlotte News & Observer

"Engaging . . . enjoyable . . . [a] high concept plot."
Publishers Weekly

"Lowell manages to balance the right amount
of intrigue, romance, and research. . . .
[Her] characters come alive."
Columbia State

"I'll buy any book with Elizabeth Lowell's name on it."
Jayne Ann Krentz

By Elizabeth Lowell

AMBER BEACH • DIAMOND TIGER
DIE IN PLAIN SIGHT • JADE ISLAND
MIDNIGHT IN RUBY BAYOU
MOVING TARGET • PEARL COVE
THE RUBY • RUNNING SCARED
SECRET SISTERS

AUTUMN LOVER • BEAUTIFUL DREAMER
DESERT RAIN • EDEN BURNING
ENCHANTED • FORBIDDEN
FORGET ME NOT • LOVER IN THE ROUGH
ONLY HIS • ONLY LOVE
ONLY MINE • ONLY YOU
REMEMBER SUMMER • THIS TIME LOVE
TO THE ENDS OF THE EARTH • UNTAMED
WHERE THE HEART IS • WINTER FIRE
A WOMAN WITHOUT LIES

And in Hardcover

THE COLOR OF DEATH

ELIZABETH LOWELL

DIE IN PLAIN SIGHT

AVON BOOKS

An Imprint of HarperCollinsPublishers

This is a work of fiction. Names, characters, places, and incidents are products of the author's imagination or are used fictitiously and are not to be construed as real. Any resemblance to actual events, locales, organizations, or persons, living or dead, is entirely coincidental.

AVON BOOKS
An Imprint of HarperCollins*Publishers*
10 East 53rd Street
New York, New York 10022-5299

Copyright © 2003 by Two of a Kind, Inc.
Excerpt from *The Color of Death* copyright © 2004 by Two of a Kind, Inc.
ISBN: 0-06-050411-0
www.avonbooks.com

First Avon Books paperback printing: June 2004
First William Morrow hardcover printing: July 2003

Avon Trademark Reg. U.S. Pat. Off. and in Other Countries, Marca Registrada, Hecho en U.S.A.
HarperCollins® is a registered trademark of HarperCollins Publishers Inc.

Printed in the U.S.A.

10 9 8 7 6 5 4 3 2 1

To the Voglesong family,

Whose complex journey through the little-known disease called GS/FAP has inspired more people than they know

 **Prologue**

With each stabbing, slashing stroke, the painting took shape in violent shadows and searing spurts of water like screams flung against the night. But the woman in the painting couldn't scream.

A blunt masculine hand had forced her head under the steamy surface of the spa. Blond hair floated like golden light on the seething water. Her right hand raked a scarlet trail across her murderer's forearm. Something on her wrist sparkled against the overwhelming blackness swirling around her, devouring her life.

She was just one more to die in plain sight and never be seen. One more to fall prey to what the tabloids called the Savoy Curse.

Pausing, he glanced at the other paintings lined up in a bleak row along the studio wall for comparison. He deftly adjusted the shade of blond in the new canvas, intensified the contrast of darkness and diamonds, added a blood-red moon reflection, and set aside his brushes without signing his name. He would send this one naked.

That was rare.

That was part of the fun, keeping everyone off-balance. Making them nervous. Making them wonder if the next one would be sent to them, the press, or the police.

They shouldn't have killed you, dancing girl. You were mine. I can't kill them for you, but I can make them pay. And pay.

And pay . . .

If there is a God in heaven, they will live in hell.

With a bleak smile he looked at the calendar. He didn't need to see the death date in order to remember it, but looking at the brittle page was part of the ritual, part of the revenge. He painted the month and day in blood-red, circled it, and closed his eyes.

Burn in hell, you bastards.

Burn.

1

Lacey Quinn looked around her parents' gracefully remodeled old Pasadena home and gave herself a moment to prepare for the coming storm. Her mother and father were enjoying a sun-dappled weekend brunch in the garden room. Lacey had driven over from the coast and dropped in without warning, figuring it would be easier to tell them that way.

Now she wasn't so sure.

"Remember that art auction benefit for the Friends of Moreno County I mentioned last time I was here?" Lacey asked.

Her mother made a noise that said she was listening despite the boring subject. Although charity benefits were Dottie Quinn's meat and drink, her daughter's relentless interest in art baffled Dottie as much as it irritated her. Except at the very high end of the trade, art was indelibly messy; she preferred life well ordered and tasteful.

"What about it?" her father asked.

Part of Lacey wanted to drop the subject. The rest of her tensed for a fight. "In addition to bringing two of her paintings for a showing, Susa Donovan is going to paint a canvas onstage and then auction it off right there, with the money going to Friends of Moreno County."

Coward, sneered her inner self. *You didn't drive all the way from the beach just to announce that.*

Brody Quinn grunted, shuffled the legal papers he was reading, and said, "That's nice."

"Nice?" Lacey put her paint-stained hands on her equally paint-stained jeans. "Dad, even postcard-size paintings by La Susa sell for more than a quarter of a million a canvas."

"So she gets a nice write-off giving one to charity," Brody said. "So what?"

"In addition to donating the painting," Lacey said through her teeth, "she has generously agreed to look at any old paintings people bring in. Sort of like *Antiques Roadshow.*"

"Clever idea," Dottie said instantly. "Everyone is sure they have a treasure hidden away in the family junk, so there should be a huge turnout and lots of press for the event. Excellent approach. I'll put it to work for my next charity auction. I'll even use the name of your little shop, Lost Treasures Found."

Lacey managed not to wince. Her shop wasn't huge, but it kept her and her partner, Shayla Carlyle, employed and paying taxes while they scoured estate sales and craft fairs both local and distant for stock.

Figuring the conversation no longer needed to include him, Brody went back to the legal brief he was reading.

"The point is," Lacey started, when she got distracted by a lock of her curly hair springing free of the clip she used to tame the chestnut mass. "Damn!" Automatically she jammed curls back in place and reset the clip.

"If you'd just have it cut short and styled, dear, it would be easier to control," Dottie said.

"Then I'd have to do it every few weeks."

"And?"

"The point is, it only costs twenty dollars a painting to have Susa look at them."

Dottie adjusted to the changed subject without a pause. "Even better. All money donated, yes?"

"Yes, and I'm going to take three paintings in for her to see," Lacey finished in a rush.

"I'm sure she'll be quite kind to you," Dottie said. "After all, she has family of her own, I believe. Didn't *High Style* magazine mention six children and various grandchildren?"

"Not my own paintings," Lacey said, setting her teeth. "Granddad's."

A legal brief slammed down on the patio table as Brody stood up. The family cat shot out from under Brody's chair and vanished into the lush undergrowth of the garden.

"All over again," Brody said. "From the beginning."

Lacey's chin came up. "You have a good legal mind. Do I really need to repeat it?"

"What you need to do is convince me that I shouldn't—"

"Not again, Dad. We've had this argument so many times we could speak each other's lines. For whatever reasons, you think your father's paintings aren't worth wall space. I do. I think he is—was—" She swallowed.

His death two years ago was still fresh for her, still hurtful. Sometimes she still thought she saw him from the corner of her eye or across the street or turning down the aisle of the grocery store. "Grandfather was a very fine artist, equal to if not better than any of the California Plein Air Impressionists that are hanging in museums on both coasts. I believe in him. *He believed in me.*"

"Honey, I'm sure your father—" Dottie began.

Lacey kept talking. "Without my grandfather I'd be trying to be something I'm not, a society woman instead of an artist. I don't ask you to support my choices with money or hugs. But, damn it, don't act like I need your permission, either. He left the paintings to me, not you. He died before I understood how much he meant to me. The least I can do is try to resurrect him from undeserved anonymity as an artist."

"Still dying to do *David Quinn: Biography of an Unknown Artist?*" Brody asked.

"I want to know where I came from. I love my family, but I don't fit in. My sisters do." She grinned wryly at her mother. "Two out of three ain't bad, right?"

"Lacey," her mother said, hugging her. "We love you."

"And I love both of you," she said, returning the hug. "But that doesn't mean we're the same kind of people. The older I get, the more like myself I get and the less like either of you. Grandpa Rainbow understood that. He understood me at a time when it meant . . . everything. Now I want the world to understand how great he really was."

Brody sat down at the table and put his head in his hands. *What a royal mess.* But all he said aloud was, "Okay, you want to find out all about your beloved grandfather, my father, who was as self-absorbed a bastard as ever came down the road." He looked up at his baffling daughter. "You're the only one he really noticed, you know. He just tolerated the rest of us."

Lacey didn't know what to say.

"He wasn't a nice man," Brody said finally. "Finding out more about him won't help you, but it sure could make you sad. Leave it alone, Lacey. Some people aren't what you want them to be."

"He was an extraordinary artist," she said stubbornly. "I'm sorry he wasn't a good father or husband, but . . ."

"You're going to do it anyway."

She nodded. "That's why he left everything to me. Even though he never signed a painting, he knew the value of his art. So did I. You didn't."

After a moment Brody said, "What happens if this fancy painter at the auction doesn't see anything special in my father's paintings?"

"I'd be shocked."

"I wouldn't. If ever a man deserved obscurity, he did."

Lacey smiled sadly. "Art and deserving don't go together much. Look at history."

Brody didn't have to. He had his own problems. The less the world knew about his reprobate father, the better. A man bucking for a judicial appointment didn't need any skeletons crawling out of the family closet.

"Lacey," he said slowly, "I ask you again. Leave it alone."

"I'm sorry, Dad. I can't. But don't worry, I've made sure that I'll be anonymous, so you won't need to worry about . . ." She paused, then shrugged. "You know, the wrong kind of publicity for you when you're at a crucial point in your career."

"Anonymous," her father said. "I don't understand."

"Grandfather never signed his paintings, so we don't have to worry about that. Instead of bringing the canvases under my name or my store's name, I taped an e-mail address to the back of the canvases as a contact number. The address is a new one under an invented name, January Marsh. And if anyone manages to track me down despite that and asks where I got the paintings, I'll just say I found them at a garage sale. Given my line of work, it's an obvious way to account for my possession of Granddad's art."

Brody made a sound that could have meant anything, then let it go. If she was wrong about her grandfather's genius, this would all die a quiet death. If she wasn't . . .

Well, he'd burn that bridge when he came to it.

2

Ian Lapstrake hadn't been raised by fools. When Dana Gaynor, copartner of Rarities Unlimited, started in on him with a voice like an ice-tipped whip, he stood up straight and paid attention.

"Listen, boyo," she said, borrowing one of her partner S. K. Niall's favorite nouns, "I'm getting damn tired of you ignoring your e-mail. How are we supposed to keep you up-to-date on your projects?"

"I always have my pager turned on."

"Screw your pager."

"I'm not that desperate yet, but thanks for the thought."

Dana glared at Ian's dark eyes and gentle trust-me smile. She opened her mouth to tear a strip off him, but snickered instead. He looked as innocent as a puppy.

He wasn't.

"You and Niall," she said, shaking her head. "I always end up laughing when I should be furious."

That wasn't quite the truth, but Ian knew better than to point it out. The times when Dana had *not* ended up laughing were vivid in his memory, like a fresh brand.

She watched him with eyes as dark as his own and said simply, "I've been trying to get in touch with you. The Donovan is worried."

"Kidnap threat?" Ian asked instantly.

"No one is threatening to steal Susa and ransom her for a few mil," Dana said. "Your job is to be real visible so that it stays that way."

"So he wants a guard for her, not her paintings."

"As her husband, the Donovan, put it, Susa can create more paintings but no number of paintings can create more Susa."

Ian smiled. "A man with priorities."

Dana all but winced. "And not shy about sharing them. Normally one of the Donovan men would be traveling with Susa, but . . ." she shrugged. "Sometimes a husband, four sons, and two sons-in-law just aren't enough to go around."

"What are friends for?" Ian said, accepting the quiet assignment with grace. "One strapping gofer coming right up. What about the Lazarro icon shipment?"

"Niall's problem, not yours."

"The Kenworth scrolls?"

"Belong to Mary."

"The possible Louis Fourteenth—"

"As of now," Dana interrupted, "Susa Donovan is your full-time assignment. Your other projects have been parceled out."

Ian grinned. "You're really determined to get all the

Donovans into the Rarities Unlimited fold, aren't you?"

"Haven't the faintest idea what you're talking about." Dana winked and walked away. "Check your e-mail for details of where and when you pick up Susa this afternoon."

Ian watched the smooth locomotion of Dana's hips with a male appreciation that didn't need to fondle in order to enjoy. Then he shoved his hands in the pockets of his slacks and headed for the coffee machine. Right now it looked like caffeine was going to be the only excitement in his life until Susa Donovan's big charity bash was over.

That and checking e-mail.

Savoy Ranch
Southern California
Tuesday morning

3

Even the stately colors and textures of Ward Forrest's big dining room couldn't soothe him this morning. Watched by the worried brown eyes of Honey Bear, his golden retriever, Ward was up and pacing the Persian rug. He avoided the antique furniture without even seeing it, and didn't spare a glance to the paintings of founding ancestors. They weren't his anyway, as his dead wife had taken great pleasure in pointing out. Even if the paintings had been of his blood kin, he would have ignored them. Right now he was riding a real hard mean.

He hadn't run a profitable land-based empire into the twenty-first century by being sweet-tempered and churchgoing. Hell, in all his seventy-odd years, no one had expected him to act like a sugar cookie.

Until now.

Angelique White was a pain in the ass. Too bad she held the future of Savoy Ranch in her pious little fist.

Talk about a Savoy Curse. Christ. There was one for the supermarket headlines.

"God damn all women to hell anyway."

Honey Bear thumped his tail enthusiastically at the sound of Ward's voice.

Rory Turner, sheriff of Moreno County and Ward's former son-in-law, looked up from the report he'd brought to the ranch house. Unlike Ward, who was dressed to go pheasant hunting, Rory was in uniform, right down to side arm and hat.

"What are you talking about?" Rory asked.

"Saint Angelique makes Mother Teresa look like a party girl."

The ripe disgust in the older man's voice made Rory want to laugh, but he knew better. Ward had really wanted some dirt on the CEO of New Horizons, who happened to be the only daughter of a televangelist and a Savannah socialite. NH was a cash-rich investment fund looking to diversify by building communities with "room for family, community, church, and God." Savoy Ranch had been courting NH and Angelique for ten months, but every time it got down to signing papers, something happened. Blissy, usually. His daughter had a genius for hitting the headlines at all the wrong times. Or one of his grandkids would be on TV spouting something offensive to somebody—Christians, usually—and Angelique would draw back.

Each time she backed away, she screwed another concession out of Ward before she returned to the bargaining table. She might spend a lot of time in dim places with her head bowed while she talked to the air, but she was one of the coldest negotiators he'd ever sat across the table from.

"Well, she's as near to sainthood as anyone I've ever

investigated," Rory agreed, tossing the report on the table in front of Ward's empty chair. "No lovers of either sex, no drugs, no booze, no bad loans or overdrawn accounts or maxed credit cards. No tickets or outstanding warrants. She tithes regularly and goes to church twice a week. Dresses well, and why shouldn't she? She can afford it. She runs the family business and does it damned well. Pays all her taxes and then some. Drives her accountants and lawyers nuts demanding that they stay cleaner than clean. Doesn't even break the frigging leash law with her dogs."

Ward scooped up the report and read the summary. "Jesus. The woman really should have been a nun."

Living up on that kind of high moral plane—or even appearing to—was a tightrope act and the Forrest family couldn't afford to fall. The merger had to go through. If it didn't, Savoy Ranch would be just one more big family ranch holding nibbled to death by taxes, environmentalists, and generational incompetence.

Not that he was worried about incompetence. Blissy and Savoy might have control of Savoy Enterprises, but their daddy still held the purse strings. After he was dead they could piss it away—if they could get around his lawyers—but by God they wouldn't fuck it up while he was alive to see it.

"Keep digging," he said to Rory. "We've got a little time until the final negotiations. Get me just one handful of mud on Saint Angelique and I'll sit down at the table with real pleasure."

"You better have a fallback position," Rory said bluntly. "Getting dirt on her isn't looking likely."

"You do your job. I'll do mine."

Corona del Mar
Tuesday

4

Lacey Quinn stood in the middle of her partner's large storage unit and wondered how she could ever select only three out of the hundreds of her grandfather's powerful paintings. So much depended on finding the right ones, the best, for Susa Donovan to appraise.

But choosing just wasn't possible. *Maybe I misread the rules,* Lacey thought hopefully. She glanced at the flyer in her hand. Nothing had changed. The paper still discreetly insisted NO MORE THAN THREE PAINTINGS PER PATRON, PLEASE.

"Damn," she muttered.

"Now what?" Shayla Carlyle asked from the other side of the room.

Lacey started. She'd forgotten that her business partner and old friend was with her. Painting—and paintings—had that effect on Lacey's brain, as people had pointed out more than once. Guiltily, she looked over her shoulder. Shayla was sitting cross-legged on the cement floor, price stickers clinging like confetti to her black bike tights and red sweatshirt. Her sleek laptop computer balanced uneasily on her long legs as she updated prices and inventory for their shop. That was work Lacey should be doing, or at least helping with.

"Oh, I just was hoping I'd read the pamphlet wrong," she muttered.

Shayla glanced up. "Huh?"

"The charity auction. They only let you bring three paintings for Susa Donovan to look at and I can't get past these six."

Shayla bent over the computer again. "I don't blame you. I like all your paintings."

"Not mine. Grandfather Quinn's."

"You're better than he is."

"You're sweet, but you're no judge of art."

"I know what I like, and it's your paintings I like. So there. Sue me for lewd and dissolute taste."

Laughing, shaking her head, Lacey turned back to the six Quinn canvases and rearranged them yet again. Maybe this time a different angle of light would reveal flaws or flatness or slightly skewed compositions— anything to put three paintings out of the running.

Five of the six paintings were solidly in the tradition of southern California Impressionism, lyrical yet muscular evocations of a landscape that had long since gone down beneath D9 Caterpillars and belly dumps gouging out pads for upper-class McMansions overlooking the ocean. *Sandy Cove* was a case in point. The paintings done by her grandfather showed a landscape more than fifty years in the past. There were golden beaches with no human footprints, coastal bluffs with no houses. The ravines were green with grass from winter rain and graceful with eucalyptus trees dancing in the breeze, instead of the modern cement culverts lined with chain-link fences.

Whether David Quinn painted coastal mountains, beaches, grasslands, or chaparral canyons, most of the canvases celebrated southern California before the huge population leap at the end of World War II. The land was filled with light and distance and clean air.

Then there were his other paintings, the ones that Lacey could admire professionally but wouldn't hang in her own home to be part of her life. Perhaps a tenth of his work was in the dark, brooding school of social realism that had supplanted the plein air painters after the Depression. Not that Quinn's bleak canvases really fit in that category, either. There wasn't any handy art history label for the grim side of her grandfather's talent.

The Death Suite.

Her artistic conscience wanted her to include a painting from each of the three kinds of death—fire, water, and earth/car wreck—but she hadn't been able to bring herself to do it. She'd settled on one of the water paintings with its chilling contrast of blood-red scream, blond hair, turquoise water, and inky night. The figure's humanity was clearly visible, the death struggle intimate and terrifying.

With a sigh, Lacey kept on trying to pick the three best paintings out of the six she'd set aside. She rearranged them, leaning two against the big fire extinguishers that she insisted be kept in the storage area. Her grandfather's phobia about fire in the studio or storage room had been thoroughly drilled into her.

When the silence got to Shayla again, she stretched her back and looked over at her friend. As always,

Lacey's hair was a glorious whirl of cinnamon-colored chin-length loose curls, the kind women with straight hair would kill for. The rest of the package was equally casual—faded jeans, sandals, no socks, and a flannel shirt that could have come from one of the garage sales both women haunted, looking for new merchandise for their shop. Old paint stains made startling patterns on both shirt and jeans.

Then Shayla noticed the six paintings lined up. "Hon, you aren't going to show *that* one in public, are you?"

Lacey jumped again, having forgotten again that she wasn't alone. She looked at the dark, savage painting. "I don't know."

"It creeps me out."

"That's what it's meant to do. That's what makes it so good."

"Well, yippee-skippy. Give it to a horror museum or the public morgue. Should fit right in. How many of those damn things did he paint anyway?"

"I don't know," Lacey said. "I inherited thirty of the dark ones, but they're numbered one through forty-seven. So my grandfather either sold, gave away, or destroyed the seventeen missing paintings. Or some combination of the three. The man was nothing if not unpredictable."

"I'm voting for destroyed."

Lacey sighed and swept her hand through her unruly cloud of curls. "I'm not. Even though the subject matter of the paintings isn't exactly warm and cuddly—"

Shayla snorted. "Ya think?"

Lacey ignored her "—the Death Suite—"

"Now there's a name to draw little children."

"—is nothing short of brilliant," Lacey finished loudly.

"What about the others? Just because they don't make you want to scream, does that mean they're not good?"

"Of course not. The landscapes have the same emotion and energy and finesse as the bleak paintings. Quinn painted light and dark, yin and yang, heaven and hell with equal skill and emotion."

"Maybe he was bipolar," Shayla said, bending over her inventory again.

"Could be. My dad said as much once. But I think my grandfather was simply a gifted artist who was able to create both sin and salvation with equal power."

"Give me heaven every time."

"Hey, I didn't say I was going to hang any of the Death Suite in my apartment. But that doesn't make those paintings bad. Just uncomfortable to live with."

"Uncomfortable. Yeah. The way a bed of razor blades is uncomfortable."

Lacey ignored her friend and went back to staring at the six canvases. *Well, Grandpa Rainbow,* she thought, using the nickname she'd given him for the paint splatters on his clothes, *you've given me an impossible job. I've been hovering over these six paintings forever, and they all still look equally good to me.*

She turned the paintings to a wall, shuffled them like a con artist moving a pea beneath walnut shells, and then picked three paintings at random. The first one portrayed breakers foaming on the beach and the ocean in every shade of blue and green imaginable. The rocky cliffs were darkly textured, a solid masculine presence against the fluidly feminine sea. Though no people appeared in the painting, Lacey loved the canvas for its sheer sensuality, almost sexual in its impact.

"Now that one is worth looking at," Shayla said.

For the third time, Lacey jumped.

Both women laughed.

"Score one for blind chance," Lacey said, pleased that *Sandy Cove* would be one of the three she presented to Susa Donovan.

"What else is going with it?" Shayla said.

"Don't know yet." Lacey reached out to the second of the three blindly selected paintings. "Let's find out."

The second painting was an untitled portrait of eucalyptus trees silhouetted against sunrise. The shadowed, textured masculine strength of the trees stood in stark contrast to the fluid, multicolored sigh of dawn. Again, the near tangible sensuality of the painting left Lacey with the feeling of having been stroked by a lover who savored the difference between male and female.

"Excellent choice," Shayla said dryly, like a waiter approving a dinner selection. "Or is it just that it's been a long dry spell in the XY department for me?"

"Does it really seem that sexy to you?"

Shayla fanned herself. "Your granddaddy might have been twisted, but he knew that a woman's mind is her most erogenous zone. Probably because when it comes to sex, a woman's imagination is always better than reality."

Lacey made a face. "I hear you. I never started out to spend my life alone, but men keep changing my mind. After some of the specimens we've known, being single looks real good." With a shrug for the state of manhood in modern America, she added, "Give me a good painting any day. Speaking of which . . ."

She reached for the third painting and turned it around.

Scream Bloody Murder.

Shayla grimaced and went back to her stickers.

"Um," Lacey said, her brown eyes intent on the canvas. "Maybe not. It's brilliant, no doubt, but this is a charity event and . . ."

Her voice trailed off. The savage, almost abstract whirl of turquoise water and black night, pale hair and blood-red mouth distorted in a death cry stunned Lacey each time she saw it. It made her stomach clench as if she'd stumbled onto a murder scene too late to do anything but close the eyes of the dead.

Art, like humanity, wasn't always kind.

"Do you think he really saw that?" Shayla asked reluctantly, drawn in spite of herself to the raw reality of the painting.

"I think he dreamed it."

"They call those kind of dreams nightmares."

Lacey couldn't argue that. "But anyone who can look at this and not feel something doesn't deserve to be called human."

"Some really sorry pieces of mobile protein are called human." Shayla turned away from the painting. "It's too real. The difference between being able to imagine something that violent and actually doing it seems small enough to make me nervous."

Lacey didn't answer. Part of her had always wondered if her grandfather—who always painted from life "en plein air"—had once seen violent death. But most of her really didn't want to know what his inspiration had been.

Maybe that was what her father had meant when he told her: *Leave it alone, Lacey. Some people aren't what you want them to be.*

Southern California
Tuesday afternoon

5

Glass walls on all sides of Savoy Tower's penthouse conference room showed the colorful sprawl of Moreno County's high-tech industrial parks, world-class shopping centers, skeins of freeways, and subdivisions that ranged from six-bedroom McMansions to luxury beach condos for the itinerant and truly rich. Low mountains, chaparral-choked canyons, rolling hills where white-faced cattle grazed, citrus groves, strawberry fields, marinas, and a few highly endangered saltwater marshes were interlaced like fingers through the various developments. Bounded by mountains to the northeast and ocean to the southwest, the Savoy Ranch was both fulcrum and lever of a power that reached to the state governor and the United States Senate, and had a hefty down payment on the present vice president.

The portrait above the head of the sleek cherry conference table was as imposing as the view: old man

Benford Savoy himself, the merchant who had made a fortune selling twelve-dollar eggs and thirty-dollar women to forty-niners. Mining gold from other men's pockets was a lot easier than crouching in icy water and panning for gold from "can see to can't see."

Benford had taken the gold and bought up an old Spanish land grant. Land and wealth had passed from generation to Savoy generation for almost one hundred years without a hitch. Said hitch was the third generation's bride, Sandra Wheaten Savoy, who had the gall to leave part of her Savoy inheritance to her sister's children. It was an irritant to have someone "not of the blood" sit on the board of Savoy, Inc., but when the cause was important enough, those of proper Savoy blood unbent enough to acknowledge their shirttail Pickford cousins.

Another hitch in the proud Savoy tradition occurred in that same generation. Benford Savoy III, called Three by his close friends, had the bad fortune to beget a daughter rather than a son for his one and only child. The next best thing to a son was to have his daughter marry the son of an old friend. Gem Savoy and Ward Forrest duly tied the knot. And if they didn't live happily ever after, they multiplied in a way their parents and grandparents hadn't. Four children came along in short order. Two of them contracted severe cases of Moonie religion and were completely excised from the family. Not even cards at birthdays or Christmas.

That left the much married Bliss and her younger brother, Savoy, to play tug-of-war with the family fortunes. Bliss's interest in running the family business was erratic. When she was between husbands and/or lovers, she meddled in her brother's business life and ignored her three grown children. Savoy managed to keep his marriages to two and his offspring to three.

The six cousins weren't present at today's important meeting for the simple reason that as long as Bliss and Savoy lived, corporate control was theirs. Like their own father, Savoy and Bliss were very much alive. The Savoy Curse of accidental death hadn't visited them, probably because they weren't as reckless as some of their ancestors.

The chair at the head of the conference table was empty when the door at the far end of the room opened. With a nod here and a word of greeting there, Savoy Forrest walked confidently to the waiting chair. His dark blond hair was like his clothes—casual, expensively cut, and hinting of the sun that flooded southern California's saints and sinners with equal light and warmth.

Bliss closed the book she'd been reading, *Powerful Women in the Twenty-first Century*, and glanced at her solid gold digital watch, which she always wore with the gold-and-diamond heart design bracelet she'd inherited from her mother along with a diamond necklace that showed well at the opera. "You're seven minutes and forty-four seconds late."

"Thanks, Blissy," he said, putting a thick folder on the table. "I gave the governor your best regards."

"Fuck her."

"She'd be one of the few you've missed," Rory Turner said.

"Fuck you."

"Been there, done that, remember?"

"No," Bliss said. "Was it good for you?"

The rest of the people around the conference table sighed, shifted, or looked impatient, depending on their mood. In addition to being sheriff of Moreno County, Rory was one of Bliss's four ex-husbands. The other three had taken their money and run for more welcoming pastures. Rory hadn't. The two of them fought more now than they had when they were married. But since this was family rather than civil business, Rory had changed into a suit and tie and left the khaki uniform at his office.

"Thanks for the update," Savoy said ironically to the two of them. "Can we keep it above the belt while we take care of business?"

Rory shrugged and smiled. "Sorry. Old habits and all that."

Bliss ignored her ex-husband. She'd had a lot of experience doing that, as Rory had worked for her father before, during, and after their marriage. Ward Forrest had never quite forgiven her for divorcing Rory, "the only one of the lot with balls." She had to admit that the sheriff did indeed have an impressive pair, but he never used them on her behalf outside of sex. *Yes sir* was all he ever said to his father-in-law. It was pretty much the same when it came to her brother, too.

What was the point of having a badge and a gun if all you did was kiss ass?

Savoy looked around the table. As always, at least one of the Pickford arm of the "family" was present. Sandra Wheaten Savoy's nephew Steven the accountant or his son Jason the lawyer didn't miss a meeting, or a trick, when it came to making sure that the Pickfords' fifteen percent of the action produced every possible dime of money. Today it was Steven who waited to argue pennies, his eyes and pencils sharp, calculator at the ready.

Also present and ready to fight were the Savoy

Sharks, the two New York lawyers who kept minutes, digital recordings, and score at every Savoy Enterprises meeting. The men had names, but only Savoy remembered them. To the rest of the family, lawyers were as interchangeable as they were important.

"Sorry to keep you waiting," Savoy said to them.

Both lawyers smiled graciously. They were on retainer and Savoy Forrest was the man who signed their checks.

"The governor wanted to know if she could count on our support for her re-election," Savoy continued, looking around the table. "I assured her that she could."

Bliss made a rude noise and smoothed her hair, which was several shades of blond and cost four hundred bucks a month to keep that way. She resented the governor because she kissed Savoy's ass instead of hers. But then, so did everyone else at the table except Pickford. He was simply a pain in everyone's ass. He liked the governor well enough, though. She'd quietly pushed some amendments through the state legislature that resulted in a tax windfall for Savoy Ranch—and thus for the Pickfords' fifteen percent. The vice president of the United States was trying to do the same for the Savoy Ranch at the federal level.

"Now, for the first item of business," Savoy said, shuffling through the soft leather folder in front of him and pulling out papers. "You know how honored the Savoy-Forrest family is that the Savoy California Impressionist Museum has been selected to receive the—"

"Christ," Pickford said loudly, "is this going to cost us more money? At last count you'd spent twenty million of our corporate money building a museum and acquiring so-called art for your private collection of—"

"Not private," cut in one of the Savoy Sharks. "The museum is a tax-exempt, nonprofit organization funded and run by Savoy Enterprises for the cultural enrichment of the community, county, state, and nation. The museum is open to the public on a regular, published basis and—"

"Spare me the legal bullshit," Pickford said over the lawyer's words. "Everyone knows that Savoy Forrest and his daddy pick all the paintings and some of them hang in the Savoy Museum Wednesday through Saturday. Only fifteen paintings are on display at any one time, and you've got more than two hundred of the things. If that isn't private use of Savoy Enterprises money, it sure as hell looks like it to me."

"Your legal opinion didn't hold up in court," one lawyer said coolly, shooting his cuff.

"Only because Savoy Forrest owns the bench and the honorable ass on it."

"Thank you for your input, as always," Rory said. "Do drive safely and well within the speed limit on your way home."

Pickford shifted his suit coat and shut up for the moment.

Savoy reached out, checked his sister's watch, and said, "Almost thirty seconds without an argument. A new record. My compliments, Steven."

Rory snickered.

Bliss bit her lip against a smile. Savoy knew just how to jerk the Pickford chain and look innocent as an egg while doing it.

Savoy lit a cigarette and waited. Smoke rose swiftly, sucked away by the air-filtration system.

No one spoke.

"Shall we try for thirty-one?" he asked.

"Just cut to the chase," Pickford said, tapping his well-manicured fingers on the table. "This isn't a press conference called to congratulate the *true* Savoy blood on their civic virtue. You have the power, so you have a tax-exempt hobby that takes money away from tax-payers in general and the Pickford family in particular. Next topic, please."

"You're welcome to visit the museum," Rory said. "I'll make sure you get a free pass."

Pickford gave him a slicing sideways look.

Savoy drew on his cigarette, then placed it in the smokeless ashtray Bliss had nagged him into using. "I'm afraid the next topic won't please you, Steven. This board has been invited to host a table at the Friends of Moreno County charity dinner and auction."

"Charity is only free if you're poor," Pickford said. "How much will it cost?"

"Ten thousand dollars for a party of eight."

Pickford rolled his eyes: fifteen percent of $10,000 was $1,500.

"Cheap. Good publicity, too," Bliss added, yawning. "Buy two tables and put Rory at the other one with Daddy."

"Excellent suggestion," Savoy said. "Sure to improve everyone's digestion. Rory?"

"He wants the family together, in public, and not arguing or getting drunk."

Rory carefully didn't look at his ex, who had almost made headlines taking a swing at the cop who arrested her for drunk driving. Fortunately, the cop had been a sheriff's deputy who knew which side his bread was buttered on. He'd tossed Bliss in the back of the squad car and drove her home to her daddy.

"If he wants a public love feast, separate us," Bliss said.

Rory shook his head, making light slide and shine over the gray temples that turned a rather boyish face into a dignified one. "Mr. Forrest was pretty clear that he wanted a united Savoy table for the press to see." *And more important, to reassure Angelique White that the family was in accord on the subject of the merger.*

But Bliss was dead set against anything that had to do with developing the ranch, so talking about Angelique wouldn't increase the peace.

Rory also didn't say aloud what everyone at the conference already knew—Ward Forrest might be more than seventy, but he looked and acted like a fit fifty. Although he'd willingly handed over the reins of corporate power to his two favorite children ten years ago so that he could pursue various hobbies and interests, the bulk of the actual wealth was still under Ward's control. The leash on Bliss and Savoy was long, but it was real.

"If press coverage is the issue, tell Daddy to sit at La Susa's table," Bliss said, using the media's name for Susa Donovan, who signed her paintings with a simple *Susa.* "The Donovan matriarch is the driving power behind the auction as well as being the celebrity that reporters will line up five-deep to interview."

Rory ignored her.

So did everyone else.

"Fine, one table," Savoy said, making a note in the margin and turning to the next topic.

"Where is my side of the family sitting?" Pickford asked. "These tables aren't big enough for more than eight, and I'm sure the Pickford women will want to attend with us."

"I thought you didn't like art," Savoy said.

"I don't. Make sure there's room for at least eight Pickfords at a Savoy Enterprises table."

"Two tables," Savoy said, making another note. "At opposite ends of the room." He looked up at Rory. "Unless Dad wants to include collateral relatives in the love feast?"

Rory laughed. "Only if it's their funeral he's attending."

Savoy smiled slightly. Ward had hated the Pickford family at first look forty years ago. Nothing had changed since then.

Nothing would.

"The next item on our agenda," Savoy said, shifting papers, "is the suit filed against the corporation by Concerned Citizens for Sane Development. We have to decide whether we want to settle out of court and agree to cut the density of our planned Artists Cove community by two thirds, or spend the next decade in court while continuing to pay taxes as if the land is already developed. Or we could put the land in Agricultural Reserve, save tax money, and in all probability lose the ability to ever develop that tract of the ranch in the future."

"You can develop whatever you want, as long as it isn't on *my* half of the ranch," Bliss said. "That half includes Sandy Cove, which is the real name of Artists Cove."

"You don't own half of anything," Rory shot back, "and Sandy Cove doesn't exist on any map. Artists Cove does."

"Keep your goddamn bulldozers out of the old family land where our ancestors lived and died," Bliss snarled.

"Waterfront is the most profitable land to develop on the ranch, and Artists Cove is just a small part of what should be on the table," Pickford said loudly. "We're getting eaten alive by taxes and—"

Bliss, Pickford, and Rory started talking over one another.

"Ladies first," Savoy said, rapping the ashtray sharply on the table.

"That would be you," Rory said to Pickford.

When the accountant came halfway out of his chair, Savoy sat down, picked up his cigarette, and took a long, soothing pull. He would need any help he could get not to lose his temper. The meetings resembled nothing so much as the family brawl they were. It had always been that way. It always would be. The only thing that changed was the names of the players snarling at each other, wasting time when there wasn't any to waste.

He hadn't even brought up the New Horizons merger yet. When he did, Bliss would really go ballistic—most of the proposed development was on land she thought of as "hers."

But there was no choice. Angelique White had made it clear that the suit with Concerned Citizens for Sane Development had to be settled before she would consider a contract merging the future of Savoy Enterprises with that of New Horizons. From what he had seen of the balance sheets, there wasn't any choice about that merger, either. In the brave new world of the twenty-first century, it was merge or die.

Savoy took another drag on his cigarette. Even if nothing else went wrong, it was going to be a hairy bitch of a month.

6

Lost Treasures Found was located off Pacific Coast Highway, several blocks up on the inland side where monthly rents weren't the same as the national debt of an emerging nation. The streets weren't swept as often as they should be and the homeless people took up informal residence at night, but there were no drugs or prostitutes. Yet.

One day Lacey fully expected to own a shop facing traffic on the water side of the heavily traveled highway. One day, but not this one. Today she was happy to meet the rent with enough left over from her half of the profits to buy groceries and finance her twice-weekly forays to flea markets, garage sales, thrift stores, and estate sales. Along with handicrafts that Shayla found in the United States and South America, informal noncommercial sales were the major source of the contents of the store—the lost treasures of other days and places, waiting on the shelves to be found in the here and now.

Awkwardly Lacey let herself in the back door of the shop, juggling three bundled-up paintings along with a big cloth purse that often did duty as an overnight bag. The frisky ocean wind wasn't any help. She felt like a kite without a string.

Lacey kicked the door shut behind her and listened for the sound of her partner, who had left the storage unit earlier to take the afternoon shift in the store. But even with the door shut, she couldn't hear anything except the muted steel river of Pacific Coast Highway traffic pouring by a quarter mile away.

"Shayla?" Lacey called out.

"Back here, admiring your latest painting."

"Ouch. Sounds like a thrilling day at the retail level."

Shayla's laughter floated from the apartment over the shop. "Between one and two o'clock, we made overhead and then some, and we don't close for a couple hours yet."

"Thank you, Lord."

"You need any help getting that stuff upstairs?" Shayla asked.

"So far, so good."

Lacey headed for the back staircase that led to the upper floor where she lived, painted her own kind of plein air dreams, and kept extra merchandise when the downstairs got too full and Shayla's brother didn't have any spare storage units to give them rent-free.

The sound of something bumping against the walls brought Shayla to the head of the stairs. She saw her friend struggling under bundles that were half as big as she was.

"Told you I should have taken at least one of them," Shayla said.

"Nope. Anything happens to these suckers, I want to be the one in line for the butt-kicking."

"Hon, they aren't that valuable."

"We'll leave that for Susa Donovan to decide. As far as I'm concerned, my grandfather is the undiscovered genius of California plein air painters."

Shaking her head, Shayla descended the stairs in time to catch a painting that wanted to cartwheel off into the great unknown. "Which one is this?"

"Don't know." Lacey blew a chestnut curl out of her eyes.

"I'd hate to think I rescued that wretched murder painting."

"Then don't."

"Rescue it?"

"Think."

Shayla started to say something, then shook her head. Following her friend's unexpected turns of thought was more than Shayla was up to right now. Between packing for her next buying trip to the Andes and trying to catch up on inventory, she had a headache big enough to share with a stadium.

"Right," she said. "I won't think."

Lacey propped the wrapped paintings against a stack of unframed finished canvases—hers, not her grandfather's. When the paintings started to slide, she stopped them with one of the big fire extinguishers she kept in her upstairs apartment.

The shop door chimed cheerfully.

"My public calls," Shayla said, heading for the stairway.

"I'll take it," Lacey said, talking as she raced out and

down the stairs. "You deserve a break after the inventory stuff. There's some fresh orange juice in the fridge. Or beer, since it's been that kind of day already."

She was going so fast that most of what she said was overheard by Ian Lapstrake, who was browsing downstairs. He voted in silent sympathy for the beer and *that kind of day*. Then he went back to cruising the shop for his own personal idea of treasure: Western movie posters from the time before southern California and the Southwest was paved over, smogged out, and generally screwed up by growth.

That was why he'd left L.A. early and cut over to Pacific Coast Highway before going to the John Wayne airport to pick up Susa Donovan—if you looked fast and not too hard, there were glimpses of the old California just off the coast highway. That was how he'd discovered Lost Treasures Found, a twenties bungalow wedged between a fast-food business and a con artist selling control of your own karma through the shop called Cosmic Energy. As far as Ian was concerned, it was earthly bullshit. But then, people had accused him of being a cynic in the past.

Lacey spotted her new customer before she reached the bottom of the stairs. Uneasiness flared in her. Though his back was to her, it was clear that he was at least six feet tall, with shoulders wide enough to fill out his black denim jacket. She was suddenly glad that Shayla was upstairs. Most of her customers were women alone or dragging a bored and boring husband along. Whatever this man was, he wasn't boring.

"May I help you?" she asked professionally.

"Just looking for old movie posters," Ian said, turning around.

At first glance the girl standing a cautious five yards

from him didn't look old enough to work. A second glance told him what he already knew—looks were deceiving. Beneath the mop of loose curls were measuring cinnamon-brown eyes and a mouth that waited to see whether it would smile. Not a girl at all. A woman dressed in paint-spattered shirt and jeans and totally unaware of it.

"Old movies," she said. "Film noir?"

"Westerns."

"I should have guessed."

He looked at his feet. "How? No cowboy boots."

"Denim jacket."

He smiled and decided not to tell her it was great cover for his shoulder holster. "Dang, I keep forgetting about that."

Lacey absorbed the man's slow smile and wondered why she'd ever been nervous. The smile she gave him in return was more appreciative than professional. Automatically she walked closer.

"Most of the people around here still worship at the altar of film noir," she said, waving to the three framed posters that hung over the cash register, protected from the sun by special glass.

Ian glanced up at the posters. Though they depicted black-and-white movies, the cinema moguls had known that color sells. Most of the posters had been printed with at least some bright elements. For every man in dark hat and jacket—no tie—cigarette dangling at a just-so angle from his world-weary lips, there was a woman with smooth yellow hair, hourglass body, creamy skin, and wearing a cocktail dress that was as red and close-fitting as lipstick. Some kind of handgun—usually wrong for the period—smoked in the foreground. Everything but the babe's dress and hair was in shades of darkness that owed more to philosophy than to the reality of shooting in black-and-white film.

"I prefer my black-and-white with more color," he said dryly.

Lacey laughed. "So do I, but I'm in business and noir sells." She pointed toward the side of the store. "My Western and musical posters are in the bin just beyond the Deco-style vases. I'll help you, but have to wash my hands first. I've been grubbing around in the storeroom."

"Pretty colorful storeroom."

She looked at her hands and then at her clothes. "Oops. I forgot. I was painting before I went through some canvases to choose three for a charity event and then I came back and—oh brother, talk about too much information. Go look in the bin. I'll be right back."

Instead of telling her that she could keep talking just for the pleasure of hearing the laughter in her voice, Ian walked over to the bin and began flipping through the cardboard-backed, glassine-shielded posters. Musicals and more musicals. Though he didn't collect them, he smiled at the colorful exuberance of the singers and dancers coming and going beneath his fingertips. Like Westerns, musicals celebrated a less world-weary America. He was all for that. Christ knew that the world had enough brutality without making movies about it.

The scent of soap and something feminine drifted to him even as he heard footsteps behind him. She wasn't nearly as wary of him now. She came up almost close enough to kiss. He'd always enjoyed women like her, unself-conscious and intelligent. The fact that there was definitely a female body wrapped around the package sure didn't hurt.

He would have to browse this store again. Soon. Since the charity art show wouldn't happen until the end of the week, he should have enough time to explore the shop, and maybe even the woman. There hadn't been any rings under all the paint and grime on her hands. But then, maybe she didn't wear jewelry while painting or working in storage sheds.

"Any luck?" she asked, watching his mouth, wondering idly if his kiss was half as warm as his smile.

"Not yet. Nice collection, though."

"Thanks. A lot of them were my grandfather's."

"Was he in the movies?"

"Nope. Unless set painting counts."

"Keeps bread and beans on the table," Ian said. "That always counts."

Lacey's smile slipped. She remembered more than one loud argument between her father and grandfather on the subject of how the elder Quinn earned his living.

"Now here's a prime one," Ian said.

Laccy stepped around him and looked. The poster was indeed prime. "John Wayne in *Hondo*." She started to say that her customer bore more than a passing resemblance to the younger Wayne. At the last second she changed her mind. He might take it as a come-on.

He might be right. It had been a long time since she'd seen anything as deep down interesting as this man's smile, obvious pleasure in the posters, and offhand intelligence.

"That was one of my grandfather's favorites," Lacey said.

Ian glanced at the discreet sticker on the back of the cardboard and sighed. "You know what you have, don't you?"

"You bet."

"Any give on the price?"

"Not much."

"How much is not much?" he asked.

"You live in California?"

He nodded.

"I'll eat the sales tax," she said.

He glanced at his watch. There was just enough time to make Susa's plane and still buy the poster. "Bon appétit," he said, smiling. "Check or credit card?"

Lacey blinked. There it was, slow and warm and so gentle it had to be seen to be believed. A smile like that should be registered as a lethal weapon. Mentally she shook herself and focused on the business at hand.

"Local check?" she asked.

"If Upland is local, I'm local."

She hesitated. Upland wasn't exactly local, but it wasn't that far away, either. And she really hated giving the credit card barons two percent of her hard-won sales.

"Pleased to meet you, neighbor," she said, holding out her right hand. "I'm Lacey Quinn, half owner of the shop."

"Ian Lapstrake, neighbor at large."

He shook her hand. Its competent feminine strength reminded him of Dana. He released Lacey's hand before she could feel uneasy about her humorous gesture of "neighborliness" when they actually lived one to three hours apart, depending on how clogged the freeways were.

"Will you be taking the poster with you or do you want it shipped?" she asked.

He glanced at her left hand—freshly scrubbed, no visible rings or ring marks—and decided he would come back for the poster. "Could you hold it for a day or two?"

"Sure."

He pulled a folding checkbook out of his jacket pocket, and braced it on his thigh. "Can I borrow your pen?"

She patted her jean pockets. "I don't have one."

"How about this one?" Deftly he pulled a pen out of the curls dancing around her right ear.

"What are you, a magician?"

"Only in my dreams." He wrote swiftly, tore out the check, and tucked the pen back into its nest of curls before she could react. "I didn't know hair came in that many shades of dark and gold and almost red. It's beautiful."

Before the compliment registered, he was on his way out the door.

"Who was that?" Shayla asked from the stairway.

"I was wondering the same thing myself."

Lacey was also wondering if she had really seen the outline of a shoulder holster beneath the denim when he bent over to write the check, stretching the cloth across his back.

Over Moreno County
Tuesday afternoon

7

It was the type of sunny January day that made people in the Blizzard Belt pack their cars and head for southern California. Though Seattle rarely had any snow to flee from, it did have a thousand shades of winter gray. Susa Donovan was happy to see the sun again, even through an airplane window.

Sitting in the comfortable cabin of a Donovan International executive jet gave her an uninterrupted view of the coastline far below. These days she rarely painted humanity's marks on the landscape, but the contrast between the wild fluid blue of the sea and the pale man-made grid of subdivisions, freeways, and industry made her hand itch to hold a paintbrush. Viewed from a distance, the image was abstract and dramatic, like a human storm poised on the edge of breaking over the endless ocean.

Yet if she almost closed her eyes, she could see the land as it once had been, green ravines and velvet shadows of eucalyptus, orange and yellow evenings, a young woman's smile as she painted her lover holding out his hand in silent offering.

Sometimes it was hard for Susa to believe she'd ever been that young, but she had. Years before it became fashionable in the late sixties, she'd abandoned school and home for an unconventional life of late nights, exotic cigarettes, the smell of turpentine and sex; and painting, always painting, more important to her than all the rest of it put together.

She'd been born much too late to participate in the glory days of California Impressionism, yet she'd known some of the great painters, had learned from them, had heard them talk over endless bottles of wine about the glories and scandals of the Painter's Beach art colony at its height, Benford Savoy III, called Three, a rich man's son who supported artists because he enjoyed the bohemian life.

Sometimes she wondered what had happened to those unknown artists, the talented ones who lost their art in booze, or the women whose art disappeared under the weight of cultural disinterest and the intricate demands of motherhood. So many of them tore themselves apart and left nothing to mark their passage from art to death.

A feeling of foreboding went through her, the kind of rippling of the skin that her kids laughingly called sure evidence that not all the witches had been burned in Salem. Even as she tried to dismiss the chill beneath the warmth, she wished that her husband was beside her and her children and grandchildren gathered around. She felt . . . haunted.

Something was wrong. Somewhere.

Of course there is, she told herself briskly. *Some-*

*thing is always wrong somewhere. No need to take it
personally, even if I do have witches in my ancestry.
Well, druids, actually, but they burned just the same.*

Whatever. Everything is fine with those I love.

And if she told herself that often enough, she might
believe it. Part of it was that she hated having Don half
a world away. And most of it was something else,
something that couldn't be touched or known, simply
accepted.

"Ms. Donovan?"

The pilot's voice came over the intercom. Susa
flipped a switch on the seat arm. "Yes?"

"The Donovan requests that you 'turn on your goddamned cell phone.' "

"Oops," Susa said, reaching for her big purse. "I
didn't expect him to be awake. Isn't it the middle of
the night in whatever godforsaken hunk of real estate
he's visiting?"

"Trust me. He's awake."

"I'm calling him as we speak."

The pilot, whose ears had been singed, sighed gratefully. "Good. We're landing in twenty minutes. I'd
hate to try to juggle both the Donovan on a rant and
the air controller at John Wayne International."

Susa was still smiling when her husband answered
his phone.

"Susa?" The voice was rough yet warm.

"I'm here, love."

"I miss you."

She caressed the phone with her fingertips as though
she could reach through time and space and feel the
warmth of her husband's mouth. "Same here. I'm one
lucky woman."

"Because I'm not around to harass you?"

She laughed softly. "That's not harassment. I was just thinking about the painters in Moreno County."

"BWM," he said.

Before We Met. It was the way Susa and Donald Donovan divided their lifetimes.

"Yes," she said. "I look down at the land and I'm haunted by the talented men who never found what they were looking for and stopped painting, and the talented women who weren't fortunate enough to find a mate who supported their work, praised their abilities, and made painting part of raising a family. I was so lucky to find you. Have I ever thanked you for that, my love?"

"Every time you smile."

"I wish I could kiss you." She hadn't wanted him to go and had told him so more than once before he left. *For God's sake, Don, why do you think I put up with our strapping, looming sons and quick-witted daughters if not to let them take over the business so we can play?* But Don was as stubborn as she was, which was why they were still individuals and still together. "How are the negotiations going?"

"Slowly."

"You're going to miss the auction." It wasn't a question.

"I'm afraid so."

"Afraid? Ha! You're chortling."

"Well, smiling maybe, but not chortling. I never chortle." He yawned hugely. "Couldn't sleep until I heard your voice."

"Are you saying I put you to sleep?" she teased.

"Eventually. Damn it, honey. I should be with you, not over here talking through interpreters to people who see dollar signs when I walk in the room."

"Then come home."

"Always."

"But not tonight, huh?"

"No." He sighed. "I swear I'm going to put a leash on one of our kids and make them take my place."

"Remind me to be somewhere else when you try."

He bit back a laugh. "Be safe, my beautiful Susa. Call me even if you think I'm asleep."

"Same for you. Don't let down your guard, love."

"Don't worry. Uncle Sam assigned me some company. Three guys. They remind me of Jake and Archer, cool around the eyes and always ready to jump in any direction."

Susa's heartbeat quickened. Their son Archer and their son-in-law Jake had once spent time in the kinds of government service that Congress didn't oversee. "Don't worry?" she asked in a rising voice. "What's going on?"

"Nothing. The government just thought it was easier to keep an eye on me than to find me if I got lost," he said.

She let out a long breath. "Good for them."

"You think it's a good idea?"

"Anything that keeps you safe is a good idea."

At the other end of the line, her husband grinned. *Gotcha.* "Then you'll cooperate with Ian Lapstrake."

"Who?"

"The man who's meeting you at the airport. He's Lawe's friend."

"Oh, *that* Ian."

"He's also one of Rarities' top security men. I'm sure you'll enjoy his company every minute of the time you're hauling yourself and your half-million-dollar paintings all over the southern California landscape."

"Are you saying—" Susa began hotly.

"I love you."

Being a wise man, the Donovan hung up before Susa could answer.

8

The room was more than a hundred years old, a symphony of brass and polished wood, thick Persian carpets and heavy draperies, brown leather couches so deep that only a fit man could get out of one without grunting. A wood fire leaped and licked at the huge hearth. Ward Forrest hadn't changed any of the Savoy decor when he married Gem and united the Savoy fortune with the Forrest ambition. He'd even left the trophy heads on the walls—mule deer, bighorn sheep, elk, antelope, moose, bear, cougar. Though he'd personally shot bigger game, he'd never felt the need to stare at the results over coffee and brandy.

Ward went back to studying the contract-labor arrangements for the Savoy Hotel. Although it wasn't well known, the conglomerate that owned the hotel was largely owned by one of the many arms of Savoy Enterprises. It was a belated—and probably too late—attempt to diversify from an entirely land-based business. Because Ward had insisted on overseeing every detail of the hotel personally, down to the kitchen equipment, uniform sources for everyone from cooks to concierge, and security arrangements on every floor for every reason, the Savoy Hotel had taken up a large part of his working days. He would be glad when the damn thing was launched and he could stay home and go back to being semiretired.

The grandfather clock chimed repeatedly like someone humming the opening note for a choir of angels. The dog at Ward's feet wagged its tail, dreaming along in key.

"You lazy old son," Ward said, and thumped the dog fondly on its well-padded ribs. "Too fat to hunt and too old to care."

Honey Bear opened one eye, slicked his tongue over Ward's fingers, and went back to sleep. Ward smoothed his hand down the dog's coat several times. He'd had a lifetime of Honey Bears romping at his heels: different dogs but the same sex, breed, and name, the same eager-to-please nature, and the same unquestioning love for the hand that fed them. Smooth coats, too. The older he got, the more he appreciated that silky canine warmth and reliability.

In his opinion, when it came to company on a lonely night a good dog was worth twenty women. Dogs didn't ask fool questions, didn't argue about how the ranch should be run, and didn't throw a shit fit when they didn't get what they wanted. His wife had done all that and more.

Being widowed had its good points.

"Ward? You back in your den?"

Rory Turner's voice lifted Ward out of his reverie. "What took you so long?" he called out.

"Got here as soon as I could," Rory said, yanking off his tie as he walked into Ward's sanctuary. "Why don't you just come to the meetings or wire me for sound?"

"Because I keep hoping my kids will grow up and get the fucking job done."

Disturbed by the tone of voice, Honey Bear lifted his head and nosed Ward's calf. Absently Ward gave the dog's head a go-away kind of pat. Honey Bear took the hint and went back to sleep.

Rory knew better than to comment on the business abilities of his ex-wife or his former brother-in-law, so he just unbuttoned his shirt collar, shifted the shoulder harness he wore in or out of uniform, and settled into a chair.

"Well?" Ward said. "What happened?"

"Blow-by-blow, or leave out the sniping?"

"Jesus" was all Ward said.

"There will be two tables at the art auction—one Savoy, one Pickford."

Ward's mouth flattened at the Pickford name. Every time he thought of how his mother-in-law had finessed fifteen percent of the Savoy Ranch out of his control, he wished all over again that he'd known in time to change things. But he hadn't, so now he had to live with "relatives" he'd rather bury than kiss.

"Do you want the tables together?" Rory asked.

Ward just gave Rory a look out of glittering blue eyes that hadn't faded one bit in more than seventy years.

"Right. Opposite sides of the room, as requested," Rory said, hiding his amusement. "Savvy surprised me," he continued, calling Savoy by his childhood nickname. "He said he'd negotiated a more generous settlement in the Artists Cove development and would appreciate our support. Bliss started screaming that he couldn't get away with that, Sandy Cove was sacred to her, that she'd see him in hell before it got developed, and stormed out. Meeting over."

"What about the New Horizons offer?"

"We didn't get to it."

Ward shot out of his chair with a speed that brought a startled yip from Honey Bear. "Are you telling me that—"

"Yo, Dad, are you back there?" Savoy called from the front of the house.

Honey Bear stood, stretched luxuriantly, and started for the hall door to greet Savoy.

"Damn, I thought the nitpicking Pickford would keep Savvy longer than a few minutes," Rory said, standing up hastily. "Cribbage tonight?"

"Unless I'm in jail for killing my stupid son," Ward muttered.

"Not a chance. I'm the sheriff, remember? See you after dinner."

The outer door closed behind Rory a few seconds before Savoy walked into the den. While everyone knew that Rory reported to Ward, everyone got along better if their noses weren't rubbed in it.

"Hi, Dad," Savoy said. He bent down and scratched the dog's ears. "You, too, Honey Bear."

The dog looked more enthusiastic than Ward did.

"Well?" the older man demanded.

Savoy gave the dog a final pat and sat down in the place recently vacated by Rory. If he noticed that the seat was still warm, he didn't mention it. As for loosening his tie to be more comfortable, he didn't have to. One of the perks of being the business head of the

Savoy Enterprises was that he didn't have to wear a tie. Ditto for a suit. His silk sport coat was soft and unstructured, like the sleek slacks that were the same toast brown of the leather chair he sat on.

"We'll all be gathered around a fancy table Saturday night," Savoy said. "With luck, none of the knives will be buried in anything but dinner."

"It's not funny."

"No, but it's damned ridiculous." Savoy held his hand up, forestalling a lecture from his father. "Bliss will be there because she knows this is important to you. It would have helped smooth things along if Rory hadn't been the messenger."

"She should be used to it by now."

"She isn't. She never will be."

"Too bad. She had her chance and she blew it when she divorced him."

Savoy felt like asking when he had blown his chance to be his father's confidant, but knew there was no point. The son had the clean blond looks of his mother, and however his parents' marriage had begun, it had ended with indifference punctuated by contempt.

"What about the New Horizons offer?" Ward asked.

"Bliss walked out before I could bring it up."

"Shit, boy, you could have romanced the Pickford contingent and then presented it to Bliss after she had a few drinks."

"The last time I tried to cut a private deal with the Pickfords, you had a—"

"That was then," Ward cut in. "This New Horizons deal is more important than anything I've ever done. I'd rather have Bliss on board, but if you have to get in bed with the Pickfords for a majority vote, then by God you will."

"Or you'll cut off my allowance?"

Temper burned along Ward's cheekbones. "It could happen."

"It could," Savoy agreed.

Ward blew out a breath. "Hell, you're just like your mother was. Sit there calm as marble and throw everything back in my face."

"And Bliss is just like you, fast on the trigger. If you'd quit jabbing at her through Rory, we'd have a better chance of getting her cooperation on the New Horizons merger."

Eyes narrowed, Ward drummed his fingers on his leather desk chair. He doubted that Savvy knew how important the merger was to the future of Savoy Enterprises and everyone who drew a corporate paycheck. To be fair, Ward hadn't told his son anything beyond the obvious: the merger would benefit both parties.

But right now Ward didn't feel like being fair. He felt like taking a bite out of something and his son was handy. "Get the Pickfords to agree to the merger or I'll get myself a new chairman."

"CEO," Savoy corrected. "I've been studying the New Horizons offer. It calls for opening up parts of the ranch to development that we agreed years ago would remain in trust for future generations."

"Does the phrase 'land poor' mean anything to a fancy Stanford business school graduate like you?" Ward asked sarcastically.

"Then donate it to—"

"You aren't listening," Ward cut in coldly. "Just like your mother, so sure that what she wanted was right and proper and the rest of the world could go to hell. Well, listen to me and listen good. The profits on all the agriculture on the Savoy Ranch don't pay the fucking taxes on the cropland. When we try to develop a piece of land to pay a dividend, we end up in court while three-hundred-dollar-an-hour lawyers argue over how many politicians can dance on the devil's pitchfork."

Savoy looked at his father's stabbing finger and bit back a sigh. As long as he could remember, his father had complained about taxes and newcomers who wanted him to keep the ranch as a pretty landscape for suburbanites to admire. There was plenty of truth in Ward's complaints, but that didn't mean Savoy wanted to hear them all over again. The land was what it was. Taxes were what they were. Citizens would always line up to spend somebody else's money.

"I believe I made some headway with CCSD on a conference call," Savoy said when his father took a breath.

"Which wild-eyed bunch is that?"

"Concerned Citizens for—"

"Oh, them," Ward interrupted, looking as disgusted as he felt.

"Yes, them. The group that has pro bono representation from one of the most expensive law firms in L.A."

"Only because the four partners in that firm want a different governor of California than we do, because a different governor would nominate them and their buddies to fill judicial vacancies."

"The point is," Savoy said evenly, "that CCSD is receiving high-level free legal advice on the ways and means of forcing delays in development." He reached into his sport coat and pulled out a folded sheaf of legal papers. "This is their latest—and probably last—proposal before we let the courts sort it out. Bliss won't like it, but she'll sign it. She just had to throw a public fit."

"Bottom line. What's in it for us?"

"We get to develop the hills above Riker and Artists Cove at forty percent of our original proposed density. The remainder of that parcel, approximately fourteen hundred acres, becomes Savoy State Park, the newest jewel in the California State Park system."

"That's the best you can do? We give up a half a *billion* dollars worth of prime beachfront property and in return we get to develop a handful of houses with an ocean view you need fucking binoculars to see?"

Savoy leaned forward and put the proposal on his father's desk. "You forgot the hefty tax write-off. Here's the profit/loss I did."

Ward's fist slammed down on the papers. "That's bullshit!"

"It's a way of not being in court when New Horizons wants to close the merger. You know how wary Angelique White is of any negative publicity."

Ward went still. "You're blackmailing me."

"No. Bliss is. She's the one who cut the CCSD deal that left Artists Cove intact."

"Bliss did this? *Bliss did this?*"

"Like I said, you really should stop jabbing at her with Rory. I squeezed another seven percent density out of CCSD. Take it or leave it."

"That's not a deal, it's a hose job!" His fist slammed onto the table.

"It's the best deal we're going to get. Think of the positive publicity if we make the gesture of donating an incomparable piece of California history and land-scape to—"

"Fuck that. I'd rather think about how long Blissy will last without money."

"I take it you agree to the deal?"

Ward's mouth thinned. "Hose job. Yeah, do it. And if you see your sister, ask her how she likes paying her own bills."

9

Some women made a dinner ring out of the wedding or engagement diamonds left over from past loves and lusts. Bliss Savoy Forrest had a splashy diamond pin created from the postmarital jewelry. She also had frown lines between her eyes that no amount of expensive shots could wholly erase. She'd reverted to her maiden name of Forrest after her first divorce, and had kept that name through three more husbands, but she hadn't forgotten what it was like to be in Rory Turner's bed. What really pissed her off was that she didn't know if he thought of her in any way but as a rich man's spoiled daughter.

Blue eyes narrowed, she tapped a manicured nail on the kitchen counter of the oceanfront condo she leased. She had several such homes-away-from-no-home scattered throughout California, plus one in New York, London, Hawaii, and Aruba for those times when only a complete change of scene would lift her spirits.

Now, for example. She would turn fifty soon. No matter how many nips and tucks, shots and peels and ego-boosters she paid for, the mileage showed. The half-century mark was coming at her like a freight train from hell. If it wasn't for her money, she wondered if any man would even buy her a cup of coffee.

The ringing phone startled her. She grabbed the receiver, grateful to have something to concentrate on besides unhappy thoughts.

"Hello?"

"Hi, Bliss. Buzz me up."

"Rory?" she asked, though she knew his voice all too well.

"No, it's frigging Santa Claus. Ring me up. It's cold down here."

"I'm out of gin."

"I brought my own."

"I'm not dressed," she said.

"I'll take off my clothes."

Without really intending to, Bliss found herself smiling and punching the button that released the lock eight floors down. She and Rory were divorced, but they weren't exactly strangers. She wondered if the blue lonelies had ambushed him the way they had her.

When the elevator opened, she was waiting in the doorway.

"You're dressed," Rory said, giving her a lazy, masculine once-over.

Bliss hoped he couldn't see through the baby-blue silk wrapper she wore to the carefully hidden surgical scars and insecurity beneath. It was so damned unfair that men got distinguished and women got old.

"You don't have any gin," she said, looking at his empty hands.

"Since when have we ever told each other the truth?"

Before she could change her mind, he walked by her and into the front room. Thirty feet ahead, a wall of glass showcased the darkly lustrous Pacific Ocean. Occasional searchlights stabbed across the breakers. A strong southwest wind was piling up twelve-foot swells. Salt spray made a fine mist that haloed everything, even the streetlights.

"Nice view," he said as he always did. Then he added, "Must cost you a bundle."

Bliss raised her eyebrows. That comment was new. "I'll ask my accountant."

"Then you have one. Good."

"An accountant?"

Rory turned and faced her. "Yes."

Uneasily she crossed her arms over her D-cup chest. He wasn't smiling. His brown eyes didn't have the edgy gleam that came when he was deliberately getting in her face. If anything, he looked tired. New lines on his forehead, new gray in his hair, new wrinkles in the clothes covering his lanky body. The veins stood out on the back of his hands as he shrugged off his jacket and dumped it over the back of the nearest chair. His movements were tense.

"What's wrong?" she asked.

"You really out of gin?"

She looked in his eyes for a long moment and saw what she'd never found in any other man except her father—confidence. All right, arrogance. But in both men, not without cause. In their lifetimes they had accomplished more than most men.

"Tonic?" she asked.

"Lime?"

She nodded.

"Tonic and rocks," he said. "Thanks, Blissy. One way or another, it's been a long day."

Her smile was weary, wary, and real. They had a lot of history together. Some of it was good. "Coming up. Sit down and kick off your shoes. Have you eaten dinner?"

"Not yet." He sank into a sleek Italian leather chair and began rubbing his face the way he did when he was worn out.

"Want an omelet to go with the gin?" she asked.

He looked up suddenly. "Would you cook for me?"

"Sure."

"How'd I let you get away?"

"You didn't. I did it all by myself."

He smiled faintly. "Oh, yeah. It's coming back now."

Bliss retreated to the kitchen before their brittle, unstated truce could blow up in her face. She didn't feel like fighting with anyone right now. Even her fiery ex. She was as tired as he was, tired of many things. Most of all, she was tired of being alone.

Rory listened to the sounds coming from the kitchen, sighed, and toed off his shoes, enjoying the peace while it lasted. With Bliss, it was never long. But then, he was never bored. If he could have found a woman that he wanted more, he'd have married her and written "the end" to the part of his life that had included Bliss. But he hadn't found anyone and he'd decided he wasn't going to.

Whatever Bliss's faults, he loved her. A lot of the time he even liked her. He sure didn't want to watch while her father plucked off each of her beautiful feathers and shoved them up her pampered ass.

She didn't understand her father. Rory did.

"You awake?" Bliss asked quietly.

He opened his eyes. "More or less."

"Here," she said, handing him a glass of ice and mostly gin, just enough tonic to make the lime taste good. "Kill or cure."

He took a sip, blinked at the burn, took another sip, and sighed with pleasure. No one made a drink like Bliss. Somehow she knew when to be liberal and when to be light on the booze.

"Fantastic," he said, lifting the glass in a silent toast to her. "Want to get married again?"

She did a double take, laughed hesitantly, and retreated to the kitchen. "Would the aliens who stole the real Rory Turner please bring him back?" she said. "This one is scaring me."

"Hey, I wasn't that bad as a husband, was I?"

"You want validation or eggs?"

"Eggs. Want me to make toast?"

"It's toasting."

"Damn, you're good."

He took another healthy sip of the drink and felt his nerves begin to uncurl. As he did, he thought it was funny how Ward, for all his shrewdness, hadn't noticed how upset his former son-in-law was. But Bliss, who was rarely shrewd about people, had seen his edginess right off.

Score a first for Bliss. Maybe getting older really did turn people into adults. Finally.

"Want to eat there or in the kitchen?" she called.

"Kitchen."

He stood and walked in his stocking feet to the cool

tile floor in the kitchen. There was nothing awkward or slow about his movements. One of the things he had done as sheriff of Moreno County for the past fifteen years was to get rid of the doughnut-gut brigade. Any man—or woman—who wanted to rise under his command was as fit as their fifty-four-year-old boss was.

He slid into a chair whose cushions were striped in orange and gold and lime. The omelet Bliss set in front of him on an elegantly simple white plate was light, fragrant with some exotic cheeses, and filled with chunks of ripe tomato and tender ham. Fresh chives were scattered across the top. He picked up a fork, cut off a mouthful, and bit in. Heat, textures, and something spicy zinged his tongue.

"Oh, man," he said, forking in another mouthful. "Sure you don't want to get married again?"

"That's it. I'm calling the *Enquirer* to come and interview my alien."

"Yeah, well, before they get here, think about it. We had more going for us than most."

Silently she refreshed Rory's drink, poured a mild gin and tonic for herself, and waited for him to get around to whatever it was that had brought him to her door in the first place. Though she would have undergone torture rather than admit it, she loved watching him enjoy her food. Cooking was her one domestic accomplishment. That and sex.

Come to think of it, the sex hadn't been at all domestic. Not with Rory. She'd had other men, but none of them had been as good for her as her ex, damn him. She couldn't live with the man and couldn't stop thinking about living with him.

Marriage.

Again.

What if he was serious?

What if he wasn't?

"You're biting your thumb," Rory said.

Guiltily she put her hand behind her back. She gnawed on her thumb only when she was feeling unusually insecure. And only Rory noticed it. She didn't know whether that irritated or enraged or reassured her. All three, probably. Just one of the many things about their relationship that kept it from dying a simple, painless death by indifference.

In silence Rory finished the omelet, ate the toast she'd brushed with olive oil and herbs and a hint of cheese, and carried his plate to the sink. With the economical motions of someone who was used to cleaning up after himself, he soaped the dish, rinsed it, and set it on the rack to dry. Then he scooped up everything else in the kitchen that she'd used to prepare his meal and began washing them, too.

Bliss wanted to gnaw on her thumb again. She didn't know what was on Rory's mind, but she knew she wasn't going to like hearing about it. What intrigued her was that he wasn't eager to tell her, either.

"Spit it out," she said when he began cleaning the counters with a soapy sponge.

"How much money do you go through every month?" he asked.

She shrugged. "I don't know."

"You just send the bills to Ward and he pays them."

"Not all of them. I have a trust fund from Mother and Grandmother."

"How much is it?"

"What the hell is this all about?" Bliss asked.

"Concerned Citizens for Sane Development."

"Shit. I knew it. You came here to chew on me for Daddy."

Slowly Rory shook his head. He dumped the sponge in the sink, dried his hands on a towel in the same cheerful colors as the dinette chairs, and went to stand close to her. Very close. Close enough to smell the perfume she always put on at night after her shower. He wondered how many other men had stood like this, scenting her, wanting her, and then peeling off one of her silk wrappers and diving in. But thinking about that would just piss him off.

"You may or may not get to keep Artists Cove."

"*Sandy* Cove. And I'll keep it."

"Maybe. And maybe Savvy will cut a deal with the Pickfords."

"Then I'll raise the kind of holy hell that will make the kind of headlines Daddy doesn't like."

Rory just shook his head wearily. He knew Ward could just stall signing the Artists Cove compromise until the merger was complete. Then he could tell his daughter to go to hell. And he would.

"You think Daddy's going to beat me on this one, don't you?"

"Yes."

"Is that why you came here?" She crossed her arms defensively. "You never used to like singing in the I-told-you-so choir."

"I came here to find out how much cash you have that isn't attached to your father."

"Interest on the trusts. A few investments." She crossed her arms over her chest. "Why? Is he threatening to cut me off again?"

"He hasn't ever threatened that and you know it."

"I know it's always there, like a gun at my head. If that isn't a threat, what is?"

"Then why do you keep poking at him?"

"Because I'm an adult and I shouldn't have to run to Daddy for money!"

"Try living on your income."

She made a disgusted sound. "Saint Rory. Why should I live like dirt? He never did. All he did was marry into Savoy money and he had the world at his fingertips. I'm a Savoy by *birth*. I deserve better than to be kept at heel like Honey Bear."

The corners of Rory's mouth turned down. "The blood thing again. Jesus, Blissy. Maybe if Gem hadn't rubbed Ward's nose in her wealth and bloodlines, they'd have had a marriage instead of an armed truce."

"The only people who sneer at bloodlines don't have any."

"As usual, this is going nowhere." He sighed and rubbed a hand over his face. "You're too much like your father. That's why you drive each other nuts."

"Just because I don't spend my life saying 'yes, sir, whatever you say, sir' doesn't mean—"

"We've been around this track," Rory cut in, turning away. "Thanks for the omelet."

Bliss hesitated, then stretched out a hand he didn't see. Hastily she withdrew it. "Rory."

He turned toward her.

"I . . ." Her voice died. She began gnawing on her thumb. "Oh, hell. Is he really mad?"

"He's really determined. Different thing entirely."

"He wants to develop the Savoy Ranch in his own image, a monument for the ages."

"Maybe. And maybe he just wants to make enough

money to keep all the Savoy-Forrests in beachfront condos. The deal you cut with CCSD will cost half a billion in land alone, not to mention what the developed property would be worth."

"But the tax write-off—"

Rory's laugh wasn't humorous. "Blissy, you should talk to that accountant of yours. If we can't develop the ranch, we won't have any profits to write off taxes against. If you don't sell off or develop big chunks of the land, all that Savoy wealth everybody is busy spending won't amount to a fart in a tornado."

10

The high school gymnasium smelled vaguely of old socks and sharply of fresh floor cleaner. Instead of the usual crowd of teenagers working painfully hard to be cool, there was a swirling, ever changing flood of people holding paintings from their attic or basement for Susa Donovan to anoint as worthy of cultural as well as familial interest.

"Sweet God," Ian muttered. "I haven't seen this much crap since I raised geese for a 4-H project."

"Geese?" Susa asked.

"No room for a pig or a pony. Besides, the geese mowed the lawn for me."

Susa laughed and felt like hugging him. For the past hour she'd been smiling and trying not to hurt someone's feelings about the cultural worth of Great-Aunt Sissy's fabulous study of a rose from bud to petal drop . . . in mauve, of course.

"Uh-oh," he said, spotting a woman with a look of hope and determination on her face.

"Remember," Susa said quietly, "these are treasures to the people who brought them."

"Lost Treasures Found."

"What?"

"The name of a shop I was in earlier. Bought a nifty old movie poster. No bargain, but in great condition."

As Ian spoke, he stepped in front of Susa to protect her from a woman who was carrying more paintings than the average county museum. One of the event organizers and a leading figure in the American Figurative Artists Association, Mr. P. E. Goodman fluttered around her like a balding, scalded moth.

"I'm so sorry," Goodman said to Susa, rolling his eyes toward the matron. Then, in a hissing undertone, "She's a big supporter of local artists. Wouldn't hear of only three to a customer."

Susa smiled through her teeth. There were some in every crowd who just *knew* that the rules didn't apply to them. The fact that Susa was built more like a pixie with laugh lines than an Amazon with fangs probably had something to do with the fact that everyone assumed they could just walk all over her.

"Ms. Donovan will be happy to look at all your offerings," Ian said, smiling gently at the matron even as he blocked her access to the table.

"I knew she would. My grandmother's paintings are of a much higher quality than—"

"We'll start with these," Ian said over her. As he spoke he took three paintings from the woman's armload and put them on the table in front of Susa. "There, that was easy, wasn't it?"

Before the woman could get past Ian's smile, she

found herself being escorted by him back to the auditorium doors, where the end of the line awaited her.

"We'll see more of these paintings in no time at all." Ian patted the matron's armload of family pride. "I know Susa is particularly eager to look at everything you brought."

"But I'm . . . the line is so . . ."

Ian was already gone, blending into the crowd even as he speared through it back to Susa's side.

The red-faced Goodman stared when Ian reappeared alone as swiftly as he'd left. "How did you do that?"

"He smiled," Susa said.

Goodman glanced at her.

"Killer smile," Susa assured him.

"Want a job?" Goodman asked Ian.

"I have one, thanks."

"If you ever—" Goodman began.

"If he ever wants another job," Susa cut in, rapidly assessing and rejecting the first of the three paintings in front of her, "he'll apply to Donovan International."

Goodman wasn't stupid. He went back to lining up people and making certain that a name or address or contact number of each owner was somehow attached to every painting.

Ian's dark eyebrows lifted. "Donovan International, huh? Sounds like an order."

Susa half smiled. "My son Lawe said you were bright. What's more important, so did Dana."

"I'm flattered."

The sideways glance she gave him was amused. "I don't believe you."

"Lawe said you were quick."

She laughed out loud. "I like you, Ian Lapstrake."

"Now I'm flattered."

She stood, gave him the kind of quick, smacking kiss she bestowed upon her family males, and sat back down to study the paintings left by the matron, who was still wondering how she ended up at the back of the line again.

"This one isn't by the same hand as the other," Susa said.

Ian looked from one painting to the next. Flowers. Lots and lots of flowers. "How can you tell?"

"A century of experience."

"Bull. You haven't been around longer than forty years."

"Flatter me some more, I'm amenable. I'm also old enough to be Lawe's mother, remember?"

"I'm working on it. So tell me, is the Donovan as tough a bastard as his sons say?"

"Absolutely." She set the second picture on the table behind her, with the few she had decided merited more study. "Better looking, too."

"Well, dang. How am I going to win you away?"

Snickering, shaking her head, Susa moved on to the third painting. "I wish I had another daughter for you."

"Something wrong with the ones you have?"

"Husbands." She tilted her head to one side and slanted the painting in her hands so that it caught the light from all angles. "Remarkable."

"Is that good?"

"In this case, no." She put the third painting on the reject table, looked at the long line of eager humanity in front of her, and questioned her own sanity for agreeing to thumb through Moreno County's attics in quest of fine unknown artists. As a publicity boost for the Friends of Moreno County, it was a great idea. Now that she had to actually do the looking . . . well, she'd get through it somehow.

"Time for a break," Ian said. It wasn't a question, or even a suggestion.

Susa's head snapped up. "Have you been taking lessons from my husband?"

"Your oldest son, actually."

"Archer?"

"Yep," Ian said cheerfully. "He called and told me to be sure you didn't get tired."

"Told you? He didn't ask?"

"Told."

"That's Archer," she said, but she was smiling a mother's affectionate smile. "I'll do fifteen more people."

It wasn't a suggestion; it was a fact.

In that moment Ian understood how Susa managed her hardheaded sons and equally hardheaded husband. She smiled. She coddled. And she didn't budge worth a damn.

"Yes, ma'am. Fifteen it is."

Ian stepped away from the table and began counting bodies. He had gotten to thirteen when he spotted Lacey Quinn.

11

Lacey shifted from one foot to another while balancing the three bubble-wrapped paintings and fending off random surges of the crowd. She glanced at her watch. Four people waited ahead of her, holding one or two paintings each. Maybe ten more minutes at most. Susa Donovan sized up paintings the way she painted—with energy, intelligence, and economy. Rarely did she take more than a minute with any of the canvases that people had brought to her for judging.

But what really rocked Lacey back on her heels was the man standing between Susa and the crowd. Except for the suit, he looked just like the guy who'd bought an old Western poster at Lost Treasures Found a few hours ago.

Nope. Can't be, she reassured herself. *I'm hallucinating because I'm nervous.*

Then the man smiled at something Susa said and Lacey's nerves ratcheted up several notches. Different clothes, same heart-stopping smile, same man: Ian Lapstrake. Under other circumstances she'd be happy to run into him again, but not now, not with her arms full of paintings she'd promised couldn't be traced back to her. The fake name she'd invented to go with the e-mail wouldn't do any good if Ian remembered her.

Maybe he won't recognize me. Or if he does, maybe he'll forget my name. He sure wouldn't be the first man to do that.

Watching him from the corner of her eye, Lacey tried to decide if Ian was one of the Donovan family Susa's biography had mentioned. Maybe a son-in-law. Then Lacey remembered the outline of a shoulder holster beneath his jacket and wondered if he was Susa's bodyguard.

The crowd heaved, pushing Lacey a foot closer to the table where her grandfather's work would be judged. Susa looked very elegant with her short, silver-streaked dark hair and sleek black pantsuit. An unusual twisted rope of semiprecious gems hung around her neck to her breasts. Deep green gems winked in her earlobes.

Lacey wished she'd taken time to do more than gather up her hair and clamp it in place with a holder the size of her hand and the colors of the rainbow. At least it was a match for her paint-stained jeans, ankle boots, and the vivid, loosely swirling blouse she'd fallen in love with at a garage sale two weeks ago. A bulky, colorful jacket hung over her arm beneath the paintings. The jacket was a wild patchwork of velvet scraps. It didn't actually "go" with anything in the fashion sense, but seeing it always made her smile.

I'm not here for a wardrobe critique, Lacey told herself. *The paintings are on display, not me.*

And thank God her mother wasn't in the auditorium. She would have been mortified by her daughter's outfit. Appearance and the lack of a country-club husband were the two major reasons mother and daughter fought. Every time Lacey thought her mother had finally gotten used to the idea that the oldest of her three daughters wasn't the cashmere-and-pearls type, she'd get another lecture on her pitiful fashion sense.

Must you look like you just crawled out of a paint tube?

Do you really style your hair with a hand mixer?

If you can't afford anything but garage-sale shoes, I'd be happy to take you shopping.

"Lacey? Ms. Quinn? Hello? Anyone home?" Ian fanned his fingers in front of her face.

"Oh. Sorry. Is it my turn?" Then she blinked and focused on the man who was talking to her, calling her by name. *Hell. There goes Ms. January Marsh.* "Ian, right? Neighbor Lapstrake?"

"At your service. Susa will be finished with the two folks in front of you real quick. Why don't you step up to the table and let me help you unwrap your paintings. Things will go faster that way."

When he reached for the paintings, her arms tightened protectively around the canvases.

"I'll be gentle," he said gravely. "I promise."

The humor underlying his reassurance flustered Lacey. Or maybe it was the smile. She stuck out her lower lip and blew a stray curl away from her eyes.

"Family treasures?" he asked, waiting for her to release the bundles.

"No! I found them at a garage sale."

Again Ian smiled even as he wondered why the

pretty lady with the summer-garden shirt and clear brown eyes was lying. All the "tells" were there— looking away, defensive posture, restlessness.

"Whatever," he said. "Take them over to the table and unwrap them. Unless you trust me to help?"

Lacey felt like a fool. "Sorry. It's just—" She blew fiercely at the curl that kept tickling the corner of her eye.

With a motion too swift and impersonal for her to take offense, he tucked the stray curl back in place.

"It'll just come unsprung again," she said. "I'm a walking fashion disaster."

"Good. I hate models."

Her quick smile changed her features, adding an electric element to her face that was both intelligence and intensity. "Here. Take the top one. I'll handle the other two. And don't mention my name to anyone, okay? If it turns out badly, I don't want, um, the wrong publicity for my . . . um, shop. Just call me . . ." Hurriedly she tried to remember her e-mail pseudonym. "January," she said, "January Marsh."

Ian barely managed not to laugh out loud. He didn't know what game the lady was playing, but he was certain it had to be as innocent as she was. She couldn't have lied successfully to save her life.

"Okay, Ms. Marsh," he said, pointing with his chin. "This way."

From behind Ian, where Susa was judging paintings, came a man's rueful laughter. "A student exercise, huh?"

"Straight from a *You Can Too Paint* book. The frame, however, is quite old." It was quite awful, too, but Susa felt no need to point that out.

"Oh, well, back under the bed with it."

"Actually, if you wouldn't mind leaving me your name and address, I know a professor who is doing a study of painting books and their influence on the popular culture of their time. I'm sure he'd be fascinated by this painting and its history."

"Sure." He ripped the business card off the back of the painting and handed it to her. "Here."

Susa tucked the card into a small file that sat next to her left hand and smiled expectantly at the next person, a middle-aged man who was sweating heavily in the overcrowded auditorium.

"I think the lady was next," he said, gesturing toward Lacey.

"Go ahead," Ian said as he wrestled with the generous tape job. "We'll be a minute."

"Thank you!" The man hurried forward, clutching some paintings.

Considering the man's nervousness, Susa decided the offerings were probably his own work rather than that of an ancestor.

"They're very unusual," Susa said, hoping that you didn't go to hell for white lies, because she sure had told a lot of them tonight. "Clearly in the genre of modern studio art, which is unfortunate. The purpose of this"—she waved a hand at the crowded auditorium—"is to discover old plein air artists, not new studio artists."

"I'd be glad to donate the paintings for the auction," the man said quickly, "like it said in the pamphlet."

Ian had already figured out where this interview would end. He signaled to one of Mr. Goodman's assistants, all of them local artists. This one was a cat-slim male dressed entirely in shades of black except for an unusual gold earring clinging to his left ear. He trotted over eagerly.

"That's very generous of you," Susa said to the hopeful studio artist. "One of the assistants will give you the forms."

"Would you help this man carry his paintings to the auction table?" Ian said. "We're trying to move things along so Susa can have a break."

"For La Susa, I'd move mountains," he said with a bow that would have done credit to an eighteenth-century French courtier.

Ian covered his laugh with a cough.

It took Susa less than four minutes to reject the next three paintings. Each one was a still life of the type beloved by middle-class Victorian women who believed that painting roses on china and playing the piano were the hallmarks of good breeding.

"You want to take your break now?" Ian said, tugging at more of the stubborn tape. "Ms., uh . . ." He hesitated.

"Marsh," she supplied quickly.

Ian smiled slightly. "Ms. Marsh has these things wrapped up like the lead in *Revenge of the Mummies*."

"You just have to know where the zipper is," Lacey retorted, pulling a painting free with a flourish.

Susa took one look at the canvas and felt years fly away. *She was breathless, young, standing frozen in a violent storm of discovery as she looked at a Lewis Marten painting for the first time.* Hand against her throat, she made a small sound of wonder and surprise.

"Susa?" Ian said instantly. "What is it? Are you—"

She held up her hand, cutting him off. "Where did you get this?" she demanded without looking away from the canvas.

Lacey moved uneasily. "A garage sale."

Deftly Susa turned the unframed canvas over without touching the face of it. All she saw was an e-mail address and the words *Sandy Cove*. There was no artist's title on the back. No date. But then, many artists didn't date their work.

"A garage sale," Susa said. "Where? When?"

"I, um, I don't remember."

Susa pinned the younger woman with a clear hazel glance that seemed to look right through to her soul. "How can that be?"

Lacey cleared her throat. "I go to twenty or thirty sales a month, so it's hard to keep track."

"Do you have any more Martens?"

"Martens?"

"Paintings by Lewis Marten," Susa said.

"I don't even have one. These are—" Lacey stopped just before she blurted out something about her grandfather. "There's no name on the paintings, so I'm sure they don't belong to anyone called Marten." Especially as she'd watched her grandfather paint *Sandy Cove*, a fact that she wasn't going to reveal.

Susa flipped the painting back over and for the first time looked for an artist's signature. Her arched eyebrows lifted when she found none. She tilted and turned the canvas to catch the light, looked at its back, and turned it faceup again, fascinated and bemused by seeing the past live again in her hands, a past brought to life by someone who had lived at the time when Painter's Beach was called Sandy Cove.

"Well, a rose is a rose is a rose and all that," Susa said. "No matter that it isn't signed, this was painted by an extremely talented plein air artist who worked in Lewis Marten's time." *More likely, in his body.*

Lacey grinned. "I knew it!"

"A garage sale. My God." Susa laughed triumphantly. "My ancestors strike again."

"What?" Ian asked.

"Long story," she said, shaking her head. "Put it this way—I just *knew* I'd find something wonderful if I did the triage for the charity auction. But this—this is like pulling weeds and finding diamonds in the roots. Extraordinary." She looked at Lacey and started laughing. "A garage sale! Lord, but life is sweet." She held out her hand. "I'm Susa Donovan and I'm delighted you came here tonight, Ms.—"

"January Marsh," Ian said before Lacey could get over the shock of shaking hands with a painter whose name was often mentioned in the same breath as Georgia O'Keeffe.

"Are the others like this?" Susa asked, releasing Lacey's hand.

At first Lacey was afraid that Susa had somehow read her mind and knew that there was a storage unit filled with hundreds of unframed canvases by her grandfather. Then Lacey realized that Susa was looking eagerly at the two other wrapped packages.

"They're all unsigned," Lacey said carefully.

"Well, open them up!"

Ian smiled at Susa's enthusiasm. "I've just about got this one out of its cocoon."

"Here," Lacey said, leaning in over his right arm and pointing to a piece of red tape. "Yank on that and it will all come off. Mostly."

He yanked. Bubble wrap slithered down the canvas. Stately, elegant eucalyptus trees rose against a radiant slice of dawn.

"Oh, my," Susa murmured. She took the canvas and turned it slowly in a circle, letting light flood over the painting from all angles. "Superb. Just superb. Muscular, graceful, energetic, serene. Emotionally vivid, technically fluid. Everything you could ask of a plein air painter. And so very like Marten."

Ian looked from the canvas and Susa's rapt face. "Should I know that name?"

"Lewis Marten?" she asked.

"Yes."

"No reason to, unless you have a doctorate in obscure California Impressionists. All anyone ever knew was that Marten was a teenage runaway who showed up in Laguna Beach before World War Two," Susa said. "The local artist community took him in and then watched in amazement as a skinny child painted them right into the ground."

"Ouch," Ian said.

"Oh, they didn't admit it aloud. There were some excellent painters around at the time and their egos weren't tiny. But still, when you confront huge unselfconscious talent like this, it just takes the world away."

"That's how I felt the first time I saw a painting by you," Lacey said, "It . . . burned."

Susa glanced at Lacey, saw sincerity rather than flattery, and smiled. "Thank you. I love knowing that one of my paintings reached out and grabbed someone."

Lacey started to say that her grandfather had been a great fan of Susa's paintings. Instead, she said, "Anyone who isn't 'grabbed' by your work must be dead between the ears and the ribs."

"It would be lovely to think so," Susa said dryly, "but I know better. After you cut away all the intricate intellectual rationalizations, art is a matter of taste. No single flavor works for everyone. Nor should it, despite what the critics and academics would have us believe."

"Don't tell me you had problems with the critics and academics?" Lacey asked before she thought. Then she winced. "Oops. Sorry. I didn't mean to be rude."

Susa was laughing too hard to hide it. "I came of painting age during the last hurrah of postmodern abstract minimalism. I painted 'scenery.' Believe me, I had a long procession of teachers, fellow artists, and critics telling me I was painting the wrong thing."

Lacey smiled. "I get some of that, too."

"I thought you were a painter," Susa said with satisfaction.

"How could you tell?"

"Hands."

Lacey looked down. Sure enough, she hadn't been able to get all the paint off her skin. "Mother would kill me."

Wordlessly Susa held out her own hands. Neatly trimmed nails, no manicure, scrubbed skin . . . and indelible, colorful shadows of the last oils she had used.

"Don't forget the chin," Ian said.

Both women looked at him.

Gently he touched just under Susa's chin, then Lacey's. "Different colors, same place."

"When I'm in a hurry, I switch brushes and tuck the extra ones under my chin," Lacey said, trying not to be embarrassed.

"Me, too," Susa said. "My husband teases me about it. Says it's a good thing I'm so short that no one will ever see the bottom of my chin." She gave Ian a measuring kind of look. "But you noticed."

"Lifetime of looking at pretty women," he said blandly. "The prettier they are, the closer I look."

Lacey rolled her eyes.

Susa just laughed. "With that kind of focus, you should have been a painter yourself."

"If you'd ever seen me draw, you'd bite your tongue clear through before you suggested that again."

She looked at his hands. Large. Competent. Callused. Clean. "Ah, well, you're either called to paint or you aren't. What's in the last package? I feel like a kid at Christmas."

Lacey thought of the painting still shrouded in bubble wrap and wondered all over again if she had made the right choice. "It's not like the others," she said slowly.

"Not the same painter?" Susa asked, disappointed.

"Same painter. Different mood."

Susa waited for a moment, realized that Lacey was hesitating for some reason, and said, "Stop torturing me and unwrap it."

Mentally crossing her fingers, Lacey pulled the red tape and waited for Susa's reaction to *Scream Bloody Murder*.

But it was Ian who responded first. "Jesus Christ, is that what I think it is?"

"Quiet," Susa said. It was a voice her family rarely heard, but when they did, they shut up.

So did Ian. He studied the painting and waited, wondering what was going on. He was no painter, but he knew a murder when he saw it in black and blue and red in front of him. What he didn't know was who had killed, who had died, and why it had been painted.

"Incredible. He's fully mature in this one. Nothing blurred. Nothing hiding. Nothing bridled. Pure talent driven by even purer rage." Susa let out a long breath. "It's a vision of humanity that I wouldn't be comfortable hanging in my home, yet as an artist I can only say, 'Bravo!' Were you planning on auctioning any of these, Ms. Marsh?"

It took Lacey a moment to realize that she was Ms. Marsh. "I—I hadn't thought that far ahead."

In fact, she was just realizing that she hadn't truly thought beyond the instant when her belief in her grandfather would be vindicated. Now that it had happened, she was frantically wondering how she would manage to stay anonymous. She certainly hadn't counted on being recognized by a customer from Lost Treasures Found who knew Susa Donovan.

The only good news here—beyond Susa's enthusiasm—was that no one had questioned the garage sale story. And if someone did, she'd stick to it and dare anyone to prove otherwise.

"My advice would be to get a professional appraisal before you sell these paintings. Ian can put you in contact with an excellent house, Rarities Unlimited."

"He's an unknown artist," Lacey began, "so I don't think—"

"If he's Lewis Marten," Susa interrupted calmly, "and I believe he is, his paintings, if you are lucky enough to find one, start at three hundred thousand dollars."

"Holy shit." Lacey heard her own words. "Ah, I mean . . ."

"Holy shit indeed," Susa said, laughing.

Lacey looked at Ian. "Rarities Unlimited? Is that the

company I think it is, the one that works with museums and collectors around the world?"

"Buy, sell, appraise, protect," he said. "That's us."

"Can't afford you."

"If those paintings are what Susa thinks they are, you can afford us."

"They aren't," Lacey said flatly.

"You sound very sure," Ian said.

She just shrugged.

"Why?" Susa asked.

"It doesn't matter," Lacey said. "I'm just sure."

Gnawing at her lip, she looked at the three canvases and wondered how long her father had known that Grandpa Rainbow was a forger.

12

Stacks of paintings leaned haphazardly against the wall and one another in the elegant ballroom of the Savoy Hotel, the latest in a series of four hundred dollars a night and up—way up—hotels studding the glorious southern California coast. The hotel wasn't open for business yet. Electricians still chased ghosts in the wires and decorators were still unwrapping crates of "accents" to add to the public areas. But for a few very important people, the hotel was open for business. Any member of the Forrest family was one of those important people. Any guest of theirs was another.

Savoy Forrest looked at the chaos and wondered how the place would be ready in time for the auction on Saturday, but he knew it would be. His father had made it a personal crusade, and nobody wanted to face Ward Forrest with a handful of excuses as to why a job wasn't done on time. Ward would listen, say something savage, and fire people. Failure wasn't a word that he accepted, especially on one of the few Savoy development projects he'd managed to get built despite all the protests.

"Mr. Forrest, how wonderful of you to stop by," Mr. Goodman said, all but rubbing his hands together at having one of the wealthy art-buying Forrests within reach.

"I kept hearing rumors that Susa Donovan was excited about some of the paintings," Savoy said. "If anyone would know about it, I figured the past president of American Figurative Artists Association would."

Goodman nodded. "Absolutely. I do."

Savoy smiled. It wasn't likely there was any connection with the paintings and those that the Savoy Museum already owned, but if they were by the same elusive artist, he wanted to place the first and last bid before some collector or art gallery beat him to it. It wasn't often he got a chance to give his father something he'd really love to have.

"If she's excited, I'm damned curious," Savoy said as he surveyed the chaos. "Are the paintings here?"

"No, these are the donated paintings for the auction. The exhibition-only paintings are in the main conference room."

"Anything that might be of interest to the museum in this lot?" Savoy asked, waving a hand toward the leaning paintings.

"Actually, there are several rather nice early landscapes," Goodman said, smoothing a long strand of hair across his otherwise bald head. "Not world-class, of course, but La Susa thought enough of them to write a note and tape it to the back of each canvas.

That alone should add several hundred dollars or more to the final price of each painting."

"Let's see them. I'm always on the lookout for art for our museum. We own quite a few works by relatively unknown painters."

Goodman smiled eagerly. The Forrests were the foremost—and most unpredictable—collectors of plein air paintings in a state full of wealthy, eccentric art collectors. "I've set aside some of the most interesting paintings over here."

He led Savoy to a corner overlooking the zero-rim swimming pool at the cliff's edge and the whitecapped ocean beyond. Savoy dodged a decorator and two carpenters stringing a long, tight wire above eye level across the wall to hang the canvases. At the moment, some of them were leaving marks against the base of the newly painted wall. Goodman stopped at a long eighteenth-century library table where paintings were carefully stacked.

"This one is especially sweet," he said, lifting up a small landscape.

Savoy took the landscape and shifted position until he found the best light pouring through the floor-to-ceiling windows. The surface of the landscape badly needed cleaning, but beneath decades of grime the colors of golden light and equally golden hills whispered of lazy, sunny afternoons and a time when steam trains were the fastest thing on earth. On the back there was a piece of paper taped to the canvas that gave Susa's reasons for singling the painting out for special attention. She mentioned elegance and simplicity of composition and "unself-conscious, almost naive brushwork. This is a genuine act of creation rather than simply an imitation of a popular artistic style."

"I believe that's the hill where the Savoy Tower stands now," Goodman said. "This painting would fit nicely into the Before and After wing of the Savoy Museum."

Savoy nodded and set the painting down. "I'll keep it in mind."

Goodman pulled out several more landscapes that had caught Susa's eye, including another one that depicted a piece of the Savoy Ranch that hadn't changed. "This one is—"

"Picnic Bluff," Savoy cut in, taking the painting.

He'd seen more accomplished plein air paintings—a lot of them—but not one of them had been painted on Picnic Bluff. It was his own personal time-out place. Whenever family, business, or life in general got to him, he would go to the bluff, lie on his back with a stem of grass in his teeth, and listen to the ocean foaming softly below and the wind whispering secrets to the hills. It didn't cure the problems of the world, but it went a long way toward making them tolerable.

Picnic Bluff was square in the center of the land that was slated for development into Ward Forrest's visionary twenty-first-century city. Part of Savoy regretted that. The rest of him knew that unless the majority of the land was developed, the ranch would have to be broken up and sold off for taxes to keep the family in money. If the developed land included Picnic Bluff, so be it. There were a lot of bluffs on the ranch; he'd find another one to retreat to.

"Put a five-hundred-dollar minimum on this one," Savoy said. "I'll guarantee that much."

"Excellent." Goodman pulled out a business card, scribbled on the back of it, and stuck it into the frame.

Savoy looked at a few other paintings, but didn't find anything he wanted to own for himself or for the museum. He glanced pointedly at his watch. Goodman got the hint and unlocked the door to a room that was furnished as an intimate conference area.

"Reporters," Goodman said apologetically as he walked across the room to another locked door. "Word of Susa's enthusiasm got out and we've been buried in calls for photo ops of Susa with the paintings."

"Great publicity."

"It certainly would be," Goodman said, working over the lock on a door to an executive retreat that was bathroom, sitting room, and changing room combined, "but the owner of the paintings refused reprographic rights, even to the press."

"Not uncommon."

"No," Goodman said, "but usually owners of unknown artists aren't so reluctant for publicity." He shrugged. "Artists are an unpredictable lot."

"The owner is an artist?"

"So I understand. At least the person who brought the paintings to Susa last night is an artist."

"Who?"

"Ms. January Marsh."

"Never heard of her."

"Neither have I." The lock finally gave way. "Ah, here we go. Have to remember to have Maintenance oil that. They don't have room for paintings in the hotel safe, you see."

Savoy didn't answer. He'd just seen the three paintings that had been hung carefully on the opposite wall. Between the two landscapes the violence of the center painting was almost surreal.

This definitely was the same artist his father collected at every opportunity. Paintings came on the market so rarely that it had been years since he'd seen one.

"The woman, January Marsh," Savoy said without glancing away from the art.

"Yes?"

"What is she asking for these?"

"They aren't for sale."

Savoy turned and gave Goodman a look. "Not for sale? Wasn't that the whole point of this charitable exercise—raising money for the Friends of Moreno County?"

Goodman shifted uncomfortably under Savoy's cool eyes. "Well, yes, but not all people decided to auction off their paintings for charity. Their donation is the twenty-dollar-per-painting fee for having La Susa look at their family treasures."

"I see." Savoy turned back to the paintings. "I take it that Ms. March is local?"

"I don't know."

Savoy spun around. "Excuse me?"

"Our contact is an e-mail address."

"No telephone? Not even a P.O. box?"

Goodman shook his head. "La Susa had a difficult time getting Ms. Marsh to agree even to exhibit the paintings."

"Odd." He went closer to the paintings. "Well, give me the e-mail then. I'll contact Ms. Marsh. I want my father to see these paintings before I do anything, but I'm sure he'll agree that they would be excellent additions to the Savoy Museum."

Then perhaps Ms. Marsh could explain why there was no signature on Marten's paintings—and how they had survived the fire that killed Marten and burned his life's work to smelly ash.

13

Frowning, Lacey clamped a brush between her teeth and looked at the landscape she was painting. It wasn't working. Maybe it was the fact that she'd been thinking about Susa and David Quinn's paintings. Maybe she was just having a bad day and shouldn't be trying to paint.

And maybe she was spending all her energy wondering what to do about a string of e-mails from one of the most powerful men in the state of California.

Ignore him. He'll go away.

She blew fiercely at the curl that kept dangling over her right eye, switched brushes, and added a touch more yellow to the green already on her brush.

Dad would shit a litter of green lizards if he knew.

And that's what the painting she was working on looked like—a litter of excreted green lizards.

"The hell with it," she said, throwing down her brush in disgust.

"It's not that bad," Ian said.

Lacey gasped and turned around so fast she almost tripped. "What are you doing here?"

"I came to pick up my poster and—"

"It's downstairs."

"Your partner sent me up here," Ian continued, ignoring the interruption. "Susa wants you to come and paint with her out on the Savoy Ranch."

Lacey just stared at him. "What?"

"My poster," he said, beginning all over again. "You know, the one that—"

"Not that," she cut in. "Susa wants me to *paint with her?*"

"Yeah." He tilted his head and took in her shocked brown eyes. "Something wrong with that?"

Lacey took a breath, then another. "Susa is a goddess."

"I'll have to tell her sons. They haven't figured it out. Archer is sure she's a mortal in need of tender loving care." Ian smiled slowly.

"Don't smile like that," she said, groaning. "I'm having a hard enough time thinking as it is."

He laughed and wound a shining chestnut curl around his finger. Letting the hair go, he stroked the back of his finger down her cheek. "You're one of a kind, Ms. Marsh."

"More like one of thousands who get lost in that smile."

"No one ever had any trouble finding her way out again real quick."

"I'm terrible at mazes," Lacey admitted.

"This is supposed to discourage me?"

"Think of it as a warning." She smiled crookedly and drew in a deep, cautious breath. Lord, but the man was good. He hadn't crowded her at all, yet her heart was doing the double-time thing. "Does Susa really want me to paint with her?"

"Don't take my word for it. Ask her yourself."

"Wow."

"What?"

"Nothing. Just wow. I'll be all thumbs and squirt oils everywhere." Lacey sighed. "But La Susa has taught classes and done videos, so I guess she's used to awed students getting clumsy around her."

"After ten minutes, you'll never think of her as La Susa again. She'll just be Susa, a wife and mother and woman with a great sense of humor and a mind like a steel trap."

"You left out the part about being beautiful," Lacey said, thinking of Susa's petite elegance.

"She's happily married to a man who would clean my clock if he caught me flirting with his wife."

"In that case, when do we go painting?"

"The hotel put up a fancy picnic so we can go whenever you're ready."

"Which hotel?"

"The one that's opening Saturday with the charity auction."

"Savoy Hotel? Am I dreaming?"

Lazily Ian reached out as though to pinch her.

Lacey swatted his hand away. "No, I don't want to wake up. I get Susa *and* a catered lunch from a five-star chef?"

"Five stars, huh? No wonder the stuff smelled so good."

Behind Lacey, her computer beeped, telling her that another e-mail had arrived.

"Something important?" Ian asked.

She shrugged and said under her breath, "More like some*one*."

Ian glanced at the screen. Her e-mail program was open. Five e-mails were lined up, three unread. A sixth was displayed on the screen.

"Are you always this nosy?" Lacey asked as he leaned toward the computer.

"Yes."

"Anyone ever tell you it's rude to read other people's mail?"

"Constantly, but my own is so boring."

She hit a button on the keyboard and the mail program vanished.

"Dang," he said. "Just when it was getting interesting. What does Savoy Forrest want?"

"To buy my paintings."

"That's great!" Ian looked around at the canvases stacked against or hanging on the wall. "Which ones?"

"Not ones I've painted. The ones my—the ones I found at a garage sale," she corrected quickly.

"Oh. That explains it."

"What?"

"Why the e-mails were addressed to Ms. Marsh."

And why there were only six listed e-mails, all of them within the past twenty-four hours. Obviously "Ms. Marsh" was a very new identity that had been activated recently, probably for the mystery paintings. Ian had pretty much figured that out already, but in his line of work independent verification was always good. What he really wanted to figure out was what Lacey was hiding, and why.

He wondered if a champagne picnic would loosen her tongue.

14

The dirt road wound out of the grassy canyon and up the chaparral-covered flanks of the coastal hills. Although the ranch had three guarded gates close to public roads, the back country had few fences, many twisting tracks, and no guards. Anyone who knew the back roads of the county could bypass the gates and have a lovely drive through open land—until one of the ranch hands noticed and put out an alarm. Then a county deputy or ranch employee would show up and escort the trespassers back to public highways.

Overhead, wind stirred the clouds into swirls of shadow and light, drama and tranquillity. Ian drove the ragged ranch road with the ease of a man who had seen a lot of dirt tracks in his childhood. The vehicle he drove could have belonged to his childhood, too. It was a GMC SUV from the time before SUVs got their name. He called it a truck and dared anyone else to do otherwise. Truck chassis, bench seat in front, backseat ripped out to make room for more covered cargo area, four-wheel drive that didn't go sour with hard work—Ian's baby was dusty, battered, smooth-running, and tough. Everything that mattered to performance was in top shape, from the new safety windshield for the new wipers to the well-tuned engine and expensive off-road tires.

Even after all Ian's hard work, when put next to the fleet of white Savoy Enterprises vehicles that the ranch hands used, his ancient truck looked like an accident waiting to happen.

Susa and Lacey loved the truck at first sight.

He just enjoyed one of the perks of having a pretty woman in the center of the seat—in spite of the aftermarket seat belts he'd installed, every time he swerved right, Lacey slid across the slick old bench seat and into him.

The tires bit into a hard right curve, spitting dirt and gravel. Susa laughed like a girl and hung on to the "chicken bar" above the passenger window. Lacey didn't have a chicken bar, so she braced herself against the dashboard and occasionally against the driver's hard thigh. When she did, he gave her a pirate's grin and gunned the truck just enough to make her hold on to him tighter.

Sunlight spilled like glory through ghost-white naked sycamore branches in the canyon below. Mist was a silver whisper sighing through the trees, caressing every crease and hollow, shimmering with time and secrets.

"Oh my," Susa breathed. "It squeezes your heart, the beauty."

"Want to stop?" Ian asked.

"If we stopped at every beautiful place we saw, we'd never make it to the top," Susa said.

"There are worse fates," Lacey said.

"Ah, but I know where we're going," Susa said, smiling. "It's worth getting there. I can't wait to capture it on canvas again. And fail miserably, again."

Lacey glanced at the artist who was a living legend and didn't seem to know it. Or maybe she just didn't care. "Have you been here before?" Lacey asked.

"Yes, when I was much younger than you."

"I thought your biography said you were born in Sacramento, not around here."

"I was. But I was the wrong child for my parents, so I lied about my age, moved to a shack out in Laguna Canyon, and started painting. Those were the days—turpentine and starvation." She laughed wryly. "I cleaned every house but my own to survive. I made a lot of friends, painted until I couldn't see the canvas, and sat up all night solving the problems of the universe while drinking bad wine with other lost souls."

"Sounds like me. Parents and all." Then Lacey added hurriedly, "Not that I'll ever be nearly as good a painter as you."

Susa waved off the words. "It's the pursuit that matters, not the labels people put on it. Although I'm quite human enough to prefer praise to brickbats and eating to starving," she added, winking at the younger woman.

Lacey grinned. "Me, too."

As Susa looked through the windshield at the canyon that had changed far less than she had through the decades, her face settled into lines that weren't quite sad. "Time is the greatest mystery. Here and not here. Memory and regret. I took my first lover on a grassy knoll not far away, broke my heart over him, and then I went on to break other hearts. I painted at the feet of California Impressionists like Alfred R. Mitchell and Charles Fries, talked to men who studied under William Wendt and Edgar Payne, fell in love with a Lewis Marten painting, and wept when they told me he was dead." She half smiled. "Where does the past go? Is there a cosmic museum filled with the beauty we've forgotten? It was all so urgent then, so misty now."

"How did Marten die?" Ian asked. "From what you've said, he must have been fairly young."

"He died in a studio fire, one of those pointless tragedies. He was mourning the death of Three Savoy, his patron and close friend, as well as a hard drinker whose car couldn't drive itself. When Marten heard about the accident, he got drunk and went to his studio to paint out his grief. Alcohol, turpentine, and cigarettes." She shook her head slowly, thinking of the wasted talent. "He fell asleep painting. The cigarette he was smoking dropped onto paint rags and touched off his studio. He never woke up. And his paintings . . ." She sighed. "All those extraordinary paintings burned."

"Three Savoy?" Ian asked. "I remember that name. My great-uncle worked as a deputy sheriff in Moreno County. Same for his son later on. They had some odd stories to tell."

Susa looked at Ian with new interest. "I'll bet they did. It was wild in those days. Kind of an early version of the Don't Ask, Don't Tell policy. Everybody seems to think sin was invented in the hippie sixties, but I'm here to tell you that the good ol' boys of Moreno County could have taught sin to the devil."

Ian snickered. "Yeah, that's what my uncle said." He put the truck into second and ground up a steep turn. "Three Savoy was what my great-grandmother used to call a rounder. Never met a bottle or a whore he didn't like. Nobody mentioned that he was a painter."

"He wasn't," Susa said, hanging on to the chicken bar again. "Oh, he dabbled, but from the paintings I've seen, he was quite ordinary. I suspect he was more drawn to the life than to the art."

"He could afford it," Ian said.

"Oh, yes." Susa laughed. "I used to wish I'd been born in time to run with Three's crowd—great food and booze, no worries, no limits, just the untouched landscape to paint and like-minded friends to celebrate the night with."

Suddenly Lacey grabbed at the dashboard and said, "Hey, back up, you missed a pothole."

Ian hit the brakes and threw the truck into reverse.

"No! I was kidding!" Lacey said, laughing even as she braced herself.

"Are you saying I'm a bad driver?" he asked.

"Would I say that to the man with his hands on a lethal weapon?"

Automatically Ian started to check his shoulder holster, then realized she meant the steering wheel. "Relax," he said, shifting into first gear and then rapidly into second. "I used to drive in dirt races when I was a kid in Bakersfield."

"Demolition derbies?" Lacey asked dryly.

"How'd you guess?"

Susa laughed.

Lacey decided to ask the question that had been eating at her since shortly after she'd met Ian Lapstrake. "Would it be rude to ask why you're carrying a gun? Yikes!" Lacey almost hit the roof as the truck swerved and hit a bump. "Do you shoot the cars you can't demolish?"

"He carries a gun because my husband is a worrier," Susa said.

Lacey opened her mouth, shook her head, and said, "I'm sure that makes sense to someone."

"Remember the 'protect' part of Buy, Sell, Appraise, Protect?" Ian asked.

"Um, yeah." She slanted him a sideways glance. "So you're protecting a culturally significant work of art called Susa Donovan?"

Susa laughed into her hands. "She's got you, Ian. No matter what you say, one of us is going to hit you."

Ian grinned. And didn't say a word.

"What Ian is protecting is my paintings," Susa said.

"You bet," he said earnestly. "That's why I left them in a hotel room a sharp six-year-old could crack and came along to watch you smear oil paints on yourself."

"Um, I sense an area of disagreement," Lacey said.

"No shit," Ian said. "But I can guaran-damn-tee that if my brief was to watch the paintings, you two would be out here alone or the paintings would be in a bank vault."

"I'm not going to waste painting time waiting for the banks to open," Susa said patiently.

"It's always painting time for you," Ian muttered.

"So glad you understand. I knew you were smart."

Ian was too smart to say what he was thinking, so he shut up. No wonder the Donovan thought his wife needed a keeper. She did. The woman just didn't think the way the rest of the world did.

Lacey stared at Susa. "You left a million dollars in paintings in your hotel room?"

The older woman shrugged. "They're not worth anything until they're sold."

"But—holy shit."

Susa just laughed. "The look on your face. I'll be sure not to invite you to my annual burning."

"Your what?"

"Every year I go through my paintings and decide what's worth keeping and what isn't."

"And you burn the rejects?" Ian asked, intrigued.

"Right down to the staples holding canvas to stretcher," Susa said cheerfully.

Lacey put her hands over her ears. "I'm not listening to this and I'm sure not believing what I'm not hearing."

"How long have you painted, Jan?" Susa asked.

Guilt streaked through Lacey. She really wished she hadn't promised her father anonymity. Lying to Susa about her identity was getting more and more uncomfortable.

"Grandpa put a paintbrush in my hand before I was three," Lacey said, grabbing the dashboard. "Dad swore I was going to be a housepainter, the way I covered everything in sight with paint. Including the cat."

"I've tied a few things to a cat's tail in my time," Ian said, "but I never painted one. What did you do, knock it out first?"

"Nope. Canned tuna in one hand, brush in the other, and presto! One house tiger emerges from the boring cocoon of a formerly white Persian."

Susa laughed and gave Lacey a one-armed hug. "I

hope your parents appreciated you. I always wanted more daughters than chance brought me."

Lacey's smile faded as she thought of all the old arguments over her own painting, and the much newer ones over her grandfather's work. "Oh, my parents and I bumped along okay. I wasn't what they wanted, but they've gotten over it. Mostly."

"Consider yourself adopted," Susa said. "Both my daughters are very creative, but neither of them would have thought to paint any of our cats." Then Susa paused and looked thoughtful. "Well, let's just say I never found out about it if they did."

The truck breasted the last curve. Ahead lay a rumpled bench of land sloping gently down to rocky sea bluffs a mile away. The ocean was the color of hammered silver beneath the clouds and sapphire where the sun stabbed through. The land was covered with grasses whose seed heads were already forming on the sunny slope, making the landscape a tossing, silver-tipped sea rippling beneath the restless wind. Ravines snaked down from the coastal hills in shades of dark green and shadows. A hawk soared overhead, impaled on sunlight and utterly free, shining like heaven.

Lacey had never wanted so much to have brushes and canvas and time to paint.

"Soon," Susa said, patting the younger woman's knee. "Almost there."

"Sorry. I didn't mean to—"

"You didn't do anything but act like the painter you are," Susa said. "Views like this make the hand and mind itch, don't they? When the first painters arrived, the Pacific Coast Highway was a dirt wagon track along the top of the bluffs. Now it's lane after lane of rolling steel. But the rest of the countryside here hasn't changed. Wind and color, sun and sea and land. Those things outlive us."

"If they aren't developed," Lacey said.

"Private property. Public need. Human greed." Susa shrugged. "That hasn't changed in all of history, and I don't think it will start changing now. We do what we can to save the best of what remains."

"That's why you're doing the auction," Lacey said. "To save this."

"I *paint* to save this. I'm doing the auction so that others might someday stand where we're standing and remember their own youth, their own time when the world was bright and untouched. It never was, of course. But it pleases us to think so. Turn right, Ian."

"Here?"

"Yes."

"Glad this baby is a four-by-four," he said. "Whatever 'road' was once here is more in your mind than on the ground. Hold on tight."

"To what?" Lacey asked.

He smiled slowly. "Me."

"I want to paint you," Lacey said before she thought about it.

"Naked?" he asked instantly.

"Your smile."

"Dang. Here I was going to get all hot and bothered at the thought of you making a tiger out of little-old-house-cat me."

Susa snickered. "Lawe is right. You should be under lock and key."

"I'd never speak ill of a son in the presence of his mother, but Lawe has it the wrong way around." Ian downshifted and crept along the path that was little more than indentations in the grass where ruts used to be. "How that boy has stayed out of the clutches of some lucky woman is a wonder to me."

"And an inspiration?" Susa asked tartly.

"Take the Fifth," Lacey said. "It works for me when my mother is on a why-aren't-you-married rip."

Ian grinned at Lacey. "Good idea. I'm pleading here, Susa."

"Lock and key," Susa said. "Both of you."

Truck wheels spun on grass, then got down to dirt for better traction.

"Hope that champagne is corked real good," Ian said as the truck lurched.

Lacey risked a look into the interior storage compartment behind the front bench seat. The fancy hamper supplied by the hotel was askew, but the ice chest was still in place.

"Nothing's bubbling out," Lacey said.

Ian concentrated on driving cross country over ruts that had filled in about the time he'd been born.

"Just another few hundred yards," Susa said. "If the spring hasn't dried up, there should be some feral eucalyptus growing in Cross Country Canyon. More of a ravine, really. Narrow enough in parts for a good hunter to jump, which apparently is what the Savoy matriarch was doing when something went wrong and she died."

"There are worse ways to go," Ian said.

"I'm sure she would have agreed with you," Susa said. "She'd outlived her husband and her only child, her daughter-in-law hated her, and her only granddaughter was as wild as the wind. The Savoy Curse."

"Too many dollars," Ian said.

"Not enough cents," Lacey added innocently.

He groaned at the pun.

"I'm going to take you home with me," Susa said, smiling at Lacey. "Don will love you. Stop about twenty yards up from here, Ian. There should be a level spot where we used to build campfires."

Ian parked the truck where Susa pointed. While he wouldn't have pitched a tent there, it was level enough that he didn't have to put rocks under the tires.

"Let me help with that," Ian said as Susa dragged her easel out of the pickup bed.

She shooed his hands off like irritating flies. "You'd just be in the way."

He looked at Lacey. She was already heading out into the grass, her arms full and her eyes fixed on the view.

While the women set up easels and small folding tables for their paints and brushes and palettes, Ian lowered the dusty tailgate and put out a five-star feast. Colorful little vegetables and piquant dips, meat pies in airy pastries, something that looked like tiny popovers and tasted like heaven, finger-size columns of bread smelling of herbs and cheese, a dessert of brownies and lemon bars, and enough fine champagne to put them all on the wrong side of the law.

"Anybody hungry?" he called out hopefully.

Nothing answered but the wind.

He took it as agreement. "So am I."

Reminding himself that he was working, not playing, he filled two hotel plates with an assortment of food and took it to the women. He started to add the linen napkins that had been provided, then looked up in time to see both women absently wipe their hands on their jeans.

"Right. They're wearing their napkins."

Susa barely nodded when he eased the food within

reach on her paint table. When he set a plate near Lacey, she gave him a vague smile, a muttered word, and went back to painting. Same thing when he opened bottles of water and put them out—*Hello, good-bye, do I know you?*

Ian left the champagne corked. No way he was going to waste Grande Dame on two women who wouldn't know if he was feeding them pork rinds and home brew. Uncapping a second bottle of water for himself, he filled a third plate, leaned against the side of the truck, and ate with enough appreciation for himself and the women combined. As he ate, he catalogued the surrounding land with the eye of a man who had once jumped out of planes at night behind enemy lines. Then he'd jumped once too often and broke his right ankle in too many places to ever jump again.

He couldn't say that he missed it.

No matter where he looked, nothing moved but the wind and a red-tail hawk looking for lunch. None of the fleet of white vehicles showed on any of the dirt tracks that wound over hills and through valleys and canyons. No trespasser was running his dog in the open country. The cattle and farm machinery that had once cropped the hills were gone. He was alone with two beautiful women who didn't even know he was alive.

"Welcome to my life," he muttered, shaking his head. "I really should get a dog or a cat to talk to. Or goldfish. They don't care if you go off for a week at a time. Maybe some ivy or dandelions or something. Nope, you have to water plants. Where are pet rocks when you need them?"

If either of the women heard, neither answered.

They were as lost in their painting as the wind was in the sky.

Ian reached under the front seat and pulled out the binoculars he'd bought when he realized that his bodyguarding of Susa required excursions into unpopulated ranch lands. Not that he expected any trouble. He didn't. And he was paid to make sure it stayed that way.

He finished his second bottle of water, opened a thermos of coffee, and quartered the land with the binoculars while he sipped rich coffee from a plastic cup. No matter where he looked, he saw nothing but gentle hills, lush grass, outcroppings of boulders, occasional eucalyptus or chaparral in the ravines, and what looked like an old piece of machinery rusting at the bottom of Cross Country Canyon. It was too early in the day for deer or coyotes, and way too early for teenagers sneaking out into the wilds with six-packs of illicit beer under their arms.

He brought the binoculars back to the shadowed ravine, intrigued by the rusting machinery. In addition to old movie posters, he collected old baling hooks, branding irons, license plates, and less identifiable bits of metal left over from forgotten farms. It wouldn't take but a few minutes to skid down the slope, check out the rusty ruins, and get rid of all the water he'd been drinking.

He searched the surroundings a final time. Nothing in sight that shouldn't be. He put the field glasses on the seat.

"Susa, I'm going into the ravine for a bit," he said. "You holler if you need anything."

She might have nodded. He wasn't sure. He went up to Lacey and said right into her ear, "I'm taking a bio break. You yell if you see anything new. Okay?"

She jumped, gave him a deer-in-headlights look, and said, "Uh. Sure. Whatever."

For a moment he considered grabbing her and kissing her senseless, just to see her reaction. Then he decided his ego couldn't take it if she ignored that, too.

"I'll be right down there," he said, pointing to the ravine. "Think you can remember that?"

"Sure. Why wouldn't I?"

"Jesus. I give up."

Lacey winced. "Sorry. I, uh, get a little distracted when I'm painting."

"Really? I hadn't noticed."

"Have I been that bad?"

"Yeah. Susa's worse. Now, listen up. I'm going down in the ravine for a few minutes. If you see anything human besides us, let me know in a real loud voice. Okay?"

Lacey frowned and glanced around at the beautiful empty land. "Do you really think—"

"I'm paid to be paranoid and I'm good at my job," he cut in. Gently he rubbed a smear of blue paint off the corner of her mouth and touched the center of her lower lip with the pad of his thumb. "Don't worry. Go back to painting."

"Did I almost get a pat on the head?" she muttered.

"No. You almost got kissed."

She looked at his dark eyes and wide, tempting mouth, and wondered if it was too late. Then she realized she'd said it aloud and wanted to bury her face in her paints. "Sorry. I don't have any, uh, social graces when I'm painting. Or any other time. I just say whatever I think."

Ian brushed a tender, tasting kind of kiss over her lips. "You ate dessert first."

She blinked and looked into the nearly black eyes that were so close to her own. "What?"

"Lemon bar."

"You've been drinking coffee. Tastes good."

"I'll get you some," he said.

"Only if you drink it first. I hate coffee."

His eyes darkened to a hot kind of black. "If I weren't on duty, I'd take you down in that ravine and . . . play."

She blew out a breath. "Whew. Do you come with warning labels?"

"Do you?"

"I've never needed any."

"Neither have I," Ian said. "Guess we have a bad effect on each other."

She licked her lips. "If that's bad, heaven is overrated. Now go away before I do something embarrassing."

"Like what?"

"Reach inside your jacket and see if your gun is loaded," she retorted.

Ian laughed out loud.

"Knock it off, you two," Susa said, trying not to laugh herself. "You're distracting me and Don is half a world away."

"Does that mean if I tell you I'm taking a walk in the ravine you'll hear me this time?" Ian asked.

"I hear you," Susa said. "Now I don't want to hear you for a while."

"I'm gone," he said, but he gave Lacey a tasting kind of look before he loped off toward the ravine.

Then he paid attention to the footing. Running shoes were fine for sidewalks, well-combed athletic tracks, and pavement. On long grass and a steep slope, the shoes were a little like two surfboards. He managed to stay right side up and landed at the bottom with only a twinge or two from his bad ankle.

The rusting hulk that had intrigued him from a distance wasn't farm machinery after all. It was an old two-door Chevy of the kind once loved by hot-rodders. Even overgrown with grass and covered with eucalyptus leaves and bark, it was obvious that the car had burned either before or after it had bounced down the steep ravine. Rusted, heat-warped metal was scattered over the ravine. Whatever had happened had been a long time ago. Only the biggest eucalyptus growing nearby showed any trace of fire scars; all the younger trees were untouched.

He watered one of the trees while he eyed hunks of wreckage. What looked like a bumper lay upside down by the one of the rocks poking out of the other side of the narrow ravine. He zipped up and went to investigate. There was a patch or two of chrome shining among the swaths of rust. When he pried the bumper out of the undergrowth, he saw a battered license plate beneath.

"Cool," he said, grinning at the half-century-old plate. "I don't have one like this in my collection."

He picked it up, rubbed off dirt and frantic sow bugs, and looked around again at the collapsed, burned body of the car. Even fifty years later, one thing was clear.

Whoever had been behind the wheel hadn't walked away.

15

Mr. Goodman shook Ward Forrest's hand with a combination of enthusiasm and gratification that he'd finally gotten the chance to meet the big man himself. Around them the Savoy Hotel's lobby was like a kicked-over anthill with workers scurrying right, left, and center. Ward's presence didn't fluster any of the regular staff or workers. He'd been in and out—and underfoot—so much that the busy staff hardly noticed him anymore.

"I'm so sorry Susa couldn't join us," Mr. Goodman said to Ward. "The hotel staff said she was out painting. On your ranch, I believe?"

Ward looked at Rory, who was in uniform, right down to the shiny Sam Browne belt wrapped around his narrow hips. Rory looked at Savoy, who was casually elegant as always, turning female heads wherever he went.

"We okayed her painting excursions before she arrived in southern California," Savoy said. "Naturally, we're hoping for some paintings of the ranch."

"She painted the ranch before, I believe," Goodman said.

"Yes, back when she was an unknown artist," Savoy said. "I suspect that's why she was willing to participate in your auction—a trip down memory lane."

Ward straightened his Western string tie with its beautiful Zuni medallion of coral and turquoise and silver, depicting the gods of rain and wind. "I can't say as I'd mind adding a Susa to our collection. It'd be worth the money just to hear the Pickfords scream."

Mr. Goodman smiled warily. The fights between the Pickfords and the Forrests were the stuff of Moreno County legend. "It would certainly be a fine feather in our county's artistic cap," Goodman said. "As president of Moreno County Artists, vice president of California Plein Air Coalition, and former president of the American Figurative Artists Association, I'd be happy to help in any way I can."

"We'll keep it in mind," Ward said, glancing around at the quiet frenzy of activity. "The auction going to come off on time?"

"Absolutely," Goodman said. "The hotel manager assured me not half an hour ago."

Ward grunted. He'd believe that when he saw it. And he damn well better see it, or a lot of folks would be looking somewhere else for their next paycheck.

"I know how pressed for time you must be with the auction breathing down your neck," Savoy said to Goodman, "so why don't we just get to the paintings?"

"Of course. Would anyone like coffee or something else sent in?"

"Nothing, thanks," Ward said.

Rory wouldn't have minded some coffee, but it wasn't worth the trouble. Ward was in a mood. Savoy knew it; he was practically oozing soothing vibes. Rory didn't blame him. Ward could be a mean son of a bitch when he felt like it.

Savoy looked expectantly at Goodman.

"Right this way," Goodman said, ushering Ward across the busy lobby. "I don't know if you're aware of it, sir," he said to Ward, "but the Artists Association is looking for sponsors for its scholarships for deserving children, with emphasis on the large immigrant community of southern California."

"Send a note to my office," Savoy said before his father could take a bite out of Goodman. "We'll get back to you on it."

"Thank you. It's a very worthy cause."

"They all are," Ward said. "Some day someone's going to pitch an *un*worthy cause to me and I'm going to kiss the bastard on all four cheeks."

Goodman took the hint.

Rory glanced around the lobby, paying particular attention to the discreet cameras that were being installed. Since he partially owned a security firm that handled the hotel, he knew that the cameras—when they were working correctly, and they were finicky bitches—gave about ninety percent coverage. It would take a real pro to sneak through the missing ten percent.

"Did you want to show Mr. Forrest some of the other paintings you looked at earlier?" Goodman asked Savoy hopefully.

Savoy knew he wasn't the "Mr. Forrest" in question. When his father was along, there was only one

Mr. Forrest. "No point in wasting my father's time right now," Savoy said blandly. "Those paintings could be acquired out of the museum cash drawer after a slow day."

Rory smiled faintly and thought if Savvy would show his teeth more often, Ward wouldn't have to.

Goodman unlocked the conference room with a master electronic key and headed toward the executive bathroom beyond. Before he could open the door, Savoy took the key from his hand.

"Thank you," Savoy said. "We'll return the key at the front desk after we're finished."

"Damned waste of time," Ward muttered. "They make 'em by the gross. About as secure as a sieve."

Goodman hesitated, then took his dismissal with the grace of a man who was accustomed to begging for grants and scholarships among the wealthy. "Of course. If I can be of any further assistance—"

"We'll call you," Ward cut in impatiently, taking the key from his son. "Thank you and good-bye. Let's get to it, Savvy. I don't have all day to spend on this."

Savoy gave Goodman a smile and a shrug that invited him to be understanding of a spoiled old man's impatience. "Be sure to send your scholarship information to my personal attention," Savoy said. "I'll put it at the top of my requests pile."

Goodman smiled and forgot to be annoyed. "Thank you, sir."

Savoy waited until Goodman was out of earshot before he shut the automatically locking conference room door and turned to his father. "Your manners need some work. Goodman may be a pushy twit, but he's well respected in the art community, whose support is important to the Savoy Museum, which is important to the family's philanthropic image, which is very important to New Horizons, which is feeling goosy about the upcoming merger."

"What you don't understand about power, boy, is that you have to exercise it. Respect is better than a friendship award every time." Ward jerked his thumb toward the bathroom. "Now open the fucking door, *please*."

"You have the key."

"You bet I do." Ward smiled. "Don't ever forget it." He shoved the plastic rectangle in the slot.

Rory snickered. The old man was a pistol, no doubt about it. He might drive them all crazy, but he hadn't lost a step to the years.

Ward shoved the door open and stared at the three paintings. "I'll be a son of a bitch. You were right, Savvy." He whipped reading glasses out of his suit coat and checked for a signature on the dark painting. "What the hell is this? He didn't sign it?"

"That's why I brought you. You have a better eye than I do," Savoy said evenly. It was only the truth. "Is this a Marten?"

Ward lifted the painting and flipped it over, peering along the thin edge where canvas wrapped around stretcher. He grunted. "Number twenty-seven. Jesus, how many did he paint before he died?"

"So it's a Marten?" Savoy asked.

"Marten or Santa Claus, signed or unsigned, I'm buying it."

"We have nineteen already," Savoy said. "Burning house, burning car, drowning woman. Sixteen are signed. Don't you think that's enough?"

"The thing about collecting is that you ain't finished until you have it all." Ward set the painting down. "Buy it."

"I told you," Savoy said patiently, "it's not for sale."

"Bullshit. Everything's for sale. Just a matter of finding out the price."

"That could be difficult."

"Why?"

Savoy bit back his rising temper. He knew very well that his father's memory was better than a computer's. The old man was just doing what he did best—pushing his son's buttons. So Savoy reached into his sports coat, pulled out his cell phone, and pushed some buttons of his own. After a few moments the screen showed what it had been showing ever since the first e-mail: no response from the elusive Ms. Marsh.

"She's not answering my e-mails."

"So call her."

"No phone number," Savoy said through his teeth. "Remember? No address, either. Remember?"

A flush of temper appeared on Ward's cheekbones. "I'm not senile."

"Then don't act like it," Savoy shot back. "We've been over this ground five times since I first told you about the painting. Now, I'd love to get it for your birthday—or rather, the company would—but I can't buy what's not for sale."

Ward turned to Rory. "Find her."

"A description would help," the sheriff said mildly.

"Goodman saw her," Savoy said. "Talk to him."

Rory flicked a sideways glance at Savoy and waited for Ward to speak.

"Do it," Ward said.

"When I find her, what then?" Rory asked.

"Savvy will take it from there."

Rory sighed. "Wouldn't it be easier just to wait until Saturday? She's bound to show up for the auction."

"Maybe, but I'm not counting on it," Ward said.

"Why not?" Savoy said. "It's only logical."

Ward turned on his son. "Christ Jesus, haven't you learned anything? Logic isn't what turns people's screws. *Find her.*"

16

Now I remember why I left," Susa said, waving a hand at the rush-hour mess on Pacific Coast Highway. "So many people, so few places to put them."

Lacey looked at the traffic stacked up in all directions, waiting for a light to change so that the idiot in the intersection who was blocking everyone could move on through.

"Aren't there laws against that?" Ian asked, looking at a Jaguar crouched across traffic lanes with no place to go.

"Stupidity?" Lacey asked. "Last time I checked, intelligence was the endangered species."

"There are streets in D.C. where pushing a light like that will cost you four hundred bucks," Ian said.

"Voice of experience?" Lacey asked.

He gave her a dark glance in the rearview mirror. "Nope. That's why they give cops sirens."

"Doesn't work in Manhattan," Susa said. "Any

emergency vehicle caught in rush-hour traffic doesn't get a break from the other drivers."

"No wonder people get shot," Ian muttered. "Stupid bastards. What if they were the one who needed help?"

"It always happens to the other guy," Susa said. "First article of faith in cities."

"Water-hole theory of risk," Ian said, smiling slightly.

"What's that?" Lacey asked.

"Every animal has to drink, so predators lie in wait at water holes. When thirsty time comes, someone's going to get eaten, but everyone figures it will be someone else."

"Wow, that's a cheery outlook," Lacey said. "Turn right at the next street and I'll show you a back way to my shop."

The twists and turns Lacey took them through showed Ian a bit of the pre–World War Two California he found in old Westerns. He had to stare past rows of parked cars to see it, but at least it was there.

"Look at that little cottage," he said. "Isn't it great?"

Lacey glanced at the run-down place that someone had turned into a tattoo parlor. The picket fence was more memory than reality. The tiny window gardens were bare of all but a few tough weeds. The small wooden porch sagged at one corner. So did the steps leading up to the door.

"Heaven help them if the termites all sneeze at once," Lacey said.

"It has great lines," Ian said.

"So does a mummy. Turn left into the alley, then right."

"Are you saying you don't feel the poetry in that old cottage?" Ian asked.

"That's what I'm saying."

"Thank God."

She gave him a questioning look.

"I was afraid you were perfect," he explained.

Susa laughed and decided January Marsh was right—Ian should come with warning labels.

"If Shayla isn't here, you can park in back," Lacey said. "Otherwise, just let me out." She stretched to look around Ian's wide shoulders. "She's still here."

"You sure you won't have dinner?" Ian asked.

She hesitated, then sighed and did the right thing. "I have to help Shayla with inventory. But thanks."

Ian double-parked and put on the emergency flashers so that he could help Lacey unload her gear.

"You stay with the truck," Lacey said as she slid across the bench seat. "Newport supports itself on parking tickets. I'll be right back."

She made several trips into the store with fresh field studies while Ian sorted out the rest of her things from Susa's. When it was down to an easel and a box of brushes stacked against a box of oils, Lacey ran up and gathered everything into her arms. "Thanks for everything."

"Wait. Don't forget these," Ian said, holding out two bottles of champagne.

"What? They're not mine. They cost a fortune!"

"Susa has two more in her suite refrigerator, compliments of the management," he said.

"Then you take them."

"Champagne and side arms don't mix."

Lacey blinked. She kept forgetting that this easy-laughing, gentle-smiling man wore a gun beneath his denim jacket. She shifted on the sidewalk, getting a better grip on her gear—and herself.

He tucked the two bottles of expensive bubbly into her arms. "Don't drink it all it once."

She tilted her head and looked at him with clear brown eyes. "Do you always wear a gun?"

He smiled slowly. "I've been known to take it off for close friends."

"Here." She nudged one of the bottles out of her arms. "Go get close to a friend."

He caught the bottle before it hit the sidewalk and became a pricey pile of foam and broken glass. "How long will you and your partner be working on that inventory?"

"Until it's done or we go nucking futz."

"Now that I'd pay to see." He brushed her stubborn shiny curl aside and kissed the spot on her eyebrow where the curl had been. At the same time, he tucked a piece of paper into the pocket of her wildly colorful jacket. "If you decide you need help, that's my cell phone number."

"Help with the inventory?" she asked, shivering at the warmth of his breath feathering over her temple.

"With anything at all. Okay?"

Hesitantly she nodded.

"Call me, no matter what the time," he said. "I'm used to it."

"Women calling you?"

He smiled and wished the time and place were different. But they weren't. "No. Odd calls at odd hours from odd people."

"Are you calling me odd?"

"Yeah."

She blew back the stray curl. "Good call. And good night."

Ian waited until Lacey went through the shop door before he slid behind the wheel of the truck, turned to Susa, and said, "Well?"

"She didn't forge those three paintings."

He let out a long breath. "Thank you, God."

"Didn't want to seduce a crook in the line of duty, even an appealing one?" Susa asked, partly joking and mostly not.

Ian turned off the flashers and drove carefully down the narrow street.

Susa waited for an answer.

"I'm real picky about who I get naked with," Ian said in a level tone. "So you're saying she isn't good enough to have painted those Martens or whatever the hell they are?"

"She's talented, no doubt about it. If she keeps painting, she'll shed the last of the academic shackles and fly."

"Then what makes you so certain she didn't paint those landscapes? I'm no specialist, but what she painted today looked damned good to me. Hell, it looked better than good. Maybe she was soft-pedaling her ability so that no one would suspect what she was capable of."

Susa was silent for the space of several breaths. Then she sighed. "It's possible that she might have consciously shifted her brush strokes and managed to paint the two pure plein air landscapes she brought to me. Barely possible, in my opinion."

"But possible all the same."

"Don't you want her to be innocent?"

"I want to play blues guitar like B.B. King. So what?"

Susa rotated her head on her shoulders, trying to loosen muscles tied up by decades of painting. Or by decades, period.

"Field studies," she said, "which is plein air painting by another name, are by their very nature looser and less academic than studio works. In that sense, someone might argue that field studies are easier to forge. I'm not saying I would argue that myself, simply that an argument could be made."

Ian wanted more than faint reassurance. He didn't like to think that he could have been so completely taken in by a paint-spattered con artist.

"Did she or didn't she?" he asked bluntly.

"I'd say no."

"Much as I'd like to agree with you, I flat don't believe she got those paintings at a garage sale."

Susa shrugged. "Stranger things happen all the time. In fact, one of my old paintings turned up in a flea market a few years back."

Ian grunted. "She didn't act like she was comfortable talking about the so-called garage sale."

"How about this? Even if she was working from a photo or copying directly from another painting, I don't believe she could have changed her basic style enough to produce the drowning woman canvas. Brushwork is as individual as handwriting and much harder to forge successfully."

"Keep going."

"Do you want a declaration signed in blood and notarized?" she asked impatiently.

"Rarities Unlimited exists because forgers, good forgers, exist."

"People who are excellent copyists often are like good actors—they don't have their own vision, so they borrow someone else's. You saw her paintings today. What do *you* think?"

"She didn't wait around to see what you would paint. She just went out there and set up her easel and started thinking. Not painting. Not right away. She looked at the land, her brushes, the canvas, her paints, and then the land again. Once she started to paint, she never came up for air."

Susa smiled. "You're a very noticing kind of man, Ian Lapstrake."

"It's not like I had a lot else to do today."

"Am I detecting a faint whine?"

"Yeah. And thanks, I've already had plenty of cheese to go with it."

Susa took pity on him. "You don't have to come to the dinner with me tonight. I'll be in the midst of southern California's art glitterati and the spendy sponsors who go with them. The only thing threatening me is terminal boredom. That's why I wanted Jan along."

"That's the other thing bothering me about her," Ian said.

"What?"

"Her name isn't January Marsh."

17

Ward got out of the car and shot his cuffs, freeing them from the sleeves of his navy blue suit coat. He fingered his maroon silk tie, found it smooth against the handmade linen shirt, and didn't know whether to laugh or swear at having to get tricked out like an executive flunky just to have dinner. But unless you were born with a platinum spoon clamped between your gums, the well-dressed social game was necessary to business success.

"Very handsome," Savoy said to his father.

"Go ahead, say it. Too conservative."

Savoy shrugged, shut the car door, and gestured the driver on. "This isn't Hollywood."

"Couldn't tell it by you." Ward waved at his son's sport coat and slacks, shirt and no tie. At least he hadn't worn running shoes. "The only people who can afford to ignore society's conventions are the children of the spoiled wealthy, like you and Blissy. I'm the son of a working man. Nobody handed me anything."

"You married well."

"You think that wasn't work?" Ward shot back. "Every day of her life, Gem shoved my lack of good breeding in my face."

"Couldn't have been all that bad," Savoy said. The whole topic of bloodlines bored him almost as much as his mother's pathetic, drunken insistence on good breeding had. "Your father was a close friend of Mother's father—and she married you, didn't she? Stayed married, too."

Ward made a sound of satisfaction. "She sure as hell did, common blood and all." But it had taken some real persuasion on his part.

In his younger days, he'd been good at charming the upper classes. Good enough to win a place by marriage in the Savoy family. Good enough so that his children would inherit the Forrest name and the Savoy fortune, minus the fifteen percent his ever damned mother-in-law had given to her sister's kids. Of course, knowing where all the family bodies were buried hadn't hurt him, either.

The maître d' of the Hunt Club rushed forward to greet Ward and Savoy. "This way, sir. Your private room is waiting. Mr. Goodman, Ms. White, and the Birch-Andersons have already arrived."

Ward nodded.

As his father had taught him, Savoy put a folded fifty-dollar bill in the maître d's palm and shook hands with him. "Thank you, Charles. I trust the fish came through on time?"

"Yes, sir," Charles said. "Fresh Dover sole, gulf prawns, and Maine lobster. A Mr. Lapstrake called and asked if there would be room for a Ms. Marsh, a friend of Ms. Donovan, to attend. I assured him there would be, but then he called again to say it would be just himself and Ms. Donovan, that Ms. Marsh had an engagement she couldn't ignore."

Savoy wondered if Ms. Marsh's first name was January, but before he could ask, Ward was talking to the maître d'.

"How's your son?" Ward asked. "Heard he'd been injured playing football."

"Much better, sir, thank you." The maître d' smiled widely. "You should have seen the other guy."

Ward gave a crack of laughter. "You tell that boy of yours to keep kicking ass. It's the only thing real men understand."

"Yes, sir!"

Savoy watched the maître d' and his father walk away, exchanging football lore. The old man should have been a politician. Savoy was the one tipping the maître d', yet a single question from his father about the man's son had him smiling and preening and actually *liking* Ward Forrest. Maybe you had to be raised with the common touch to have it. If not for hunting and target shooting, he wouldn't have anything to share with his father but an accident of birth.

With a stifled sigh, Savoy walked toward the private dinner room. Times like this he really missed his mother; Gem had understood him in ways Ward never would. Not for the first time, Savoy wondered why his parents had stayed married as long as they had. It must have been that old thing about opposites attracting. God know that the two had been about as opposite as could be.

And here Savoy was, by all accounts a gentle and

charming scion of wealth, waiting for his second wife to meet someone else and divorce him. They had seemed so compatible ten years ago. Now they lived separately and, for the most part, peacefully, appearing together only when it was necessary to present a united front for special birthdays, corporate events, and the like. This coming Saturday, for example, when the family would strut their' unity for Angelique White.

Speaking of the New Horizons devil, there she was, her lean model's body clad in a little black number that Coco Chanel and Gem Savoy Forrest would have loved.

"Angelique," Savoy said, smiling and holding out his hands while Ward went on to greet the other three people. "How lovely that you could come. My wife will be sorry she missed you, but the Volunteer Guild at the hospital only meets once a month."

"Believe me, I understand," Angelique said as she took Savoy's hands. "Charity always comes first."

Savoy felt the faint brush of her cheek almost touching his. Angelique knew how to air kiss with the best of them. Close to Bliss in age but with a lot less mileage—or a better plastic surgeon—Angelique was as shrewd as she was devout. It was an unsettling combination in a businesswoman. Savoy wasn't used to working with a chief operating officer who wouldn't pick up a phone on Sunday unless it was to report directly to God Almighty.

"Congratulations on finally settling that CCSD problem," Angelique said. "And a very generous settlement it was. Well done, Savoy."

He smiled and hoped she didn't mention it in front of Ward. "We're pleased with it."

She smiled like the businesswoman she was, but couldn't help looking eagerly around. "I can't believe I'll get a chance to talk with one of the most famous painters America has ever produced. La Susa *is* coming, isn't she?" Angelique asked.

Savoy smiled and silently congratulated himself on arranging the dinner tonight. It was the historic and artistic lure that had drawn New Horizons to Savoy Enterprises in the first place. The association of his grandfather Three Savoy with California Impressionism helped to separate Savoy Enterprises from others courting the cash-rich New Horizons. Presenting Angelique to Susa Donovan would definitely put a rosy glow around the Forrest name.

And unless Bliss got over her pique real soon and lined up with the rest of the family, the name was going to need all the help it could get.

"La Susa and her escort should be here momentarily," Savoy said.

"I saw the easels. Is she really bringing some paintings?" Angelique asked.

"At least three. It's her way to thank people for their patronage of the arts. How is your own painting coming?"

Angelique laughed and shook her head. "It's just a hobby. A series of art teachers have assured me that I'm not even in the gifted amateur category. But that doesn't prevent me from enjoying the talent of a true artist like La Susa."

A stir behind Savoy told him the guest of honor had arrived. That, and Angelique's murmur, "Oh, my, she's petite."

As Savoy stepped forward to handle all the introductions, he speculated about Susa's "escort." While hardly a boy, the man still looked young enough to be one of her sons.

"Just set them up over there, Ian," Susa said, gesturing toward the end of the room. "Then you can stand guard over them like a junkyard dog or you can eat with the rest of us." She leaned close enough not to be overheard. "But if you stay with the paintings I'll put ground glass in your breakfast coffee."

"I'm your Siamese twin."

"Good answer." Susa put a gracious smile on her face and turned to greet the rest of the dinner guests.

Ian went to the easels and began carefully unwrapping the unframed paintings Susa carried around with less fanfare than most women would a purse. There were four easels and four paintings. Two of them were from the early stages of Susa's long career. The other two were so fresh they still smelled of the oils that had been used to create them. Ian didn't know which made him more nervous—older paintings worth close to a million bucks or art so new it was barely safe to handle, despite the metallic salts Susa and Lacey had added to their paints to accelerate the drying process.

"Extraordinary," Savoy said. Even without the spare signature— ʃUʃA —in the lower left-hand corner of each painting, he could see that it was the same painter no matter the differences that artistic development had brought.

He stared at the paintings of the dark, narrow ravine where his grandfather and great-grandmother had died in separate accidents. This was Bliss's "sacred ground," land that she would rather drag the family into ruin than develop. His mother had died a lot closer to home in another accident. At least that's what the coroner's report had said, but when the coroner/sheriff was a close friend of the family, it wasn't hard to switch death by suicide to accidental death by overdose of drugs and alcohol, and let tongues wag until they bled about the Savoy Curse.

"The old and the new are different, yet no one else could have painted them but La Susa," Savoy said.

"I'll take your word on it. I only saw her paint these two," Ian said, setting up the second new canvas.

"I'm relieved," Savoy said dryly. "The other two were painted before you were born, and well before suburbs crowded up against the sea."

Ian looked at the paintings. Savoy was right. Beneath the differences in execution, season, and color, the land was the same except for the amount of buildings in the background at the edges of the modern paintings.

"Have you worked for Susa long?" Savoy asked.

"No."

Savoy waited, but Ian didn't say anything more. "The maître d' said you were bringing a third person, a Ms. Marsh?" Savoy asked.

"It didn't work out. Sorry, I guess the maître d' didn't have time to tell you."

Savoy shrugged. "Any guest of Susa's would be welcome. Is that the same January Marsh who brought the paintings that so excited Susa?"

"Yes."

Again Savoy waited. Again Ian didn't offer any more information. "I've been trying to get in touch with Ms. Marsh."

Ian made a sound that meant he was listening.

"Do you have her phone number?" Savoy asked.

"January Marsh's? No." He had Lacey Quinn's, but it wasn't up to him to spread that fact around.

"If you happen to hear from her, tell her that the Savoy Museum is very interested in acquiring at least one of the paintings she showed to Susa."

"Sure, but I got the impression Tuesday night that she wasn't interested in selling."

"If she cared enough to bring the paintings in the first place, perhaps she'll care enough to see that they are properly housed and passed on to future generations. The Savoy Museum can do that."

"Good point." Ian shifted his dark suit coat. The fabric kept wanting to hang up on the damned shoulder holster. That's what he got for buying the coat a size larger instead of having the right size properly tailored for the harness. "It might help if she saw the museum. When is it open?"

"For Ms. Marsh, it's open whenever she wants to visit." Savoy got out a business card and wrote quickly on its back. "This number is always the fastest way to reach me."

Ian took the card and wondered how much Savoy would pay for one of the paintings. Lacey wasn't poor, but anyone who worked for herself the way she did could always use money. The good news was that she hadn't put her talents to work forging old masters or more recent Impressionists for quick cash.

He hoped.

"Savvy, you have a minute to talk to Susa?" Ward asked from across the room.

"Excuse me," Savoy said.

"No problem. I'm just the hired help."

"So am I," Savoy said under his breath.

Ward watched impatiently while Savoy greeted two couples who had just arrived—very big spenders on the art circuit—and wove through the other people with a smile and a promise to come back soon.

Savoy held both hands out to Susa. "Your paintings are magnificent," he said, "but I didn't mean to ignore the artist."

There was no polite way for Susa to say that she'd rather be ignored than feted, so she pressed his hands gently, released them, and changed the subject. "Your father was just telling me that the Savoy Museum was interested in acquiring some paintings at the upcoming auction."

"January Marsh's paintings," Ward added.

Susa frowned at the name. She still didn't understand why such an otherwise open young woman would want to have a fake name. As a personal matter, Lacey certainly didn't have the sort of artistic fame that would make anonymity welcome. Perhaps it was simply that she couldn't afford to insure such fine paintings. The thought cheered Susa, even though she couldn't quite believe it.

"We have our eye on several pieces of art," Savoy said to Susa, "including those you painted on our ranch. They're an almost inevitable acquisition for the Savoy Museum, don't you think?"

"Since it was on the Savoy Ranch that I first found, absorbed, and understood what it meant to be a painter, I would be happy to make a gift to the museum of a painting created on your ranch," Susa said.

Savoy didn't bother to conceal his surprise. "That's very generous, but hardly necessary."

"As my daughter-in-law Hannah would say, 'No worries.' I'll just paint another one."

"If only it was that easy," Savoy said, remembering

the times he'd painted before his mother convinced him that he should focus his talents on business. "But you can't ever capture the same thing twice, can you?"

Susa smiled at his understanding. "No. You just go on and hope to capture something new. Sometimes you do, most times you don't. So you burn the bad ones on New Year's Eve and get ready to try again."

"You burn money?" Ward asked.

"No. Failed paintings."

"Would anyone but you think of them as failures?" Ward asked.

"I know the difference. That's what matters to me."

"Son of a bitch," Ward said, shaking his head. "Well, I suppose you have enough money to burn some now and then."

Her eyebrows raised. "I've been burning paintings for as long as I've painted, and I was plenty poor until about fifteen years ago."

"You have guts," Ward said. "Not much business smarts, but plenty of guts."

She smiled, amused rather than insulted. "Actually, I'm smart enough to know that it's important to understand the past but not to be owned by it. Burning canvases is a way for me to be free as an artist."

"Like burning bridges?" Ward asked.

"Exactly."

"Well, I sure as hell know about that. Some bridges just have to be burned, no matter what the rest of the world thinks about it." Ward laughed and winked at Susa. "The trick is to know which bridges to burn, and when, and how not to get caught with the matches in your hand."

"My father has a unique take on the world," Savoy

said wryly, shaking his head. "No frills, no fancies, just get the job done."

"My take isn't so unique that I'm going to pass up Susa's offer of a painting," Ward retorted. "It would be great publicity for the corporation."

"And for the arts," Savoy added quickly, turning to Susa. "You might not believe it after listening to him, but my father is the force behind the Savoy Museum. It was his vision, his dedication, and his willingness to fight other board members to free up funds that resulted in the museum's establishment and its continuing acquisitions."

Susa made an appropriately polite sound. Privately she doubted that Ward Forrest had a single artistic sensibility in his flinty soul. Not that it mattered in the long run. Throughout history many of the most famous patrons of the arts wouldn't have known what to buy if some well-dressed salesperson hadn't pointed out the art and told them what words to use when discussing their new acquisitions with their equally clueless peers.

Ignorance combined with acquisition shouldn't have annoyed Susa, but sometimes it did. She couldn't help wondering how many of the people in this room would have bought one of her own paintings if they'd stumbled over it in a flea market twenty years ago. Ian, perhaps. He had a good eye.

And where the hell was he, by the way? He was supposed to keep her from getting bitchy out of sheer boredom.

Oh, quit whining and do your job, Susa told herself impatiently. She wasn't here for her own benefit, she was here because she'd once been among the legions of talented, hungry, hardworking artists who were consumed by their need to paint. The more support she could send their way now, the better the chance that they would keep painting long enough to be "discovered." Then they could quit their day job and follow their fey talent as far as it would take them.

"Have you been to our museum?" Savoy asked.

"Not yet," Susa said, snapping back into focus. "I'm hoping to fit in a trip before the auction."

"I gave your man my card," Savoy said.

"My man? Oh, Ian." She pressed her lips against a smile.

"Whenever you want to come, just call that number. I'll see that you have a full guided tour. And feel free to bring guests such as Ms. Marsh."

Ward's eyes narrowed. "Marsh? The one with the—"

"Yes," Savoy cut in, not wanting his blunt father to say too much. No point in paying more than they had to for an unsigned painting. "I understand that Ms. Marsh is reluctant to sell her paintings. I hope after she sees how well they would be cared for in the museum, she'll change her mind and sell us at least one."

"We're going painting tomorrow," Susa said. "I'll mention it to her."

"Then you know where she lives?" Ward asked.

"She's meeting us at the hotel," Ian said, walking up in time to hear the conversation.

Susa's eyebrows went up, because she'd heard Ian make arrangements to pick up Jan—Lacey, damn it!—early in the morning. But Susa wasn't the Donovan's wife for nothing.

She knew when to talk and when to shut her mouth.

18

When the telephone rang, Brody Quinn looked up from his notes on his most recent case—a woman who had decided that being an accountant wasn't as lucrative as being an embezzler. With each motion of his pen, the cat's white paw swatted at the flashing metal. Brody didn't even pause in his notes. He would have noticed only if the cat hadn't been there. Tag-the-pen was part of a nightly ritual that man and feline enjoyed.

"Can you get that, honey?" Dottie called from the direction of the master suite spa. "I'm up to my chin in bubbles."

He muttered something, checked the caller ID, and sighed in relief. Just Lacey, not another business crisis.

"Hi, Lacey," he said.

"Sorry to interrupt your work," she said. "I know

you look forward to evenings without the phone yammering at you."

"I'm always glad to hear from my girls."

At the other end of the line, Lacey almost smiled. It had been a long time since she'd qualified as a "girl," yet to her father she would always be just that. "How's everything?" she asked.

"Same as always at this time of night. The fur ball is teasing my pen, I'm behind on my work, and your mother is up to her lips in the spa."

Lacey hesitated. She wished her father would be as enthusiastic about the good news as she was, but she didn't think he would be.

"Everything all right with you?" Brody asked.

"Everything is wonderful. Susa went nuts over Grandfather's paintings. Said they were as good as Lewis Marten's work."

Brody's eyes closed and his hand clenched on the phone. *Damn it, Dad, couldn't you have picked someone else to copy?* "That's nice."

"Nice? It's incredible! Lewis Marten is a fine, nearly unknown California Impressionist who would have been world-famous if he hadn't—"

"—died a long time ago," Brody interrupted impatiently. "Your grandfather died two years ago. Why would anyone believe it's great that my father painted just like some dead artist? Better he should have had his own style, don't you think?"

"You don't understand. Susa agrees with me that Granddad is a fine artist. The leading collector of California plein air artists wants to buy at least one of his paintings. Susa says that I should have them appraised, because they could be worth hundreds of thousands each."

"Only if they were actually painted by Lewis Marten," Brody said flatly. "But they weren't painted by Marten. They were done by a man who was old enough to know better but couldn't resist making money the easy way."

"What are you talking about?"

"Something you don't want to hear and I sure as hell don't want to tell you. Leave it alone, Lacey."

"Tell me anyway."

"Always pushing. Always have to do it your own way."

"I'm sorry, Dad, but it's too late for me to change. Are you going to tell me or not?"

Brody bit back a curse. He'd always been afraid that this skeleton wouldn't stay in the closet forever, but he really wished it had come rattling out at some more convenient time.

"When cash got short," he said, "your beloved Grandpa Rainbow forged Lewis Marten paintings and sold them—unsigned—to unsuspecting galleries at cut rates."

Lacey opened her mouth. Nothing came out through her painfully constricted throat. She swallowed and tried again. "But I saw him paint," she said hoarsely. "He was magical. He didn't need to copy anyone."

Angry and unhappy, Brady swept off his reading glasses and pinched the bridge of his nose. "Damn it, honey. I didn't want this to happen. I didn't want him to make you cry like he did everyone else."

"I'm not crying." *Yet.* Lacey bit down hard on her emotions. "I can't believe it."

"You mean you won't."

Lacey drew a ragged breath. "I know he was a lousy husband and father, but he was an *artist*."

"He was a forger," Brody said, "and all your stubbornness won't change that fact. Now the whole world will know. When the shit hits the headlines, I'm going to deny all knowledge and hope to hell you will, too. It's the only way I might salvage my professional reputation."

"But that's crazy. Even if you're right about Grandpa, you can't be held accountable for what your father did or didn't do."

Brody laughed without humor. "Lacey, how old are you? This is politics, not church. Guilt by association is the name of the game."

She wanted to argue but knew there wasn't any point. He was right. "God, I'm so sorry. I never meant to—"

"I know that," Brody interrupted roughly. "Hell, maybe it's for the best. After the doctor told me to slow down, your mother wasn't crazy about the idea of me being a judge. She's been after me to cut back on work and spend more time traveling."

"But you've always wanted to be a judge."

He shrugged. "You don't always get what you want."

"No one has to know," she said urgently. "No one knows my name. I'll just withdraw the paintings and vanish."

"It won't be that easy."

"But—"

"Forget it," Brody cut in, his voice raw and weary. "The cat's too far out of the bag to shove it back in. Save your energy for salvaging your own reputation when people start wondering if the granddaughter is as big a cheat as the old man was."

"I told you—nobody knows who I am!" *Well, al-*

most nobody. Ian didn't count, did he? "It will be all right, Dad. I'll just withdraw the paintings and everything will be fine."

But everything wasn't fine. She finally understood why her Grandpa Rainbow never signed a canvas.

Forger.

19

Bliss stared at the credit cards and debit cards on her kitchen table. Every time she'd tried to use one of them today, the "request" had been denied. She'd had to pay for the all-day spa treatment out of her own checkbook. She hadn't really understood how much it cost until she sat there and wrote the check. Three thousand dollars plus six hundred in tips. Thirty-six hundred dollars for a facial, pedicure, body peel, botox shots, haircut and three-color frost, body waxing, manicure, massage, makeover—all the things a woman her age needed *not* to look her age.

Thirty-six hundred bucks. Jesus.

She was used to just signing a chit and never looking at the amount, because the money all came out of Forrest family funds. Or it had, until she tried to make her father surrender some control over the land.

Is he really mad?

He's really determined. Different thing entirely.

As always, Rory had been right. Her father was going to do things his way and to hell with who got hurt in the process.

"Bliss?" Rory asked from the bedroom.

"In the kitchen," she said.

She looked up as he came into the kitchen, rumpled and too sexy to be over fifty. Life really was unfair to women, she decided all over again. Not that Rory had complained about how she looked. After dinner they had gone at each other like teenagers and finally had fallen asleep in a slippery, satisfied pile.

Why is this the one man for me when there's a world full of males I can handle without breaking a sweat?

There wasn't any answer. There hadn't ever been, but she kept asking anyway, hoping one day she would figure it all out.

"What are you doing?" Rory asked, rubbing his bare chest idly.

"Wondering how long Daddy's going to stay mad."

Rory looked at the pile of plastic cards while a combination of anger and helplessness coursed through him. Ward knew all about fighting to win. Bliss knew only how to be rich. Rory had always admired Ward's bottom-line business sense, but he hated seeing it applied to the woman he loved.

"How much do you owe?" he asked.

She lifted one shoulder.

"Guess," he said.

"I just sign, I don't look."

"Twenty thousand? Thirty?"

She glanced up at him with hurting blue eyes. "Why is he doing this? It's not like I'm asking him to give up the ranch. Just the places that are important, like

Sandy Cove and the beaches we used as children and the canyon where Three and Granna Sandra died, and—"

"The places you're describing are among the most easily developed, most accessible, and most valuable land on the whole damn ranch."

"It's *my* history even if it isn't his. It's *Savoy* money he's spending, not his own. It's *my* money, damn it!"

"Bliss . . ." Rory cursed under his breath and tried again, wondering if she would listen, really listen, this time. "Your mother argued that point most of her married life. It didn't do her any good. It won't do you any good. The only money you control is in trust funds. Saying that it should be different won't put one penny in your bank accounts."

There was a long, unhappy silence.

"He always ends up winning," Bliss said in a thin voice.

Rory didn't argue. It was the truth.

"Once, just once, I want him to lose," she said fiercely. "Is that too much to ask?"

"How much are you willing to give up for it?" Rory asked.

"I don't know."

"You willing to try marriage again?"

She gave him a startled glance and almost smiled. "Why?"

"It's the only way I can protect you. Ward respects a man's right to stand up for what is his. But an employee getting in the way of a family dispute would be fired."

"He'd never fire you. You're the son he never had. He cares for you more than he does for me or Savvy."

Rory just shook his head. "Ward would hand me

my corporate pink slip and go out hunting pheasant without a thought. And when it came time for re-election, he'd back another candidate."

Her mouth dropped open and stayed that way. Then she reeled in her astonishment. "I can't believe it."

"I can. You never knew your Grandfather Forrest real well, did you?"

"I never thought about it."

"He was a very smart man and a natural politician. Charming to anyone who could do him some good. Hard as steel underneath the smile. He ran Moreno County with a clenched fist, both as sheriff and later as district attorney. Booted out some gambling gangsters and sent them to Las Vegas at a time when it was a real dangerous thing to do."

Bliss tried to imagine her grandfather running gangsters out of town. She couldn't. When she'd known him, he was a spidery old man with nothing much better to do than sit in the sun with a cat in his lap.

"I don't imagine Theodore Forrest was much kinder to his son than Ward is to Savoy," Rory continued. "The Forrests aren't long on kindness, but if you want the job done, they'll do it. And if *they* want the job done, you'd better do it or get the hell out of their way."

"Was your family like that?" Bliss asked, curious about Rory in a way she'd never been when she was younger.

"Pretty much. Only poor, real poor. If your father hadn't liked what he saw when I turned up looking for work at the ranch close to forty years ago, I'd probably be someone's hired man today instead of the sheriff of Moreno County and a member of the Savoy Ranch corporation board."

"But you'd risk getting Daddy mad at you to help me."

"Hell, Bliss, I've always loved you. I just can't always live with you."

She laughed almost sadly. "Same here, darling. Damn, life can be a tricky bitch."

He held out his hand. "Come back to bed while we can still live with each other."

"Want something to eat first?"

"Nope. How about you?"

Smiling, she pushed back from the table. Before she could take his hand, his cell phone rang. He rummaged through the pile of clothes on the living room floor, found his belt, and looked at the number in the cell phone window.

"Speak of the devil," Rory muttered. He punched in the connect button. "Evening, Ward. Or should I say good morning?"

At home, Ward laughed curtly and scratched Honey Bear's silky ears. The dog groaned and all but slid to the floor in a puddle of pleasure.

"Have you found January Marsh?" Ward asked.

"Lots of people in the county and state with the last name of Marsh. No one called January or Jan or Janet or Jane or any other variant we could think of. No driver's license in those names. No voter registration. No property taxes. No business license. No wants, warrants, parking tickets, fingerprints, telephone numbers. No birth certificate on file in any state, no tax records either state or federal. No social security number. Offhand, I'd say the lady doesn't exist."

"Find her. I didn't get you elected sheriff of Moreno County for the fun of it."

"I have someone watching the paintings. If anyone

asks to see them, man or woman, they'll be tagged and followed. We'll find her."

"I want that painting, damn it!" As he spoke, Ward sank his fingers into Honey Bear's thick fur. The dog stirred uneasily at the sudden pressure, then settled.

"The auction is Saturday," Rory said patiently. "If we don't find her sooner, we will when she comes to pick up her art."

"Susa knows Ms. Marsh, or whatever the hell her name is. They're going painting tomorrow."

Then why are you badgering me? But Rory knew better than to say that aloud. The old man wasn't reasonable when it came to his damned paintings. He'd spend whatever it took and defy God, the devil, or the members of the board to stop him.

"Will they be painting at the ranch?" Rory asked.

"I don't know. Probably."

"If 'Ms. Marsh' shows up tomorrow, I'll have her real identity by dinner."

"How?"

"Does it matter?" Rory asked evenly.

Ward laughed and hung up.

"What was that all about?" Bliss asked.

"Your daddy has a bug up his ass about buying a painting."

Rory punched numbers on his cell phone. Talk about a waste of taxpayer money. On the other hand, one way or the other, the lion's share of the county taxes were being paid by Ward Forrest.

As soon as someone answered, Rory gave rapid-fire orders.

20

W hat's wrong?" Susa asked.

Ian glanced at the rearview mirror yet again. Still there, hanging back in the early morning traffic. "Someone's playing tag."

"What?"

He thought of pushing a yellow light just to see what happened, but decided against it as he had every other time he'd been tempted this morning. If the car had been anything other than a beige Ford, he would have tried to dump the tail by breaking a few laws. That didn't work when the guys behind you had badges.

"Tan sedan, three cars back," Ian said. "A wolf in lambskin."

She looked over her shoulder. After a few moments she spotted the sedan. It wasn't hard. In southern California, almost no one but government types drove full-size American cars.

"You broken any laws lately?" she asked.

"Not in the last few days. I'm licensed for concealed weapons here. I even have the sheriff's private number on the back of his business card if I need help from any of his boys and girls. Just one of the perks of working for someone Moreno County really wants to have around."

"Rarities Unlimited?"

Ian laughed and shook his head. One of the things he really liked about Lawe's mother was that she didn't have any idea of her own importance to the world at large.

"It's you, La Susa, not Rarities. Every local PD and county mountie is touchy about who does and doesn't carry on their turf. The fact that I work for Rarities didn't hurt, but it was being your gofer that really did the trick. Sheriff Rory Turner himself gave dispensation for me and my shoulder harness to follow you around Moreno County."

Susa rolled her hazel eyes. "Spare me the testosterone brigade. It's a good thing you aren't a lump as a companion."

"Why?"

"Because I'd really have to smack some ass the next time I saw Don."

Ian gave her a slow sideways smile. "Sounds like fun."

She snickered.

He signaled like a good citizen, turned, and drove down a side street, leaving the bumper-to-bumper grind of the coast highway behind. As soon as he found a space big enough for two cars, he pulled over.

"Forget something?" Susa said.

"Hope not."

He watched the tan sedan approach, drive by, and park half a block down. "Stay here with the doors locked," he said to Susa.

He got out and walked down to the sedan. The men inside made no effort to ignore him. In fact, the one in the passenger seat rolled down the window.

"Morning," Ian said. "Do I know you?"

"He's Deputy Glendower and I'm Deputy Harrison," the man said, pointing to the driver first, then himself.

"Mind if I see some ID?" Ian asked mildly.

Harrison pulled out a badge.

Ian nodded and looked at the driver.

"Chrissake," muttered Glendower, but he took a badge out of his suit coat and showed it to Ian. "You got something to show us?"

"No badge, sorry." Ian's smile was all teeth. "How about this?"

He took out his wallet and removed the business card with its handwritten number on the back.

Glendower looked at the card without surprise. "Say hi to Sheriff Turner for us."

"Will do. You boys have something that can take back roads?"

"No."

"In about half an hour, you're going to need it. Have it delivered to the south entrance of the Savoy Ranch."

Ian left as one of them reached for the radio to order up a four-wheel-drive vehicle. When he got back to Susa, he slid in behind the wheel.

"Well?" she asked.

"I'm double-checking."

Keeping an eye on the sedan, Ian took out his cell phone and punched in Sheriff Rory Turner's private number.

"Yeah?" Rory said, picking up, yawning.

"Ian Lapstrake. Sorry for calling you after hours, or before in this case. I'm being followed by a beige Ford sedan with two plainclothes in it. Glendower and Harrison. Are they yours?"

"Probably."

"I'd appreciate it if you'd find out for sure. I wouldn't want to put a foot in the wrong place." *A cop's balls, for instance.*

"Hang on."

Ian waited. It wasn't long.

"They're mine," Rory said.

"Have you received threats against Susa or any information that she might be at risk?"

"No, but the more I thought about her, the more I didn't like the idea of someone bothering her in any way. We aren't as bad as Mexico or Italy, but kidnap for ransom isn't unheard of here, either. It's not going to happen on my watch if I can help it."

Ian's eyebrows went up. "I see. Thank you, Sheriff. Sorry to bother you."

"No problem. If you notice any other cars or anything else odd, let me know."

Susa watched Ian as he replaced the cell phone. "Everything okay?"

"They're on the side of the angels."

She let out a breath. "Okay. Let's get Lacey and do some painting. She has to be back by eleven o'clock to open her shop."

"You're hoping she'll tell you her real name all by herself."

"Aren't you?"

"Yeah. Then I'm hoping she'll tell me why she wanted a fake name in the first place."

21

Lacey stood in the door of Lost Treasures Found and looked at Ian with eyes that were too dark against skin that was too pale. If she'd gotten any sleep last night, it didn't show. The bruises beneath her eyes were big enough to frame.

"I'm sorry," Lacey said tightly to Ian. "Something has come up. I can't go painting with Susa."

He smiled with gentle understanding and was inside the shop with the door closed behind him before she could blink.

"What could be more important than painting with the premier living artist in the United States?" he asked.

Lacey said the first thing that came to her mind. "I'm sick. I don't want to infect anyone else."

He might have bought it just on her looks alone, but she was such a bad liar that he didn't even hesitate. "You're not sick, you're worried. What's wrong? Is it something to do with your fake name?"

For an instant tears stood in her eyes. Then she turned her back and got herself under control. "Give Susa my regrets."

"No. You'll have to do that yourself."

"I told you, I don't want to infect anyone else."

"Susa's tough." He put his hands on Lacey's shoulders. "So am I. What's wrong?"

Blindly, Lacey shook her head. "I can't."

"Why not? I'm discreet. I haven't told anyone who asked me about your real name." Which was the truth—Susa hadn't asked.

The sudden stiffness of Lacey's body told Ian all he needed to know. *Bingo.*

"That's what this is all about, isn't it," he said, no question in his voice. "Your fake name."

She turned around and faced him.

His hands lifted, then settled on her shoulders again.

She felt the warm weight of his touch and wished that things were different. It had been a long, long time since any man had intrigued her on as many levels as he did. But things weren't different. They were what they were, and she had a family to protect.

"Good-bye," she said huskily. "Please give Susa my regrets. Her encouragement of my own painting is something I'll never forget."

He saw both the determination and the shadows in her eyes. "Lacey, whatever it is, let me help."

"I can't."

"That means you won't."

She closed her eyes. "If it was just me, I would. But it's not." She opened her eyes and gave him a crooked smile. "Don't forget to take your movie poster."

That pissed him off. "Here's your hat, what's your hurry, and don't come back again, is that it?"

Her smile wavered. "It's better that way."

"No, it's better *this* way."

His hands tightened, his mouth lowered, and he kissed her, surprising both of them. Neither of them stayed surprised very long. Both of them had been wanting this since the teasing kiss over her easel in Cross Country Canyon.

Lacey went up on tiptoe, pressing into the kiss. Into him. His hands shifted and drew her close, then closer. She tasted hot, exotic, ripe with possibilities. In a heartbeat the kiss went nuclear. Before he knew what he was doing, he wrapped his arms around her, turned, and flattened her between his body and the shop door.

Even as he told himself to back up and back *off,* her arms tightened around his neck and she made a throaty sound that told him she was with him every bit of the way. He groaned and went in deeper, trying to get all of her sweet female heat he could. When his hands pushed under her sweatshirt, she hesitated, then shuddered with pleasure as his thumbs teased her nipples through her bra. She twisted her hips against him, moving against the erection he couldn't have concealed if he'd tried.

Heat exploded through him. Distantly he realized that one of them had better come up for air or he would strip off her jeans and take her right where they were, right now, picking her up and wrapping her legs around his waist and watching her and driving into her until—

Lacey's hand over his mouth cut off the hot vision he hadn't even been aware of saying aloud.

"Holy shit," she said, leaning against him, trembling, struggling for breath while her heart went wild. "What's happening?"

Ian lowered his forehead against hers and grabbed at breath. "I was going to ask you the same thing."

She stuck out her lower lip and looked stubborn. "I asked first."

He laughed despite the sexual need hammering through his whole body. "You go to my head, darling, among other places."

She didn't have to ask which other places. She could count his heartbeat in the erection pressing against her belly. Normally she would have raked any man up one side and down the other for getting so intimate in such a hurry. What worried her was that she wanted more of Ian, not less. She wanted what he'd described—him driving into her, watching.

"And no, I've never tried to nail a woman the second time I kissed her," he added. "Sorry about that. I'm wondering what happened myself."

"Ho boy," she said, blowing a stray curl away from her eyes. "Don't apologize. Must be something in the air today. You got me hotter, faster, than anyone ev—" She broke off, appalled at what she was saying. Groaning, she tried to hide her blush against his chest.

Gently he lifted her chin until she met his eyes. "You're not cooling me off here," he said, but he was smiling the kind of smile that made people trust him with small children and large fortunes. He brushed his lips over her eyebrows, her nose, her cheeks, and inhaled her breath without kissing her. "Come painting with Susa, or let us stay here with you."

Thoughtfully Lacey ran her fingertips over the outline of his shoulder holster beneath his jacket. "You're really her bodyguard?"

"No, I really work on the security side of Rarities Unlimited. I protect art, not people. Sometimes my boss does favors for the Donovan family, and vice versa. This is one of them. Until I put Susa on the Donovan company plane back to Seattle, I'm on duty. Otherwise I'd be trying the old-fashioned dating thing with you, and would have been since I first heard you coming down the stairs talking about a beer kind of day." He blew the springy curl away from her eyes and kissed her temple. "Don't shut me out, Lacey. I don't want to spend the rest of my life wondering if I let something special slip through my fingers because of work."

Lacey looked up at Ian's dark brown eyes and even darker hair. He wasn't smiling. He meant every word. "Oh, God, what a mess," she said in a rush of air. "Why now, when I *can't*?" She bit her lip and looked away, then looked back at him. "Rain check?"

"Haven't you heard? It never rains in southern California."

"Does that mean no rain check?"

"I'm not that patient. Never is too long."

She closed her eyes and her generous mouth curved down.

"You said it wasn't just you," Ian said when the silence stretched too long. "Who else is in trouble?"

"It's a family matter and no one is in trouble. It's just . . . awkward." *Really awkward.*

He looked at the stubborn line of her lower lip and wondered what it would take for her to trust him. And then he wondered why the hell it should matter so much.

"Well, if it's just awkward, there's no reason not to go painting, is there?" he asked reasonably. "We won't ask any embarrassing questions." *Like why you needed a fake name, for instance.*

"Not enough time," Lacey said, thinking of her grandfather's paintings hanging out in public like dirty linen. "I have to do something else before the shop opens. It can't wait. Maybe—maybe tomorrow?"

Ian would have pushed if he hadn't sensed that it wouldn't do him any good and probably would hurt his attempt to get her to trust him. He didn't have any real sisters, but he'd been raised next door to his first cousins, all four of them girls. He knew when a female was movable and when she wasn't.

Lacey wasn't.

"Okay," he said. "Painting tomorrow, six A.M. I'll pick you up for dinner at seven tonight."

She blinked. "Dinner?"

"I know you eat." He smiled. "I've seen you. I even put the food on your paint table where you couldn't miss it."

"Um, yes, but—"

"Good," he interrupted. He wasn't going to take no for an answer, not with the taste of her still on his lips and the heat of her body reaching out to him. "Seven o'clock for dinner. That will give you time after your shop closes to add up the till or whatever."

She started to say something and found herself kissing him instead. Though gentle, the kiss was even hotter than the first one. She could feel him straining at the leash he kept on himself, and she could feel herself pulling hard right along with him. When he lifted his head, she blew out a rush of warm air and wondered why this one man could get to her so fast and so deep.

"Seven o'clock," Ian said huskily, lifting her away from the door.

She watched the door close behind him and asked herself what the hell she was doing, letting herself be seduced by Susa Donovan's bodyguard.

Susa, who could uncover Lacey's grandfather for the fraud he was.

22

Lacey leaned against the expensive rare-wood counter of the hotel and waited for the manager to get around to her. She'd been waiting for more than twenty minutes, watching people hurrying through the lobby with armloads of stuff destined for one of the hotel's seventy-nine rooms. Suites, actually. When accommodations started at four hundred dollars a night and went up fast, patrons expected enough room to spread out.

Scents from the restaurant adjoining the hotel drifted through the lobby—or perhaps the delectable odors were pushed by fans through the building's ventilation system to lure more patrons. The pricey eatery had unofficially opened two weeks ago, but the media opening wouldn't be until this Saturday.

"Ms. Marsh?" The concierge paused and said more loudly, "Ms. Marsh?"

Lacey jumped and reminded herself that she was

Ms. Marsh. She turned toward the sleek Eurasian woman who was helping out behind the registration desk. "Sorry. I was daydreaming."

The woman smiled. "It is a beautiful place to dream, is it not?"

Lacey sighed and wondered why some women got all the elegance and she got all the klutz. Her own blouse and worn fleece jacket were clean, if paint-stained, but only a connoisseur of garage-sale couture would approve of her jeans. The concierge's accent and clothing were indelibly French, her looks riveting, and she carried herself like the unusual beauty she was.

"Mr. Goodman is on his way," the concierge said. "Perhaps you would like some tea or coffee while you wait?"

"Mr. Goodman? Is he your manager?"

"No, but he is the one responsible for the security of the art for the auction. Our manager would like to help you with your request, but cannot, as it is Mr. Goodman's responsibility. He will be only a few moments. May I show you to the cafe? It would please the hotel to offer you a complimentary breakfast."

Lacey looked at her oversized wristwatch. The face of a vivid green *Tyrannosaurus rex* leered back at her. She thought the fluorescent orange teeth were a particularly nice touch, even if it made the dark hands of the clock look like roving tooth decay—and for fifty cents, who could resist? It kept hours and minutes just like the five-thousand-dollar models.

"I'm really slammed for time," Lacey said. "I had no idea there would be any problem picking up *my* paintings. Surely someone here has a key to the storage room?"

"I am very sorry, Ms. Marsh." The concierge

smiled and made a graceful gesture with her hands. "I have not the authority, especially as you have not the identification."

"I have a receipt signed by Mr. Goodman."

"Yes, but without personal identification . . ." She spread her hands. "It is difficult, you understand?"

Lacey smiled without warmth. The concierge was polite, but it was a definite *gotcha*. Lacey had plenty of ID, and none of it was in the name of Ms. January Marsh.

"Coffee would be lovely," Lacey said through her teeth.

No sooner had she been seated in the luxurious seventies retro cafe, with blandly psychedelic tableware, than Mr. Goodman came hurrying forward, looking worried.

"Ms. Marsh, this is most distressing," he said, sitting down at her booth before she could stand up. "Is it something we've done? Are you unhappy with the way we've handled your paintings?"

Lacey tried not to sigh. "Not at all. I've simply decided to withdraw them from the function."

"But why?"

"Does it matter? The paintings are mine and I'll be taking them with me when I leave."

"Oh, dear. La Susa will be terribly upset. She was so enthusiastic."

Lacey simply lifted her left eyebrow and said nothing.

"Have you talked with La Susa about this?" Mr. Goodman asked.

"No."

A server brought coffee and poured it into rainbow-hued oversized cups. Lacey ignored hers.

"Perhaps if you would talk with her," Goodman said, "she could reassure you that—"

"No," Lacey interrupted, forcing a smile. She'd learned in dealing with her mother that a polite, gentle stance simply didn't get the job done. You have to know what you want and stick to it. "I understand that you're the only one who can open the room where the paintings are."

"Ah, er . . ." He looked as uncomfortable as he sounded.

Lacey's smile thinned. "I see. Some people enjoy playing Button, Button, Who Has the Button, but I'm too old for that game. Do you have the key with you?"

Quietly Goodman cursed the Forrests for putting him in this unhappy position. On the other hand, Ms. Marsh would come and go from his life like the wind. The Forrests were forever.

"Mr. Savoy Forrest will be here soon," Goodman said.

"How nice. The key, Mr. Goodman." Lacey wasn't smiling any longer. She was getting angry—and frightened.

Always pushing. Always have to do it your own way. I'm sorry, Dad, but it's too late for me to change.

Now she was trying to do the right thing and that wasn't working, either. It should have been so easy, damn it. The paintings were hers.

All your stubbornness won't change the fact that my father was a forger. Now the whole world will know.

"The key," she repeated tightly to Mr. Goodman. "I'm running late as it is."

"It won't be but a minute."

Anxiety streaked through Lacey. She didn't want to believe that she was going to be the cause of her father's career going in the toilet.

But you've always wanted to be a judge.
You don't always get what you want.

"Mr. Goodman," she said distinctly, "are you telling me that until a third and wholly irrelevant party arrives, I can't have access to my own paintings, which I left in your care?"

Goodman smoothed the one long strand of hair that he had combed from his right ear to his left in a vain attempt to cover his balding head. "Mr. Forrest has expressed great interest in the paintings."

Lacey bit back on the rising turmoil of her emotions. That was another thing she had learned when arguing with her mother: the person who lost her temper first lost the argument as well. That was one of the two reasons she hadn't gone over the table, put her face in Goodman's, and started yelling about lawyers, police, and newspapers.

The second reason was that she didn't want the cat any further out of the bag than it already was.

"I'm aware of Mr. Forrest's interest in my paintings," Lacey said evenly, "just as he is aware of my *dis*interest in selling the paintings to him. Am I to understand that somehow he is in a position to prevent me from reclaiming my paintings?"

"Er, no, not at all. It's just that—" Goodman broke off and pushed to his feet with a relieved smile. "Mr. Forrest, how nice of you to join us on such short notice."

"I'm always ready to rush around to accommodate the arts," Savoy said. "Fortunately, my father had a set of spare hotel keys. I brought them immediately when you told me you were having a problem."

"Keys?" Goodman said blankly. "Oh, yes. The desk said there was a problem. They didn't say what it was."

Savoy smiled and held out his hand to the casually dressed young woman whose eyes snapped with temper and intelligence. "Ms. Marsh, I presume? Savoy Forrest. Sorry to keep you waiting. Things are a little crazy when you're running late on a grand opening."

Ingrained good manners had Lacey accepting the handshake even though she wanted nothing to do with Mr. Savoy Forrest.

"How do you do," she said formally, letting go of his hand almost in the same instant she touched it. "Mr. Goodman was trying to explain to me why I can't take my paintings. He wasn't very effective. Perhaps you can do better?"

Savoy smiled even as he sized up Ms. Marsh. Like Bliss, she had a temper. Unlike Bliss, she could keep it on a tight rein. Also unlike Bliss, Ms. Marsh was either not interested in fashion or not able to afford it. Considering the fact that she was supposedly an artist and had the paint-stained jeans to prove it, he rather guessed that expensive clothing wasn't high on her personal must-have list.

"Mr. Goodman was doing me a favor," Savoy said. "So I did him a favor and came here."

Lacey didn't smile. "I figured that out all by myself. Now I would like someone to do me the *courtesy* of no longer wasting my time. I came here for my paintings. Whichever of you gentlemen has the key to the storeroom, please put it to use. I'm sure both of you have other places to be. I know that I do."

"The Savoy Museum is willing to offer you fifty thousand dollars for one of those paintings," Savoy said, and watched the young woman's mouth drop open.

"Holy—er, fifty thousand for an unsigned painting by an unknown artist?" Lacey asked in disbelief.

Savoy shrugged. "As you're very well aware, the painting may or may not be by an unknown artist. If it's a Lewis Marten, the museum will have made a wise investment. If it's not, we will still have a fine example of California plein air painting to add to the museum's collection. Either way, you will have fifty thousand dollars."

Sweet God, no wonder Grandpa Rainbow sold the occasional painting when cash got scarce. And if he didn't sign them, who could prove fraud on his part?

"That's very generous of you," Lacey said. "I'll think about it. While I do, I want the paintings in my possession." She gave him a double row of teeth. "Considering their surprising value, I'm sure you understand."

Savoy almost smiled himself. She'd neatly turned his argument back on him and hadn't promised to sell a single canvas, much less the one that would fit best into his father's collection. If the old man wasn't so hard to buy gifts for, Savoy would have been tempted to throw up his hands. But his father was difficult and the son would go a long way to get the occasional pat on the head. Savoy didn't like that about himself, but he hadn't been able to change it any more than Bliss had. Both of them still craved their father's approval on a level too deep to deny or ignore.

"You drive a hard bargain," Savoy said with equal amounts of approval and irritation. "Seventy-five thousand."

Lacey looked at his hard eyes and soft smile and wondered how on earth she was going to get out of this without blowing her father's career straight to hell.

"I'll think about that, too." She looked at her watch, then at Goodman. "Now I really have to go."

Goodman looked at Savoy, who nodded.

As soon as Lacey was out of sight, Savoy went to the plainclothes deputy who had been hanging around the lobby of the hotel just in case someone wanted to see the paintings.

"Did you get photos of her off the security cameras?" Savoy asked.

"Yes, sir."

"Then follow her wherever she goes, show the pictures around when she stops, and find out who Ms. Marsh really is."

Savoy Civic Center
10:30 A.M. Thursday

23

Rory Turner picked up the phone on the second ring. It was his private phone line, the one that didn't run through his assistant's desk. The caller ID came back as Moreno County Sheriff's Department.

"Yeah?" Rory said.

"Deputy Glendower, sir, reporting as requested."

"Go on."

"No young woman met the subject, Susa Donovan, at Savoy Hotel. Before she went painting at the Savoy ranch, subject's escort drove to a shop in Newport Beach called Lost Treasures Found, just off Pacific Coast Highway in the—"

"Put it in the report unless you found Ms. Marsh there."

"No young woman came out of the shop with the escort, Ian Lapstrake. He was carrying something that looked like a movie poster from an old John Wayne flick. He handled it like it was valuable."

Rory grunted. If the Forrests started collecting movie posters, he'd care. Until then, he didn't. "Keep talking."

"Subject Donovan was then driven to the Savoy ranch, and from there over various ranch roads. At the moment, we're having an early lunch, since we all were up before dawn."

"Where are you eating? Last time I checked, there weren't any fast-food joints on ranch land."

"Ms. Donovan's escort was aware of us. He parked and introduced himself. On their second stop they bought enough food for four."

Rory laughed and silently saluted Susa Donovan's style. "How long did it take Lapstrake to catch on?"

"Less than two miles on PCH." Glendower's voice was rueful. "We didn't think we were working with a pro or we would have approached the subject in a different manner."

"No problem. He called me to double-check that you really were deputies instead of wise guys with costume badges. I told him you were real." Rory hesitated as a thought struck him. "How's the plainclothes car holding up? Some of those ranch roads are rough."

"Lapstrake told us we'd need four-wheel drive, so we called ahead. A Savoy ranch vehicle was waiting for us at the south gate."

"What you're saying is that Lapstrake's not trying to lose you or make life hard on you."

"That's correct, sir."

The phone beeped; someone else was trying to call Rory.

"Anything else?" Rory asked.

"No, sir."

"Keep me posted."

Before Glendower could answer, Rory broke the connection, picked up the incoming call, and said simply, "Turner."

"Deputy Mendoza, sir."

Rory flipped through his mental file and came up with the right man. "You're on the Savoy Hotel assignment."

"Yes, sir. At approximately nine-thirty this morning, a young woman calling herself Ms. Marsh asked to have three paintings returned to her."

Rory's hand tightened around the phone. "What?"

"She had the correct receipt but no personal identification, so the concierge stalled as instructed. Mr. Goodman came to the hotel and identified the subject as Ms. Marsh."

Rory thought of all the ways Ward could make his life miserable if the paintings vanished. "Did she take the paintings?"

"Not right away. Savoy Forrest came to the hotel. He told me to print photos of Marsh off the security cameras, then went and talked with Goodman and Marsh. By the time Marsh got the paintings and left, I had the photos and was in place to follow her."

"Good."

"She went to a shop a few blocks off PCH in Newport Beach, a place called Lost Treasures Found."

Rory made a satisfied sound. When the same place showed up twice in one day, a cop could be pretty sure he had his subject's home ground.

"She parked in back, took the paintings inside, and hasn't been out since," Mendoza continued. "I showed the pictures of her around the shops on either side of her business. Some woman wearing crystals and turquoise robes assured me it was Lacey Quinn, a part owner of Lost Treasures Found. Ditto the counterman at the deli down the street. Lacey Quinn comes in there all the time for bagels or sandwiches. Very positive ID."

"Did you run that name through our computers?"

"Of course, sir. No wants. No warrants. Valid driver, vehicle, and business license. Current voter registration. All the outward signs of a solid, tax-paying citizen."

"Home address?"

"She lives in an apartment above the shop. Should I continue surveillance?"

Rory thought quickly. Lacey Quinn had the paintings and was at her place of work, which was also her home. There was nothing to suggest that she was going to grab the paintings and run. Even if she did, she wasn't a rootless street person who would be hard to find.

"Go back into the computer and get all the information you can on her and her business partner," Rory said. "Find out if she has any family or other close friends. If she bolts, we want to know where to start looking."

24

Lacey fidgeted in front of the mirror and wished that Shayla was home to reassure her that she didn't look like an impostor wearing a chic black dress and a wonderful rope of crystal and ebony jewelry she'd found at an estate sale. But Shayla was on her way to South America to buy local crafts for their store. Lacey would just have to suck it up and be an adult.

"I don't feel like an adult," she muttered at the mirror. "I feel like a teen on her first date. And at the Savoy Hotel's five-star restaurant, of all places. Good Lord. If Mom and my sisters hadn't been giving me society-child clothes all these years, I'd be screwed."

Crystal and ebony swung from her ears as she impatiently twitched the neckline of the dress. Some cleavage was okay, but she really didn't want an outfit that looked like it was going to slide off her nipples the next time she let out a good sigh.

"Oh, the hell with it. The necklace pretty much hides everything anyway."

Lacey went to her closet and looked for something warm that wasn't covered in paint. All she found was an old velvet brocade coat with black lamb's wool around the collar, cuffs, and hem. The coat itself was a deep cranberry color. Like the jewelry, it would have been fashionable in the 1910s or '20s. Unlike the jewelry, it was wool-lined and warm. She pulled out the coat, looked it over critically, and decided that no one would notice the teensy moth holes here and there. Moths had to eat, too, right? Besides, she'd stitched up the worst of them with thread that almost matched the basic material.

She glanced at the clock, sighed, and faced the shoe issue. Not that she didn't have plenty of shoes. She did. Her mother and her sisters were forever buying pretty instruments of torture for her to wear on her feet. Needle heels and toes to match. Even though the leather was incredibly soft and twice as expensive, her toes cringed at the thought of being crammed together while she tiptoed through an evening. She looked longingly at her scuffed, comfortable sandals, but didn't reach for them. The coat she could justify on the basis of warmth. There was no justification for the sandals except sullen mulishness.

If it had been a required party thrown by her mother, she might have been a mule. But she didn't want to embarrass herself—or worse, Susa and Ian—by looking like something out of a church rummage sale. It was grin-and-bear-it time.

"Bother!" Lacey grumbled, grabbing a pair of black heels and glaring at their sleek, uncomfortable style. "Why are there so many useless rules about what to wear to this or that? And why is everything that's acceptable *un*comfortable? Who decided that women should wear heels, anyway—the Marquis de Sade?" She sighed and hoped Ian would take her straight to the restaurant, where she could kick off her shoes under the table and wiggle her toes.

The downstairs bell rang, telling Lacey that she couldn't stall any longer. She pulled on the shoes with their lethal heels, grabbed the vintage beaded envelope purse, shoved her arms into the coat, and headed down the stairs. There were just enough shop lights on to satisfy her insurance carrier. In the semidarkness, Ian's silhouette loomed black in the doorway. For an instant she remembered her first impression of him: big, broad shoulders, and not necessarily safe.

Then his smile flashed through the plate-glass window in the front door and she felt a giddy kind of happiness bubble through her blood. Only then did she understand how much she'd been looking forward to seeing him again.

You're getting in over your head, she told herself.

It's about time, too. Dating myself is really boring.

Lacey unlocked the door and opened it. "Come in. I've got to check the locks and stuff, and then we can go."

"Not so fast. You forgot something."

She opened her mouth to ask what and then felt his tongue gliding past her lips. She made a humming sound as she leaned toward him and slid her arms beneath his, getting as close to him as her bulky coat allowed. His arms tightened, helping her get nearer, holding her while the kiss burned like a fast fuse leading to an explosion of unknown force.

After a moment or five, Ian forced himself to loosen his grip on Lacey. He lifted his head slowly, with many tiny nips and tastes that made her moan. She returned the sweetly stinging caresses and bit not quite gently on his lower lip. Then she traced his lips with the tip of her tongue and tasted him again, bit him again, shared the full-body shudder that went through him.

"I want you," he said.

"Same here. If I could hear my brain above my heartbeat, I'd be scared to death."

His smile flashed again in the gloom. "Me, too. But I'm not so deaf to reason that I'm going to do what I really want to do."

"Which is?" she whispered.

"Lift you up on that counter, take off your panty hose, and go so deep into you we both want to scream."

The small sound she made was more exciting than anything he'd known before.

"Is that what you want, Lacey? Right here? Right now?"

"I—I—"

He gave her a quick, hard kiss and released her. "Lock up. Lock up real tight. I'm having a hell of a time remembering that I'm on duty here."

"Not here you aren't," she retorted, but made sure she was three steps away before she spoke. "You're not guarding anything of mine."

He blew out a hard breath and wondered why he couldn't keep his hands off a curly-haired artist in a moth-eaten cranberry coat. Then he decided the why of it all didn't matter. The attraction was as real as gravity and just as hard to ignore.

"We going out the back or the front?" he asked.

"The back."

"I'll lock up out here."

"Okay. I'm going to check upstairs again. I keep

forgetting and leaving the bathroom window open."

Ian turned toward the front of the shop, then frowned. The windows and glass-pane door that faced the street had a thin line of wire around all the panes, but that sure wasn't much of a barrier to someone who didn't mind setting off the burglar alarm.

"You ever think of upgrading your security system?" he called out.

"Why? It's not like I'm selling diamonds or drugs."

He heard her heels clicking lightly on the wooden stairs as she came back down.

"You've got some valuable stuff in here," Ian said.

"Only to collectors. The average druggie looking for a quick turnaround isn't going to haul a movie poster or a reproduction Deco lamp to the local pawnshop."

He wanted to argue but didn't for the simple reason that she was right. There wasn't much in her shop that would appeal to a smash-and-grab hype. Still . . .

"What about you?" he asked.

"What about me?"

"You're collectible and should be better protected."

Lacey gave him a sideways look and a sly smile. "Is that why you're wearing a gun, to protect yourself from being collected by a person or persons unknown?"

He laughed and gave up the argument—for the moment. As he worked deadbolts and slipped on chains, he made a mental list of some basic security upgrades she really should have. He could get her a good price on everything and the installation would be free. He had several weeks of vacation time stored up and no particular reason to use it, until now. And after he was finished with the wiring and such, maybe she'd like to go up to Bakersfield and meet some other Lapstrakes.

When Ian heard his own thoughts, he fumbled the

last lock. Then he reminded himself that while some women had found him sexy, none had wanted a long-term affair, with or without the benefit of marriage. To be honest, he hadn't wanted that kind of intimacy either—makeup and pink shaving gear in his sink and too much conversation when what he craved was the rushing silence of his small house in the foothills of the San Gabriel Mountains.

"Need some help?" Lacey asked. "One of those deadbolts is sticky."

"I've got it now."

He slammed the bolt home, followed her to the back of the shop, and waited while she armed the security system—a pathetic one, in his opinion—and shooed him outside during the eight-second grace period before the alarm registered an open door and went off.

"I suppose it's better than nothing," he said under his breath.

"What?"

"Nothing."

"You're not making sense."

He grinned. "Thank you."

She rolled her eyes. "C'mon. There's a pathway between my house and Woo-woo Central."

"Woo-woo Central? Should I ask?"

"The cosmic calamity next door."

He looked at the old clapboard building that was barely larger than a double garage and had a bunch of boxes filled with packing material stacked haphazardly around the back and side. Some of the boxes had been wilted by rain. Others were fresh and dry, though torn. All of them came from places like Mystic Crystal of Arkansas or Vortex Stones of Arizona.

"You got something against witches?" he asked,

stepping around a pile of shredded paper or straw or whatever that nearly blocked the narrow space between the buildings.

Lacey snorted. "I'm fine with witches. Blessed be and all that. But Lady Marian over there is a real piece of work. Spends her days conning old ladies into her karmic vitamin schemes and then does vodka shooters and smokes wacky tobaccy all night in the back room."

"I see what you mean," he said as he nudged an empty half-gallon booze bottle with his toe. "Doesn't believe in recycling, does she?"

"Ya think?" Lacey asked dryly as she picked her way through the trash that lay between the two shops.

"Don't see any of the wacky stuff lying around."

"You sound disappointed."

He snickered.

"When the offshore wind blows, which it does about all the time, you can smell it when she lights up," Lacey said. "The wind blows through her place straight to mine."

He took a deep breath. Brine and something else, something much sharper. "Smells more like chemicals to me."

"My paint stuff. She doesn't usually toke up until after nine." Lacey stepped out onto the cracked sidewalk. None of the vehicles looked familiar. "Where's the chariot?"

"Half a block down to the left."

Lacey smiled to herself as Ian took the street side of the walk and then laced his fingers through hers. When he squeezed gently, hot and cold thrills chased over her nerves. *Omigod, I've got it bad. Just holding hands with him makes me want to laugh and skip like a kid.* She looked up and saw him watching her, smiling. The simple pleasure in his eyes made her toes curl.

Ian kissed the flyaway curl on her temple and kept walking. It was that or drag her back to the shop and head for the nearest horizontal surface. The realization that he was hard and ready to go—and had been for some time—irritated him. He wasn't used to taking orders from his dick. Advice, sure. Urgent suggestions, sometimes. Orders? Not since he was fifteen and found out that his dick was seriously stupid.

"Whoa, that's a grim look," Lacey said.

"Just thinking."

"About what?"

He keyed off the locks and opened the passenger door of the truck. "About being fifteen and so horny I'd screw the crack of doom."

She laughed and choked at the same time. Then she went absolutely still when she saw the intensity in his dark eyes.

"But I'm not fifteen," he said. "I know all about itch-scratch-itch. If I thought it was that easy with you, we'd be back in your shop and I'd be hip deep into you, and we'd both be loving it. But it's not that easy, is it?"

She opened her mouth, closed it, tried to get a grip on her scattering thoughts. "I don't know. I've never . . ." She touched his mouth with her fingertips. "Whatever it is, I don't want it to go away."

"Does that mean you trust me?"

"Yes."

Ian leaned over and said against her lips, "I'm holding you to that, Lacey January Marsh Quinn."

He had her inside the truck with the doors locked before she realized that the words could be a promise or a threat.

25

Barefoot and still in the black dress she had worn to dinner, Lacey paced restlessly in the apartment above her shop. She considered painting and rejected it. All she wanted to paint right now was Ian Lapstrake. Stark naked.

"Damn." She groaned.

She raked her hand through her hair and threw the fat hair clip into the corner, letting her curls spring free. Maybe she should have had more champagne. Or maybe she should have dragged Ian inside when he said good night, instead of letting him drive Susa back to the hotel where they were staying.

Being on duty twenty-four/seven really sucked.

Lacey looked at the single bed in the corner and knew she wouldn't sleep. She looked at the empty canvases waiting for her. She could paint. The result might be colorful garbage, but she could still paint the hours away until she was tired enough to sleep—or until she saw Ian again.

Itch-scratch-itch. But it's not that easy, is it?

Right now she was willing to risk finding out. Too bad he wasn't. The good-night kiss he'd given her had been worthy of a younger brother.

With an irritated swipe of her hand, she turned on the CD player. From speakers as small as fists, Etta James's husky, worldly wise voice poured out, filling the apartment with dark words about breaking hearts, crooning a deceptively simple blues song, lamenting what might have been.

Perfect.

Lacey decided she would paint after all. Without a thought for the expensive dress she was still wearing, she pulled on a huge, tattered flannel shirt that served as a paint smock if the nights were cold. When she'd first found the shirt at a garage sale, the hem came way below her knees and she'd had trouble keeping the sleeves rolled up. The hem hadn't changed, but now there was so much paint on the sleeves that they were crusted in deep folds at her elbows.

No sooner had she started to lengthen the legs of her easel when a knocking sound from the front door made her jump. Cautiously she went to the window that overlooked the sidewalk in front of the shop, opened it, and stared down. The man below turned up his head at the sound of wood creaking against wood.

"It's me," Ian said. "Susa kicked me out. Said you needed protecting more than she did. Then she woke up my boss, who told me to do what Susa wanted."

Lacey started to ask why, but thought better of it. He didn't sound happy to be standing below her window in the middle of the night.

"Um, everything is fine here," she said.

"Tell it to Susa," he retorted.

A gust of wind tugged at the denim jacket Ian was wearing and flattened his jeans against his legs. It wasn't raining, but it was damn chilly.

"Is there a rule against you coming inside?" Lacey asked.

"It's either that or freeze my butt off."

"Gosh, it's so nice to be wanted for my own sweet self."

Before he could answer, she slammed and locked the window. Then she padded barefoot down the stairs and through the gloomy shop with its brooding noir posters, and unlocked the front door.

"Don't forget to lock it behind you," she said, turning her back on the very man she'd wanted to see a short time ago. But that was then and this was now, when he looked mad enough at having to be with her to take a bite out of a rabid dog. "There's coffee and champagne and beer in the kitchen. Crackers and cheese if you're hungry."

Ian watched Lacey go back up the stairs like a paint-splattered wraith and wondered what she had on under the huge flannel shirt—if anything at all. The thought had an immediate effect on his crotch, which made his temper take another steep downward dive. *Susa and her damn hunches and her cast-iron will.*

The smile lurking around Susa's mouth hadn't made the orders she gave any easier to take. Neither did the dark, sultry voice of Etta James drifting down the stairs, caressing the words of "Hold Me." Why the hell couldn't Lacey have liked retro rap or the new groups that wouldn't know a tune if it bit them on their tattooed balls?

With a sound of disgust, Ian started shoving locks into place. He wasn't hungry, didn't drink on duty, and was too wide awake to need coffee. Turning on his penlight, he stalked down the dim aisles of Lost Treasures Found, looking at the shapes of pre-Columbian gods on modern pottery, the practiced ennui of noir posters, and the equally practiced elegance of Art Nouveau knockoffs from the Roaring Twenties. He paused at an Art Deco lamp whose clean lines somehow reminded him of the open country east of the Sierra Nevadas, where sun and wind reigned supreme.

He flicked the penlight at his watch. Seven whole minutes had gone by. Whoopee. Only three hundred and sixty-seven more to go. By morning he should have the frigging inventory memorized.

"You don't have to prowl around there in the dark," Lacey said from the upstairs room. "I'm painting, not sleeping. Lights won't bother me."

He didn't have to ask if she would mind company. If she was painting, he could stand close enough to taste her and she wouldn't even know he was there. But instead of reassuring him, that irritated him. All in all, he was in one pisser of a mood.

He took the stairs three at a time.

Lacey heard the footsteps swiftly approaching and gripped the easel so hard she almost left dents. With exquisite care she finished opening the telescoping legs so that she could paint standing up. Normally she sat while painting, but not tonight. She was much too edgy.

And having Ian arrive like a thunderstorm looking for a place to break wasn't helping her nerves one bit.

"I thought all artists worked only in full daylight from north-facing windows."

"In a perfect world, yes. I don't live on that planet. Full-spectrum lighting works in a pinch," Lacey said, waving her hand at a bank of special lights overhead.

With that, she selected a fresh canvas from her file of prepared surfaces and placed the thirty-six-by-thirty-inch rectangle on the easel.

"Is that stuff really canvas?" he asked.

"The best is made of linen. Very expensive."

He looked at the canvas, frowning. "So that's linen?"

"No. Can't afford it, so I've adapted my technique to make the most of cotton."

"Virtue out of necessity?"

"Yeah. Like peanut butter. You've got enough peanuts to cover the planet, so what do you do? You mash them so they store better."

Trying not to smile, he bent over her shoulder and peered at the pale rectangle waiting to be filled with color. "Looks like it's already got a layer of paint."

Lacey told herself that she couldn't really sense the heat of Ian's body reaching out to her. "Some of my canvases are commercially prepared, so that I don't have to fill and sand and paint on the ground layer myself. But this is one of a batch that I prepared weeks ago."

When he didn't say anything, she let out a careful breath and turned to her paint table. Tables, actually. When she worked in the studio, she liked to spread out. The tables themselves were covered with dribs and drabs of old paint in every hue. The dinner plates she used as palettes were paint-free everywhere it mattered. Same for the brushes she chose.

Ian watched as Lacey put out on a separate, smaller table something that smelled like turpentine, and brushes of all sizes in a surprising number of shapes. All of them had really long handles.

"Why so many?" he asked.

She gave him a wary look as she opened the paint drawer that was part of the table. "Sorry, my mind-reading skills are on holiday."

"Brushes. And shapes."

"One color per brush."

He waited.

"Otherwise I'd be stopping to clean the brush every time I wanted a different color," Lacey explained. "And I have a separate table for the solvent because I learned the hard way that I knock the stuff over if I keep it near my easel."

"Brush shapes?"

"This one"—she lifted up a brush with pale bristles—"is flat on the edge with long bristles. I use it for medium or thinner paints."

"The others are for thick paints?"

"No. This one is for thick paint." She lifted up a brush with short hair and a flat edge. "It's called a bright."

"What kind of bristle or fur or whatever?"

"Chinese pig hair." Lacey pulled over a smaller easel and set up the field study she'd done while painting with Susa.

"Pig hair," he repeated.

"Also known as bristles to some folks. The actual breed of pig is called China White. If you want to get really hairy, there are subspecies of the pig favored by some artists."

"China, huh? Must be expensive to import."

"They're more expensive than synthetic, yes, but the pigs they pluck for brushes no more come straight from China than the black Lab down the street came from Labrador."

"So you only use pig hair?"

She shrugged. "If I was doing portraits or old master style, I'd use sable brushes, or badger, or mongoose."

"Mongoose? You're pulling my leg."

"Nope." She tested one brush thoughtfully. Clean, dry, ready to go.

"But you're happy with pig hair."

"For oils, yes." She looked from the field study to the empty canvas. "Pig hair is stiffer than the other kinds, and oil paint is stiffer than other painting media. Also, pig hair flags—kind of frays—at the end of each shaft instead of coming to a point like fur."

"That's good?"

"Sure. Frayed shafts hold more paint, give more texture. Of course, texture also depends on the canvas and the binder in the paint and the paint itself." Her voice was absent, her attention on the blank canvas. "I use poppyseed oil paints when I want heavy, fast-drying textures."

"Is that what you were painting with on the ranch?"

Lacey nodded.

"Are you using it now?" he persisted, enjoying hearing her talk without being wary of him.

"Nope. Linseed oil."

He watched her uncap a big tube of white paint and smaller tubes of red, green, blue, and yellow. She squeezed the paints as separate globs down the edge of one plate.

He looked at the plates set out on a table encrusted

with more colors than he had words to describe. Yet she didn't reach for any more tubes of paint.

"You mix all your colors out of those five?"

"Four," she said absently, slapping the long-handled brush on her palm. "Technically, white isn't a color. It's the absence of any color, just as black is the presence of all colors."

"Where's your black?"

"Don't use it. Chevreul's law of color contrast."

"Come again?"

She shifted, selected a few more brushes, and set them aside before she spoke. "Impressionism at its heart is just that—an *impression* of reality rather than a one-for-one representation. Impressionism is the art of tricking the eye into seeing shadows by using complementary colors to increase contrast rather than using the black shadows and the white light of the old masters."

"Old masters always looked just plain dingy to me."

"That's the result of bad cleaning or no cleaning at all. Or bad art. There was a lot of that going around. Always has been. Always will be. Old doesn't necessarily mean good."

"Not if what Susa slogged through Tuesday night was any indication."

Lacey smiled briefly, but the empty canvas was tugging at her.

"Susa's paints didn't come out of tubes," Ian said.

"She makes her own a lot of the time. So far I'm happy with the effect I get from prepared paints. When that changes . . ." Her voice died away as she went to work.

He watched while she mixed colors in the center of the plate, added a drop of oil, mixed again, then added a touch more yellow, transforming the bold colors at the edge of the plate into a pale, almost ghostly shade of blue.

"Looks like you're making your own paints to me," he said.

She made an absent did-you-say-something kind of sound.

"Aren't you?" he asked.

"What?"

"Making your own paints."

"Blending my own colors. Different thing."

He took her word for it.

For a few moments there was only Etta James singing "Love's Been Rough on Me" and the hushed sounds of brush stroking over canvas. The sky condensed on the canvas like a secret sigh. A different brush, a different mix of colors, and the ocean took form. A third brush, more mixing, and the green foreground took shape.

He glanced from the smaller painting she had done at the ranch to the larger painting taking shape before his eyes. Same place, same colors, yet more subtle, somehow more contained. Field study versus studio painting. He could see the difference, yet he couldn't say which appealed more to him. Each had its own vision, its own strength, its own reality.

"Susa stretches her own canvases," Ian said. "Do you?"

"I used to." She tucked the green brush under her chin and picked up the pale blue one again. "Grandfather insisted on it. His most cherished tool was the pliers he used for stretching. I still have them. Don't use them. Don't do my own sizing, either. The factories can do it better than I can. Quicker, too." While she spoke, she put down her first brushes, squeezed more paint onto another plate, mixed swiftly with new brushes, and added the contrasting swaths of color that gave sky and ocean and grass a sense of three dimensions. "He's the one who taught me to blend prepared paints, even though he made his own with a mortar, pestle, and a hunk of mineral."

Ian managed to follow the twists in her conversation—he hoped. "Your grandfather?" he asked cautiously.

"Mmm."

"He was a painter?"

"Mmm."

"Is that mmm-yes or mmm-no?"

"Huh?"

"Was your grandfather a painter?"

Her brush jerked. With a hissed word she picked up a palette knife, scraped off the mistake, and told herself that she'd better pay attention to the conversation rather than her painting. She couldn't clean up careless words as easily as careless paint.

"Just mmm," she said.

"A dabbler?" Ian pressed.

Their earlier conversation echoed in her ears. *Does that mean you trust me?*

Yes.

I'm holding you to that, Lacey January Marsh Quinn.

A threat.

Definitely.

Ian watched Lacey gnawing on the end of her brush and wondered why she was totally comfortable discussing painting yet flinched from discussing her grandfather who was also a painter—maybe. In any case, Ian decided with irritable satisfaction, at least he had her full attention now.

"So, he was a dabbler?" Ian repeated.

"You know how it is with art. One man's Michelangelo is another man's disaster."

She bent and mixed red and blue together to create a purple that would look like black shadows when placed next to the green of the foreground. She wielded the long-handled brushes with an ease oil painters had in common, because they needed the extra length to stand back and judge the result as they painted.

After a few moments, Ian leaned back with a casual ease that had put more than one subject off guard. Interrogation was really a simple art. First you find out what people don't want to talk about, and then you circle around and keep talking about it until something shakes loose. Waiting was the most important part of the art.

"Was he a Michelangelo to you?" Ian asked finally.

"Who?"

"Your grandfather."

"He was Grandpa Rainbow. That's all that mattered to me."

"Sounds like you were close."

"What do you mean?" she demanded, looking over her shoulder at Ian for the first time in twenty minutes.

"He left you his favorite pair of pliers." Ian smiled. "I don't know how women feel about it, but that adds up to 'close' in any man's book."

"He encouraged me to paint." She turned back to the canvas as though ending the topic.

Ian remembered some of the conversations Lacey had had with Susa. "And your parents didn't."

"Mom thought it was a messy, downscale way to spend time. As a hobby, she tolerated it. As an avocation? Nope."

"Maybe she'd had a bellyful of it while she was growing up with Grandpa Rainbow."

Absently Lacey shook her head, already succumbing to the lure of the canvas. "Mom came from lawyers and judges and politicians." She switched brushes, blended colors. "Grandpa Rainbow is my father's father."

"So your dad didn't mind your painting?"

Her mouth turned down in an unhappy line. "He didn't get along with his father. I was the only one who understood my grandpa."

"And your grandpa was the only one who understood you."

It wasn't a question, so she didn't answer. She simply slid deeper into the world she was creating, arcs of color that suggested sky and ocean and land stirred by wind, a day both wild and serene within its wildness. The houses along the coast were quick dashes of cream beneath dark eucalyptus trees bowing to their mistress the wind.

"What does your father do?" Ian asked after awhile.

"Law. He's up for a judicial appointment."

"Sounds like a good match for your mother."

Lacey smiled. "It is. Living with either one of them would make me nuts, but they do real well together. Go figure."

"Did your grandfather live with you?"

"On and off."

"The way you paint, it must have been more on than off."

She tapped the end of a brush against her chin and

considered the painting. Despite the distraction, it was coming along faster than any she'd done before. More free. More evocative. More swirls and less angular strokes. More . . . reckless. She liked it.

Maybe she should have Ian breathing down her neck more often.

"Was he around a lot?" Ian asked, trying it another way.

"Who?"

"Your grandfather," Ian said companionably, despite the impulse to clench his teeth.

He'd pried information out of more difficult subjects than Lacey by being the good cop. He'd hammered some out of others by being the bad cop. Whatever got the job done. Except he really didn't want to bad-cop Lacey into telling him things for no better reason than his own curiosity about why a transparently honest woman invented a fake name and didn't want to talk about her grandfather. Much better to keep casting the conversational lure until she rose to it freely. Then he would have proof of something that was only a gut certainty now.

Laccy had no more found those three paintings at a garage sale than his mother had found him under a cabbage leaf.

26

Ian decided to be patient until Lacey was wholly lost in her painting before he brought up her grandfather again. Watching and waiting wasn't exactly a hardship. Even the shapeless flannel rag she was wearing couldn't hide the bare, feminine curve of her calves, the narrowness of her ankles, and the arch of her feet. He'd never considered feet particularly sexy before, but he found himself staring at hers. They seemed so *naked*.

Outside, the chill wind pressed against windows and the old frame house shifted and groaned.

"Aren't your feet cold?" he asked finally, without meaning to. He should be talking about her grandfather.

She started. "Um, yeah, now that you mention it."

"You have any slippers?"

"Beside the bed." She tilted her head toward the end of the room.

He walked over, taking his time. The canvases

propped up everywhere kept pulling at him. Some were like the ones she'd painted at the ranch, smaller rectangles thick with paint and vivid with energy—field studies created in the heat of the moment of first discovery. Other paintings were bigger, more polished versions of the smaller scenes. Again, he couldn't choose between the two methods. Each drew him in a different way.

He finally spotted the slippers peeking out from beneath a pillow that had slipped off the bed. Black nose, eyes and ears, with pale curly wool everywhere else, the slippers looked like slightly tipsy lambs. Grinning, he picked them up and told himself he hadn't seen the inviting disarray of the bed or smelled the fist-size candle that flickered silently on a small table nearby, infusing the air with spice and mystery.

Think of your cousin's kids or Lawe's nieces wearing these silly slippers. Now hold that picture.

It worked until Ian sat on his heels behind Lacey. It just wasn't the same with a big girl as with a little one. Lacey's feet were sexy. Very sexy. They had high arches and were attached to delicate ankles leading to long legs that vanished beneath folds of ragged, faded flannel into shadows that were perfumed with something as exotic and feminine as the candle burning by the bed.

Think nieces, Ian told himself.

Gently he lifted one high-arched foot to warm the cool flesh between his hands as he did for his nieces.

Lacey stopped painting and forgot to breathe. The feel of his big, warm hands wrapped around her foot made her heart turn over and her blood heat up.

It's just my foot, damn it.

Yeah, and the Queen Elizabeth *is just a ship.*

When he eased her foot into the familiar slipper, she let out a long breath that she hadn't even known she was holding. Then she found herself letting him warm her other foot and decided oxygen was overrated. She'd just close her eyes and breathe him in—gentleness and impatience, laughter and gun harness, smile like an angel and hands like the devil himself.

"Better?" he asked, still holding her other foot.

Her tongue stuck to the roof of her mouth. She swallowed and said, "Yes."

The husk in her voice went straight to his groin. He told himself that he wasn't going to give in to Susa's obvious matchmaking.

Yeah. Sure. And he was going to fly to the moon without benefit of rockets.

He slid Lacey's foot into the waiting slipper, then trailed his fingertips up the smooth swell of her calf to the back of her knee, lingered, and then traced the lines of her leg between his thumb and his forefinger all the way down to her heel hidden in wool. And back up.

Lacey felt like she was falling into warm cream. She knew Ian wanted her, knew he was pissed off about it, yet he was so gentle with her that she wanted to give him . . . everything.

When the backs of his fingers slid up the inside of her thighs, the brush slipped from her lax fingers and fell across one of the plates with a clatter she didn't hear and he ignored. She grabbed the heavy easel for support.

"Skin as soft and warm as your smile," he said. He eased upward until he felt a different texture of silk, lingered, and then caressed down her legs again, up again, down. "Strong, long, beautiful. I want to feel your legs around me."

Her knees trembled.

He felt it and smiled despite the claws of sexual need that were sinking into him, twisting. "Do you want that?"

She opened her mouth but all that came out was a low sound when his fingertip traced the crotch of her panties, then retreated.

The inner surface of the old flannel felt like silk to him. He decided she must be wearing a slip underneath the shirt, or a nightgown. He couldn't wait to find out which. His hands eased back up her legs. "Do you want that, Lacey?"

"Y-yes," she managed.

"Risky thing to say to me right now."

"Yes."

His laugh was like he was, tender and dangerous at the same time. "That's one of the things I liked right away," he said. "There's nothing coy or cold about you."

"A lot of my dates"—her voice broke as she felt her underwear being tugged down her legs—"would disagree with you."

The smooth movement of his fingertips hitched as he understood what she was saying. Then the sight of silky underwear slithering down her legs made his mind go blank. Wine-colored. Sexy as her scent. Warm with the heat of her flesh.

Like feet, he'd never found underwear a particular turn-on. But as his fingers sank into soft, flimsy, girly cloth, he was thinking he'd been missing something good in life. The sight of the burgundy lace against the foolish slippers was so sexy he didn't know whether to laugh or drag her down to the floor. He compromised by giving her a long, openmouthed kiss just below her knee.

"Lord, you're sweet," he said huskily.

As her knees turned to water, she wondered if even her sturdy easel could support her weight. When his hands circled her right ankle and began a slow, inevitable journey toward her center, she was afraid she was going to find out.

"Wait," she said.

His hands froze.

She kicked out of her slippers and underwear. "Okay."

"Does that mean I can undress you?"

"You already have."

He nipped at the back of her knee while his hands caressed up her thigh. "I've hardly begun, darling. When I took off your coat at the restaurant and saw the neckline on your dress, I wanted to run my tongue around the edges and see if I could reach your nipples."

She made a breathless sound when his tongue slid across the crease at the back of her knee. "It's not too late."

He lifted his head. "What isn't?"

"I'm still wearing it. The dress."

His hands hesitated, withdrew, and returned between the flannel and the silky garment he'd thought was a nightgown. "You're right. It's not too late. Are you really fond of this old rag?" he asked, turning his hands to tug at the flannel.

"I've got a closet full of rags."

"Say good-bye to this one."

He grabbed a double handful and yanked. The ancient cloth gave way almost gratefully, landing in a jumbled pile around her naked feet. He found himself about eye level with the hips he'd watched with an elemental male hunger as he'd seated her in the restaurant. It occurred to him that with very little effort he could pull her down over him, sink deep into her, and just plain enjoy a lapful of Lacey Quinn.

On a surge of power that was just short of violent, he came to his feet. If he stayed crouched on his heels one second longer, he knew the fun would be over way too soon. He wanted more from her than fast sex. He wasn't sure what else he wanted, but he was damn sure that he was going to enjoy finding out.

Lacey turned toward him, lifted her hands to his face, and said, "Yikes! I can't touch you. I'm covered in paint."

"Cover me, too."

"No, I'll wash and . . ." Her breath backed up in her throat, cutting off her words. Ian's tongue was tracing the neckline of her dress, probing, proving that not only could his tongue reach her nipple, his teeth could.

He bit her very delicately, sucked harder, nibbled gently again. "Gotta say, I love your taste in underwear."

"I'm not wearing any."

"Like I said."

She laughed and reached for him. "You fond of this denim jacket?"

He smiled against her breast, licked, kissed. "Why? You going to tear it off my manly body?"

"I'm not that strong. But on my way to getting this jacket off you, I'm sure going to stain it up some."

He nuzzled. "Have your way with me."

"You do know how to tempt a woman."

"Do I?" He lifted his head and looked at her. "You're the first one to mention it."

She rolled her eyes and began pushing the jacket off his shoulders. "Yeah. Sure. And you have a bridge to sell me."

"No bridge. Just me."

Her hands stopped as she met the clear, hot darkness of his eyes. "Sold."

The smile he gave her was as sexy as the slow twist of his body helping her to pull off his jacket. She looked at the leather shoulder harness, supple and tough—and the gun, completely unknown.

"Um, is this thing on whatchamacallit—safety?" she asked.

His smile got hotter. "The one on my shoulder is. The other one is locked and loaded."

She looked down, then followed her glance with her hands, measuring his readiness. He took the sweet torture for a few moments before he dragged her hands back up his chest.

"Unless you have a hidden lust for sex with a fully dressed, armed man," he said hoarsely, "we'd better take it easy on that one."

"Okay."

He told himself he wasn't disappointed that she agreed. Then he felt her hands working on his fly and sucked at breath. "I thought you were going to take it easy."

"I've never done things the easy way. Not the things that really mattered, the good things."

"Now you're the one tempting me."

His hands reached down, slid up the inside of her thighs, and found her center. She was sultry, slick, open to him. The ripping sigh of her breath as he caressed her was like fire. The liquid heat of her response nearly brought him to his knees. He felt control slipping away and didn't care. Her fingers had already undone his fly and freed him while he'd pushed her dress up to her waist and teased her.

"How sturdy is that paint table?" he asked, pointing his chin at the nearest one.

"I stand on it to change lightbulbs, why?"

With one arm he swept the plates, paint tubes, and used brushes aside. With the other he lifted her and put her bare bottom on the paint-covered edge of the table.

Her breath hissed in.

"Okay?" he asked.

"Cold," she said huskily, "but you're going to take care of that."

She touched his erection with the tip of her finger. She liked the jerk of his response, the eager beat of his blood. She wanted more, much more from him than she'd had with anyone. And she wanted it from herself, too. Men who appealed to her enough to take a chance on sex with them had been real scarce in her life. She didn't know how long Ian would be around, but she was absolutely certain that she wanted to explore the sensual recklessness he brought out in her.

Smiling, she shifted her thighs until he brushed against her slick core. Shivering with pleasure, she looked down. He was breathtakingly close—and not nearly close enough. She tugged at the front of his jeans until he just nudged into her.

"Got something in my pocket," he said.

She laughed. "I hate to break it to you, but it's already out of your pocket."

"Oh, man, you're not helping me here." He dug in his back pocket until he found the foil packet.

"You don't mind if I watch, do you?" she said in a low voice. "I never thought it'd be fun, but you're worth watching."

His answer was a groan and a small, sleek pulse that escaped his control. Her fingertip circled him, spreading his own heat, as she watched him. Then she opened the condom and put it on him with a care that made him clench his teeth against the need crawling up his spine.

His forehead rested heavily against hers and he said roughly, "You're going to be the death of me."

"Is that good or bad?"

"Let's find out."

He lifted her legs and sank slowly into her, then retreated. Sank in. Retreated.

"I don't know which is better—seeing or feeling," she said raggedly.

"Yeah. I'm having the same problem."

Her head snapped up in surprise and something close to embarrassment. "You're looking!"

He grinned and didn't glance up. "You sure?" He drew back and eased in deeper and then deeper, only to withdraw again. "Yeah, you're right. I'm definitely looking. You're beautiful, Lacey."

A lush thrill uncurled in her like a slow whip. She forgot to be embarrassed. She held on to the leather harness he wore and wrapped her legs around him.

"Again," she said.

She could take all of him now, but he didn't go that deep because the second he did, he was afraid he'd lose it. He was sweating from his forehead to his heels, his vision was hazed, and he was heavy with a hunger that was new to him. He pushed into her and re-treated, pushed and retreated, setting a slow rhythm that shrank the world down to the room, the table, the squeeze and pulse of her around him. When he felt her begin to tip over the edge, he stopped, waited.

"More," she said, pulling him closer and arching her back. "More, damn it!"

He felt like laughing and groaning and howling all at once, but he didn't move. "You'll get more, I prom-ise you, when I'm good and ready."

"My God, you're a tease," she said, discovery and irritation and pleasure all at once.

"Only with you." He slid partway in. "Something about watching you watching me gave me all kinds of ideas."

"Like?"

"This is one."

Her breath hitched as his hands went beneath her bottom and came forward, pulling her legs farther apart until she tightened suddenly around him in a slick intimacy that came within an ace of undoing him.

The lush whip uncoiled again, faster, taking her by surprise. Her pleasure pulsed hotly, repeatedly, bathing him, burning away his control. With a groan he drove all the way into her, setting a new rhythm, hard and fast and deep. She shivered, arched, and came in a rush that blinded her. He listened to her gasp of surprise, her keening cries of pleasure, felt the clench and release of her orgasm all around him, realized it was his, too, and gave a stifled shout as the world came apart.

When he could see again, he discovered that he was braced on the table and she was collapsed against him, breathing like a sprinter. So was he. He smiled, savor-ing her female heat, scent, and textures.

"First my jacket, now my jeans," he said against her hair. "Hope you have a washing machine around here. Or at least a dryer."

She took a breath. "You bragging or complaining?"

"Bragging. You mind?"

"I'd need a brain to mind. I must have lost it with my dress."

"Your dress is around your neck. Kind of."

She blew against his chin. "How about my brain?"

He tipped her mouth up and gave her a gentle, thorough kiss. "Sexy. Female. Really fine."

"My brain?"

"Yeah."

She tilted her head back and smiled up at him. "I like you a lot, Ian Lapstrake."

Amused, he glanced down to where they were still interlocked. "I figured that out."

"No, I mean even after, uh . . ."

"The itch is scratched?"

She nodded. "Usually, well . . ."

"Same here. Things change afterward. Not bad, just different, because you know it's not what you wondered it would be like before."

Her lips brushed his. "Yeah. And this time it was."

"Would you believe I followed that?"

"Right now, I'd believe anything you tell me."

"Water flows uphill," he said.

"Naturally."

"Black is white."

"Always."

"One plus one is five."

"Of course."

"I only have one condom."

"What? *Damn.* I stopped keeping them because I

couldn't find anyone to wear them with." She stuck out her lower lip and blew hard enough to make the curls against her temple fly. "Guess we'll get to brush up on our heavy petting skills."

Ian threw back his head and laughed without restraint. "I really like you a lot, Lacey Quinn."

The kiss he gave her started slow and ended deep. Finally he lifted his head and said, "I have enough condoms to kill us."

"Standard equipment?" she asked before she could stop herself.

"Susa gave them to me when she kicked me out."

Lacey's jaw dropped. "You're kidding."

He shook his head.

She smiled slowly. "We'll have to think of a way to thank her."

"I'll bet she's hard to buy gifts for."

"Good thing we have all night to think about it."

"Yeah." Slowly Ian stepped back until they were separate again. As he lifted Lacey off the table, he looked down at her breasts flattened against his shirt and harness. "Next time I want to be naked, too."

"Only if I get to paint you that way."

His eyebrows shot up. "That would be another first."

"This is your lucky night, neighbor. C'mon, strip. We'll throw everything but the gun and holster in the washer. Won't do diddly for the oil stains, but the rest should come out just fine."

When she turned around and headed for the washer, he saw that her butt was both firm and rainbow-colored from the paint table. Grinning in anticipation, he followed her, peeling off clothes every step of the way.

27

The man had been around enough to know how street people moved—slow, a little bent over, uneven, careful. Kind of like a drunk pushing a three-wheeled shopping cart full of junk. Except the real drunks would be off the streets by now, passed out in a doorway with an empty pint tossed nearby. Newport PD didn't hassle the street people unless someone complained a lot or the local liberals started a drive to round up the homeless and give everyone a bath, a blanket, and shoes or wheelchairs or whatever. It didn't matter. Within a day or two everything but the bath would end up in a pawnshop and the money would go straight to the mini-marts that sold fortified wine; but it's the thought that counts.

Since it wasn't election time, nobody had been counting or thinking about the homeless lately. He'd passed two old ladies barricaded behind their rusty shopping carts and third-world luggage. Then he passed a guy trash-diving behind a local deli for a late-night snack. A couple of alley cats also watched with interest. A rat's eyes gleamed from beneath the wheeled trash bin.

When the man reached the last street before his destination, he waited until nothing moved, not even a rat, before he crossed in the darkness between two distant streetlights. The wind off the ocean was cold enough to make bones ache, but it didn't matter to him. He'd be warm in a little while.

And Lacey Quinn would be a hell of a lot hotter than warm.

With a narrow smile, he walked past the back of Lost Treasures Found to the trash piled up behind the cottage that was painted blue in the front and peeled down to bare, scoured planks in the back. Pressed between buildings on either side of the alley, the wind poured through the opening in an invisible, restless stream.

After a quick look around to be certain he was alone, he selected an area that was about six feet from the narrow opening between the two old houses that had been converted to shops. Not so close to Lost Treasures Found that anyone would guess it was the target, and not so far away that the shop would survive the coming fire. Satisfied, he reached into his coat, pulled out one handful after another of compressed paraffin-soaked sawdust, and scattered the chunks through some cardboard and packing material that was heaped between the two houses.

When only a handful was left, he pulled a quart bottle of gasoline out of a deep coat pocket. Using all but about half a cup from the bottle, he saturated the loose pile of trash. Next he pulled over a cracked, battered plastic trash can that stood drunkenly in back of Cosmic Energy. Then he gathered enough other cardboard debris to make the kind of bonfire that homeless people started on nights like these to keep warm. In case the local cops couldn't figure that angle out on their own, he shoved all the trash into the can, emptied the rest of the gas on it, threw in the bottle, added more paper, and lit it off. As soon as the flames bit down into the gasoline, the fire settled in to burn hot and bright.

He counted to sixty and pushed over the can with his foot. Flaming trash flowed out toward Cosmic Energy like a dragon's forked tongue. The back of the old clapboard house started to burn like the tinder it was. Another part of the tongue flicked out hungrily, licking toward the gasoline-soaked pile between the two houses.

He was three blocks away before the two fires joined.

28

Lacey and Ian woke up in a nightmarish clarity of adrenaline and smoke pouring through the open window.

Fire.

Neither knew who yelled it first. Their feet slapped on the wooden floor at the same time.

"Call 911!" Lacey said, grabbing for the fire extinguisher she kept by the bed.

Ian snatched up the bedside phone, punched in the numbers, and went through the maddening and necessary protocol of name, address, phone number, reason for call, etc., etc. While he answered questions, he yanked on jeans, shoes, and weapon harness. As he clipped his cell phone to his jeans, the emergency operator asked him to repeat the information.

"Play back the tape, I'm busy," he said and threw the receiver on the bedside table. He stuck his head out the bedroom window to measure the fire. "Oh shit, oh dear. Lacey!" he hollered. "We've got to move your car. Where are the keys?"

"On the hook by the back door. I'll get them."

"Do it before the car is toast." *And so are we if that gas tank blows up in our faces.*

Lacey didn't answer. She just grabbed the keys and shot back out in the alley. Ian snatched her sandals and his shirt for her to wear and ran down the stairs. He paused long enough in the kitchen to snag some dish towels and another fire extinguisher. When he got outside, Lacey had just finished moving the car and was running back up the alley toward him. He dumped everything but the towels near the extinguisher she'd abandoned to get the car away from the flames.

"Put these on so you don't get cut up or burned," he said.

White-faced, she jammed on her sandals, pulled his T-shirt on, and bent down to pick up the fire extinguisher. Soon the *whoosh* of carbon dioxide and chemicals spewed out of the canister again. A tongue of flame snaked around the back corner of the shop, met a blast of foam, sputtered, and died. She followed the flame back to its source, a scattering of trash blown by the wind. Then she went to work on the next outrider of fire climbing up the side of her shop.

"There's a hose by the back steps," she yelled to Ian.

"Got it."

While she chased bold flames, he turned on the water and braced the nozzle so that liquid sprayed over the side of her shop and the aisle of burning trash between the two buildings. It was better than pissing on it, but not much.

Where are the lights and sirens, damn it!

Too much fire. Not enough time.

Grimly he soaked the kitchen towels in water. As smoke masks went, it was like the hose—better than nothing, but not much.

"Don't go back in the shop," Ian said as he headed for the old clapboard house next door. "I'll go around to the front and make sure your neighbor's out."

Lacey's mouth was too dry to answer. She'd seen another licking swirl of orange glide up the side of her shop beneath the veil of water. Heart hammering, hands sweating, she pointed the extinguisher nozzle and fired. Chemicals mixed with the biting smell of smoke. With every spurt from the nozzle she thanked her grandfather's paranoia about fire. When this extinguisher died, she had four more big ones inside.

Surely by the time these are used up, the fire department will be here, won't they?

But until then, all she had was fear and prayer and chemicals and shaking hands. And Ian, a dark figure lit by flames as he ran toward her from the front of Cosmic Energy.

"Deadbolts and bars all over the front of the shop," he said. "Hope it isn't the same back here."

It wasn't. He'd never figured out why people didn't bar the alley door as heavily as the front, but most of them didn't. He kicked in the back door of Cosmic Energy and vanished inside. Although the exterior of the shop was only moments away from full conflagration, there was surprisingly little fire visible inside. The smoke more than made up for it. Breathing through the wet towel, he headed for where he thought the stairway might be. It wasn't. All he found was smoke, blinding, choking, smothering. He spun and hurried in the opposite direction, found the stairway, and raced up, bending almost double to get below the smoke. He didn't need the crackle of flames to tell him that the fire was worse upstairs. He could see it across the back of the house, pouring in the heat-shattered hall window.

One of the two rooms upstairs was empty. The other, overlooking the alley, was locked and barred. Smoke curled out from the cracks around the door. The panels were blistering hot to the touch. Whoever opened that door without full fire-fighting gear would get a lethal blast of flame.

Nor was there any reason to go farther. From the smell of it, whoever was in that room had already swallowed the dragon and died.

Crouching low, Ian ran for the staircase and air that didn't gag him to breathe.

Outside, the fire sighed and flared in fluid, deadly beauty. Lacey watched in horrified fascination as wind-driven flames leaped to consume the second-floor apartment.

I'll make sure your neighbor's out.

A new kind of fear streaked through Lacey, a razor slice of panic. Her brain knew that someone had to check on her neighbor, but the primitive part of her screamed that Ian mattered more than the drunken cosmic pothead whose carelessness likely had started the fire in the first place.

"Ian!"

He didn't answer.

Lacey grabbed a second extinguisher and ran toward the shattered back door of Cosmic Energy, canisters banging with every step. She emptied the first extinguisher on the doorway, readied the second, and leaped over the smoldering barrier.

"Ian! Where are you?"

He heard her before he saw her silhouette outlined by the flaming doorway. His heart stopped and then kicked in at twice the speed. He took her low and over his shoulder, slamming out through the doorway into the smoke-filled alley that smelled like paradise after the ghastly house.

"Of all the crazy—" he began fiercely, coughed. "I'll chew you out later. Is the extinguisher I brought down still loaded?" he asked hoarsely.

"No."

"Any more?" he asked, coughing again.

"In the shop."

"Where?"

"Here." She shoved the good extinguisher at him and sprinted for her back door. Getting them herself was easier than telling him how to.

He started to object and decided to save his breath for coughing and dragging at oxygen. While he did both, he figured out the extinguisher, triggered it, and damped down the flames in the trash piled between the two houses. The hose still sprayed on everything it could, but it wasn't enough. He repositioned the hose so that it would throw water at the roof of Lacey's shop, where windblown flames were starting to reach out hungrily from the burning house next door.

Two fire extinguishers clanked down nearby. He threw away the empty and went to work with a fresh one.

In the distance, sirens wailed their song of bad luck and death.

Lacey stood for a moment, fighting for breath, unaware that she was shaking from adrenaline and fear. The two old cottages looked like a study in light and darkness, fire and waiting. Beyond the reach of hose or chemicals, wood smoked and shimmered into flame. Some of the flames were licking at her eaves.

For the first time she understood that she was losing her shop and her home to fire.

"No," she screamed. "*No!*"

Ian braced the extinguisher with one arm and with the other pulled her close for the only kind of comfort he could offer.

"Grandpa's paintings! I can't let them burn!"

Before he could prevent it, she twisted away from him and lunged back into her shop. Breathing smoke and fear every step of the way, she raced upstairs, grabbed sheets from her bed and frantically began wrapping up the paintings. Clutching them awkwardly, she turned around and ran smack into Ian.

"Give me those," he snarled.

It was a voice she'd never heard from him. "They're Grandpa's. I couldn't let—"

She was talking to herself. Ian had grabbed the paintings and was shouldering her out and down the stairs at a speed just short of breakneck. She turned for the back door of the shop, only to be yanked off her feet and shoved through the aisles of Lost Treasures Found toward the front door. She opened the locks automatically and stumbled out into the night, tripping over fear and grief. He caught her before she fell and hustled her across the street, upwind of the fire.

"I'm all right," she said numbly. "The fire—"

"Will do just fine without you," he cut in. "Stay here."

"Only if you do."

In the light of the streetlamp, he looked at her stubborn eyes and trembling lips and knew she would follow him the instant he turned his back.

"We have maybe two minutes," he said. "What do you want saved?"

"Everything." She smiled through tears. "Nothing. I have what's important right here. All the rest can be replaced one way or another."

"Computer records?"

"Duplicates in my car."

"Clothes?"

"There are twelve garage sales this week."

"Your paintings?"

She flinched. "More where they came from."

But her expression said it wasn't true.

"Guard these until I get back," he said, pointing to the three canvases he'd put on the sidewalk.

He ran back into the shop before she could argue. He couldn't save all her work, but he could rescue some of it. He snatched the painting drying on the easel, scooped up others at random until he couldn't carry any more, and clattered back down the stairs and out the shop door.

The night was alive with sirens and red lights and men yelling orders while laying hoses. He dumped the paintings at Lacey's feet and turned to go get more before the cops who were screaming in from all sides could barricade the entrances.

"No!" Lacey's surprisingly strong hands clamped over Ian's forearm, nails digging in.

"There's time."

"You're worth more than a few paintings."

"There are more than a few paintings up there."

Her lips trembled into a smile. "You're still worth more."

"Don't tell the IRS."

Then he pulled her close and held her, just held her,

while squad cars slammed to a stop and uniformed cops poured out. Two of them spotted the couple on the sidewalk and came toward them.

Ian braced himself for the questions that would begin raining down. As he did, he wondered if the answers the cops eventually found would include who had started the fire.

And why.

**Newport Beach
Early Friday morning**

29

The ringing of his phone jerked Rory awake. Bliss, who was sprawled across him, grumbled sleepily and burrowed closer to his warmth. He reached around her and fumbled for his cell phone. Damn, getting older was a bitch. Once he would have awakened completely, mind and fingers nimble. Not anymore.

"Yeah," he muttered.

"There's a fire down in Newport."

"Jesus, Ward, what are you doing awake?"

"You get to be my age, you spend a lot of time awake."

"Listening to the police radio," Rory said, understanding what had happened.

"Better than television."

With a sigh, Rory shifted beneath Bliss's thighs. He couldn't believe he was getting an erection—not after the last few nights. But damn, it felt good to have her pussy snuggled up to him.

"You hear me?" Ward said irritably.

"There's a fire in Newport Beach, which is in Orange County, which wasn't a part of Moreno County last time I checked."

"You didn't have any trouble assigning men to cover Susa Donovan, did you, and she went to Orange County."

"What do you want me to do, drive down and pee on their fire?" Rory said impatiently.

"I want you to get your well-paid ass out of my daughter's bed and go see where the fire is."

Idly, Rory wondered how Ward had found out who was sleeping with Bliss. "Your daughter, my future wife."

There was a pause. Rory smiled. He could almost see the old man's calculating frown.

"When?" Ward demanded.

"As soon as the blood tests come back."

Ward grunted. "Didn't know she had the guts."

Rory didn't bother to hide his yawn. "Anything else on your mind?"

"The fire in Newport Beach. From the address called in to 911, it sounds close to that girl's shop."

"A lot of girls have—"

"The one with the paintings," Ward interrupted. "Quinn or whatever the hell she's calling herself now."

Rory rubbed his hand over his face and told himself to be patient with his once and future father-in-law. Then he told himself to wake up and start thinking about his boss rather than how good it was going to feel to spread Bliss's knees and dive in.

Girl. Paintings. Quinn.

Damn. No wonder Ward's dick is in a knot.

"Are you saying that Lacey Quinn, the young woman whose paintings you want to buy, that her shop—where she's keeping the paintings now—is on fire?" Rory asked.

"How the hell would I know?" Ward shot back. "All I remember is that the place your men followed her to is in the old section of Newport and there's a fire burning in the old section of Newport right now. Get up and find out if my paintings are safe!"

Rory didn't bother to point out that the paintings weren't Ward's yet—if ever. From all Savoy had been able to find out, the lady wasn't interested in selling. On the other hand, Rory couldn't think of the last time the old man had taken no for an answer.

"I'll make some calls," Rory said, and hung up.

30

Wrapped up in a thick terry cloth hotel robe, Susa glanced at the closed door of the second bedroom and then at Ian. "How is Lacey?"

"She was asleep when I left her. Hope she still is." He raked his fingers through his hair and wondered if he would ever get the ghastly smell of death out of his skin and his mind. "Losing everything is a bitch, but at least Lacey didn't roast like her neighbor."

"From what you told me about it, I doubt that the woman ever woke up."

His mouth flattened. "Sure as hell hope so."

"Are you certain Lacey lost everything? She said they got the fire out before it got into her shop."

"Smoke and water damage," Ian said succinctly. "Some of the durable stuff, glassware and jewelry and metal and such, can be saved. Posters and textiles . . ." He made a sharp gesture with his hand. "Dead loss."

"What about her paintings?"

"Mostly ruined, I'd guess. Maybe not. I don't know much about the staying power of oil and canvas."

"Better than pastels or watercolors." Susa frowned. "I'll help Lacey go through her paintings when she's ready. She might throw out something that could be saved with proper treatment. Did you ask about insurance?"

"She has it. Whether it pays anything helpful is up to the claims adjuster and the lawyers, if it comes to that."

Susa looked at Ian's spiky hair and grim eyes. "How about some food or coffee or a drink?"

"No thanks. I'm still digesting smoke."

"Some salve for your burns?"

"Been there, done that. Smeared Lacey all over while I was at it." He almost smiled. That part, at least, had been enjoyable.

"Sleep?"

"In a while. I'm waiting for a call from the arson investigator."

Eyes narrowed, Susa watched Ian pace. "Arson? Lacey didn't say anything about that."

"All fires are routinely investigated."

"Nice try, doesn't fly," she shot back. "You wouldn't be waiting up if you didn't expect something more than routine."

"Bet your boys never got anything past you, did they?"

"Constantly, but nothing that mattered."

Ian looked over his shoulder at the closed door, then walked over and stood next to it, listening intently. If Lacey was awake, she wasn't moving around.

Susa waited with the patience of a mother or a hunting cat. Sometimes there wasn't much difference.

"From what I could see, the fire started in a trash barrel," Ian said. "Then someone dumped the barrel and the fire poured over the aisle between the two shops. Just in case that wasn't good enough, some kind of accelerants were used—kerosene or gasoline—plus what looked like chunks cut from those paraffin-and-sawdust logs folks use for fires when they don't want to bother with wood. Stuff burns like a bastard, even in a downpour."

"Why would anyone set fire to Lacey's shop?"

"It wasn't Lacey's shop, it was Cosmic Energy next door."

"Then why are you sending out the kind of feelings that make my Druid ancestors twitchy?"

Ian shot her a dark look. "What kind of feelings would those be, Ms. Donovan?"

"Bad. You might as well tell me the rest of it."

"Nothing to tell." And he hoped there wouldn't be.

"Bullshit."

He blinked, then smiled slowly, his first real smile since he'd half carried, half dragged a smoky, hollow-eyed Lacey into Susa's suite an hour ago, dumped her in Susa's arms, and gone back for the paintings he'd left in the lobby.

"Okay," Ian said, "but I don't know how my speculations are going to make anyone feel any better."

"Did I ask to feel better?"

He whistled very softly between his teeth. "Lawe told me you were a rapier, but I didn't really believe it until now."

"You can wiggle like a worm on a hook and try to change the subject, but it won't work."

Ian had already figured that out. "Something that looked a lot like burning chunks of sawdust log lay in an arc from the trash can to Lacey's shop. I thought I caught a whiff of gasoline, too, but nothing I could take an oath on. But I just flat out don't like how it adds up."

"Anybody ever tell you that you're paranoid?"

"Occupational hazard."

"Unfortunately, I've got a gut feeling you're right."

It took a moment for Susa's calm words to sink in. "Damn, I was hoping you'd disagree."

"So was I. What are we going to do about it?"

"You aren't going to do anything," he said, "except what you came here for, and that doesn't include messing with arson."

She lifted her eyebrows. "You and my husband have something in common—arrogance."

"Good thing you like that particular trait," Ian said easily, smiling.

"I think it's time to call my new friend Dana Gaynor of Rarities Unlimited. Your boss, I believe."

"Dana might send me out at your say-so for some slap-and-tickle that she thinks is long overdue, but there's no way she's going to put your artistic tush in danger." He pulled out his cell phone and punched a speed-dial number. "Ask her yourself."

"And while you're doing that," Lacey said from the bedroom door, "Ian can tell me what the hell you're talking about."

31

Rory shifted the weight of his side arm as he waited at a table in a cafe overlooking the ocean. Coffee steamed in front of him, black as hell but a lot better tasting. The weather outside was the other half of January in southern California—sunny, with a warm Santa Ana wind from the desert, and blue sky forever, or until the smog crept back over the land as soon as the inland wind stopped blowing.

He drank more coffee, glanced up, and saw Dick Merle approaching. He looked like a vampire in need of a quart of blood, and was the chief arson investigator for Newport Beach Fire Department.

Rory stood and held out his hand. "Morning, Dick. I want to thank you for taking time out of your busy schedule for me."

Merle shook hands and grinned wearily. "Man's gotta eat," he said. "Since Moreno County is buying,

I'm one hungry son of a bitch. I've been working most of the last three weeks."

"Yeah, we've been watching the string of arsons you've had in Orange County. Bad news. Hope you catch him soon."

Merle sat down with a heaviness that told its own story of too much work and not enough sleep. "So do I. Until then, I'm living on coffee."

The server appeared, watched Merle inhale a cup of coffee, poured him another, and set the pot on the table, ensuring her tip. After the server took their orders and left, both men drank in silence for a moment, watching ocean waves flattened by wind blowing from the land.

"Now that your arsonist is up for murder after last night's fire," Rory said, "you might get more manpower."

Merle drained the second cup of coffee, poured more, and sighed. "I'm kind of iffy about last night."

"What do you mean?"

"Different MO entirely. If you can even call it a MO."

Rory picked up his coffee cup and settled in to listen.

"Our serial arsonist likes empty buildings, cigarettes, matches, birthday candles, and kerosene," Merle said. "A real slow fuse leading to kerosene-soaked rags. He gets off waiting for the party to begin, see?"

Rory nodded.

"Then he gets off all over again watching it burn and seeing us run around like ants with our feet on fire," Merle said.

"But not last night?" Rory asked.

"Dunno." Merle yawned until his jaw cracked. Then he yawned again and rubbed his bloodshot eyes.

"Don't think so." He fixed Rory with pale blue eyes. "This is all very preliminary. We've barely even begun a proper investigation of the one last night."

"I hear you. I'm not making any reports. I'm just damned curious. If the asshole comes calling in Moreno County, I want to know what his act looks like."

"Okay. What we have is a cold, windy night, an alley with small businesses on both sides, two old houses that are shops on the first floor and owner's quarters above."

Rory had figured that out from the police reports, but didn't say a word.

"We have a few resident homeless, a couple old ladies. Then a couple of drifters looking for a place to piss and sleep out of the wind." Merle rubbed his eyes and poured more coffee. "Nobody else around but the shop owners who were asleep in the two old houses."

"Did the street people see anything?"

"What do you think?"

"I think they all slept the sleep of fortified wine."

"Yeah. Didn't see, didn't hear, didn't know shit until the sirens woke 'em up."

The server came and put breakfast platters in front of the men. Rory was eating toast, fruit, and scrambled eggs. Merle was eating everything but the hand that fed him—eggs, pancakes, steak, potatoes, toast, biscuits and gravy, a side of ham, and two glasses of milk.

"More butter, please," Merle said to the server. "And jam."

"Man, you're something," Rory said. "I've known you for years and you never gain an ounce."

"Clean living, constant prayer, and twenty-hour

workdays." He shoveled in the first of the food, chewed, and said, "So the boys questioned the bums—excuse me, the domicile-challenged—and found out nothing."

Rory chuckled and shook his head. "If your job depended on votes, you'd be mopping floors."

Merle chewed and didn't disagree. His impatience with politics of all kinds was an article of personal faith. "My men found indications of petroleum products, which was hardly a shocker—it's an alley and people park cars there and change oil there and take out their household garbage and such. Plastics are made with petroleum, you know. They also found a plastic trash can that was pretty well slagged."

"Fire source?"

"Yeah." Merle cleansed his palate of pancakes and syrup with one glass of milk and went to work on the salty part of the meal. "There was enough trash around to burn down half the city. No surprise that the wind tipped over the can and the fire spread. I'm guessing the drifters that started out warming their hands over the barrel ended up running down the alley with their asses on fire."

"So it wasn't your arsonist?" Rory asked.

Merle swallowed coffee and went back to steak, talking and chewing with startling efficiency. "Buildings were inhabited, not empty. No cigarette butts stubbed out while he stood back and waited for it all to get going. No empty rainbow package of birthday candles left to taunt us. Nope, not our boy."

Rory settled back and got to the part of the conversation that interested him, or rather, Ward.

"What about a Louie the Torch?" Rory asked, referring to a contract arson purchased to collect insurance on a losing business.

"Possible, I suppose. Didn't look like anything much in the place where the woman died. How much are crystals and bogus vitamins worth to an adjuster? Besides, so far there's no sign of any insurance on that one."

"What about the other place?"

"The artist's business?" Merle shrugged, swallowed the last of the steak and eggs, and concentrated on the biscuits and gravy. "Insured. Kept the policy in a bank safe deposit along with some other papers."

"How much?"

"Dunno, but she said business had been good enough to pay the rent and then some, and the insurance wouldn't be worth more than that. We're checking on it."

"What about the merchandise itself?" Rory asked. "Was it worth burning down the place to collect on insurance?"

"She had some old movie posters that apparently were worth something, and some stuff that was too old to be junk but not old enough to be antiques. Nothing big. Anyway, she said she got the most valuable things out before it burned."

"What was that?"

"Three old paintings."

Smiling, Rory nudged his plate over toward Merle. "Have some more breakfast."

32

For the past hour, Lacey's parents had sat in Susa's suite and grilled their daughter more thoroughly than the police, but with a different intent.

"Lacey, you're just being stubborn," Dottie said with a sad sigh. "There's no reason on earth you can't wrap up whatever's left of your little shop and come home with us right now. We *do* have telephone service for you to handle all the details. Oh, honey, I knew from the start that you shouldn't have rented that ratty little place."

"So you've said before, many times." Lacey rubbed her eyes. "Look, I appreciate your concern, but I'm staying."

"You don't have a place to live," Brody said. It wasn't the first time he'd pointed that out. "Be reasonable. You have no money, no home—or are you planning to sleep out of your car?"

Ian had been trying to be invisible in the second

bedroom, but that did it. He hung up on his great-uncle—who had been regaling him with tales of the old days in Moreno County—and made a fast call to the bellman. Then he stalked into the suite's sitting room. The bedroom door shut real firmly behind him. He crossed over and stood beside Lacey's chair, stroked his palm over her wild brown hair, and caressed her cheek in silent support.

"I know y'all mean well," he said, "but I haven't seen anything this relentless since my two cats tagteamed a baby bird."

Brody looked at the tall, relaxed man with short dark hair, unflinching eyes, and a weapon harness hanging from his broad shoulders. "Who the hell are you?"

"Ian Lapstrake," Lacey said quickly. "Remember?"

"Oh," Dottie said and smoothed her pink St. Martin's knit suit. "You're the one who was, uh, *with* Lacey when the fire broke out." She stood and held out her hand. "I'm Dottie Quinn. I want to thank you for helping our girl. She's not very practical about life."

Ian was real tempted to tell this nice, tightly wrapped piece of Pasadena society just how fine her impractical daughter looked wearing nothing but paint on her shapely ass, but decided against it.

"My pleasure," he said, shaking Dottie's hand, and smiling. He didn't understand why his smile worked on people the way it did, but he sure didn't hesitate to take advantage of it. Especially at times like this, when butter was going to accomplish a lot more than bullets. "You have a fine and talented daughter, as I'm sure Susa Donovan will tell you when she gets off the phone with her husband."

Dottie smiled. "Yes, well, we love our Lacey."

Ian didn't doubt it. That was the only thing that had kept him from kicking a hole in the outer wall and shoving Lacey's parents through it. He turned to Lacey's father. "Mr. Quinn, glad to meet you."

Before he knew what was happening, Brody found himself shaking the hand of his daughter's lover. Not that it should have mattered—she was over thirty. But some reflexes die hard in a father. Bristling in the presence of a male who'd seduced his daughter was one of them.

"You don't have to worry about Lacey sleeping out of her car," Ian said. "The suite next door is being made up for her right now. It's hers as long as she wants it."

Lacey made a startled sound. "But I can't afford it."

"No worries. It's free."

Her brown eyes widened. "Since when is a Savoy Hotel suite free?"

"Since I called Rarities and told Dana about the paintings."

Lacey shook her head like a dog coming out of water, making loose curls dance. "Excuse me? I'm kind of slow this morning."

He smiled, tipped her chin up, and brushed a gentle kiss over her lips. "Darling, one thing you never are is slow."

She closed her eyes, blew out a breath that sent stray curls flying, and tried to gather her thoughts. "What's happening?"

Brody smiled. Any man who could sidetrack Lacey with a light kiss had more going for him than the average bedroom jockey. About time, too.

"Susa told Dana about the paintings," Ian said.

"You remember? The ones you ran back into a burning building to save?"

"It wasn't burning," Lacey said.

"What would you call it?"

She stuck out her lower lip. "Almost burning."

"Correct me if I'm wrong," he said, "but isn't that the same *almost* burning building you wouldn't let me go back into for your paintings?"

"That was different."

Instead of being irritated, Ian grinned. "Oh, well, that explains it."

Lacey looked warily at him. "It does?"

"Sure. Different things entirely." He looked at her expectantly.

"Ah . . . what are we talking about?"

"You got me, darling. Mustn't have been important."

Brody snickered and winked at Dottie, who was watching openmouthed as a strange man got around Lacey's stubbornness as though it didn't exist. Then Dottie noticed Ian's steady, dark eyes and knew that her daughter hadn't heard the last of the subject, but it would be settled later, in private.

"Before you forget what your name is," Brody said, "I wanted to tell you that I'm withdrawing my objections to you displaying the paintings."

"What? Why?" Lacey asked.

Dottie answered, "He decided that it's time to slow down and smell the golf courses. He withdrew his name for the judicial vacancy."

Lacey hesitated. "Are you sure this is what you want, Dad?"

"Yes." He smiled wryly at his wife. "It just took me a while to figure it out."

A knock came from the hall door, followed by a voice announcing the arrival of the bellman.

"Get that, would you, Lacey?" Ian said. He turned to her parents. "It was real nice of you to drive here with clothes for Lacey. The bellman will need one of you to show him what to bring up for her."

"I'll do it," Brody said.

"I'll come along," Dottie said. "I could use something to eat."

"I'm sorry, Mom, I didn't think that you'd be hungry," Lacey said, overhearing. "I'll have something sent up to—"

"We'll join you as soon as Lacey has something more to wear than a bathrobe," Ian said over her words. "The cafe is excellent. Be sure to try the Welsh cakes."

He shut the door firmly after her parents and the bellman. Then he went to the locked double doors that led to the adjoining suite. When he opened them, the matching doors on the other side were also open, creating a giant suite that could sleep twelve and host thirty more.

"How did you do that?" Lacey asked.

"Easy. You turn this deadbolt and then—"

"No. I meant how did you get rid of my parents without making them mad?"

"They mean well and they love you and don't understand you. You mean well and you love them and you don't understand them. You all push each other's buttons without even trying. I just short-circuited the old playlist."

"You're scary."

He took the lapels of her plush robe and pulled her slowly closer. "That's not what you said last night."

"Last night you let me paint you naked."

"Any time, darling."

She stood on her tiptoes and leaned into the kiss, luxuriating in his strength and his willingness to let her be herself. It was an experience as heady as any sex, any liquor, anything.

"When I bought her more painting supplies," Susa said, "I didn't have performance art in mind."

Lacey would have jumped back like a guilty teenager, but Ian didn't let her. He ended the kiss as slow and tender as he'd started it. Only then did he lift his head.

"How's the Donovan?" Ian asked.

"Lonely. Like me."

"Time to go painting?"

Susa looked out the window, hesitated, and then smiled. "You're an understanding kind of man, Ian. I feel like painting, but not outside."

His dark eyebrows lifted. "Okay. Where?"

"Here." Susa smiled at Lacey. "What do you say we paint him?"

Lacey stared. All she could think of was last night, when she'd done a swift study of Ian watching her from the bed, his arousal as clear as his pleasure in watching her.

Susa laughed out loud. "Oh my, the look on your face. But I'm not thinking about getting naked and rolling around in the paints. I'm thinking of you as you are now," she said to Ian, "T-shirt and shoulder holster, all gentle and hungry around the edges, with those bleak eyes and trust-me smile."

Ian looked like a man whose shoes were too tight.

Smiling, Susa crossed the room, grabbed his face between her hands, and gave him a smacking kiss. "I didn't know men still blushed."

"You'd embarrass a statue," he muttered.

"Good thing you're flesh and blood," she said. "I'd like you over by the window, I think."

"Lacey," he said. "Help."

"I plan to, just as soon as I get the new paints Susa gave me."

He started to point out that Lacey's time would be better spent salvaging what was left of her shop, but he liked seeing light come back to her eyes too well to spoil her mood.

"How about I give y'all a rain check?" he said instead. "I've got to make arrangements for those three paintings to be locked up."

"They're not worth guarding," Lacey said.

"I disagree," Susa said.

"Look," Lacey said wearily, "I appreciate all you've done, but you're wrong about the paintings. They're not by Lewis Marten."

"Have you had them appraised?" Susa asked.

"No."

"I've made arrangements for Rarities Unlimited to appraise them," Susa said. "If you're right, I'll bite my tongue and slink off into the sunset."

The light that had returned to Lacey's eyes was gone as though it had never existed. "No. No appraisal."

"Why?" Susa asked mildly.

Lacey simply shook her head.

"What would you say," Ian said to Susa, "if I told you that the paintings originally belonged to Lacey's grandfather?"

"What are you talking about?" Lacey demanded. "I never said anything like that."

"You never meant to," he agreed. "But before you went back into your shop, you yelled something about saving your grandfather's paintings. Then you came out carrying those three paintings. Nothing else. Not even your own work."

Lacey went pale, then red streaks of anger appeared over her cheekbones. "You're wrong. I—I painted them!"

"Show me."

"Go to hell. I painted them."

He almost smiled. "Darling, you don't lie worth a damn."

"But you do, don't you," she said bitterly. "You act all gentle and kind, and all you can think about is springing an ambush so that your poor victim trips and falls flat, spilling everything."

He didn't move, yet somehow he seemed to loom over her. "Is that what you think, that I seduced you to get some answers?"

"Yes!" Then she remembered last night, the laughter and the passion and the peace. "No." She crossed her arms over her chest and turned away. "Jesus, what a mess."

Susa looked at the tears of anger, fear, and exhaustion standing in Lacey's eyes. "We want to help you. Do you believe that?"

"Yes," she said hoarsely. "But I can't. I just can't."

"But—" Susa stopped at a gesture from Ian.

"Your grandfather's dead," Ian said. "What's the problem? He collected some paintings and passed them on to you."

Lacey almost said that he hadn't collected them, he'd *painted* them. Big difference. Then she realized that Ian was offering her an out, whether he knew it or not. "Look, Grandpa Rainbow was something of a, uh, character. Colorful. Really, really colorful."

Ian waited and wondered if she would ever trust him enough to stop lying, or at least trying to. She was so god-awful at it he would have laughed if he hadn't been pissed off.

"He drank too much sometimes," Lacey said.

Ian started listening because her body language said she wasn't lying now.

"And he went off on trips."

Ian waited.

Lacey took a deep breath and stuck to as much of the truth as she could. "Sometimes he came back with paintings, but he never had any bills of sale from a gallery or an artist or anything like that."

"Where did he go?" Susa asked.

"All over California."

"Any favorite places?" Susa asked.

"Palm Springs, Anza-Borrego, San Francisco, Death Valley. Why?"

"But not Laguna Beach or Painter's Beach or Savoy Ranch?"

"No. Why?"

"Two of the three paintings you showed me were painted on the ranch," Susa said. "Several galleries in Laguna and Newport feature early plein air painters who worked locally."

Lacey shrugged. "He never mentioned any part of southern California but the desert, so if he got anything anywhere else, I don't know about it."

"I'm still not understanding the problem," Ian said.

"What problem?" Lacey asked.

"Why you don't want the paintings appraised."

She put her hands on her hips and glared at him. "How would you like your grandfather to be proved a crook?"

"I'm not following you."

"What if he stole the damned things!"

"What if he painted them?" Ian retorted. He watched color drain out of her face and swore. "Shit, I was afraid of that. He was a forger, wasn't he?"

"I never saw him copy anything," Lacey whispered.

"But he sure did paint in a famous dead man's style, didn't he? A man whose paintings sell for three hundred grand and up?"

She hesitated, then nodded painfully. "Yes. Dad's going to kill me."

"Why?"

"I can see the headlines: SON OF ART FORGER AL-MOST APPOINTED JUDGE." She tilted her head back but tears fell anyway. "Poor Dad. A life's work ruined because of a father he couldn't control and a stubborn daughter who just had to open Pandora's box."

A knock came on the door. "Bellman."

Lacey pulled her robe closer around her. "That's my clothes. I'll get dressed and break the news to Dad."

Ian glanced at Susa. She looked thoughtful, the way she did when she confronted an entirely new landscape.

"Go with her, Ian," Susa said. "I have some calls to make. And Lacey?"

"Yes?"

"After you talk with your parents, we'll sort through the paintings in your shop. Then we'll take our sad hearts and go back in time to paint."

"What?"

"We're going to paint a sunset on a bluff overlooking several hundred years of history. I'll call ahead and arrange it with the ranch's majordomo."

Lacey hesitated, then smiled wanly. "Thanks. I'd like that."

"Good. While you talk to your parents, think about this—I still want Rarities to look at the paintings."

"Why?"

"I believe they are Lewis Marten's work. They must have survived the studio fire or been painted before his death. Don't you see? If your grandfather was a copyist, he had to have some templates to work from, and those templates would have been *true* Lewis Marten paintings. Those paintings still exist somewhere. They belong to the generations, Lacey."

Ian started to ask a question, but a look from Susa shut him up.

Too heartsick to argue, finally believing what she didn't want to believe, Lacey said, "Fine. Whatever. Nothing will change the fact that Grandpa Rainbow was a forger." A tear slid from the corner of her eye. "All I wanted to do was get my grandfather's painting the recognition it deserves. Now my father's reputation is on the brink of ruin and my grandfather will soon be infamous as a forger and a crook." She laughed oddly. "The road to hell really is paved with good intentions, isn't it?"

33

Wearing the dressy slacks and pullover sweater her parents had brought, plus a head-to-toe coverall borrowed from hotel maintenance and her own beat-up sandals, Lacey stood on the sidewalk looking at the front of her shop. Except for the CLOSED sign on the door during what should have been prime business hours, some puddles here and there, and the burned wreckage next door, last night could have been a bad dream.

"It doesn't look like anything happened to my shop," she said. "After all the hoses and fire axes and tramping around last night, I expected to see an ungodly mess."

"You will," Ian said. He'd spent time at enough fire scenes to know what waited inside. *An ungodly mess* just about covered it. "You sure you don't want me to take care of this for you? I could bring all your paintings out and—"

"No," she interrupted firmly. "My shop, my responsibility."

Saying nothing, he stroked his palm over her curly hair. Behind her brave front, he knew that she was running on adrenaline, emotions, and old-fashioned grit. He also knew that seeing the extent of the damage from the fire and firemen would feel like a fist to the gut.

He glanced over at the small woman standing on Lacey's other side. "You tamed those sleeves yet, Susa?"

"I'm working on it." Like Ian and Lacey, Susa was wearing borrowed coveralls. None of the hotel maintenance crew had been remotely close to her size, so she'd rolled everything up at the ankles and wrists, and then rolled them up some more.

"You don't have to do this," Lacey said. "I can sort through my own paintings. The rest of the stuff . . ." Her voice trailed off. She drew herself up sharply. *I'm not going there. It's just things. Crying over them won't do a damn bit of good.*

Chin high, shoulders squared, Lácey walked toward the tranquil front of her shop, opened the door she'd locked again before going to the hotel last night, and stepped inside. The smell was an overpowering mix of cold smoke and wet everything. She flipped a switch. Miraculously, the lights came on.

She wished they hadn't. Gloom had been friendly to the shop, concealing the fallen plaster, water, and just plain gunk that covered every surface. The farther into the shop she walked, the worse everything looked.

"Stay here while I check out the upstairs," Ian said. "The firemen told me there wasn't any structural damage, but I want to be sure. Then I'll take photos and board up the broken windows."

Numbly, Lacey nodded. *The shop didn't burn down, so just suck it up and stop sniveling. It can't be as bad as it looks.*

Susa put her arm around Lacey's waist and hugged her like she was one of her own daughters, silently telling the younger woman that she wasn't alone.

Ian came back down the stairs with a carefully neutral expression. "Okay, it's safe up there. Are you sure your paintings aren't covered by insurance?"

"According to the IRS, I haven't sold enough to move from the hobby category," Lacey said matter-of-factly. "Galleries don't want you until you sell, and you can't sell until you're in galleries." She shrugged and started for the stairs. "Which is a long way of saying I'm sure my paintings aren't insured because they have no market value."

Susa stared at Lacey's back. It had never occurred to her that an artist of Lacey's talent wasn't represented in galleries. "Well," Susa said distinctly, "that's going to change. You'll be exhibiting in galleries up and down the coast."

Lacey stumbled on one of the steps. She looked back over her shoulder. "Excuse me?"

"You heard me. I won't have talent like yours hidden in the loft of a secondhand shop." Susa walked briskly toward the stairs. "Your first exhibit will be called From the Ashes. It will open in the Visions Gallery in Seattle on Thanksgiving and run through Christmas."

"What are you talking about?" Lacey asked.

"A gallery exhibit, what else?" Susa passed her on the stairway. "Put a boogie on it, girl. We only have an hour or so before we have to change and go painting. This gallery owner is one picky bitch. She'll only want your best work, so you have a lot of painting to do in the next few months."

Lacey just stared after Susa.

"Better hustle," Ian said, grinning. "Susa on a mission is something to see."

"But Visions is one of the most famous galleries in the United States for debuting new plein air artists. She can't just . . ."

"Sure she can. She owns the place."

Lacey's jaw dropped. "Holy shit."

He leaned over and kissed her swiftly. "You're good, darling. Your parents might never get it, but it's way past time that you do. Now go help that picky bitch do triage on your paintings."

She blinked back sudden tears. "Grandpa's the only one who ever believed in me."

"Now there are three."

She looked questioningly at him.

"Susa, me, and your grandpa." He kissed her again. "Get going before I indulge in a new fantasy of mine."

"Which one?"

"Sex in the mud."

She looked around. "It's plaster."

"Okay. I'm easy."

She gave him a shaky smile and a big hug. "I'm glad you're here, Ian. Really, really glad. You make everything better."

Before he could respond, she was hurrying up the stairway. He watched her freeze at the top, when she got her first look at what had been her apartment and studio. For a long moment he thought she was going to fold. Then her head came up and she walked into the ungodly mess to see what could be salvaged.

34

The bellman pushed a large covered cart into the elevator, put in the override key for the top floor, and waited. Several large floral pieces crowded the top of the cart.

When he got to the top floor he pushed the cart down to the corner suite. Ignoring the DO NOT DISTURB sign, he knocked three times, and said, "Bellman."

No one answered.

He knocked and called out again.

Silence.

He pulled a passkey from his uniform pocket and slid it into the slot. A green light blinked, the lock released, and he walked in. As soon as the door closed behind him, he went rapidly through the rooms, including the adjoining suite, making sure they were empty. Then he went through again, collecting paintings. He chose seven rectangles of varying sizes. Any more wouldn't fit beneath the cart's stylish rose linen covering with the hotel's name embroidered in gold around the edges. He checked to make sure nothing showed, picked up one bouquet, and set it on a bedside table.

As he went to the elevator, he kept the gigantic floral arrays on the cart between himself and whatever security cameras were in the vicinity. He did the same across the lobby and out through the employee elevator into the valet parking lot below the building. There he loaded the paintings into a white van whose only ID was a magnetic sign attached to the side. The words advertised locksmiths available at any hour of the day or night. A temporary license plate was taped to the back window. There were no other plates on the vehicle.

Inside the van, beyond the reach of the security cameras, he changed back into the workman's coveralls and cowboy hat he'd worn to drive into the garage, stripped off the exam gloves that had covered his hands, put on huge sunglasses and some dark face fur, and started the van.

Beneath the unblinking eyes of the video cameras, the van backed out of its space, turned right, and headed south on Pacific Coast Highway along with about fifty thousand other commuters.

35

Ian keyed open the door to Susa's suite and waved in the bellman pushing a luggage cart stacked with painting gear. The message light on the phone was blinking impatiently. He swallowed a curse. While the women painted, he'd spent most of the time draining his patience and the battery of his cell phone on various public servants wearing badges and attitudes of one kind or another.

"Probably my insurance company," Lacey said unhappily. "I left this number because the phone next door wasn't working."

"I plugged it in," Ian said. "Works fine now."

"Oops. Details. I'm not good at them."

"What do you mean?" Susa said. "You gave the insurers an inventory printout before we went painting. They won't do anything meaningful until their adjuster goes through your shop and sees what's what, and she won't be there until Monday afternoon."

Lacey's lips flattened. "My insurers heard the word 'arson' and ran like bunnies."

"It's called 'use of the money,'" Ian said. "You give it to them and they use it until you can prove they have to give some back."

Lacey swiped back a curl with paint-stained fingers. "They didn't say anything outright, but reading between the lines, you'd think I set fire to the place myself."

"Don't take it personally," he said. "Arson for insurance money is a favorite scam. You get burned often enough, you get real testy on the subject. In fact, you get real—Whoa, look at those flowers!"

"Where?" Susa and Lacey said.

He gestured at a wall mirror in the sitting room. Reflected in it was an array of flowers standing like a frozen fountain of color on Susa's bedside table. Someone had given her the kind of floral arrangement that made headstones look small.

"You and the Donovan have a fight?" he asked Susa.

"No. Besides, he knows everything but orchids make me sneeze."

Lacey looked at the silent explosion of flowers. "I'll be happy to help you out with these. Looks like they came from the same florist who did the display at the concierge desk. Must turn them out like clones."

"Take them," Susa said, waving her hand. "Please. And put them in a distant corner of your bedroom."

Ian reached for the flowers.

"Wait," Lacey said. "There must be a card saying who they came from."

"Don't see one."

Lacey pawed delicately through the petals. "Me, either. Maybe the desk knows."

"Call," Ian said to Susa. It wasn't a suggestion. "Be sure to tell them that the DO NOT DISTURB sign was on the handle and it was ignored. Some eager bellman needs his knuckles rapped. If he does it again while I'm here, he might just get shot."

Susa lifted her eyebrows, picked up the receiver, and punched the number for the front desk. While she did, Ian took two tissues to keep from leaving fingerprints and carried the vase of flowers into the hallway.

He came back empty-handed.

"Well?" he asked.

Susa gave him a sideways glance. "They're checking."

Lacey looked at him. "You left the flowers out there?"

"Until we know where they came from, yes."

"You really *are* paranoid."

"Everybody's good at something."

He went into Susa's bedroom, checked the closet, and swore silently. Without a word he went to Lacey's side of the joined suite, checked the closet, and walked back out into the sitting area just as Susa hung up the phone.

"The concierge desk has no record of a flower delivery," she said. "They're checking the delivery schedule now."

He wasn't surprised. "Don't suppose either of you ladies put some of your paintings under the bed or anything?"

"No," Susa said.

"Same here," Lacey said.

That didn't surprise him, either. He muttered something foul under his breath.

"Excuse me?" Lacey said, her eyes wide.

"Check your closets" was all he said.

A few moments later, both women confirmed what he already knew: seven paintings were missing. Four of Susa's, plus the paintings that had belonged to Lacey's grandfather.

"Okay, here's the drill," he said. "We're going to the restaurant."

"What?" Lacey said in disbelief. "Our paintings are gone and you want us to eat *dinner*?"

"I want both of you out of here and in a public place. The hottest new restaurant in town is about as public as it gets."

Lacey and Susa looked at each other, shrugged, and headed for the door.

"I think we've just been sent to the sandbox," Lacey said.

"At least this sandbox has a good wine list," Susa said.

Ian followed them out the door. As he walked down the hall, he pulled out his cell phone and did what he really hated to do when he was on a job. He called the cops. In the unincorporated resort community of Painter's Beach, that meant Rory Turner.

Turner picked up his private number after only two rings. "What?"

"Ian Lapstrake, Sheriff. Several million bucks worth of Susa's paintings have gone missing on your watch."

"Christ. Anybody hurt?"

"No. We were at the ranch when the theft occurred."

"Thank God for small favors. When did you leave the hotel to go to the ranch?"

"About two," Ian said.

"Have you told the desk?"

"No. Most robberies like this are inside jobs."

"Ain't it the damned truth. I'll be there in fifteen. After I get the security tapes and duty roster, I'll come up."

"I'll meet you at the front desk," Ian said, stepping into the elevator that had just arrived. "I'm reviewing the tapes with you."

"You trying to say you don't trust me?"

"Trust you? Sheriff, I don't know you well enough to exchange Christmas cards."

Rory laughed. "Do I need to tell you not to touch anything?"

"What do you think?"

"I'll see you at the front desk in fifteen minutes. And send the ladies down to the restaurant or something so they won't get in the way of my crime scene technicians."

Ian's eyes narrowed. Paranoia quivered. Probably totally unnecessary, but there was always the long shot that made everyone cry. "The women aren't leaving my sight."

He cut the connection and called Rarities. He was put through to S. K. Niall very quickly. As head of Security, Niall was technically Ian's boss, except when Dana stepped in and preempted him for one of her pet projects. When Niall answered, Ian didn't try to put lipstick on the pig before he shoved it into the spotlight.

"I fucked up," Ian said. "Susa's paintings are gone."

"Bullshit," Susa said loud enough to carry into the cell phone. "It's not your fault. I'm the one who insisted on leaving the damn things in the room."

"Sounds like Susa's intact," Niall said. "No damage to her?"

"Underneath her gracious manner," Ian said, "she's mad enough to eat steel plate. Otherwise she's fine."

"Then you didn't fuck up."

Ian said something fully suited to his mood.

Niall ignored it. "You need backup?"

"To help nail shut the barn door? No, I think I can handle that all by myself."

"Ease up, boyo. If the Donovan had wanted a lock on the paintings, he'd have asked for two of you. He knows his wife. Now quit feeling sorry for yourself and put her on. She can describe the paintings to me and I'll send out the word right away. We'll get the bastard when he tries to unload them."

"Always assuming it wasn't a commissioned theft, in which case they'll never hit the market." With that cheerful thought, Ian handed the phone to Susa. "Say hello to S. K. Niall. Describe missing pictures to him. Pray for the good guys."

Susa picked up the phone. "It wasn't Ian's fault."

"You know it. I know it. When he gets over his temper, he'll know it. I'm turning on a recorder. Describe what was stolen."

Susa started talking.

36

Rory Turner walked into the lobby with long, impatient strides. He was dressed in casual clothes except for the badge holder hanging out of his pocket and the weapon harness playing peekaboo beneath his unbuttoned jacket. Two men and two women followed him. They were in uniform and carrying the lights, cameras, measuring instruments, and other equipment that was required to investigate and record the crime scene. Two more uniformed deputies hurried through the imposing lobby doors and across the lobby. Judging from the rolls of bright yellow tape they carried, their job was to secure the crime scene.

"Can the TV cameras be far behind?" Ian muttered. "This has all the earmarks of a class-A cluster job."

Lacey gave him a wary glance and finished describing her grandfather's paintings to S. K. Niall.

Giving rapid, concise orders to the deputies, Rory grabbed the night manager and hustled everyone into an elevator. Only after he'd dispatched everyone to the top floor did he acknowledge the three people waiting by the desk.

"Follow me," he said tersely. "I kept this off the police radios but somehow the damned press always finds out. After the investigators are through, the manager will transfer your belongings to new suites. Unless you want a different hotel?"

Ian looked at Susa.

"Why bother?" she said. "I'm leaving Sunday after the auction is over. I'm sure the security will be tighter here than anywhere else for the next few days."

"You can take that to the bank," Rory said grimly.

He led them through a door marked EMPLOYEES ONLY and down a short hall with office doors on either side. In front of the one marked SECURITY, he stopped, pulled a plastic rectangle out of his pocket, and swiped the card through a reader. The lock released.

"Nice," Ian said.

"I own nineteen percent of the firm that put in the low bid for the hotel's security contract," Rory said, "a fact that has been thoroughly aired in the press and ignored by everyone else."

The room was empty except for TV screens, computers, machines, and a startled man in a hotel security "uniform" of dark suit and tie. The ID badge hanging around his neck was also an electronic key. It said GATEMAN.

"Sheriff? What can I do for you?"

"Anyone come into this room on your shift?" Rory asked.

"Not until you. 'Evening, ladies," he added, nodding to Susa and Lacey.

"When did you start your shift?"

"Uh, two o'clock. Bob wanted an early jump on the weekend traffic, so I said I'd cover for him."

"So you think it's an inside job," Ian said too softly for anyone but Rory to hear.

"I think a million dollars worth of bad publicity is coming down on Moreno County and my ass is going to get reamed for it," Rory said distinctly. "Anyone call you away for any reason?" he asked Gateman.

The security guard, who had the build of a former linebacker and the gut of a computer jockey who liked beer, shook his head. "No, sir. What happened?"

Rory ignored the question and asked one of his own. "All the systems working?"

Gateman did a fast survey of the status lights. "All green."

"Show me the top floor from noon until now."

Gateman's broad face creased in a frown. "Is something—"

"Just do it," Rory cut in. "If I want conversation, I'll tell you."

The head of second-shift security for the Savoy Hotel shut up and went to work on his computer. Although everyone called the result "tapes," the images were digital rather than taped. Since most of the cameras were triggered only in the presence of movement, there wasn't a lot of hard drive storage wasted on photos of blank hallways.

Everyone watched while a bellman went from elevator to hall and stopped in front of Susa's suite. Moments later Susa, Ian, and Ms. Quinn began loading stuff on a luggage cart.

"Slow it down to quarter time," Rory said.

Gateman's hands moved over the keyboard.

Rory watched canvases loaded onto the cart. All of

them looked blank on both sides. Still, it never hurt to be absolutely certain. "Again."

The picture switched to the beginning. Nothing but blank canvases and paint-smeared boxes that were too small to hold the missing paintings.

"Okay. Normal speed."

Ian smiled slightly. The sheriff probably didn't expect La Susa and the man from Rarities to be running an insurance scam, but "inside job" had more than one meaning.

On the monitor, the cart and four people vanished into the elevator.

An instant later in the viewers eyes', and almost three hours by the electronic clock that showed at the bottom of every camera sequence, a bellman pushing a room service cart loaded with big flower arrangements emerged from the elevator. He went down the hallway under the scrutiny of various cameras and never showed his face or any other identifiable part of his body.

Gateman shifted and narrowed his eyes at the screen playing back in black-and-white. He didn't like the looks of what he was seeing. "Dude knows where the cameras are," Gateman said.

"No shit."

The guard took one look at Rory's cold eyes and decided that the sheriff really didn't want—or need—input.

The cart and the unidentifiable bellman stopped in front of Susa's suite. Ignoring the DO NOT DISTURB sign, he knocked, waited, knocked, and took an e-key from his pocket. A few moments later the lock opened.

"Hold there. Get today's electronic record for that lock," Rory said.

Gateman shifted to another computer and accessed the record for Susa's suite. "Guest, guest, guest," he read off the screen, "guest . . . security."

"When?" Rory demanded.

"Sixteen hundred."

The exact time the "bellman" had opened the lock.

"*Shit*. Which security card?" Rory asked.

"Thirteen."

"Whose is it?"

Gateman checked, grimaced. "Never issued, sir. Nobody wanted an unlucky number."

Ian bit back a comment about how bloody wonderful it was that the hotel security was a superstitious lot.

"Well, isn't that just sweet," Rory said neutrally. "All right, Gateman, show me the rest of the record on the can't-see-who bellman and the invisible security guard."

Lacey winced and felt sorry for Gateman, who had been unlucky enough to be on duty when the theft occurred.

Gateman turned back to the computer keyboard and wondered if he would have a job tomorrow. He'd never seen the sheriff so pissed off.

Cart and bellman vanished inside Susa's suite. Five minutes and forty-one seconds later, they reappeared.

"Hold," Ian and Rory said simultaneously.

The picture froze.

"Some flowers are missing," Lacey said.

"The bouquet on my night table," Susa said. She eyed the sides of the cart critically. "I assume the paintings are beneath the cloth."

"Would they fit?" Rory asked.

"Unless the bellman is a dwarf, yes," Lacey said.

Rory looked at her, but it was Susa who answered.

"The proportions of the cart would be large enough to hold the paintings if the bellman was at least of average height," Susa explained. "Artists are accustomed to viewing things relatively rather than on an absolute metric scale."

Rory grunted. "Man or woman?"

"Man," Ian said instantly.

"You sure?" Rory asked.

"I've never seen a woman with that flat a butt. Man must have to strap a board on so he doesn't fall in."

Rory snickered.

"What are you talking about?" Lacey asked.

"Sex," Ian said.

She rolled her eyes. "I should have guessed."

"Ready?" Rory asked Ian.

"Yeah. Can't wait to see where he goes. Ten to one it's the valet parking lot."

"Sucker bet," the sheriff said. "It's the only covered parking around."

"Cameras?" Susa asked.

"Of course." Rory's mouth flattened. "Bet he knows where they are, too."

"No bet," Ian said. "But it's damned hard to hide a vehicle behind a flower cart."

"Run it," Rory said to Gateman.

Silently they all watched the bellman enter the elevator. The doors closed and the floor display above the elevator lit up.

"He's going to the lobby," Lacey said.

Gateman started working the keyboard, shifting to the lobby record, beginning at the instant the man entered the elevator. The screen divided itself until it was like looking at the lobby through the eyes of a distorting prism that divided the world into squares. Some of the squares were blank. All of them winked in and out of existence in a seemingly random sequence.

"Yikes," Lacey said. "That's the stuff of nightmares."

"Fascinating effect," Susa said, studying it.

Ian leaned forward. "I haven't seen a system like this before."

"It's not available on the market yet," Rory said, watching the intricate patterns. "We're testing the setup for the inventor, along with some other businesses. It's a pretty flexible program. In the lobby, where there's too much traffic for motion-sensor activation on the six cameras to be cost-effective in the storage and coverage area, the cameras are programmed to fire randomly. It's a way to cover a lot of ground without having to buy millions of bucks worth of monitoring, computer, and data-storage equipment. Since it's all digitized, we can enhance by extrapolation, so the cameras don't have to have expensive, fancy lenses to zero in on areas of interest."

"How much coverage?" Ian asked.

"About ninety percent of the lobby over a one-minute period. More than the average hotel requires. And there's our man." Rory pointed to one of the screens. "Freeze it and tell the computer to follow him."

A fine sweat showed on Gateman's lip as he worked over the keyboard, circling the bellman and cart with the cursor, instructing the computer to extrapolate what those items would look like from various angles, and finding matches in the camera records for other areas of the hotel in the ensuing minutes. He'd spent a month learning this security system backward and forward, but this was like a final exam. He fumbled, backed up, cursed, and entered the correct sequence of commands.

The bellman and cart moved in a series of jerks and stomach-swooping changes of viewing angles.

Gateman almost groaned when the cart vanished through the door marked EMPLOYEES.

"Cut to the valet lot, same time," Rory said. "If we don't find him there, we can always back up."

Gateman went back to sweating over the keyboard.

An underground parking lot appeared. The view didn't divide into six, but it did click around the lot like a fast slide show.

"Got him," Ian said.

"When he gets to his vehicle, do it in quarter time," Rory said.

"Bastard knows where the cameras are," Ian said.

Rory didn't answer. He didn't have to—the evidence was in front of him.

The room was silent as the bellman went to a white van, unloaded the paintings, pushed the cart aside, and got in back. When he reappeared in the cab, he was wearing coveralls, a cowboy hat, and a beard.

"This one's really cute," Ian muttered.

The last shot was at the hotel gate, where the van turned right onto Pacific Coast Highway and headed south.

"Now what?" Lacey asked.

Ian looked at her with dark, angry eyes. "Now the sheriff runs the van's temporary plate, finds it's a yo-yo; runs the stick-on business sign on the side of the van, finds it's a yo-yo; then thinks about running the white van and decides to call the California Highway Patrol instead, because sure as shit one of those guys will tag the van as an abandoned vehicle somewhere between here and the Mexican border."

Rory gave Ian a long look. "You a cop?"

"Not anymore, as I'm sure you'll find out when you run me through your computers. You'll get a buttload of hits and not a one of them will help you solve this robbery, and you'll do it anyway."

"I sure will. You're a pro. You know security systems. You piss me off. That puts you number one on my hit list."

"What about your security staff and the hotel staff?" Ian said coolly. "You know, the folks who'd have access to the magic-key machine."

"They're tied for second."

37

After the first reporter's call, Ian told the hotel desk to stop connecting outside calls unless it was Sheriff Turner himself. The last thing Susa needed to deal with were newshounds baying at the heels of a celebrity story. *Tell me, World Famous Artist, how does it feel to have a million dollars in irreplaceable paintings stolen from your room? Do you feel angry? Violated? Better yet, Will you cry during the interview? Spill your guts for the bored public? Get the reporter a promotion? Separate ads with juicy sound bites? Give us sensation disguised as the public's right to know?*

About ten minutes after Ian hung up on the hotel desk, room service brought a lovely meal, compliments of the hotel. The food might as well have been dog chow for all the attention it got. Susa took a polite bite of everything, drank half a glass of the fine wine, and went to a comfortable chair where she sat staring at nothing. Sadness came off her in waves that were almost tangible. Every time Lacey looked at her, she wanted to cry.

If Ian noticed, he didn't let it get in his way. He addressed dinner with the speed and precision of a machine taking on fuel. "Eat," he said to Lacey between bites. "You'll need it."

Lacey ate what she could and pushed the plate away. She wanted to comfort Susa but didn't know how, because she knew only too well that there was no replacement for lost paintings. Despite her own carefully indifferent front, she felt as though part of herself had been ripped out after the fire. If it hadn't been for Susa's gentle persistence in sorting through the water- and smoke-damaged paintings, Lacey would have thrown out everything in a rage of pain. But Susa had understood the emotions seething beneath the quiet. She had helped, and in helping, healed.

Lacey wanted to do the same for her.

"Well, the good news is that you won't have to sweat your father's or grandfather's reputation," Ian said, pouring himself more coffee and then going to work on Susa's dinner.

Lacey looked away from Susa's still, unhappy face. "What are you talking about?" she asked, although she already knew. Guilt snaked through her because Ian had figured it out, too.

"The paintings you were so worried about are gone." His voice was matter-of-fact. "Your family's home free."

The only thing that kept Lacey from clawing at Ian was the anger burning in his dark eyes. "I'd rather have Susa's paintings back."

His fork hesitated. "What about your grandfather's?"

"Susa's are original. Irreplaceable. Grandfather's . . ." She shrugged. "Well, we all know what they were."

"Susa's not mourning the loss of her paintings," Ian said.

"What?"

"Are you, Susa?"

Susa turned toward the table. Tears glittered in her eyes. "No. I'm mourning a past I can touch only through memory and art. Memory fades. Paintings don't. The artist who painted Lacey's three canvases was someone who lived and loved and wept and laughed and raged and put it all into landscapes of places that time and man have paved over. Art is all that's left of what once was." Tears magnified her beautiful eyes. "Now some of that art is gone. Some of me is gone with it."

"But they were only forgeries," Lacey said hoarsely.

Susa simply shook her head.

Lacey's conscience warred with her emotions. As usual, her conscience lost. Susa wasn't family, but she felt like it to Lacey. She'd held Lacey when she finally wept in the stinking, dripping mess that had once been her studio. Then Susa had pushed up her sleeves and gently, relentlessly, forced Lacey to keep on sorting through her paintings.

Seven of the canvases had been set aside for the November show. Susa's expertise and real enthusiasm had moved Lacey from the dripping ruins of the present to a future bright with possibility.

It was a gift Lacey could return.

"How would you like to take a trip with me to a storage unit?"

38

Ward Forrest pinched the bridge of his nose and cursed the years that had made him need glasses to read print that had once been as plain as a whale in a parking lot. Even the fire in the hearth, which usually soothed him, was making his eyes hurt.

"We can do this tomorrow," Savoy said.

"No." Ward settled the reading glasses back on his nose and picked up the legal papers once more. "I can't believe that bitch wants to screw more land out of us for the same amount of stock in New Horizons."

Savoy didn't bother to answer. "Bitch" was the nicest thing Ward had called Angelique White tonight. "She senses weakness and wants to know how bad it is."

"You think I don't know that?" Ward retorted. "If I didn't need her cash, I'd tell her to piss up a rope."

Honey Bear's tail thumped against Ward's ankles.

He nudged the dog with his foot. The tail thumped faster.

"But we do need her cash," Savoy said for the tenth time in an hour, "especially after that settlement with Concerned Citizens for Sane Development. Besides, it's a good business fit. New Horizons has cash and no land. We have land we can't sell or develop without costly court battles, and no one is willing to lend money at a rate that would turn a profit for us."

"You're preaching to the choir."

"I'll leave that to Angelique. Are you going to sign this 'agreement to agree' tonight or do you want to sit on it for a while?"

"Damn that bitch anyway," Ward said bitterly. "If she hadn't dragged her feet about developing, a lot of this would already be done."

"What bitch are you talking about now?"

"Your mother. Always whining about her precious land and then spending money hand over fist like it grew on trees. Should've been born a frigging queen."

Savoy's fingers tightened on the contract he was reading. "My mother, your wife."

"Don't remind me."

"Then don't remind *me*," Savoy said in a clipped voice, standing up. He flexed fingers that weren't as supple as they once had been and ached every time the wind turned cold. Unlike his father, he felt every year of his age, even if he didn't look it. "I can't touch the past and I'm sick of hearing about it."

"Huh. Well, the past sure as hell can touch *you,* so you might open up your damned ears and learn something."

Only if you have something new to say, Savoy thought.

But he knew better than to speak it aloud. That would just lead to a shouting match. He didn't need that. More important, the future didn't need that. The future needed Ward's agreement, no matter how reluctant, on the New Horizons deal. The longer Ward delayed, the more likely it was that something would come spectacularly and publicly unstuck in the family, and Angelique would bolt all over again.

"Are you going to restore Bliss's credit?" Savoy asked, his voice carefully neutral.

"Has she agreed to quit fighting me over the ranch?"

Savoy managed not to flinch. Sooner or later Ward would see the new clause Angelique's lawyers had appended to the deal. Then his father would throw a shit fit.

According to the "agreement to agree," the merger couldn't go through without Bliss's written approval.

"I don't know. What does Rory say about it?" Savoy asked.

"They're getting married again."

"Really? When?"

"Couple of days."

Savoy shrugged. "He might as well. He's your son in everything but name."

"Not if he takes Bliss's side in this."

"Does he know that?"

"He knows." Ward's finger stabbed at the sheet he was reading. "What the hell is *this*? Since when does this merger need an eighty percent agreement of all private shareholders in Savoy Enterprises!"

Savoy pinched his nose in an unconscious echo of his father. In some cases, headaches were indeed catching. "Since Angelique realized how deeply Bliss is against developing certain portions of the ranch, Angelique doesn't want 'to be a source of familial discord.' "

"How the hell did she find out?"

"Jesus, Dad, the woman would have to live under a rock not to know Bliss's stand on developing the ranch. Radio, TV, newspapers—take your pick. They've all featured our dirty laundry at one time or another, and Blissy makes a wonderful poor little rich girl."

Ward hurled his drink into the fire, glass and all. The explosion of sound sent Honey Bear scrambling for a calmer place to sleep.

"That bitch Bliss has twenty-four hours to sign this deal," Ward said to the fire. "Then I'm going to the lawyers. All she'll inherit from me will be ten dollars and my sincere hope that she roasts in hell. Tell her, Savvy. Tell her tonight."

Savoy gathered the papers and left without a word. He'd seen his father mad before, but not like this. Not since his mother was alive. Cold, not hot.

Blissy, what have you done now?

39

Turn left, turn right, run in circles, repeat sequence," Ian muttered.

Susa ignored him.

Lacey didn't, but she didn't say anything, either. She could see his reflection in the rearview mirror. His eyes were darker than night. His mouth was flat. She knew he was irritated that she wouldn't tell him why the trip to the storage unit was necessary, but she couldn't help it. The paintings would speak for themselves. They would have to. She didn't know how to explain them, and she didn't feel like answering all the questions they would raise if she told everyone about them before they got there.

Too late for second thoughts now, she told herself.

Hoping she was doing the right thing, she pulled the cashmere coat her parents had brought closer around her. It was a lot warmer than the velvet-patch coat, but not nearly as colorful. Black was pretty much black, and she preferred bright.

Ian checked the mirrors. His faithful escort had gotten careless. Instead of running a streetlight to stay on Ian's bumper, the deputies had stopped two blocks back like good little citizens.

Ian didn't feel like a good little citizen. He opened the gap between the two cars, pushed the next light, and turned right into a residential area without signaling. Then he put the accelerator on the floor and did the rocket-sled routine for two blocks, turned left, shot down two more blocks, whipped onto another side street, and shut down the car.

"Well, that achieved target heart rate," Susa said dryly. "Tired of being followed?"

"Yeah." His tone didn't encourage comments.

"Any particular reason?" Susa asked.

"No."

"Ah."

Silence descended in the car.

"What do you mean, 'Ah'?" he asked finally.

"Ah, as in, ah, of course, testosterone," Susa said.

Ian didn't argue the point as he watched the deputies cruise through an intersection one block over. He knew it was petty of him to feel good about losing them, but there it was. He felt good.

The deputies didn't reappear. After a few minutes Ian started up the truck again and cut over to a road that would loop around to Corona del Mar.

Lacey began giving instructions again. "Turn right at the next light."

Finally they came to an area where small businesses struggled to survive, motels became cheap apartments, and storage yards for the rich and overstocked thrived.

"There," Lacey said. "Universal Storage, on the left. Just pull up to the gate. I'll enter the code."

Lacey got out, punched in her private code, and got back in before Ian drove through the electronic gate. Bright lights illuminated six rows of storage units, each row two units tall.

"Shayla's brother-in-law owns the place," Lacey said. "We get a couple of units for free, unless he needs them. Then Lost Treasures Found gets crammed to the ceiling again."

Susa glanced around curiously and didn't ask any questions.

Ian grunted. So far Lacey had been willing to talk about everything but why she'd decided to take a late-night jaunt to a storage unit. "Why the big mystery?" he asked.

"Number one-twenty" was all she said, pointing to the right. "Second row of buildings, first story. You can park right in front of the freight elevator."

No one else was around, which wasn't surprising. Most people had better things to do late on a Friday night than check out the contents of their storage unit. Lacey winced at the thought of how many weekend nights she'd spent doing just that. She hadn't realized how predictable—okay, *boring*—her social life had become until Ian appeared and put the moon and stars back in her nights.

She wondered how long it would last. If he was mad at her now, she couldn't imagine what he'd be like when he saw the contents of number 120.

Ian looked around the designated parking area, rejected it, and went farther down the row to a point where the truck couldn't be spotted from the street.

Lacey walked up the row, looked at the wide storage door that opened like a garage door, and pulled out the key that would open the padlock. The closer she got to the paintings, the more she wondered if she was doing the right thing.

And the more she was afraid she wasn't.

"If you chicken out after all this," Ian said conversationally, "I'm going to pry that key out of your paint-stained little fingers and go in alone."

Her chin came up in a "You and who else, big boy" gesture that made him smile despite his irritation. He tugged at the lock of her hair that never stayed in place.

She didn't know whether to smile or smack his hand.

Susa snickered.

Lacey opened the padlock, stuck it in her coat pocket, and tugged up on the door. Most of the units had rolling doors that shrieked like Halloween. Hers didn't. The sound of metal on metal made her teeth ache. That was why the door rose up with hardly a sound. She kept it as well oiled as a bodybuilder's pecs. Saying a silent prayer that she was doing the right thing, she flipped on the light and stepped aside.

It was a big unit. A quarter of it was packed with shelves and racks of items waiting to be needed at Lost Treasures Found. The rest was Grandfather Quinn's paintings and closed cupboards lining the far wall. The racks for the paintings were so closely packed that it was all a person could do to squeeze between the rows.

Ignoring the shop goods, Susa looked at the unframed paintings that were stacked in racks along the walls and aisles, leaning against the racks, and wrapped in paper and piled on or under cheap tables. Then she made a startled sound and turned the nearest painting toward the light. *A hillside waist-deep in golden grass, green eucalyptus with pale bark peeling in graceful ribbons, a wild sky alive with rain and wind . . .*

"My God," she breathed. "Another Marten."

"No. Another David Quinn," Lacey said. "A roomful of them, as a matter of fact."

Susa shook her head like a woman coming out of one dream and into a deeper dream.

"I saw him paint that one," Lacey said, pointing to the canvas Susa was holding.

"*En plein air?* Or was it painted in his studio from a field study?" Susa asked.

"Studio and field study."

"Where is it?"

"The field study?" Lacey asked.

"Yes."

Lacey frowned and looked around the unit. "I don't know. It might not have survived. Like you, Grandpa destroyed paintings all the time."

"Probably a good idea in his case," Ian said. "If the original is gone, it's harder to prove forgery."

Lacey flinched and didn't disagree.

"How could anyone destroy an original Marten?" Susa asked. Then, quickly, "Never mind. That was my heart talking, not my brain. But still . . ."

"I didn't bring you here to make you feel bad all over again," Lacey said. "I just wanted to prove to you that you didn't have to mourn those three stolen paintings. They weren't Martens. They were Quinns, and there are a lot more where they came from. And maybe, just maybe, an original Marten or two or three is waiting to be discovered somewhere in the hundreds of paintings I inherited. Since I was raised with the paintings, I don't think I'd be able to tell the difference between original or forgery. But maybe you can separate the wheat from the Wheaties."

"Or Rarities could," Ian said. "It's what they do and they're damned good at it."

"Sure. Send them the whole bloody lot," Lacey said unhappily, "but don't ask me to pay for it. I can't."

"I can," Susa said. She glanced around. "Looks like another triage job," she said, mentally rolling up her sleeves. "Let's get to work."

40

You lost them twenty minutes ago?" Rory repeated into his cell phone. He looked at his watch. Almost nine o'clock. He hadn't been with Bliss long enough to kiss her properly and already something had gone wrong.

The irritation in Rory's voice made Bliss look up from the cheese pastries she was making. Glumly she wondered if he was going to have to rush off and leave her watching TV alone. The drop in her spirits surprised her. It told her how much and how quickly he'd become part of her life again.

The best part.

"How'd it happen?" Rory asked. "You get out to take a crap or what?"

The deputy at the other end of the conversation swallowed hard. "The subject had been cooperative, so we didn't worry when he went through a yellow light. It was busy—Friday night and all—so we just let him go rather than endangering civilians by taking the light red."

"Uh-huh," Rory said, understanding their predicament but not real sympathetic at the moment. "So, did the light stick on red?"

"No, sir. He rabbited. Turned off the highway into a residential area. By the time we got there, he was gone."

"If I were you," Rory said, "I'd pray to God that nothing happens to Susa Donovan before she gets back to the hotel, where you and your partner will be waiting for her."

"Yes, sir."

"Call me when you pick them up again."

Rory didn't wait for the deputy's agreement. He punched out and called Ward.

"Hope I didn't wake you," he said when Ward answered the phone.

Ward snorted. "That'll be the day. You fight with Bliss and decide to play cribbage tonight with an old man after all?"

"Not yet. Just got a call from my men. They lost Susa Donovan."

"How'd they lose her in a hotel?"

"It wasn't in the hotel. It was PCH on a Friday night."

Silence.

Mentally Rory prepared himself for the abrasive edge of Ward's tongue. It wasn't a happy prospect. Rory was still raw from the explosion that had come when Ward realized that the paintings he wanted to buy had been stolen.

"No big deal," Ward said, "unless you think she

stole the paintings herself or had it done, and is going to pick them up again."

"If she did, I'm a long way from proving it. Besides, why would she do it? It's not like she needs money. Ian Lapstrake, now, maybe there's a possibility. But I got to tell you, nothing in the information I've dug up on him suggests he's anything except the answer to a mother's prayer."

"Huh? You making any progress at all on the theft?"

"I said I'd call you if we had any breaks on the case."

"So you can't follow a truck on PCH and you can't catch a brass-balled thief. What the hell good are you to me, Sheriff?" Ward hung up.

Rory grimaced and turned off the phone.

"You have to go?" Bliss asked.

He turned toward her. The rosy silk wrapper she wore brought color to her skin and made her eyes look incredibly blue. "I'd have to be a fool to leave a beautiful lady alone on Friday night."

She smiled almost sadly. "I'll be here when you get back."

"I'm not going anywhere." He tossed the cell phone on the counter and unbuckled his weapon harness. He draped it over a kitchen chair and went to Bliss, drew her close, and kissed her. "Mmm, you smell good enough to eat."

"Is Daddy mad at you because you're here?"

"No." Rory nibbled on her ear. "The paintings he wants to buy were stolen today."

"And he blames you?"

"A firm I own part of was responsible for security at the hotel where the paintings were stolen."

"So? Does he blame you every time a bank gets held up?"

Smiling, Rory kissed her carefully shaped eyebrows. "Nope. But he really had a yen for those paintings."

"Do him good not to get something he wants."

"Speaking of wanting something," Rory said, sliding his hands into the deep neckline of the silk wrap.

"You want food or sex?" she asked, but she arched her back to make it easier for his hands to find her.

"Dinner in bed."

She laughed and kissed him hard.

No sooner had she gotten his belt unbuckled than her phone rang.

"Ignore it," she said against his neck.

"I was planning to."

The phone rang again. Then again. Then the answering machine kicked in.

They heard Savoy's voice. "Bliss, if you're screening calls, let me in. It's important. Really important."

"Well, shit," Rory said. Slowly he withdrew his hands. "Better get it, sugar. Savvy doesn't sound happy."

She sighed, touched his lips with her fingertip, and went to the phone. "Hi, Savvy."

"Ring me up."

Bliss's mouth settled into sulky lines. "I've got a man with me."

"Your future husband?"

"Who told you?"

"Our father, who art *not* in heaven." Savoy's tone said more than words. "Ring me up. I promise it won't take long."

A long, rosy fingernail stabbed at the number pad,

opening the downstairs lock. By the time Bliss had her wrapper rearranged and Rory had his shirt tucked in, Savoy was knocking at the front door. Bliss opened the door and looked at her brother.

"You look tired," she said.

"Spending time with the old man when he's on a rant will do that to you," Rory said.

"Yeah." Savoy pinched the bridge of his nose again. The headache that had begun at the ranch had really taken hold.

"What do you want to drink?"

"Scotch. Neat. And some aspirin if you have it."

Rory went to the wet bar just off the kitchen.

Bliss crossed her arms under her breasts and waited. Then she saw the new lines on her brother's face. "Oh, damn, Savvy. Sit down. I can't throw you out when you look like this. You hungry?"

Savoy hesitated, thinking about it.

"Did you eat dinner?" Rory asked, handing him the drink and some white tablets he'd taken from the bottle behind the bar.

Savoy knocked back half the drink, threw down the tablets, and finished the drink. "No, I don't think so. I've been going over the latest version of the New Horizons agreement with Dad. Took away my appetite."

"How does country soup sound?" Bliss said. "I've got some left over from dinner, and some bread to go with it."

"You don't have to feed me," Savoy said. He smiled slightly, "I know you have better things to do. And by the way, congratulations to both of you." *Hope you get it right this time, but I'm not holding my breath.* He glanced at Rory. "You were the only one of the crop that didn't kowtow to Blissy. Drove her nuts."

"Went both ways," Rory said. "She didn't kowtow to me."

"And it drove you nuts," Blissy said.

"Only sometimes." Rory looked at his future brother-in-law. "Another drink?"

Savvy shook his head. "Thanks, but I promised Bliss to make this fast." He reached into the breast pocket of his wool blazer and pulled out the ten-page "agreement to agree." "Sign this and I'm gone."

Bliss's eyes narrowed into glittering slits as she read the heading on the first sheet. "I'm not going to sign away my birthright to that sleek little church-talking bitch so that Daddy can have a fucking monument built to his everlasting memory."

"Your choice," Savoy said evenly. "But if you don't sign this deal, your birthright will consist of ten dollars and your father's fervent hope that you roast in hell."

Bliss's head snapped up. "What?"

"You heard me."

"I don't believe it."

The corner of Savoy's mouth turned down. "Believe it."

She stared at her brother for a long moment. "He'd do that to his own daughter?"

"After what happened to our Moonie siblings, do you have to ask? Dad hasn't so much as spoken to them for thirty years. Hell, he won't even listen if I speak *about* them."

"Jesus, thirty years." Bliss shook her head, staggered by all the time. Where had it gone? "Has it really been that long?"

"Yeah. And nothing has changed since," Savoy said

wearily, "except that Dad's gotten less patient with people who get in his way on business."

Rory put a comforting arm around her waist.

"When you sign," Savoy said, "you'll get your credit cards back. He's a no-holds-barred son of a bitch when it comes to running the ranch his way, but he doesn't hold grudges."

Bliss tilted her head back. Tears fell anyway. "Damn, damn, *damn him*. He always wins."

"Marry me," Rory said. "I can't keep you like a queen, but you won't starve."

She gave him a watery smile. "You keep making me wonder why I ever walked away from you." She looked at her brother and the smile faded. "Where's a pen?"

Savoy reached into his breast pocket and gave her a pen.

"You don't have to," Rory said. "Money isn't—"

"I won't deny money is part of it," she interrupted, her voice as defeated as the line of her back. "I'm too old to be happy on the pension of a public servant, and I know it. You wouldn't be happy having to find another job flipping burgers, and you know it." She looked up and met Rory's eyes directly. "Just like you know that if Daddy thought you were standing between me and my signature on this, he'd crucify you. So there's no real choice, is there?"

Savoy didn't disagree.

Neither did Rory. He'd never wanted to be one of the "retired" senior citizens working in fast-food joints to make payments on their medical prescriptions.

Silently Bliss signed the New Horizons papers and handed them back to her brother. "Well, it was fun while it lasted."

"What was?" Rory asked.

"Yanking his chain." She smiled thinly at both men. "It was a hell of a lot more satisfying than being one more Honey Bear licking his feet."

41

Hands on hips, Susa stood back and looked at the various paintings. So did Lacey. It reminded her of what a hard time she'd had picking just three canvases for Susa to view.

"You've selected as many as you've rejected," Ian said.

"More, actually," she said.

"I was trying to be tactful," he muttered.

"Don't strain anything." But she smiled at him to take the bite out of her words. "Truth is, I'm having a hell of a time choosing. Each painting pretty much looks better than the others. He must have been ruthless when he culled his work through the years."

"No originals?" Ian asked.

Susa shrugged. "Nothing that leaped out at me. Would Rarities rather have a handful to work with or a whole bunch?"

"I don't know." He looked at his watch. By now,

Dana and Niall would probably be kicking back over garden catalogues, arguing about what to plant next spring. Niall would be looking for new varieties of peonies or violets. Dana would be back in the herb section of the seed magazines, licking her lips over the culinary possibilities and wondering how to sneak *those bloody weeds* into Niall's gardens. "Want me to call and ask?"

"No," Susa said. "If they need more from me, I'll handle it after the auction tomorrow."

"You're leaving tomorrow," Ian said.

She shrugged. "I'll stay an extra day or two if Dana wants it."

"I take it the Donovan is still in Uzbekistan?" Ian asked, trying not to smile.

"Eating mystery meat from communal pots," she agreed. "Everything that was once the eastern reaches of the USSR is rediscovering—or reinventing—tribal rituals to sanctify daily life of all kinds. It would be amusing if they had a sense of humor about it."

"The newer the state, the greater the need to be taken seriously," Ian said.

Susa sighed. "What do you think, Lacey?"

"About global politics?" she asked, startled.

"About my choices," Susa said, gesturing toward the various paintings.

"Don't look at me for help. It took me weeks to pick the paintings I brought to you."

"Well, I've done all I can until I know what Rarities needs."

"Uh, there are more," Lacey said.

"Paintings?" Susa asked. "Where?"

"In the cupboard. Shayla hates them so much I hide

them so she doesn't have to trip over them when we're getting new stuff for the shop."

Susa's eyebrows lifted. "Everyone's a critic. Have you heard from her yet?"

"No. I don't expect to until she gets out of the back country of Peru and into a place where there's cell phone coverage. That could be ten days." Lacey headed for the far wall, picking her way through paintings. "Besides, she couldn't do anything I haven't already done, except maybe help me kick butt at the insurance company."

"A worthy cause," Ian said. "If you need backup, I've got size thirteen boots at your disposal."

She looked over her shoulder and smiled slowly. "Save them for kicking the deputies who are looking for Susa's paintings." Lacey opened the first cupboard and began pulling out the Death Suite. "Help me pass these out to Susa, will you?"

"Sure." He walked with surprising delicacy through the mess, considering the size thirteen boots he wore.

The light in the storage unit wasn't great, but it was plenty bright enough for Ian to see the subject of the paintings as he handed them along to Susa.

"Man, your grandfather must have been a cheerful bastard," Ian said as he looked at the fifth version of the drowning woman.

"He had his moments," Lacey mumbled.

Susa didn't say anything. She just took each dark painting and propped the canvas against whatever she could so that she was able to compare them at the same time. There were eleven of the water.

The twelfth painting was different.

"New topic," Ian said. "Finally." He shifted the painting Lacey had just handed to him and whistled through his teeth. "This time he's burning 'em to death."

"There isn't a human figure in his fire canvases," Lacey said.

"That's your story," he said. "From here, it looks like a cremation." And it reminded him far too much of the fire last night.

Susa glanced at the painting, frowned, and began stacking it in a new area, away from the first eleven.

Silently Lacey handed out six more paintings of a house or a cottage or something burning down. Despite her defense of her grandfather's works to Ian, she was all too certain that the heaped shadows in the background of each canvas had once been human.

Shaking his head, Ian passed the paintings along to Susa, who kept her silence.

"Last batch," Lacey said.

"For these small favors, Lord, we give thanks," Ian said under his breath. He'd seen violent death in his time, yet somehow the painter had managed to capture and vividly enhance the suffering, the rage, and the finality of the act of murder. "He might have been a forger," Ian said, looking at a car wreck where what could have been a slack white hand dangled against the crumpled, sprung door. A trail of fire led down the slope to the car, marking the leakage from the ruined gas tank. Flames and a full moon leered down at the scene, competing to give ghastly illumination to death. "But he was damn good at it."

"Talk about small favors," Lacey said under her breath.

Ian kept staring at the painting, tantalized by the

sense of something not quite seen. Something . . . familiar.

"Hello?" Lacey said, holding out another canvas to him.

"Huh?" He looked up. "Oh, sorry. Something about this . . ."

"Pass it along," Susa said. "The light's better out here."

"And there are ten more of them to look at," Lacey said.

Ian handed the painting over, and the ten that followed it. When he was finished, he was more certain than ever that the paintings were somehow familiar.

Yet he was positive he'd never seen them before in his life.

"Ian? You want to see the pictures in better light?" Susa asked.

"Uh, yeah." Frowning, he picked his way between shelves and racks of items that his great-aunt called "dust catchers."

"Here they are," Susa said, gesturing with graceful fingers at the eleven paintings.

Lacey followed Ian and stood at his side while he stared at the car-wreck paintings.

"What are you looking for?" she asked finally.

"Don't know."

"Well, that makes it easier."

A smile flickered over his mouth. "I feel like I've seen these before, or something like them."

"It's possible," Lacey said.

"It is?"

"Yeah. Assuming Grandpa only painted fourteen— an assumption I can't prove—there are three missing."

Susa and Ian stared at Lacey.

"How do you know?" he asked.

"I'd like to say I'm psychic, and open my own woo-woo shop and sell vitamins," Lacey said, "but my knowledge is more ordinary than that. The paintings are numbered along the stretchers on the back. Two is the lowest. Fourteen is the highest number. There's no guarantee there weren't paintings numbered higher than fourteen. I only know I don't have any."

Ian began checking the back of each car-wreck painting. "One, seven, and twelve are missing."

"It's the same for each, uh, topic." *What a genteel way to describe three separate takes on death and murder. Mom would be so proud of me.* "A broken sequence of numbers."

"What's the other number written on the opposite side?" he asked.

"I can't be sure, but I think it's the total number of the Death Suite."

"The *what*?" Susa asked.

"It's my name for the dark paintings, not Grandpa's. I don't know if he separated them from the rest of his work in his own mind."

"But you do," Susa said.

"Wouldn't you?" Lacey asked.

Susa looked thoughtful. "Yes, of course. Are the other works numbered in any way at all?"

"You mean the landscapes?" Lacey asked.

"Yes."

"Not that I've found. No numbers. No dates. Only the dark ones are numbered and dated, or maybe dated—hard to tell. Two.six, four.six, and nine.two aren't exactly the same as April eighth, nineteen-ninety. It could have been the numbers of attempts he made before he got one he liked, or it could have been a code as private as the vision he was painting. The paintings lend themselves to a more, um, ritual than rational explanation."

"Tactfully put," Ian said, his voice sardonic. "Rituals could be another name for psychoses, right?"

Lacey compressed her lips and shut up. Seeing the paintings through the eyes of people who hadn't grown up with them gave the art a new dimension. It wasn't a happy one.

Grandpa, did you imagine these or . . . ?

She refused to finish the thought. Rubbing away the goose bumps that prickled coldly over her arms, she stepped back into the shadows and let Ian and Susa absorb the paintings.

Ian paced silently from the drowning pool to the fire to the wreck. Each time he stopped in front of the wreck and studied the paintings as though he was trying to squeeze something out of them.

"If those are dates," he said, "there are only three of them. One for each way of dying. That's a lot of painting in one day."

"Impressive but not impossible," Susa said. "If an artist is seized by a theme, he or she might paint nonstop in a frenzy of creation. Ten paintings, twenty, thirty. As long as the body can take it."

Ian grunted. "Frenzy about covers it."

"Not pleasant," Susa said, looking from painting to painting, death echoing. "Not cozy. Brilliant the way a sword is brilliant. It's the steely essence of intelligence and tradition. It's also a punishing reminder of man's spotted soul."

With an impatient sound, Ian picked up one of the car-wreck paintings and shifted it slowly, letting light play over its dark surface. Night and hills and eucalyptus lifting like black torches to the moon-bright sky. The suggestion of parallel lines, perhaps tire tracks, rushing down a steep slope, straddling fire. The landscape shuddering as though at a blow. Every ripple of force came from and led back to the car.

Except one line. As though the wind touched only a single tree, it bent like a finger pointing to the top of the slope, where something stood and watched. Caught within the shadows that might have been chaparral or a man, a single glow came from what might have been the ember of a match.

Ian shifted the painting slowly, then shifted it again. The tiny glow winked in some lights like a firefly; in others, the glow was barely visible.

Saying nothing, he set aside the painting and picked up one of the canvases that depicted a fire raging in a cottage. Again, fire and moon were the only illumination. The moon wasn't quite full in this one, but the fire more than made up for it. The little cottage burned like a torch, an explosion frozen in time.

Once he got past the sheer violence of the flames, he could see nuances that had escaped him before. The shadow outline of a burning figure. The deeper shadow of a fleeing figure with one foot off the canvas and something dark and bulky under his arm. Or hers. They could have been women. They could have been demons. They could have been nightmares.

"Jesus, Joseph, and Mary," Ian muttered. "If it was any more real, you'd smell it."

"As I said, brilliant." Susa picked up one of the water paintings. "Nothing defined, everything suggested. Limitless, and all the more horrifying because of it." Still holding the painting, she turned to face Lacey.

"Having seen these, I feel more strongly than ever that they should be exhibited."

"But they're forgeries!"

Susa shrugged. "No matter. They're brilliant. Since the originals are probably lost to us, it's better to have something brilliantly copied than nothing at all of Marten's work."

"Then list me as the painter," Lacey said.

Susa's skin rippled in a primal wave of uneasiness that she neither understood nor questioned. "I don't think that's a good idea."

Ian glanced at Susa. "Why?"

"Your grandfather's dead. If these are forgeries, it won't matter to him, will it?"

Lacey hesitated.

"Do you think it will be easier on your father to have his living daughter flogged as a forger rather than his dead father?" Ian asked.

"No," Lacey said unhappily. "Besides, he's going to retire instead of being a judge. I'm just not thrilled about blackening my grandfather's name."

"You aren't doing one damn thing," Ian said. "Any trash that gets passed around because of this is his fault, not yours."

"I won't put these forward as your paintings," Susa said. "Your career is too valuable to destroy over this. The world has lived without many of Marten's paintings so far. I suppose it can bump along without him until you change your mind or die."

"Oh, hell," Lacey said, throwing up her hands. "Do it. I'll live with my whiny inner child."

Susa grinned. "You sure?"

Lacey blew out a hard breath. "Yeah. But let's keep

it to a handful for now. After seeing your reaction to the dark ones, I'd just as soon not dump them all out in public at once."

"How about if we just sort of replace the three paintings that were stolen?" Ian suggested.

"Good idea," Susa said. "That way we'll stay within the spirit of the original event."

"No more than three paintings per patron, please," Lacey muttered, remembering. "I went through it once already. This time *you* do the selecting."

"Sold," Susa said quickly. Her glance skimmed through the aptly named Death Suite. "I agree with your original selection of the drowning," she said. "The woman is an immediate emotional focus for people unaccustomed to art. By the time they figure out what the canvas is depicting, they'll already be trapped in its power."

"This is good?" Ian asked.

Susa and Lacey ignored him.

"This one," Susa said, selecting one of the drowning pool paintings, "has the desperate clarity of the scream you can't hear."

Ian blinked and kept his mouth shut. He didn't want to get into the Zen thing right now.

Lacey pulled the painting out of the lineup and waited while Susa, muttering, paced up and down the narrow walkways between the racks where she had left her favorites of the landscapes jutting out into the aisles.

"Just two," Susa said. "Dear Lord. How can I choose?"

Ian sighed. Sometimes Zen was quicker than anything else. "Close your eyes."

"What?" Susa asked.

"Close your eyes and see better. The Zen thing."

She gave him a sideways look. "Out of the mouths of babes . . ."

"Hey, I'm fully grown."

"That's what makes you a babe."

Laughing, shaking his head, Ian crowded past Susa and took the first two paintings that were sticking out into the aisle. "Here," he said. "Now let's go back to the hotel and get some sleep. Tomorrow will be a long day."

Susa took the first painting. It was a study of the desert east of the San Jacinto Mountains. The smoke tree growing out of the sandy wash was essentially feminine, grace and endurance in a deceptively fragile-looking body. Behind the tree, the mountains loomed in angles and shadows softened by the rose-colored glasses of dawn. But the brutal coming of the sun was implicit in the sparse plant life and the cryptic tracks left in the sand by animals that chose to live in the seamless night rather than in the searing light of day.

"Fascinating," Susa said. "The oil is so thinly applied that it's almost transparent on the canvas, yet the result has the kind of depth most artists achieve only with palette knives and gobs of paint."

Gently Ian pried the painting from her hands and gave it to Lacey. "Glad you like it. Let's go."

"Show me the other one," Susa said to Ian.

"Light's better at the hotel."

She raised her eyebrows and waited.

He gave her the second painting. He no longer wondered how such a delicate little flower had held her own with the Donovan men. In fact, he was wondering how they'd held their own with *her*.

"Perfect," Susa said. "Not the same angle we painted, but the same place."

For the first time Ian looked at the painting. "Cross Country Canyon," he said, recognizing the lines of the land even though the trees were in slightly different places. Then he frowned. "Hold it for a minute. I want to compare something." He went to the Death Suite, selected one of the car wrecks, and came back to Susa.

"What is it?" Lacey asked.

"Can't be sure, but . . ." Ian compared the two paintings. "What do you think? Same place or not?"

Susa and Lacey compared the trees and the lines of the land.

"My vote is yes," Lacey said. "But the daylight view came first. Otherwise you'd see scars from the fire."

"I agree," Susa said. She looked at the intensity of Ian's eyes and the brackets around his mouth. "Why does it matter?"

"While you two were painting, I picked up a license plate at the bottom of the ravine," Ian said. "Just thought it was curious, that's all. Can't have been too many wrecks there."

Goose bumps rippled as Susa felt the familiar but never comfortable sensation of time's cool sigh through her core. She looked at the Death Suite lined up in horrifying celebration and wondered all over again where genius ended and madness began.

42

In the imposing drawing room of the ranch house, Angelique White sat on a butter-colored brocade couch and stroked Honey Bear's soft ears. He watched her with complete adoration shining in his round, dark eyes. The fact that she was nibbling on crackers and savory country pâté didn't hurt the dog's focus one bit.

"Honey Bear, move your lazy butt," Ward said, giving the retriever a hard nudge with his boot. "You're crowding the lady."

The dog leaned harder against Angelique's knee.

Savoy grabbed Honey Bear's collar and pulled him back.

"Really, I don't mind," Angelique said. "He's so beautiful."

"Tell me that after he drools all over your designer dress," Savoy said dryly, gesturing toward the ecru silk she wore. "At least it isn't black. Honey Bear just loves shedding on dark fabric."

Angelique smiled and made cooing sounds at Honey Bear. He sniffed her fingers hopefully. She slipped him a bite of pâté. The dog licked it up and drooled on the papers lined up across the coffee table.

Savoy bit back all the things he wanted to say about ill-behaved, spoiled pets. It was a good thing the ink on the deal was waterproof. He hadn't come this far just to have a golden retriever screw up everything.

"Champagne?" Ward asked.

"No, thank you," Angelique said, refusing the drink again. "I have to drive."

"Some fruit, then?" Savoy asked, passing her an artfully arranged platter of fresh fruit. "Coffee?"

"Coffee, please," she said. She reached toward the table. To Honey Bear's dismay, she picked up a handful of paper rather than pâté. "If you'll give me a moment, I'll just flip through this."

"Take your time," Ward said while Savoy poured coffee all around.

Ward watched his son and Angelique from the corner of his eye. No leaning toward each other. No brush of hand over hand. No press of leg against leg. No private meeting of eyes. Silently Ward gave up the hope that his son would charm Angelique into a compromising position in time to do any good on the ultimate agreement. Nor had Rory come up with anything useful. The deal, such as it was, would stand—not all that Ward had hoped for, but a hell of a lot better than watching his empire nibbled to death by civic ducks.

Angelique read through the papers with the speed and precision of the top executive she was; then she initialed the bottom of each page next to Savoy's mark. Only two changes had been made. Neither was important to her. After she read the last page, she signed on the line above Savoy's signature, wrote in the date, and smiled at him.

"I can't tell you how pleased I am about this," she said. "It's precisely the forward-looking, community- and family-oriented enterprise that I envisioned for New Horizons."

"We're pleased, too," Savoy said. "There were times we wondered if there was a deal to be made."

Angelique's smile widened. "That's what makes business so interesting, don't you think? The uncertainty."

Ward smiled through his teeth. He had to hand it to her—she was one hard-nosed negotiator. But it was all wrapped up now. Finally. Everything he had worked and schemed for during his lifetime was secure. The name and accomplishments of Warden Garner Forrest would echo through the history of southern California.

Forrest, not Savoy.

Always assuming nothing else went wrong before the final deal was signed, of course.

Nothing will go wrong, Ward promised himself. *I've spent a lifetime of eating Savoy shit for this, and so did my father. It will happen.*

Angelique quickly dealt with the remaining copies, stacked them neatly, and put all but one in the sleek leather briefcase that she'd brought. "I believe I'll have a sip of champagne after all. This is a day worth celebrating. A historic collaboration of land and vision, plus dinner tonight with a great artist." She smiled at Ward and Savoy equally. "Isn't it wonderful that some of the missing paintings have been found?"

Ward sat up straight. "What?"

"Well, not found exactly. Not the exact same paintings, from what Susa said when I met her in the hallway," Angelique explained, accepting the champagne flute that Savoy handed to her. "The young woman—Lacey, I believe—who brought the paintings Susa was so excited about apparently has a whole stash of them. So between that and Susa's painting while she was here, the auction will proceed as expected. With all the publicity after the theft, it should be a complete sellout."

"Are you telling me that the Lacey woman has more paintings?" Ward demanded.

"Yes. Isn't it wonderful?"

"Where?" he said curtly.

Angelique hesitated, surprised by Ward's intensity. "Where does she store the paintings? I haven't any idea."

"My father," Savoy said quickly before Ward could speak again, "is a collector. He loves the painter that did Lacey's canvases. You've heard how collectors are—rabid." He smiled. "Whether you know it or not, you've just waved a plate of pâté under a wolf's sensitive nose."

She laughed. "I see. I'm rather obsessive myself about certain things." She looked at Ward. "You'll get to see the paintings tonight, plus some that Susa painted since the theft. Such a lovely hotel you have." Angelique's smile flashed. "Thank you for arranging it so that I could stay there, too. You meet the most interesting people."

Ward smiled with the automatic reflex of a man who'd climbed to the top the hard way. "Our pleasure."

Savoy smiled even though it irritated him that Angelique had poked into every bit of the Forrest holdings, including the paper trail that led to the Savoy Hotel.

"So where are they keeping the paintings now?" Savoy asked Angelique.

"Susa didn't mention it. Rather close to her, I'd imagine."

"No need," Ward said. "If the hotel hadn't been turned upside down getting ready for the auction, the theft never would have happened." He stood up. "Excuse me. I'll check on security right now."

And while he was at it, he decided grimly, he would drill Rory a new asshole for losing track of Lacey Quinn just when she would have led him to a stash of Lewis Marten paintings.

Christ, can't anyone do the job anymore? Seems all I do is wipe asses and tie shoes for the next generation. Not a man in the lot of them.

Angelique watched Ward stalk out, then turned back to Savoy. "Goodness, I didn't mean to insult him."

"Not your fault. He just gets mad every time he thinks about those paintings getting away from him. He's probably calling the sheriff and raking him over the coals while we speak." Savoy smiled with bittersweet amusement at the thought of what Rory must be going through. *Serves him right to be on the receiving end for a change.* "Come hell or high water, I can guarantee no more paintings will be stolen before Dad has a chance to buy them."

43

Although no one had said anything about it, Susa, Lacey, and Ian had decided to keep all the paintings in their sight until midafternoon, when they would go downstairs for Mr. Goodman to hang for the auction. So rather than trying to eat at the restaurant with a painting under each arm, they called room service. Two pizzas, a salami sandwich, and a huge Cobb salad with extra chicken had arrived with gratifying speed. It helped that there weren't more than a handful of guests in the hotel at the moment. By tonight, the place would be full and room service would begin the fine old tradition of serving food as overpriced as it was cold.

Susa and Lacey pulled designer pizza apart and began licking their fingers before taking even one bite. Ian could only eye his lunch longingly, because he was talking to the sheriff of Moreno County.

Ian was watching Lacey hungrily, too, but there was nothing to be done about that until after the auction.

"Thanks for the offer," Ian said, ignoring the sound of his stomach gnawing through his backbone and the quiet ache in his crotch, "but there's no need. We can watch over the paintings for a few hours. After the auction, the exhibit moves to the Savoy Museum for a month, right?"

"Yes," Rory said. "As soon as the dust settles tonight, I'll personally escort the paintings to the museum."

"Sounds good to me. Anything new on the robbery?"

Rory made a ripe sound of disgust. "You called it right. Nothing panned out. The van was abandoned on southbound I-5 about ten miles from here, close to an off-ramp."

"Ownership?"

"The temporary registration was fake. Engine numbers were taken out with acid. Dude wore gloves. Not a print anywhere."

"Dead end," Ian said.

"Yeah. We figure he had a car parked near the off-ramp. If not, there's a bus stop right there."

"Or a buddy picked him up," Ian said.

"No matter which way, he's long gone."

"Mexico?"

"Probably," Rory said. "Could have been San Diego, but it's a lot easier to move goods through Mexico."

"Hell, it could be the Russian *mafiya* in L.A.," Ian said. "They've been bringing stolen art in from all over the former Soviet Union. Lately they've started sending stolen American art back. Smuggling routes work two ways."

"Jesus," Rory muttered. "Welcome to the new global crime village. How the hell can we keep a lid on international crooks when we can't even keep our own backyards weeded?"

"That's why organizations like Rarities Unlimited exist. They go after the exotic weeds locals don't have time, funds, or training to take care of."

"Regular civic Boy Scouts, huh?"

Ian smiled narrowly. "That's us. Let me know if you turn up anything, Sheriff. I'm sure Susa's insurance company will be in touch with you real soon."

"They've already sent a representative. He's not happy about our lack of progress."

"If you stood to lose a couple million bucks, you'd be unhappy, too."

"By the way, when I questioned a man called S. K. Niall about your honesty, he laughed so hard I thought he'd swallow his tongue," Rory said. "Then he told me I'd have a better chance of pinning it on the pope than on you. Said the only one you might have trusted enough to team up with on a robbery was Lawe Donovan, and if he wanted Susa's paintings, all he had to do was ask. Then Niall told me to quit wasting his time and hung up."

"That's Niall. A bottom line kind of guy."

"So, has Rarities come up with anything on the paintings?" Rory asked.

"Not that I know of. And I'd know."

"Yeah, well, if you hear anything—"

"I'll tell you. And vice versa. Right?"

"Sure," Rory said, and hung up.

Ian tossed the phone into its cradle. " 'Sure,' my bleeding arse," he said under his breath. "Cops never share anything important." He stalked over to the table where lunch waited.

"Did the sheriff have anything new to report?" Susa asked.

"All the leads are dead ends." He sat down next to Lacey, tilted her chin, and neatly licked up a smear of pizza sauce. "Mmm, garlic and cream. My favorite. Artichoke and basil, too. Doesn't get much better unless you put a pound of pepperoni on top. You going to eat all that?"

She swallowed, told herself that her heart hadn't really turned over at the warm flick of his tongue, and managed to speak. "You have a salami sandwich the size of a TV and a gi-normous salad of your own that you haven't even touched."

"Your point?" He eyed the pizza on her plate.

"I should have ordered a bigger pizza."

"I'll let you nibble on my salami."

She looked at his dark eyes and lazy smile and forgot to breathe. "You will?"

"Any time."

A piece of Susa's pizza plopped down on top of Ian's salami sandwich. "Quit tormenting her," she said.

"Does that mean you want some of my—" he began, turning toward Susa.

"No," she cut in ruthlessly. "I have a fine salami source of my own."

Ian snickered and began eating. Lacey watched in fascination as food disappeared. Even the messy salad didn't slow him down a bit.

"Why are you staring at me?" Ian asked finally.

"I only have sisters. My dad is a couch potato. I had no idea how much an active man could eat."

"Wait until you have dinner with the Donovans," Susa said. "Appalling." She looked at Lacey. "Did your parents bring something fancy you can wear to-night? Don't ask me why, but people always dress up for art as though it somehow makes everything more valuable."

"God, yes, Mom brought everything she ever wanted me to wear," Lacey said, rolling her eyes. "I'm going to be painting in designer dresses unless I hit a few garage sales."

"It's a shame that little black dress couldn't be saved," Ian said, smiling down at his salami. "Great neckline. Hemline wasn't bad, either."

Lacey tried not to laugh or blush, and failed both ways. She lobbed her napkin at Ian, who caught it, tucked it into his shirt collar, and dived back into his lunch.

"Thanks, darling," he said. "I couldn't find mine."

"It's in your lap," Lacey said.

"You sure? Maybe you better check."

"This tricycle is about to be turned into a bicycle built for two," Susa said, winking at Lacey. "If I'm not awake by four, pound on the door until you get a coherent sentence from me. Not just a word or two, mind you. An intelligible whole sentence. Otherwise I'll just roll over and go back to sleep."

Susa picked up her pizza and beer, went into her bedroom, and closed the door. A moment later the radio began blaring out a reggae retrospective on a local station.

"Should I feel bad?" Lacey asked.

"Why?"

"I didn't mean to drive her away."

"You didn't. One thing I've learned about Susa is that she does pretty much what she wants. Another thing is that she likes spending time alone. Before your place burned down, we went to separate ends of the suite after an early dinner. Her choice."

"So you were just giving her an excuse to get away gracefully?" Lacey asked, her voice almost wistful.

"You haven't checked for my napkin yet."

She looked at his eyes and felt her heart do the back-flip thing again. Slowly she leaned forward and checked under the table for his napkin. It was there. So was he. Right there.

"Oh," she said.

"Is that 'Oh, shit' or 'Oh, boy'?"

"You finished with lunch?" she asked.

"You have something in mind?"

"Oh, yeah."

44

Wrapped in a huge bath towel, Lacey shook out a dress and stared. "What was Mom thinking?"

Ian wandered out of the bathroom with a towel tucked around his hips, rubbing his freshly shaved jaw. "What's wrong?"

She held out the dress. "This!"

"Nice color."

She snorted. "Why do men always love red?"

"A Y-chromosome thing, I suppose. Anything else wrong?"

"There's not much of the damn thing and what there is *stretches*. No way to wear a bra and not have every stitch show."

Ian grinned. "Better and better. Let's have a look."

Ignoring her hands batting at his, he took off Lacey's towel and pulled the dress over her head. With a roll of her eyes, she wiggled and jiggled and pulled at stretchy fabric until everything was mostly where it should be.

His jaw hit the floor. "Holy shit."

"That's my line."

"Sue me," he said huskily.

He reeled in his jaw and told himself he was out of his mind. They had just destroyed the bed and each other, and he was thinking about peeling off that siren dress and sinking so far into her that they both would want to scream. It would be good, so damn *good*.

"Promise you'll wear that for me later," he said.

Lacey quit tugging at the fabric and looked at him for the first time. His half-lowered eyelids and smoky voice made her feel like the sexiest woman alive.

"How about if I wear it now?" she asked.

"You wear it and you don't leave the room until I'm too weak to lick your lips. I'm thinking that would be some time next week." He blew out a hard breath. "What else did your mother bring?"

Lacey told herself she didn't swing her hips that extra bit when she walked to the closet, but she knew she did. If she'd had any doubt, it was erased when Ian stood so close behind her that she could feel his heartbeat against her back.

"Lots of little black dresses," she said. "I was feeling more . . . frisky."

"You're killing me."

She laughed and pulled out a dress that was as much blue as black, and an electric blue jacket that went with it. "Is this mother-of-the-bride-ish enough for you?"

"Is that neckline legal?"

"Since when do you have a thing against a little décolletage?"

Ian opened his mouth to deny the onset of prudery. Then he shut it. "It's recent. Should I be worried?"

"The jacket buttons."

"Then we should make it through the evening without me hauling you off into the nearest closet."

Lacey laughed. "You make me feel like a sex kitten."

"You are."

"Only to you." She stood on tiptoe and kissed him. "Thanks. In case you hadn't noticed, you're a sexy man. Really, really sexy."

His eyebrows lifted. "Learn something new every day."

A knock came on their bedroom door. "Ten minutes," Susa said briskly.

"We'll be ready," Ian said.

"Yes, but will you be dressed?" she retorted.

"Dang, you are one picky woman," Ian said.

"So I'm told. Nine minutes."

Ian and Lacey gave up and hurried into their clothes. She put on some basic makeup her mother had included with the wardrobe, stepped into the kind of toe-cramming, skyscraper heels she hated, and pronounced herself ready.

Ian was just pulling his suit coat on over his shoulder harness. He was wearing the male equivalent of the little black dress: blue-black suit, cream shirt, maroon tie, black shoes.

Lacey whistled. "You clean up real nice."

He gave her a sidelong look.

She grinned and went out the bedroom door. Susa was in the adjoining sitting room wearing a devastatingly simple turquoise dress and a spiderweb necklace of South Seas pearls.

"Wow," Lacey said.

Susa smiled. "Thank you." She tilted her head. "I'll be right back. I have some jewelry that would be perfect with your dress."

A moment later Susa came out of her bedroom with a pin in the shape of a single peacock feather. The eye of the feather was a magnificent black opal. The rest of the feather was made of tiny colored pearls.

"I can't wear that," Lacey said hastily. "It's too expensive."

"You can wear it better than I can," Susa said matter-of-factly. "It's too big for me, but I promised Faith and Honor—my daughters—that I'd display it anyway as a way of advertising the family businesses. They're jewelry designers and my sons gather the gems from all over the world. So when people compliment you on the pin, tell them who made it. You're doing us all a favor, you see."

"Oh." Lacey stroked fingertips over the pin and smiled at the sheer sensuous playfulness of the piece. "Okay. Just don't tell me how much it cost. And you fasten it in place."

Ian came out, saw the pin, and kicked himself for not thinking of it sooner. "Did you have your jewelry with you when the room was robbed?"

"No. I left it in the room safe."

"You were lucky. The safes are better than nothing, but they won't keep out a pro."

"I suspect the man wasn't shopping for random items," Susa said.

"Yeah. Which makes it less likely that we'll recover the paintings anytime soon."

"Why?" Lacey asked.

"Pros don't steal well-known art and then try to

fence it cold. They have a buyer or buyers in mind before they ever plan the robbery."

"Lovely," Lacey said. "What lice."

"You're slandering insects," Susa said. She looked at Ian. "Since the paintings aren't here, I presume you got away long enough to take them downstairs?"

"Yes." He patted the breast pocket of his suit coat. "I have a signed receipt complete with Polaroid photos of each painting."

"That was nasty of you." Susa smiled. "Well, are we ready to face the mob?"

"The mob isn't here for me or Ian," Lacey pointed out.

"But we'll protect you," he said.

"I'm whining, aren't I?" Susa sighed and looked at her watch. "Let's go see the paintings before dinner. If they haven't displayed them properly, there's still time to fix it."

The moment they stepped into the hall, it was obvious that the auction would be a success. Expensively dressed people were everywhere—leaving their hotel rooms, waiting for the elevator, chatting with friends. The lobby was crowded with glitter and flash and hummed with excitement. Bits of conversation drifted by like wind-driven leaves.

"—seen the latest girlfriend? My God, she has to be fifty years younger than—"

"I rather fancy the dark painting, so brutal and—"

"If she gets another face-lift, she'll have a goatee."

"If *he* gets another one, he'll have two."

"—dreadful art at that show, just dreadful. It could have been left by the janitor when he changed the lightbulbs."

"Look, isn't that La Susa?"

"Omigod, look at those shoulders."

"Hers?"

"*His*. Great butt, too."

"Do you suppose they're lovers?"

"Actually," Ian said under his breath, "my shoulders and butt have been very close since birth."

"Behave," Susa said mildly.

"Why?" he muttered. "Nobody else is. I feel like meat in a deli."

Lacey smiled. "You *are* meat in a deli, my beautiful salami."

"Get used to it," Susa said, winking at Lacey. "Most of the good-looking single men here are gay. But if any of the old ladies pinch you, I'll smack their bony fingers."

Ian wondered if it was okay for a good-looking single man to roll his eyes.

The fragmented conversations went silent in the elevator, only to resume with redoubled volume in the lobby.

"Stand on my right," he said to Lacey, "but don't get in the way of my right hand, okay?"

"Why?"

"Guess."

Belatedly she realized that he wanted to be free to reach beneath his suit coat for his weapon.

"Oh. Got it," she muttered, and went to stand on his right side. But not too close. "So much for holding hands, huh?"

"That's why they call it work."

Ian put his left hand on Susa's elbow, a grim look on his face, and stared down anyone who tried to approach her as they crossed the lobby. When a look wasn't enough, he simply told the person that Susa would be available for conversation after the auction.

"Thank you," Susa said after he had turned away the fourth person. "You're as good at that as Archer or Jake. Not quite rude and certainly not friendly."

"It's something you learn in Junkyard Dog 101."

Lacey grinned.

"This way," Ian said, steering Susa toward a hallway that was discreetly marked as the Surf Ballroom.

"Nice carpet," Lacey said, eyeing the intricate, vaguely Persian pattern that had been done in shades of aquamarine and gold. "Wonder what it will look like in a few years."

"Used," Ian said.

"Gee, you're really fun when you're working."

Mr. Goodman came out of the Surf Ballroom, spotted Susa, and hurried forward. "Ms. Donovan, you look marvelous."

"Thank you," Ian said before Susa could speak. "If you'll excuse us, we're on a rather short clock. Seating at the head table begins in five minutes and Susa hasn't had a chance to see the auction layout."

"Oh, of course. If you have any questions. . . ." Mr. Goodman was talking to Ian's back.

There was a uniformed deputy standing outside the entrance to the ballroom and two more covering other exits. The small raised stage at one end of the room featured Susa's paintings. The forgeries were prominently displayed on movable panels just in front of the stage. The rest of the "Found by Susa Donovan" paintings formed an art maze that took up a third of the ballroom. The remainder of the big room was filled with plush folding chairs whose rubber feet left no marks on the gleaming wooden floor. Each seat held a paddle with huge numbers to identify bidders for the auctioneer and his assistants.

Ian gave the art maze a jaundiced look. It could hide a platoon of Uzi-carrying goons.

"Down boy," Susa said.

Ian glanced at her. "What?"

"I know that look. They teach it in Advanced Paranoia. Just remember that you're here to make the Donovan feel good, not because there is any credible or even *in*credible threat against me."

Ian grunted.

Lacey left them to sort out bodyguard protocol and went to the three panels that held her grandfather's art. The canvases were displayed the same way she'd brought them to Susa—unframed.

The lack of framing only enhanced the raw, edgy energy of the paintings. The desert scene bristled with the silent, endless battle to survive. Cross Country Canyon looked almost ominous, as though the land knew it would be an untimely graveyard. The drowning pool sent out dark waves separated by a horrifying scarlet scream.

Against her will, Lacey was drawn to the grim painting. Here in the sumptuous ballroom and clever lighting, her grandfather's work took on greater detail, greater power, becoming both more specific and more universal. The woman was Everywoman, the bracelet on her right wrist suggested intertwined hearts. Instead of being more distinct, the killer's hand became simply male, strong without being huge, deadly without weapons, a dark force taking light from the woman. The suggestion of a spa was more distinct in the special lighting; Lacey could almost see the outline of tile work and lush plantings. Yet if she didn't look closely, it could have been Hawaii or the Caribbean, any place where the greenery was lush and the water pure.

Gradually Lacey became aware that someone was standing next to her, staring at the painting as intently as she was. At first glance the woman looked thirty-something. A closer look upped the age a decade or more. She was expensively turned out in blended shades of blond hair, an oyster-colored silk dress whose lines whispered Paris, and a diamond and sapphire choker that enhanced the startling blue of her eyes.

As Lacey watched, the woman slowly lifted her right arm until her bracelet was next to the painting. The jewelry she wore was made of white gold with diamond-set hearts, intertwining. Every third heart was a larger solid metal one.

The woman leaned closer, looking from her arm to the painting. Suddenly her hand trembled. *"That's my bracelet."*

45

"You're sure?" Ian asked as he seated Lacey at the head table.

"Positive." She shivered. "It creeped me out. Didn't do much for her, either. She turned around and left like her heels were on fire."

"Who was it?"

"I don't know."

Ian sat down between Susa and Lacey. "Interesting. If you see her again, point her out to me."

"No problem," Lacey said instantly. "She's coming up the aisle right now. The blonde."

He looked and saw a striking blonde hanging on Rory Turner's arm. An even more striking blonde followed on Ward Forrest's arm.

"Which one?" Ian asked.

"The first one. I never saw the second one before. Those gossips in the hallway were right. He's old enough to be her grandfather."

"Never would have pegged him for that kind of fool."

"What does age have to do with it?" Lacey muttered. "Just because he's gray around the edges doesn't mean he's smart about women."

"I suppose—just hate to see a walking cliché."

Savoy Forrest brought up the rear of the party with an elegant brunette in tow. Their body language said they might have been intimate once, but didn't feel comfortable rubbing up against each other right now.

"Well, well," Ian said softly. "Putting two and two together, we're looking at the happy Forrest family. I'm guessing the first blonde is Bliss, Savoy's sister and the sheriff's ex- and soon-to-be-again wife."

"I'm missing something."

"You should talk to cops. Biggest gossips in the world."

The Forrests came up to the head table and chatted while introductions were made all around. When Lacey and Bliss were introduced, Lacey managed not to give Ian a sidelong glance.

"I understand you own the painting of the drowning woman," Bliss said bluntly.

"Yes," Lacey said cautiously.

"Where did you get it?" Bliss asked.

"Why?" Ian asked before Lacey could speak.

"Because that's my bracelet."

Ward's head whipped toward his daughter. "We should be sitting down at our own table."

Bliss ignored her father. She might have her credit cards back, but she was still pissed off at him for winning again. "It belonged to my grandmother Sandra Wheaten Savoy. It was given to her to celebrate my mother Gem's birth. When Mother was twenty-one, the bracelet became hers. It came to me when she died. It's one of a kind."

Bliss pulled back the long, draped sleeve on her right arm and held the bracelet under Lacey's nose.

"Very pretty," Lacey managed.

"You're damned right it is. So why is it in that ugly painting?"

"Blissy," Ward said softly, "it's time for us to *sit down*."

Savoy stepped between father and daughter as he'd always done. "Excellent idea. I'm sure you and Ms. Marsh—excuse me, Quinn—will have lots of time to talk about art before and after the auction."

Rory looked at the stubborn set of Bliss's mouth, mentally calculated how many drinks she'd had, and decided to risk it. He ran his index finger from her shoulder to her fingertips. "Come sit by me, sugar. I've had a long day and need to rest up for the night."

For a moment Bliss resisted. But when he picked up her hand and kissed her palm, she sighed. "All right." Then she looked at Lacey. "Later."

Lacey made a sound that her mother often mistook for agreement.

Bliss and Rory left for a nearby table. Ward waited patiently while Angelique asked Susa something about which brushes were best for water and which for clouds. He didn't hear the answer, but he did see Mr. Goodman quivering in the aisle like an anxious sheep dog.

"Sorry to interrupt," Ward said, smiling at Susa, "but the organizer of the event will wet his pants if we don't sit down pretty quick."

Angelique looked startled, then laughed. "Naughty man."

He smiled. "Somebody has to be or else nobody would appreciate good people like you."

With a light touch on her arm, Ward guided Angelique toward the table. Ignoring the discreet place cards, he seated Angelique so that he would occupy the empty chair next to Bliss. This put Angelique at the end of the table rather than in the center of things. Savoy gave him a sharp glance but didn't protest the new arrangement.

It took twenty minutes, but Ward finally managed to get his daughter's attention without attracting anyone else's.

"Blissy?" he murmured.

"What?"

"I know how much you loved your mother."

Bliss's fork hesitated over her salad. "You sure you want to go into this with Ms. Angel fanning her wings so close by?"

Ward's smile was as hard as the silverware. "Savvy's son has her attention, talking about saving earthworms or some such crap. No doubt the boy will have a check in his pocket before the evening is out."

Bliss smiled at the lettuce with its little vegetable shavings. "Go on. I promise not to choke up at the thought of how close Mother and I were *not*."

"In some ways, you're a lot like me."

"Frightening thought."

"For both of us," he shot back softly. "So do us both a favor. Drop the subject of the damned bracelet."

"Why?"

"Jesus, Blissy, why do you think?"

She shrugged. "Tell me."

"The last thing I want right now is to air any more

dirty skivvies in front of Ms. Angelique. You go holler-ing about that bracelet, and pretty soon all the old gos-sip about your mother's death is going to be on the front pages again and our rich little angel will fly the hell out of here. Then I'd be almighty pissed off at you in a way that will make every other disagreement we've had look as bland as banana pudding. You get it?"

"You'll cut me off."

"You better believe it."

"Shit," Blissy hissed under her breath. "Always pulling strings like some damned puppeteer."

He laughed and ruffled her hair as though she was five instead of nearly fifty. "You're finally figuring it out."

"What?"

"If you ain't pulling strings, somebody is pulling yours. But don't sulk, Blissy. Someday I'll be dead and you'll be rich enough to buy your own puppets."

46

After dinner the guests sifted through the maze of freestanding panels, noting which paintings were for sale and which weren't. People read Susa's handwritten cards next to each painting, made notes, and moved on. Mr. Goodman did the sheep dog bit, gently and relentlessly herding people along the aisles of art. With an eye to the bottom line, he praised the ordinary and the indifferent, and emphasized how valuable Susa's comments were to future owners.

Lacey let herself be herded. Away from Susa there was a blessed anonymity in being one of the crowd musing over paintings. On the stage, Ian practiced his barely leashed junkyard dog routine while a smock-shrouded Susa painted what had once been called Sandy Cove from memory. She wasn't going to let a thief stand in the way of keeping her word to the Forrests about donating a landscape of the ranch to the Savoy Museum.

"Enjoying the show?" Savoy asked from beside Lacey.

"Some of these paintings are amazing."

"Is that good or bad?"

"Works both ways."

Savoy laughed and studied the painting Lacey was looking at. It was an unusual treatment of storm clouds and cattle. Energetic and undisciplined in equal parts. Primitive, yet arresting.

"Have you heard anything more about the robbery?" Savoy asked, moving on to the next painting when Lacey did.

"Since you ate dinner with the sheriff, I was going to ask you the same thing."

"At dinner he was acting in his capacity as former and future family," Savoy said wryly. "Nothing official."

She glanced aside at Savoy. "Former and future?"

"My sister is his ex-wife. They're getting married again tomorrow."

"Oh, I remember now. Good for them. I hope." Lacey heard her own words and winced. "I didn't mean that the way it sounded."

"Don't worry. We're all holding our breath on this one."

For a moment they both stared at a watercolor that suggested seagulls in flight. Then Lacey found herself out of the maze and face-to-face with her grandfather's forgeries.

"I understand you have quite a few of this artist's paintings," Savoy said.

"Yes."

"Might I ask how many?"

She turned toward him. The forgeries were a subject

she would love to avoid, but didn't see any graceful—
or even moderately polite—way of doing so. "Why?"

"As I've said before, my father collects works by
this artist. He particularly focuses on the darker
work." Savoy gestured toward the drowning pool.

"No accounting for taste," Lacey muttered.

"You don't care for them?"

She sighed. "They're brilliant. I just can't see living
with them on a daily basis."

"Them? You have more than this one and the one
that was stolen?"

Damn, not much gets by this man. "Yes."

"Since you don't want to hang them yourself, and
you have an ample supply, the foundation would love
to acquire one or more for our museum."

"I figured that out," Lacey said. "I'm not ready to
sell."

"If you change your mind before the auction is over,
I'll give you one hundred thousand dollars for the pool
painting and an equal amount to the Friends of
Moreno County."

Her eyes widened. "Holy—er, that's a lot."

Savoy smiled narrowly and cursed his father's ob-
session. "Yes, it is. But art collectors are very passionate in their pursuits. And I am very passionate about
pleasing my father."

Crossing her arms over her chest, Lacey turned and
faced Savoy fully. "Look, I'm going to be blunt because I'm no good at being subtle."

His smile gentled, reaching his eyes. "I could like
you, Ms. Quinn."

"Promises, promises." But she smiled back. "Dealing with these paintings in a public manner is new to

me. I have to get used to the idea of their value. It isn't easy. And I have to be sure that they *are* valuable before I go selling them for thousands of dollars."

"I'm willing to take the risk."

"I'm not. I'm sending all of them to Rarities Unlimited to be appraised."

"Excellent firm. I'll be interested in what they have to say." He paused. "You're sending all of them, even the ones that are here tonight?"

She nodded.

"The museum had hoped to display them," Savoy said. "I believe that requirement was mentioned on the entry form."

"Requirement?"

"Perhaps that's too strong a word. Urgent preference might be more appropriate."

Lacey thought about it for a moment, then shrugged. "Until Rarities asks for those three paintings, I'll leave them in your hands."

"Thank you." Savoy smiled brilliantly. "My father will be pleased."

"That means a lot to you, doesn't it?"

"Do you get along with your father, Ms. Quinn?"

She thought about their recent arguments, and some of the not-so-recent ones. What she was thinking must have showed on her face.

"Neither do I, much of the time," Savoy said. "That makes it all the more important to please him when the possibility arises. If you'll excuse me, I'll tell him that you're considering selling a painting as long as a matching contribution goes to Friends of Moreno County."

Before Lacey could answer, Savoy stepped into the crowd that had gathered at the edge of the stage to watch Susa paint. A moment later he was talking to a man who didn't resemble him at all, except for a certain hardness around the eyes. Ward Forrest, the father that the son was trying so hard to please.

Lacey wished him luck.

"Ms. Quinn?"

She turned quickly and saw the expensive blonde. "Ms. Forrest?"

"Not for long. I'm giving up my maiden name all over again for Rory Turner."

"So I heard."

Bliss smiled as narrowly as her brother had. "Gossip flies."

"The price of being the first family of a county and a state."

Bliss shrugged with grace and impatience. "I'm used to it. Hell, I've added to the fires just to watch my daddy spit and sputter."

Lacey tried not to laugh.

"He turns red and then he turns off the money spigot," Bliss said. Her cleverly painted mouth turned down in a sulky, stubborn line.

"Um" was all Lacey could think of to say.

"Look, I'm really curious about the artist," Bliss said, gesturing toward the painting of the drowning woman.

"So are a lot of people."

Bliss nibbled at her lip, then at her thumb. "Just thought I'd warn you about my father. He really hates gossip and that painting is going to send the gossips into a frenzy."

"What are you talking about?"

"My mother was blond, she wore this bracelet all the time, and she died in our spa at night. Alone. The coroner said it was accidental, drugs and alcohol and hot water. The gossips said it was suicide because her latest lover had left her for a younger woman. And that painting—" Bliss drew in a swift, broken breath. "Daddy's not going to be happy about that. Neither is Ms. Fucking Pure Angelique White."

Lacey said the first thing that came to her mind. "Why?"

"That painting says my mother was killed."

Lacey was too shocked to say anything. It didn't matter. Bliss was still talking.

"And who would know better than the man who did it?" Bliss asked bitterly. "Too bad the bastard didn't sign the painting. There's no statute of limitations on murder."

47

No sooner had Susa shut the door to her bedroom than Ian turned and pulled Lacey into his arms. Instead of giving her a lover's kiss, he just rocked her against his chest.

"Spit it out, darling. What's wrong?"

She buried her face in his chest and hung on. "Nothing."

"Bullshit."

Lacey fought against the indefinable sense of panic that had been growing in her since she'd talked to Bliss. "Talking about it—I can't. It'll make it worse."

"Not talking about it is eating you alive. But that's okay, I'll call sweet little Bliss and ask her what she said to you."

Lacey's head came up so fast she nearly clipped Ian's chin. "How did you know it was her?"

"I was watching you from the stage. I figured it was her or Savoy. Got lucky on the first try."

"You trapped me."

"It's what I'm good at." He kissed her slowly, tenderly. "You look so shattered, it's tearing me apart."

"Don't be nice. I'll start crying and my nose will turn red and start running and . . ."

"I'll let you use my shirt as a hanky."

She made a choked sound that could have been laughter or tears or both together.

He held her and smoothed his cheek against the loose curls of her hair.

"My dad was right," she whispered. "I shouldn't have pushed. People aren't always what you want them to be."

Ian couldn't have argued that if he felt like it, so he just held her and said quietly, "Are we talking about your Grandpa Rainbow?"

She didn't speak for a moment. She didn't have to. Ian could feel the heat of her tears against his neck.

"I'm sorry," she whispered. "I never cry and lately I'm sniveling over everything."

"Hush," he said against her lips. "You lost a home and business, discovered that your grandfather might be a famous forger or a collector with millions in art, or both, and—"

"Bliss's mother was murdered," Lacey cut in starkly.

"*What?*"

"She said my—my—she thinks whoever painted that picture did—did it."

"Judas bleeding Priest."

Ian picked up Lacey, took her into their bedroom, and kicked the door shut. He set her on the bed before he went into the bathroom for a cold washcloth. When he came back out, he gathered her close and put the cloth against her hot tear-wet cheeks. Then he held her until she was calm again.

"Damn," she said. "I don't know where that came from."

He kissed her red nose. "Hearts are unpredictable things."

She smiled crookedly and settled against his weapon harness. "Yeah, so I've heard." *And I'm going to lose my heart to this gentle warrior if I don't watch out.*

"Ready to tell me the whole story?" he asked. "Or do you want to wait for me to pour some really expensive champagne?"

"Champagne?" She laughed raggedly. "Oh, damn, you do know how to appeal to my sense of the absurd. Please, pull the cork."

Ian went to the small refrigerator and pulled out the champagne that the hotel kept stocking for them as though it was mineral water. He ripped off the "Compliments of the Hotel" card, pulled the cork, and licked the champagne that bubbled over his knuckles.

Lacey looked up as he came to the bedside. Her hair was wild, her eyes were huge and dark, her cheeks were both flushed and pale, and her lips trembled. But her hand was steady when she accepted a glass of champagne, and her spine was as straight as the line of her chin.

"To the truth," she said, and touched her glass to his.

He hesitated. "Even if it makes you cry?"

"Dirty little secrets don't go away. They just grow up to be dirty big ones." Lacey took a long breath. "And if that woman was murdered, she deserves better than lies."

"Justice?"

"You say that like you don't believe in it."

Ian smiled rather grimly. "Oh, I believe in it. I just know that it's never free."

She smiled a sad, lopsided kind of smile. "I look at the Death Suite and I can't help thinking that a lot of paying has been done and there's damn little justice to show for it."

"To justice," Ian said, touching his glass to hers.

She waited until he took a small sip, then she set aside her glass, stood up, and put her arms around him in a hug. "Thank you."

He inhaled the heat and faint perfume of her hair. "For what?"

"For not making me feel like an idiot. For believing me. For comforting me. For being an all-around wonderful man."

"That's because you're an all-around wonderful woman."

She laughed softly against his chest. "I'm going to miss you when you leave with Susa tomorrow." *Way too much*. Lacey's smile faded. "Does your work bring you this way often?" Then, quickly, "Damn, I didn't mean to say that."

He held on when she tried to push away. "Lacey, what we have is too good to ignore." He tipped up her chin and kissed her slowly. "I'm not going to let go. How about you?"

"I don't want to let go."

"Then we'll find a way."

They held each other for a long time, until she shifted and felt the hardness beneath his gentleness. Then she smiled and went to work on the weapon harness that was no longer alien to her.

"We don't have to." He kissed her hair. "I can see

how tired you are. The last few days have been hell on you."

"Then bring me a little heaven."

He threaded his fingers into her hair and tilted her head back. The smoky desire in her eyes almost brought him to his knees. "I don't deserve you," he said.

"Too late to wriggle out of it now," she said. "I've got you and I'm not letting go until you beg for mercy."

"Beg, huh?"

"Beg."

"Hands and knees?"

"More like on your back." She pulled off the weapon harness and pushed him onto the bed. "Hands behind your head."

His smile was slow and hot as he put his hands behind his head. "Gonna cuff me?"

"Nope. Gonna trust you."

She straddled him in a soft rush of fabric and perfume. Breathing kisses over his face, she undid his shirt. When she drew her open mouth down his neck and across his chest, his breath hitched. When she nuzzled through the thatch of hair to lick and tease a tight male nipple, he made a sound deep in his throat. For hushed, sultry minutes she stroked and petted and tasted. He tried to tell her how much he enjoyed it, but the words kept coming out as groans.

Then her hands unfastened his pants and he knew he was in trouble. Fingers locked behind his head, he watched helplessly while she pulled out the prize. Her head bent down, her lips brushed, his body jerked.

"Uncuff me," he said hoarsely.

"Mmm" was all she said.

Her mouth circled, her tongue stroked, her teeth nibbled, and then she took him in. His whole body tightened at the hot, teasing suction. Sweat broke out along his spine. His breath came in jerks and left as husky groans.

"Lacey, I—" He made a rough sound that could have been pain or acute pleasure. His hips arched and his breath stopped and he shuddered from head to heels. "Okay. I'm begging. You hear me? On my back. Begging."

"Mmm."

"Now, Lacey. God. *Now.*"

She slid back up him, bit his shoulder, and pulled apart his hands. Before she could take a breath, he flipped her over, stripped off her underwear, wrapped her legs around his neck, and buried his mouth in her. When she could force herself to breathe again, the sounds she made might have been begging, might have been demanding, and neither of them cared which.

The second time she came, he shifted upward until he could push into her. He held her that way, hard and deep, his body tight as a bowstring, sharing all the wild pulses and cries of her release. When she lay spent and languorous, he began to move inside her, starting slow, staying slow, watching her eyes widen as he stroked her higher and then higher still, listening to her breath break, feeling her arch up and abandon herself to him, moving with him until their shared world went red and black and wild.

Still deeply joined with him, she slid down the glittering slope of ecstasy into sleep. He felt the trust, the relaxation, the sweet sigh of intimacy as she turned her face into his neck and slept.

For a long time he simply savored it, and her. It was

a lot better than thinking about all the reasons her grandfather might be obsessed with three particular deaths. And if Ian really worked at it, he didn't think about the most common reason.

A lot of serial killers collected trophies.

48

When Ian was sure that Lacey was deeply asleep, he carefully untangled their bodies and slid out of bed, pausing long enough to enjoy the picture she made with her unruly halo of curls and fancy dress riding well above her beautiful bare legs. He pulled the covers over her, fastened his pants, and padded barefoot through the two suites, checking windows and shoving wedges between hallway doors and frames so that even someone with a security card and a bolt cutter couldn't get inside.

Then he pulled out his cell phone and called Rarities. He was tempted to use Niall's private number, but figured he'd get his head handed to him for calling late on a Saturday night. So he called the front desk instead. Because Rarities had clients all over the world, someone was always manning the phones and checking computers for e-mail.

"Rarities Unlimited, how may I help you?"

"This is Ian Lapstrake. Is Dana or Niall still working?"

"No, sir. One moment, I'll see if any lights are on in their private residences."

Ian waited. One of the good things about his bosses—or the bad, depending on how you looked at it—was that Dana and Niall lived in separate homes on the Rarities Unlimited "campus" overlooking the lights of Los Angeles.

"There are lights on at Niall's house. Should I ring him?"

"Was he in a good mood when he left?"

"I wasn't here, sir."

Ian sighed. The phone person obviously was new. Niall was only in a good mood on Saturdays if he was working in his rose garden.

"Try his house on the normal phone," Ian said. "If it goes four rings, disconnect."

The phone rang once, twice, and then was snatched up before the third ring could end.

"Well?" Niall demanded.

"Sorry to interrupt," Ian said, "but—"

"It's about bloody time," Niall interrupted. "Any news on the robbery?"

"Nothing useful. I'm putting Susa on the Donovan private plane at nine o'clock tomorrow morning."

"You called me at midnight to—"

"And I'll be starting two weeks of vacation at one second after nine tomorrow morning," Ian said. "I didn't want you to be lining up any projects for me."

Silence. Then, "Any particular reason for the rush vacation?"

"Lots of them."

"Any you'd like to share?" Niall asked dryly.

"I have at least three weeks coming to me."

"Four, actually, but it's not like you to give such short notice. What's wrong?"

"You know those paintings that Susa's nuts for?" Ian asked. "The ones that aren't signed?"

"The ones that are going to make a nice dent in our monthly overhead by the time we check them out?" Niall asked.

"Yeah. I got a look at the whole collection. There's a series that Lacey calls the Death Suite."

Niall grunted. "Lovely."

"Wait until you see them. Anyway, we were exhibiting one of them tonight, a blonde being drowned in a spa, when Bliss Forrest told Lacey that the woman in the painting was wearing the same bracelet that belonged to her mother, who died in her spa."

"Murder?" Niall asked sharply.

"Not according to the public knowledge."

"So you're taking a vacation to investigate a murder that didn't happen?"

"It's more complicated than that," Ian said.

"Bloody hell." Then he sighed. "Go on, boyo. I'm sitting down."

"Even though it's not a Rarities problem, I'd like permission to access your computers. I could get the same information out of the county library archives, but it would—"

"Take three times as long," Niall interrupted impatiently. "You have clearance for the computers. Go in through the address I'll leave in your e-mail. Do you have the skill or do you need Research?"

"I hope not. I can't afford your rates."

"Anything else?"

"Just thanks."

"No worries. Susa thinks the sun shines out your arse, which makes us look like geniuses with the Donovan."

The cell phone went dead with Niall's usual lack of ceremony. Ian hesitated, then called his great-uncle in Bakersfield. After a lifetime in law enforcement, Carl Lapstrake's hours were unpredictable. Tonight he must have been up late watching TV, because he answered on the first ring.

"Well, which one of my ten thousand relatives is it this time?" asked a raspy voice.

"Great-nephew Ian. How's it going, Gr'uncle?"

" 'Bout like always this time of year. Tule fog is hanging on. Must have had fifty wrecks on the highways this week."

"Ouch." Driving code-three in the kind of fog that hid the front end of your own squad car was something no cop liked to do, but if you worked in California's Great Central Valley, sooner or later you had to do just that. "Bet you're glad you're retired."

"Some days I like it better than others. What do you want?"

Ian grinned to himself. So much for small talk. His grandfather's brother was famous for being downright curt unless he was feeling talkative. He maintained he was much too old to waste time making nice.

"I've got some questions about Moreno County," Ian said. "Thought maybe you and cousin Chuck could help me out, since you both put in some time in uniform there."

"Long time ago. Hell, gotta be forty years now."

"At least. But you spent ten years down in Moreno County and Chuck spent, what, five?"

"Twelve for me, six for my nephew. What do you need?"

"Some background, mostly. If Moreno County is like the one I grew up in, the local deputies know who's buying, who's lying, who's screwing somebody he shouldn't, that sort of thing. The Moreno County sheriff, Rory Turner, is affable enough, but not real forthcoming, if you know what I mean."

"Rory, huh? Let me think."

While his great-uncle thought, Ian punched the built-in record button on his cell phone. If the old man got going, he was a regular talking encyclopedia.

"Rory, Rory," Carl muttered to himself. "Oh, yeah. Got it. Must be Morley Forrest's son's gofer."

Ian opened his mouth to ask for clarification, but Carl was still talking.

"The Savoy family is always tight with whoever is the county sheriff. Hell, they elected 'em, and a lot of the other county and state officials in the bargain."

"Morley Forrest," Ian said when Carl paused. "Is that Ward Forrest's father?"

"Yeah. Named after Davina's father."

"Davina?"

"Davina Berentson, Morley's wife, a socialite type. Benford Savoy the Second was Morley's real good friend, introduced him to the right people. Berentson was one of 'em. Morley Forrest wasn't even a shirttail cousin to money, but he knew how to be useful. Savoy money got Morley elected sheriff and then DA and then state attorney general. Morley might have been born rough, but nobody ever said that boy was stupid. When he wasn't sheriff, Ward was, and then whoever Ward's handpicked man was. Rory Turner, that's right."

Ian listened hard. If he interrupted to ask where Carl was going with all this, they'd never get there.

"It was real useful to the family while I was there," Carl summarized.

"What was?"

"Having Sheriff Morley Forrest in their pocket."

"Nothing new about wealth and ambitious politicians in bed together," Ian said. "Common as house dust."

"Yeah, well, the Savoy family worked it like a cow at milking time. When Three—that's the Savoy son—drove off a ranch cliff late one night, the coroner, who was also the sheriff, didn't mention the fact that Three was higher than a kite when he died. 'Mechanical failure' was tagged as the cause of the accident."

"You're saying there wasn't much of an investigation."

"Much? Shit, boy, there wasn't no investigation to speak of. Worst police work I ever saw. Same thing when some artist died a few days later on the ranch. The guy had a reputation as a drinker, a womanizer, and was one of Three's pals."

"Artist? He died on the ranch?"

"Yeah. He had a shack or a studio there."

"Would the artist's name be Lewis Marten?" Ian asked.

"Sounds about right. I can check."

"Don't bother. What happened with the artist?"

"According to the investigation, he was drinking and painting and smoking. Passed out and the place burned to ash, along with himself. Nobody claimed what was left, so the Savoy widow stepped up and did the decent thing and buried the remains."

"This was, what, a couple days after Three died?" Ian asked.

"Yeah."

"Must have been pretty hard on the widow, two deaths in such a short time."

"If gossip is true, it was damned hard on her. Not losing her husband particularly—hell, they never got along worth spit—but losing the artist. Rumor had it that he was her lover before she married. Some people say he was her lover after, too."

Ian's eyebrows lifted. Nothing like a little adultery to piss a man off enough to think about violence. "How did Three feel about that?"

"Didn't much care. He was one of them men who only liked professional gals."

"Hookers?"

"As ever was," Carl said, chuckling hoarsely. " 'Course, the amount he drank, it probably took a pro to get him up to the mark. That man was a nonstop party. Spent money hand over fist on his hangers-on."

"But Three didn't mind if his wife got some sex on the side?"

"Nope. The gossips were real disappointed there."

"So there wouldn't have been any reason to dump good old Three over a cliff to make way for another husband?"

"Widow never remarried," Carl said.

"Well, there goes that theory. How about lovers?"

"None that lasted. Widow Savoy was real close to Morley Forrest, though. Made him her adviser. Some folks talked, but some folks have nothing to do except work their tongues."

"You don't think she was Morley's lover?" Ian asked.

"Hell, nobody loved that son of a bitch. I think she was almost scared of him. He'd say 'Jump,' and she jumped. So did a lot of people. Morley was the kind of man even the devil would tiptoe around. Righteous, churchgoing, harder than Lucifer, and twice as ambitious. Even when Three was alive, Morley pretty much ran the county and the Savoy family money."

"Other than two badly investigated society accidents, anything else wrong with the local deputies back then?"

"Three."

"Three Savoy?"

"Three accidents. A few days before Gem Savoy announced her engagement to Ward Forrest, the old matriarch—the wife of the first Benford Savoy—got in a snit and raced off on her favorite hunter like she was sixteen instead of seventy-six. Took one jump too many and broke her skinny neck."

"Who was she arguing with?"

"Her daughter-in-law, who was pushing for Gem Savoy—that would be Three's daughter—to marry Ward Forrest, Morley's son. The old lady felt the Forrests were beneath the Savoys, even though she'd depended on Morley since her own husband had died in a hunting accident."

Ian frowned. "A hunting accident?"

"It was before my time. Bunch of drunks shooting pheasant. Benford the Second tripped and blew his fool head off. Stupid to mix booze and shotguns, but fools do it every year and some of 'em get hurt."

"Seems like the Savoys have had a lot of bad luck with booze."

"The newspapers and gossips call it the Savoy Curse. I call it stupidity. Any cop can tell you that booze or drugs cause damn near a hundred percent of the 'bad luck' cops get paid to clean up after."

Ian didn't disagree. It was one of the reasons he no longer worked for city, county, state, or federal police. He'd been real tired of cleaning up after stupid drunks who weren't a hell of a lot smarter when they woke up sober in a cell where the cement floor was covered with puke on good nights and shit on the rest of them.

"Any other dirt on the Moreno County cops?" Ian asked.

"Oh, the usual. A handful of local police taking protection money, winking at gambling and prostitution, after-hours drinking, that kind of thing."

"Sounds pretty normal. Not pretty, just normal. So why did you and Chuck quit the department within a few days of each other and move back to Bakersfield?"

There was such a long pause that Ian thought he wasn't going to get an answer to his question. In the background he could hear a commercial for denture cleaner on Carl's TV. The old man was hard of hearing and wouldn't admit it, so his TV was loud enough to scare sheep. Fortunately he lived out in the countryside with cattle, and they didn't give a damn.

"I was on duty when Three and the artist died," Carl said finally. "I was new to the county and I'd been butting heads with one of the other deputies over the correct way to investigate an unattended death. Morley came in, booted me out, and got on with it. Same thing on the artist's death. If it happened on Savoy Ranch, it was Morley's. He did the investigation, wrote the reports, and if you didn't like it you could find another job."

"Again, not pretty but normal," Ian said. "Money buys a lot of special attention."

"Yeah, well, twelve years later I was on duty the afternoon the older Mrs. Savoy died. I was doing the routine death scene investigation and things weren't adding up real well."

"What do you mean?"

"I was following the horse's tracks. It spooked, went sideways about five feet, like something had jumped out from a bush, except that the ground was swept clean. There was some broken shrubbery farther on where the old woman landed, got to her hands and knees, stood, walked about ten feet, and then fell."

"Yet she died of a broken neck?" Ian asked.

"That's what the coroner's report said."

"I can't see her getting up and wandering around with a broken neck."

"Neither could I, and I said so," Carl muttered. "Sheriff told me he'd seen stranger things fighting his way through the South Pacific during the war."

Ian chewed on that for a minute. Again, it wasn't something he could argue with—during times of extreme adrenaline, people sometimes performed feats that could only be called miraculous.

"What about other tracks?"

"Everybody with feet tramped around the scene. Anyway, I didn't find any human tracks besides hers. The ground was real clean."

"You think somebody tidied it up?"

"Could be," Carl said. "The sheriff wasn't much impressed by the idea. It was windy, the ground was dry. Never prove it either way now."

"Who found her?"

"Some ranch hand. Must've scared him to death. He went back to Mexico the next day."

"Did he talk with the sheriff first?" Ian asked.

"That's what the report says."

"What do *you* say?"

Again there was a pause so long that Ian wondered if Carl was going to answer. This time the TV was selling adult diapers and Caribbean cruises. Ian wondered if his great-uncle was watching reruns of *The Love Boat*.

"I didn't want any part of it," Carl said. "None of it. Not the investigation that was a joke, not the pampering of the Savoy family. I'd had a gut full of the whole damn shootin' match."

"What about Gem Savoy Forrest's death?" Ian asked.

"I was long gone by then."

"No contacts in the sheriff's department when it happened?"

"What are you after?" Carl asked.

"There's a painting of a woman being murdered in a spa. The woman is a blonde. The bracelet she's wearing resembles one that once belonged to Gem Savoy, who died about nine years ago in her spa."

"Shee-it. Where'd the painting come from?"

"Legacy from a young woman's grandfather."

"Any connection to the Savoys?" Carl asked.

"No. Just a suggestion that whoever painted it could be the killer."

"Is the case still open?"

"It was ruled as an accidental death—prescription drugs, alcohol, and too much hot water," Ian said. "An accident. Happens all the time among the rich and bored."

"Yeah, it sure does. Where do you fit in?"

"I'm . . ." Ian's voice died. The personal part of it

was most important but hardest to explain. "The young woman, the one who inherited the painting?"

"Yeah?"

"She wants to know how it came to be painted, and why."

"Boy, you know you're one of my favorite relatives."

Ian waited. When his great-uncle started talking about family, it meant things were serious.

"I'm going to tell you the same thing I told Chuck forty years ago. There's something *wrong* in Moreno County. Too many deaths. Not enough police work. Ain't nothing changed. Stay away from it, boy."

Ian thought about Lacey. "I can't."

"Then clean your gun and watch your back."

49

Struggling not to yawn after too many hours spent querying Rarities computer files and worrying about Carl's warning, Ian was about cross-eyed. If he read one more breathless account of the Savoy Curse, he was going to puke. If there was any hint, any suspicion, any rumor of murder it hadn't made print. Suicide, sure, it was between the lines in every story about Gem Savoy Forrest's death.

Murder?

Never heard of it.

So he'd taken it from another direction—finding out more about Lacey's grandfather. Since he hadn't been a powerful scion of a drunken family, chances were good that any dirt on him would have made it into public reports.

Wrong again.

Either the man was as clean as angel crap or he'd never been caught dirty by anyone who left a record.

Which was another problem. Official records dealing with David No-Middle-Name Quinn didn't appear until the guy had to be at least forty. Granted, the time before computers wasn't as easy to access as after, but there still should have been something about David NMN Quinn.

Burying another yawn, Ian waited while Susa and Lacey hugged with real warmth, obviously reluctant to say good-bye. He had a fistful of old-fashioned notes on a notepad in his denim jacket and a head full of possibilities that went nowhere.

Like my investigation of David NMN Quinn. No matter how he tickled the data or the questions, everything leading back into the past ended up at a blank wall. *Or maybe it's just my mind that's blank.*

Ian shifted impatiently. He wasn't a skilled computer researcher, but he should have been able to get routine things like date of birth, date of death, cause of death, driver's license, tax records, and all the other numbers that made up a citizen's life.

I'll try again tonight. The stuff's there. I'm just thickheaded right now.

Susa's luggage—one small suitcase and a trunk of painting supplies—was being trundled across the apron toward the private plane, but neither woman was in a hurry to leave the other.

"I want to know the instant you find out anything about those paintings," Susa said, her eyes intent on Lacey.

"Since you're paying Rarities, I'm sure you'll be the first to hear," Lacey said, smiling crookedly.

"That's not the way they work," Susa said. "The art is their first responsibility, not the person paying the bills or the one who owns whatever is being investigated. It's all in the papers you signed this morning giving them permission to examine the paintings."

Lacey's smile faded. She hadn't liked the part in the contract that made it clear that the truth, rather than what she might *want* the truth to be, was the sole objective of the Rarities personnel. "Yeah, that part was painfully clear. I didn't know it applied to the guy paying the bills, too."

"It does," Susa said ruefully.

"Always, as more than one client has found to their sorrow," Ian said to Lacey. "On the other hand, it means that a vetting by Rarities adds a lot of value to whatever passes the tests."

Lacey shrugged. "Value isn't the point."

"It should be," Ian said. "The insurance company is going to use the arson investigator's preliminary report to hold up payment until it's clear whether the fire was accidental or not, and if not, who set it." Ian felt bad about adding to the problem by mentioning the paraffin-log chunks he'd seen, but there hadn't been any help for it. The woo-woo lady might have been a scammer and a scuffler and a drunk, but she hadn't deserved to be roasted in her bed. "You'll need every dime to put your shop back together. Selling one of those paintings could mean a lot to you."

"I know. It's just . . ." Lacey's mouth flattened. "It's so damned ugly. If the woman in the painting was really murdered, I don't want to make money from it."

"So sell a landscape to me," Susa said. "No bad juju attached to them, right?"

"I'd be happy to give you one," Lacey said instantly, "but I won't sell you one."

Susa's grin said *Gotcha*. "Okay, but only if you'll accept a painting of mine in return."

Lacey's mouth fell open. "I couldn't. Yours are much more valuable."

"That's the deal. Take it or leave it. And if you leave it, I'll cry, because I've always wanted a Lewis Marten painting—or one that draws me as strongly as his paintings," she said before Lacey could object that the canvases she owned weren't really by Marten. "Art is where you find it, not who signs it."

Lacey hugged Susa again. "I shouldn't," she said, "but I'm going to take advantage of your incredibly generous offer."

"Good." Reluctantly she let go of Lacey. "I've got to run. The pilot has a takeoff slot. If we miss it, we have to wait around hours for another one." She stood on tiptoe to hug Ian and said too softly for Lacey to hear, "I don't have a good feeling about this. Be very, very careful."

"You been talking to my great-uncle?" he said against her ear.

"More like my ancestors talking to me. I mean it, Ian. Something is . . . *wrong*."

"I hear you."

She looked into his dark, steady eyes and knew that he believed her. "Bring Lacey up to Seattle to select her painting," Susa said in a normal tone of voice. "The Donovan should meet her."

Ian lifted his eyebrows. "Any particular reason?"

"If you're foolish enough to let her slip through your fingers, I have two unmarried sons." She winked at Lacey. "You're too old to adopt, but I'm determined not to lose you. Daughters are so very hard to find."

With a speed that made people used to commercial-airline schedules blink, Susa was aboard the idling plane and it was taxiing to the run-up area for its final check. Minutes later it gave a throaty howl, gathered speed rapidly, and leaped into the air.

Ian was on the phone to Rarities before the wheels tucked into the plane's sleek underbelly. "Tell Niall to stop the clock on the Donovan client," he said to the desk. "Susa is on her way home and I'm on vacation."

He disconnected and looked at Lacey. He didn't have a happy feeling about anything in the past few days except meeting her. He sure as hell didn't want to see her hurt anymore. Which meant he had to distract her, get her up to her eyebrows in the mundane details of living, and then slide off to investigate her dear departed Grandpa Rainbow, who looked to be good for three murders.

"Now what?" Lacey asked.

"Let's take another go at those paintings before we send them to Rarities."

"And then what?"

"Tomorrow we'll kick butt at the insurance company to get an adjuster out to your shop," Ian said, "and line up a contractor to put the place back together for you. Always assuming that the arson team is finished poking around, of course."

"Doesn't sound like much of a vacation for you."

He gave her a slow smile and threw an arm around her shoulders. "Oh, I'll think of something."

And the first thing he would work on was a way to keep her safe. He didn't need Susa's and his great-uncle's warnings to know that it could get ugly when he started digging up old graves.

50

Lacey leaned out to punch in her code, waited for the arm to lift, and drove Ian's truck through the wide gates of the storage area. There were more people around today, everyone from middle-aged men stripping old cars and rebuilding them for the vintage-car circuit to families storing junk until they finally decided that Aunt Effie's old furniture wasn't worth the monthly fee to keep it.

"You have any special place in mind to park?" Lacey asked, remembering when he'd wanted the truck hidden from the road.

"Close." He looked in the rearview mirror. "There's wrapping gear in the back."

"Anyone following?"

He frowned and told half of the truth. "Hard to be sure."

But he was. He'd seen the unmarked car following them to the airport. Now the car was hanging way back because there wasn't any need to work in close. Tailing an old truck on a sunny Sunday morning highway was a piece of cake. Getting away from the deputies again would be about as likely as hiding an elephant in an ashtray.

"Susa's gone," Lacey said, turning toward Ian. "Why would the sheriff care what we do?"

"Because he'd like to stick me with the theft of Susa's paintings."

"What? That's ridiculous!"

"You know it and I know it, but look at things his way. It was an inside job. His security cops were on the inside. So was I. Guess who he'd rather tag for jail time?"

"That's crap."

"A lot of cop work is crap."

"He's more likely to have stolen them than you," Lacey muttered.

"I'll be sure to tell him the next time I see him."

Lacey backed the truck into a parking space right next to her unit. Carrying armloads of tape and packing material, they lifted up the front door of the storage area and looked around.

The interior of the storage room hadn't changed. Paintings were still stacked in racks and leaning against various surfaces in a way that looked haphazard yet still managed to keep the surface of each canvas from rubbing against anything.

Ian pulled out the digital camera he'd purchased and the portable computer he'd bought to use along with it. "Let's photograph, then wrap them."

Lacey was reaching for the closest painting—another version of the drowning pool—when Ian stopped her.

"We'll do the dark ones last," Ian said. "I want to look at them all together in good light before we wrap them up."

"Then stack them to one side so we have room to pack the rest."

He started collecting the various scenes of violence and set them out of the way. As he did, he couldn't help studying them. They were alike, yet different. Sometimes the numbers on the front were painted in red, sometimes not; sometimes the numbers were circled, sometimes not; but the numbers themselves were the same on each of the drowning pool canvases.

"Did you ever see your grandfather paint one of these?" Ian asked.

"No. Hand me that roll of bubble wrap, okay?"

"Let me photograph the painting first."

She waited while he photographed, then she began wrapping. He photographed another painting while she worked, then set aside the camera long enough to tape up what she'd already wrapped while she went to work on the canvas he'd just photographed.

"I'm only going to tape once around each way," he said, "unless you really want the mummy thing."

"Mummy thing?" Lacey looked up from the canvas she was rolling into a sheet of bubble wrap. "Oh, the way I brought the paintings for Susa to look at. No need for that now. I was just worried about the crowds of people pushing and shoving."

For a time the only sounds inside the unit were the rustle of plastic wrap and the soft ripping hiss when Ian stripped tape off a roll. Shouts, laughter, and the occasional curse drifted in from the alley out front, where people shoved things from car trunks into overstuffed units. With part of his attention, Ian listened to the outside sounds in the same way a jungle animal listens to its surroundings—just another way to keep track of what was happening behind his back.

Most of Ian's attention was on the numbers on the paintings. He kept thinking they should mean something, have some logic to explain their presence, like the numbers written on the back of the canvases indicating that each was part of a series.

No inspiration came as he wrapped paintings for shipment to Rarities. He and Lacey would rent a big truck and drive the paintings to L.A. as soon as they could take the time away from putting her shop back together.

But first they were going to move the paintings to a different storage unit, one at the far end of the complex. Shayla Carlyle's brother-in-law had been curious about why the switch was necessary, and happy to settle for cash instead of answers as to why the unit would be rented to Mark Jones instead of Shayla or Lacey. Lacey was curious, too, but Ian just had shrugged and said, "Humor me."

Ian and Lacey quickly found a rhythm: after he photographed a canvas, she would wrap, tape and stack it to one side while he photographed another. When his truck was full, he drove down the row and around the corner to the new unit and stacked the canvases inside. A lot faster than he would have believed, the storage unit was down to the Death Suite. With the sun pouring through the open door, the paintings looked darker than ever. And oddly more intense, more detailed.

"It's a shame Susa didn't see these in the daytime," Lacey said. "I'd forgotten how vivid the contrasts are in strong light."

"Vivid." He shook his head. "There's a nice, neutral word."

"Would you prefer chiaroscuro?"

He smiled, but it quickly faded. "Do you agree with Susa that a man could have painted these all at once?"

"Each subject at a different time but all the same subject at once—wreck, house, pool?"

"Yeah."

"I've gone on a few painting sprees in my time, but nothing this epic. Maybe I just wasn't feeling the emotions as intensely."

Working swiftly, Ian separated the paintings into the three distinct subjects: wreck, drowning, fire. "I don't have a trained eye, but it seems odd that all these were done at once."

"Why?"

"Well, even assuming that he was stoked on drugs or some kind of manic high"—*because he'd just murdered someone*, Ian added to himself—"why would he treat the numbers differently on the same subject? Circled in red here"—he pointed to the canvas—"painted in red and circled in black there, black and black there, all red there, and so on."

Lacey walked closer. She'd noticed the small differences before, but hadn't thought much of them. The similarity of the subject matter overwhelmed everything else. Then there was the fact that she really hadn't spent much time looking at the darker paintings. They'd simply made her too uncomfortable.

They still did.

Tough, she told herself. *Pretend a stranger painted them.*

Shoving aside the mental picture of her beloved Grandpa Rainbow whistling tunelessly as he painted death after death, she squatted on her heels in front of the paintings of the car wreck. There were subtle differences among the canvases, shades of gold and orange and hues of darkness that weren't the same from painting to painting.

"If he painted these wrecks all at once," she said slowly, "there are two ways he could have gone at it. Decorator-art style or—"

"What's that?" Ian interrupted.

"You start with a batch of prepared canvases, paint one aspect of each subject—rocks or trees or beach or whatever—in the same place on each canvas with the same color of paint, then go on to the next element of the landscape, and then the next, moving from canvas to canvas so that all of them are always at the same stage of painting. Saves all kinds of time on mixing paints, and each canvas is, technically, original art, though they're actually one short step up from prints."

"Said original oil painting is then sold to decorators at inflated prices for their clients' homes or businesses," Ian said.

"Right. It's the sort of thing that gave figurative painting a bad name. Then"—Lacey grinned slyly—"modern art became so popular that motels started using it. Mortified a lot of academics."

"So you think these paintings are the result of that kind of assembly-line art?"

"No. Look at the oranges and yellows and shadows in these paintings. Granddad made his own paints from scratch. He bought the lead white for priming the canvas, but after that he ground his own pigment and combined it with turpentine and oil himself. The more pigment and the less turpentine, the more intense the color."

Ian made an encouraging sound.

"The point is," she said, looking narrowly at the paintings of the burning wreck, "if he was doing the decorator thing, all the shades of the same colors would be nearly equal because they would have come from the same batch of paint."

"Makes sense."

"But these aren't the same shades from canvas to canvas. Look at the orange in this one and in this one and in this," she said, pointing quickly. "Different shades of the same color to depict the same part of each painting. If they'd been painted at the same time, they'd be the same shade of orange all the way across."

Ian looked thoughtfully at the paintings. "What you're telling me is that your grandfather's homemade paints were like commercial dye lots."

"Exactly."

"Okay. These probably weren't painted all at the same time," Ian agreed. "Then why do they have the same numbers on the front?"

Lacey didn't answer. Head tilted slightly to one side, she studied the paintings. After a moment she said almost absently, "Could you move all the drowning ones aside?"

He wondered why but didn't ask. He just moved paintings and watched her. She was frowning. In the clean winter sunlight, her eyes glowed like fine, tawny topaz. Slowly she began sorting the remaining paintings without regard to subject.

"Would it help to think out loud?" he asked softly.

"The technique is different in the drowning paintings," she said after a moment. "Thicker paint. More use of the palette knife. More paint, period. None of the ground shows through anywhere. There's texture in the wreck and the fire, but it's not as . . . heavy."

"And they all show some form of death at night, so the different technique isn't a matter of trying to make a statement about the subject, is that it?"

Without looking away, she smiled. "Underneath the shoulders and gun, you're one bright man."

"You're just figuring that out?"

"Just saying it out loud. I figured it out about ten seconds after we met. Scary combination—brains and muscle. Then you smiled. It was all over then, no chance to run, and running was the last thing on my stunned little mind."

Grinning, he tugged lightly at one of her rebellious curls. "So why would your grandfather change technique?"

"Lots of reasons. Some artists do it deliberately, as a kind of academic exercise. But Grandfather wasn't academically trained. Self-taught all the way. The changes that came in his painting were a natural outgrowth of time and experience."

All of a sudden, Ian understood. "You think you can date the canvases by their technique?"

Lacey just kept shuffling paintings like cards whose numbers only she could read. The pouring side light made it easy. Differences in texture and technique leaped out like boulders. Between the fire paintings there were subtle differences in how thoroughly he covered the canvas, which brushes were favored and then not employed again, and whether or not he used the end of the brush to draw lines in colors; the possibilities for changing technique were infinite, but humans tended to settle into patterns that changed only slowly.

While she worked she kept glancing over to the drowning paintings, but she didn't reach for any of them. They were simply from another period in his artistic development.

Finally all the fire paintings were lined up to Lacey's satisfaction, or at least as much satisfaction as she was going to get right now. She glanced at the drowning pool canvases and again left them out of the lineup.

"It's not perfect," she said, "but it's the best I can do without spending hours at it. Now see if the numbers on the back of each painting make some kind of order the way I've lined them up. I'm betting that the farther down the row you go, the closer the match in numerical sequence will be."

Ian started at the far end and worked back to Lacey. "You're right," he said simply. "How did you do it?"

"Technique. If I had all his paintings, I might be able to link the changes in technique across the years he painted." She paused, then smiled crookedly. "More likely, I'd get impossibly confused. Human beings don't develop in linear fashion, and artists are less linear than most. Anyway, the fire canvases were painted earlier than the water canvases. Probably quite a bit earlier. Decades, maybe."

"What makes you say that?"

"When Granddad painted with me a few years ago, his technique was the same as in the water paintings. The eucalyptus painting that was stolen was created with thinner paints, so thin that the ground showed through in places. Not a fault, just a way of making the colors look transparent. The strokes are longer in the drowning paintings, too. More curved. In the fire paintings the strokes are narrower, more angular, more like the eucalyptus. There's more blending of color layers in the fire paintings, a lot less in the drowning."

"Same artist?" Ian asked sharply.

"Oh, yes."

"You're certain?"

"Very. He might have changed the thickness of the paint or the angle of the stroke through the years, but the strokes themselves have the same . . . rhythm, I guess. They start very firmly and end with almost a sigh. Even the drowning pool. It gives an unmistakable feeling of movement to the paintings that's uniquely his. My strokes begin light, thicken, and end with a swirl. Just the way I do things, I guess, but it gives a 'feel' to my paintings that is uniquely mine. Susa . . . Susa's strokes are a graceful slow-motion explosion of energy, and always have been no matter how different the resulting paintings might be."

"Both style and technique," Ian said.

Lacey nodded. "Unfortunately, it's only a way to date canvases in relation to other canvases. I can say one was probably painted before or after the other, but that's all. Granddad didn't leave a journal saying 'Today, on nine October nineteen eighty-seven, I decided to use the palette knife more.' "

"Interesting. You reversed the day and month."

She made a questioning noise, but it was the drowning pool paintings she was looking at, not Ian.

Scream Bloody Murder.

"You said nine October instead of October ninth," Ian explained.

"Hangover from Grandfather," Lacey said absently. "Like separating date and month and year with a period instead of a slash or putting a bar through sevens and Z's—his way of being classy without a university degree."

Ian didn't say anything. He was too busy digging up the notes he'd taken the night before. He flipped through them quickly. Benford Savoy III had died on June second. Lewis Marten had died on June fourth.

2.6

4.6

Pieces of the puzzle he really didn't want to fall into place fell there anyway. If he hadn't been so worried about how any investigation would affect Lacey, he probably would have seen it sooner.

"What?" Lacey asked, looking up at Ian.

Instead of answering, he kept flipping pages, hoping he was wrong. He wasn't. Gem Savoy had died on February ninth. 9.2 Just like the numbers painted across every version of the drowning pool.

"Ian?" Lacey came to her feet. "What is it?"

"The numbers on the front of each painting are death dates." He pointed to the car wreck. "Three Savoy on June second. Marten on June fourth. And then, almost forty years later, Gem Savoy died on—"

"February ninth," Lacey cut in, looking at the drowning pool canvases. "Murdered."

There's something wrong *in Moreno County. Too many deaths. Not enough police work. Ain't nothing changed. Stay away from it, boy.*

But Ian hadn't.

Digging up old graves was bad enough. Digging up old, buried murders was much worse—especially

when the more pieces fell into place, the more holes in
the puzzle he could see. But there was no help for it. It
was too late to stop digging now.

All he could hope was that he dug up the truth before it burned them alive.

"Lacey? How did your grandfather die?"

51

Bliss stood behind Rory, trying to knead the knots out of his neck and shoulders.

"What was that call about?" she asked.

"A tail. Subject spent some time in a storage yard, then got on the freeway. They just crossed the county line, headed east in an old SUV."

She paused. "Is this something to do with the hotel robbery?"

"It sure as hell would be nice. But there wasn't anything big enough to be stolen paintings in Lapstrake's SUV, and there wasn't any place to hide them."

"Doesn't sound very hopeful," Bliss said.

Rory shrugged and expected to hear his shoulders creak. "I've gone through the files of every one of the security guards who worked at the hotel, plus the guys who installed the electronic lock-card system at the hotel. Nothing popped. Ex-cops, ex-military, nothing but good recommendations in their files and no sign of anything else in the last five years."

"What about Lapstrake?"

"On paper, he's a fucking saint."

"Now there's an image."

Rory laughed and pulled Bliss into his lap for a quick, hard kiss.

"The problem is," he said, "if it's not Lapstrake, I'm shit out of luck when it comes to leads."

Bliss nuzzled his neck. "Do you think he's stupid enough, or arrogant enough, to work for Rarities, steal Susa Donovan's paintings, and drive off with them in his own truck while being followed by your deputies?"

"That's what working inside is all about—arrogance. Nobody expects the guard to be the crook."

"Good thing you're on the right side of the law." She nipped his neck.

"Why?"

"God knows you're arrogant enough to steal elevators in broad daylight."

"I'd have to be to marry you."

The kiss he gave her took her mind off the problem of inside or outside or anything at all except getting closer to him. She could hardly believe she was married again. To Rory Turner.

Again.

He was right. It took attitude. That's what turned her on in a man. Brass balls and the arrogance to make them clang.

But damn, it made them hard to live with.

52

Mother is all excited that I'm bringing a man home for Sunday dinner," Lacey said gloomily. "I told her it was more or less business, but . . ." She sighed and shrugged at the same time.

"Are you trying to say that grilled Lapstrake will be on the menu?" Ian asked, smiling.

She sighed. "Yeah. Oh, they'll be polite about the grilling." *I hope.* "But they'll want to know which of your ancestors came over on the *Mayflower* and is your mother a Daughter of the American Revolution and that sort of stuff."

"None and no. There. Wasn't that quick and painless?"

Lacey watched him as he drove bumper to bumper at seventy miles an hour with all the rest of the southern California lemmings on their way back from a Sunday outing.

"Not even a genuine horse thief hung from the old oak tree?" she asked after a few moments.

Before he answered, Ian eased through several lanes of traffic to take an off-ramp that headed up toward the expensive hills of Pasadena.

"Oh, I've got a few horse thieves in my background," he said. "When Lapstrakes weren't fishing and farming, they sort of alternated between being the cops and the robbers. Some of them were both. Made for interesting family reunions."

She saw both the humor and the acceptance in his expression. "You really don't mind about Mom and Dad, do you? Like you didn't mind when the deputies pulled us over just short of the Moreno County line and took a good look at the inside of the truck."

"It beat having them follow us up to your parents' front door."

Lacey didn't know whether to cringe or laugh at the idea of arriving home for dinner with an unmarked police vehicle right behind. And there would be no way to hide the official tail on her parents' manicured, sweeping drive.

"God, Mother would plotz."

"Sounds entertaining."

"It wouldn't be. Guaranteed."

He gave Lacey a quick sideways glance. "Don't worry, darling. I'll be on my best meeting-the-parents behavior."

"Have you done a lot of it?"

"What?"

"Meeting parents," Lacey said.

"Nope. Never been married or even engaged. How about you?"

"The same."

"Want to try it?"

She blinked. "Excuse me?"

"Getting engaged and married."

"Frankly, the whole thing scares the hell out of me."

"Me, too. Good thing we're old enough to live together without the approval of parental units." He grinned at her and then turned his attention back to driving. "How old was your grandfather when he disappeared in the desert?"

Lacey switched conversational gears as fast as Ian had. "He would have been eighty-eight last year."

"Healthy?"

"A regular poster boy for the geriatric set. Had most of his teeth and all of his wits. Said both his parents had lived to be a spry one hundred and he planned on doing at least that well."

"When you inherited the paintings, did you get anything else of his? Other than his favorite pliers?" Ian added quickly, remembering.

"Paint boxes, brushes, easels, even his old painting tables and a chair. I still use them. Then there's some other stuff in the carriage house at my parents' place. That's where he lived when he wasn't roving around, painting. I haven't had the heart to go through it. I don't need mementos of him. I have my memories and his paintings."

"So he gave you tables, huh?" Ian remembered the night he'd set Lacey's warm, naked butt on a paint table. "Any particular one?"

She gave him a sideways glance that said she knew just what he was thinking. "Not that one. It wouldn't have survived that kind of use."

He turned up the sweeping drive toward the stately brick home on its huge lot. As he pulled to a stop in front of the double doors with their heavy iron decorations, he turned toward her with a slow smile. "Did I ever tell you how cute your butt is covered with bright paint?"

Lacey knew she was blushing. "Of all the things to tell me when my parents are opening the front door." Then she laughed out loud. She couldn't help it. The idea of her butt looking like a piece of performance art was too funny to bury in silence. "You looked pretty cute yourself. Bet you had the only purple-eyed pocket snake in captivity."

"Don't forget the green racing stripes."

"I'll *never* forget the green racing stripes." Lacey was still laughing when she got out of the car.

Dottie Quinn couldn't help smiling at the picture her grinning daughter made in a cream silk shirt, camel slacks, and black cashmere jacket. So much better than her usual wretched paint-stained jeans and flea-market coats. Then the late afternoon sun flashed on a ridiculous piece of sixties beaded sun-face jewelry that totally ruined the ensemble. Dottie sighed, wondering how that particular piece of junk had survived the fire. Then she remembered that the shop's overstock items were kept in storage. No doubt the tawdry necklace came from there.

"Lacey, you look wonderful," Dottie said, ignoring her daughter's ratty sandals.

"I should. You handpicked my outfit." But Lacey hugged her mother with enthusiasm. Neither of them could help their differences; they could only accept them and move on. "It was lovely of you to fix dinner for us on such short notice."

Brody came down the steps to shake Ian's hand.

"Are you kidding? You saved me from another night of tuna surprise."

"Brody!" Dottie said, horrified. "I've *never* served you *anything* called that."

"Now that's a shame," Ian said, smiling. "All my relatives swap recipes for tuna surprise. I was wondering what the Pasadena version tasted like."

Lacey shot him a warning look.

He winked. Then he gave Dottie the smile that made people forget all the reasons why they thought they shouldn't trust him.

All through dinner and cleanup afterward, Lacey watched in bemusement as Ian charmed her parents into forgetting that he wore a gun under his cheerfully unfashionable sport coat and didn't have any ancestors worth painting and hanging on the wall. She also noticed that each time he brought up the subject of her grandfather, her parents changed the subject without really saying much of anything about David Quinn. She was sure that Ian noticed it, too.

"Did you always live in Pasadena?" Ian asked Brody.

"I have vague memories of living in Antelope Valley as a child, but otherwise I've always lived in Pasadena. Dottie and I bought this place after Lacey was born."

Ian's eyebrows went up. "I should have gone into law instead of law enforcement."

Brody looked uncomfortable. So did Dottie.

"Grandfather helped," Lacey said.

Her parents stared at her.

"Who told you that?" Brody asked.

"Grandfather. I was about five. You and he had just had a shouting match and I was crying in my room, afraid that Grandpa Rainbow would go away and never come back. He found me in my room, set me on his shoulders, and told me not to worry, he owned the house so he wasn't going anywhere he didn't want to."

"Sounds like being an artist paid pretty well," Ian said casually.

Dottie gave her husband a worried glance.

"Well enough," Brody said. "Who do you think will win the Super Bowl?"

Ian looked past Dottie to Lacey. "Sorry, darling."

"I didn't think we drove all this way for small talk and a big dinner. Go ahead," she said, though she suspected he would have anyway.

He gave her a smile, a different one, gentle and sad and admiring all at once.

"I wish I'd come here just as Lacey's . . . beau," he said to her parents, remembering his great-grandmother talking about her youth, when girls had beaux instead of boy toys and roommates. "But Lacey and I came here to find out more about her grandfather."

Dottie's smile vanished. "He's dead. That's all anyone needs to know."

Brody picked up his wife's clenched hand and put it between his own. "It's all right, honey. I've already withdrawn my name from the judge pool, remember?"

She looked even more grim. "It's so damned unfair. You always—"

"It's all right," he interrupted. "Part of me was always trying to overcome my father's lack of scruples. I don't have to be a judge to prove that I'm not what my father was. Besides, now we get to travel."

Slowly her fingers relaxed and she returned his smile. For a moment she looked years younger. "Paris first?"

"Then London, Rome, and every other place on

your list. Our list," he corrected. "First the cities, then the golf."

When Lacey's parents faced Ian, it was as a unit. They weren't happy about the compromise life had forced on them, but they weren't going to waste time and energy fighting it.

"My father was an art forger," Brody said bluntly. "Lewis Marten was his specialty. Ever since I figured out what was going on, I've known the shit would hit the fan someday. Still, for Dottie's sake, I'd like to keep it as quiet as possible. My wife's family . . . well, they wouldn't accept the scandal very well. Neither would our other daughters. They really take after their maternal grandmother, who regularly lectured the minister on his moral duties."

Lacey winced. She didn't like to think which grandparent *she* took after. No doubt that was one of the reasons she'd been so reluctant to see the truth in her grandfather's paintings.

"Don't even think it," Ian said coolly. "Any of you. Lacey is as clean and honest as sunshine. Just because she can paint doesn't mean she's some kind of social slime." He took her hand. "You hear me, darling? What our family was or wasn't has an effect on us, but it sure as hell isn't chiseled in stone unless we want it to be. Otherwise I'd be serving life for murder like one of my cousins, or be living in Guatemala with the poorest of the poor like another of my cousins, a priest. Two brothers, and different as night and day."

Lacey moved closer to Ian on the couch and threaded her fingers through his.

Dottie's chin came up in a gesture that reminded Ian of Lacey. "I never so much as *hinted* that Lacey wasn't honest. She's our daughter and we love her."

"I know that, or I'd have chucked you out the hotel room the first time I met you."

"You can be a very rude man."

"Yes, ma'am." He smiled slowly. "But I love your daughter and she's getting around to loving me, so you'll have a long time to get used to my manners."

Lacey looked stunned. Then she smiled—a slow, wide reflection of Ian's smile.

Dottie gave both of them a startled look. Then the older woman let out a long breath. "Well, I always knew it wouldn't be a doctor or a lawyer. At least he's quick and hardheaded. You need both."

Ian felt himself relax, just a little. The upcoming conversation wouldn't be fun, but at the end of it Lacey would still have a family. He hadn't been sure of that going in.

And he'd been afraid that she would shoot the messenger, one Ian Lapstrake, on the way out.

"When did you figure out what your father was doing?" Ian asked.

"Do you really think the women need to hear this?" Brody asked.

"They can decide for themselves," Ian said.

Neither woman got up to leave.

"There's your answer," Ian said.

Brody hesitated, then decided that since hiding the truth hadn't worked, he might as well empty the whole bag. "I suspected, but didn't know for sure until he shoved it down my throat about fifteen years ago, give or take."

Dottie looked startled, started to say something, and thought better of it.

"I kept it to myself for years. I knew it wouldn't help anyone and could hurt a lot of people." Brody shrugged. "After our first two daughters were born, Dottie wanted a bigger home closer to her parents. So did I. I knew it would mean the kind of life that would help me professionally and please us personally. So I borrowed money from my father to buy this place, and I carefully didn't ask him where the money came from. Not many unknown painters can come up with almost half a million in cash to buy a house."

Ian's dark eyebrows lifted. Even thirty years ago, that was a lot of money.

"Then one day, about fifteen years ago," Brody continued, "Dad and I were arguing over him pushing Lacey into paint—"

"I wanted her to spend more time with her peers," Dottie interrupted. "Spending all her time with her grandfather instead of having friends and parties. It wasn't good."

"Dad started shouting," Brody said. "Told me painting like Lewis Marten had put the fancy roof over Dottie's head and if she didn't like it she could move out. Lacey had talent and he was going to see that she wasn't flattened by the social steamroller of Dottie's snooty family."

Dottie drew in a harsh, surprised breath. That was something else she hadn't known. It was one thing not to like Brody's disreputable father; it was quite another to know that the old man had disliked her just as much.

"I was furious," Brody said. "I'd been paying back the loan on a regular basis, but not enough to have majority ownership of the house. I told him I wasn't going to gag Dottie just to make him feel better, and that Lacey was getting old enough to need more than her grandfather for company. And if he didn't like that, *he* could take a hike."

Lacey started to say something, but pressure from Ian's fingers made her stop.

"After that," Brody said, "things got fairly tense. Dad spent more and more time in the carriage house and on the road. Dottie's parents put all the girls through the university, but when Lacey wanted to study painting overseas, the education money dried up. My father went on the road with some paintings and came back with enough money to send Lacey to France. He didn't even tell us, much less ask us. He just—"

"Handed me a ticket and a checkbook, and told me not to come back until I could stand up to my parents or support myself," Lacey finished.

Dottie winced. "I didn't mean, that is—" She held out her hands. "I wanted what was best for you."

"So did he," Lacey said. "It's just that you wanted different things." She closed her eyes on a wave of pain. "And in the end, I didn't please either of you, did I? I didn't turn into a society woman like you or a vagabond painter like Granddad."

"It's not your job to please them," Ian said. "Pleasing me, now, that's different."

She blinked, then accepted his gentle, outrageous statement, letting it defuse her sadness and anger at her family. "So good to finally know my mission in life."

"I'm here to serve." He smiled, and his dark eyes were very serious. He turned back to Brody. "If I'm doing my math right, your father was about forty when you were born."

Brody nodded.

"Is your mother still alive?"

"No. And we weren't close while she was. She said more than once that if she hadn't had me, she'd have

left the son of a bitch. When I was sixteen, she decided I was old enough to take care of myself, so she
left."

"No other kids?" Ian asked.

Brody laughed curtly. "No. Just as well. Neither of
them was any good as a parent."

"Did he have a wife before your mother?"

For a moment Brody looked startled. "No. At least
I don't think so. If he did, he never talked about it."

"What about his own parents?"

"Never mentioned them," Brody said.

Ian raised his eyebrows. "Not a close family."

"I guess not," Brody said. "I think he ran away
from home. Or at least left home real early. He would
have been in his teens in the Depression years. Maybe
there wasn't enough money to raise him, so he hit the
road and never looked back. It happened to a lot of
young men like that. Go in the army or go on the bum.
He could have gone the army route. I just don't know.
He never talked about it."

Ian studied Brody in silence. "Most men talk about
themselves at some point to their son, even if it's something they'd rather not have their wives overhear. Can
you remember anything at all about your father as a
young man?"

"Other than the usual way-too-late talk about condoms, he didn't say much. You have to understand—
my father had contempt for everyone he met except
Lacey. He saw in her a reflection of himself that he'd
never seen in me. She loved painting and she loved
him." Before Ian could ask another question, Brody
held up his hand. "What's the point of all this raking
over the muck of the past?"

Before Ian could answer, Lacey did. "Murder."

53

Dottie and Brody stared at their daughter.

"What on earth?" Dottie asked sharply.

"Sorry," Lacey said, wincing. "I didn't mean to just plop it out like that. But you remember the paintings Grandfather did of death by fire, by auto wreck, and by drowning?"

"No," Dottie said, appalled. "Which ones?"

"I don't know what you're talking about," Brody said impatiently. "Landscapes, yes, sure, hundreds of them. But nothing like murder. This is really too much, Lacey. Why do you insist on upsetting your mother?"

"Hell," Lacey said under her breath. Then, to Ian. "I knew we should have brought some with us."

"The sheriff would have, um, plotzed," Ian said dryly. "That's why I took the photos instead."

He stood up and went to the table where he had set aside his small computer. He turned it on, called up the electronic files, and carried the computer back to the coffee table, where everyone could see the screen.

"What is it?" Brody asked. "A fire?"

"A car accident," Lacey said. "It happened on Savoy Ranch at a place called Cross Country Canyon."

"I ran the license plate I found just to be sure," Ian said. "I was right. Three Savoy died in the wreck."

Brody shot a narrow look at Ian. "Are you saying it was murder?"

"Alcohol, according to the authorities," Ian said. "Apparently, Three liked to get ripped and then race around the ranch in his old hot rod."

Dottie started to speak, then closed her mouth and looked away from the screen.

"What is it?" Ian asked.

"Nothing," Dottie said.

"Nothing is what we have," Ian said. "What we need is information."

"Oh, just old gossip," she said, waving her hand. "My mother's sister married a Moreno County developer. She mentioned something . . ." Dottie frowned, then shook her head. "I can't remember. Just the fact that there was gossip. Go on. It will come back to me sooner or later."

Without saying anything, Ian clicked through the other wreck paintings. Brody and Dottie looked baffled.

"Why would he paint so many?" Dottie asked after a moment.

"We were wondering the same thing," Ian said. Then, to Brody, "Was your father big on the Savoy-Forrest family?"

"I don't understand," Brody said.

"Was he a fan, a groupie, an enthusiast?" Ian asked.

"Did he follow the society pages or clip out pictures or talk about the family a lot?"

"Not to me." Brody looked at Lacey. "How about you? You spent more time with him than anyone."

"Not one word," she said simply. "He never talked about Moreno County, either. In fact, until Susa identified some of the paintings as depicting the ranch, I thought that he'd only painted in San Diego and the desert and Santa Barbara, with a few side trips to L.A. and San Francisco. Which, come to think of it, is odd."

"San Francisco or L.A.?" Ian asked. "What's odd about that, the fact that they're cities?"

Lacey shook her head. "I meant it's odd that he never painted or talked about painting on Savoy Ranch. It had, and still has, a lot of cachet with the gallery set. But he obviously did paint there sometimes."

Mentally Ian added that fact to the growing list in his head under the category of *David Quinn, artist, grandfather—and murderer?*

"Okay, here's a new take on a way to die," Ian said, opening the file holding photos of all the burning house paintings. "We believe it depicts the death of Lewis Marten."

Brody hissed something under his breath. "Why do you think that?"

"The date on the front matches Marten's death date," Ian said. "The scene matches the small amount of information we've gotten on where Marten lived and painted."

Lacey's parents looked at the screen and then at Ian. He clicked through the rest of the burning house paintings.

"I fail to see the point," Brody said.

"Marten died on Savoy Ranch," Lacey said. "The ranch that Grandfather never talked about and supposedly never painted. The ranch that is central to California Impressionism."

Brody made an impatient gesture, but before he could say anything, Ian did. "Lacey calls this one *Scream Bloody Murder*."

As he spoke, Ian opened the drowning file. If the idea of murder had been merely whispered in the other paintings, it was brutally clear in this one.

Dottie's breath came in with a hissing sound. "Dear God."

Brody's mouth turned down. "*Scream Bloody Murder*. Aptly named, Lacey. Mother of God. Whatever possessed my father to paint this?"

"We think this depicts Gem Savoy Forrest's murder," Ian said evenly. "She died on the ninth of February." As he spoke, Ian tapped a fingernail on the screen, indicating the numbers that had been painted in red: 9.2.

Dottie recognized the name before her husband did. "But she wasn't murdered. She died of an accidental overdose of alcohol and medications. That"—Dottie flicked a glance at the computer screen—"is the imagination of a sick mind."

"Always a possibility," Ian said before Lacey could fall into her reflexive defense of Grandpa Rainbow. "Note the bracelet." He clicked on that area of the photo and it zoomed into larger size, but not so large that the shape of the bracelet was lost.

Dottie leaned forward. "Interesting bit of jewelry, but I doubt if it's terribly expensive. It's hard to tell with a painting like this what size and quality the stones actually are. I would guess white gold rather than platinum. With platinum the stones are usually bigger."

"Have you seen the bracelet before now?" Ian asked.

"I've seen the heart design used a lot, of course," she said. "Who hasn't? These days it's a tacky cliché, like the love knot. I don't remember seeing intertwined diamond hearts and solid metal hearts, but there would be no reason to remember if I had. It's hardly an astonishing piece of jewelry."

"Brody?" Ian asked.

"No."

"It wasn't something your mother had or your father kept as a memento?"

Brody snorted. "My father wasn't a sentimental man. My mother had a plain gold wedding band. It was the only jewelry I ever saw her wear."

Ian didn't need to ask Lacey; if she'd recognized the bracelet, she would have said something before now.

"The Savoy Curse," Dottie said. "Now I remember."

"What?" Lacey asked.

"Accidental death due to far too much alcohol or meds," Ian said, thinking of the newspaper archives he'd searched through Rarities. "The curse of the wealthy class. The high-toned newspapers whispered it and the bottom of the pack bayed it in the headlines every chance they got."

"Yes, that's what my aunt talked about," Dottie said. "The Savoy Curse. The second Benford Savoy died in middle age in a tragic hunting accident. The third Benford Savoy died in middle age in a fiery car wreck. The Savoy matriarch died in a riding accident, although what a woman of her age was doing racing stallions over the countryside . . . well, anyway, it was tragic. Then the granddaughter, Gem, rumored to be drunk when she drowned in her fancy spa. Again, middle-aged. So sad. All that money and no happiness." Then Dottie added briskly, "Not that poverty brings bliss to anyone. It's just that people *expect* money to make them happy."

"Which brings me back to my original question," Ian said. "Why was David Quinn obsessed with these three particular deaths but not with the others in the Savoy family?"

Brody looked everywhere but at Lacey.

"It was nine years ago," Ian said calmly to Brody, "but do you remember where your father was in February then? Particularly on the ninth?"

"What?" Dottie asked, shooting to her feet. "Of all the—"

"It's all right," Brody said, cutting across his wife's anger. "Considering the paintings, it's a fair question, don't you think?"

Instead of answering, Dottie started pacing. The click of her heels over wood alternated with the muted hiss of leather soles on expensive oriental rugs.

"The man is dead. The people in the paintings are dead. What good is all this?" she demanded.

It was Lacey who answered. "If people were murdered, it's a simple matter of justice. If there weren't any murders, I want to know that. I want to know what Grandpa Rainbow was or wasn't. I *need* to know."

Dottie looked at her daughter's stubborn chin and determined eyes. "And the devil with what the rest of us need."

Lacey flinched but didn't back down. "You hated

him. What would it matter to you if he was a killer or a saint?"

"Not everyone is dying to have a murderer in their direct ancestry," her mother shot back. "If he were still alive, I'd say go find the truth and then hang the son of a bitch from the highest tree you could find."

Lacey's eyes opened in shock. She'd never heard so much as *hell* from her mother.

"But he's dead and the only ones who can be hurt are the living," Dottie said. "If you don't care about yourself, think of your sisters."

"I think my sisters will do just fine," Lacey said. "If their society friends dump them for what their grandfather did, then they weren't much in the way of friends, were they? Besides, why can't he be innocent and just a closet groupie of the rich and famous of Moreno County?"

"This is pointless." Dottie stalked out of the room.

"*Damn it*," Lacey said, smacking her hand on the coffee table. "It always ends up the same way."

There was a long, unhappy silence.

Ian was just getting to his feet to leave when Dottie strode back into the living room carrying her portable computer under her arm. Without a word, she popped open the screen and pointed to the date listed on an elaborate professional calendar.

"David Quinn wasn't here," she said. "I know, because my mother's funeral happened to be on that day."

Lacey closed her eyes. She'd hoped her grandfather had been in Pasadena. She certainly hadn't expected to be able to prove that he *wasn't* so quickly, so definitely.

"What about the other two dates?" she asked painfully.

"That was before your father's time," Ian said. "And, apparently, before your grandfather's."

"What?"

"As far as I can find, David Quinn never existed in any official file until he married SaraBeth Courtney forty-eight years ago."

54

Rory rubbed his face wearily, leaned back into the soft leather couch, and stared at the gas fire in the hearth. He hadn't wanted to bring Bliss to the ranch to discuss old death with Ward and his two children, but she hadn't been able to let go of it.

Defensively Bliss flipped through the nearly decade-old coroner's report for the fifth time and dumped it on the coffee table in front of Savoy. "So she was alone in the spa, drinking vodka on the rocks and popping painkillers. So what? She did it all the time and she didn't drown."

Ward said something under his breath and shook his head.

Savoy picked up the old report and glanced through it. He didn't find anything new. He didn't expect to. He took a drink of his beer and set the bottle on a coaster on the coffee table.

"Well?" she challenged.

"Do you really think Mother was murdered?" Savoy asked.

Bliss's mouth set in a stubborn line. Then she looked at her new husband, seeing the tension and fatigue in the line of his shoulders. She stopped pacing and went to sit next to him.

"No," she said. "I guess not. It's just . . . it was so shocking to see that bracelet." She shivered. "And I keep wondering how the painter knew about it."

"Intertwined hearts aren't exactly a rare jewelry design," Savoy pointed out.

"But the bracelet itself is unique," she insisted. "It was commissioned for Grandmother's engagement."

Ward just shook his head. "Savvy's right. Go into any jewelry store and you'll find heart bracelets and rings and whatnot. Besides, the painting's not photographic. Even if your bracelet had looked a lot different, you still could have seen it in the painting."

She knew he was right and it pissed her off. "Don't you care that Mother could have been murdered?"

Ward took a long swallow of beer, set the bottle down with extreme care, and gave his daughter a look that had her wishing she was still standing so she could back up.

"It would have been easier on me if she had been murdered," Ward said. "Rory and I spent a lot of time and political favors keeping Gem's suicide from dragging the Forrest name through every sleazy tabloid in the county, state, and nation."

Bliss went white. "I heard whispers, but I never really believed she killed herself."

Rory put his arm around Bliss. "Sugar, your mother took after her father, and he wasn't real stable after he hit the bottle. Your dad and I worked hard to keep down the gossip about her. When she wasn't drying out in one resort or another, she was drinking and partying hard. I threw the worst of her gigolos out of the county and paid off the rest of them."

Bliss looked at her brother. "Savvy?"

He looked like he'd bitten into something sour. "When Mother was sober, she was a wonderful woman, laughing and witty and beautiful."

Ward grunted. "You got a longer memory than mine, boy. All I remember is the drunk." Then he waved his hand abruptly. "Oh, hell, Gem was all right when she wasn't drinking, but she just didn't spend much time sober and refused to pull herself out of the booze."

Savoy didn't argue. It was the unhappy truth.

Bliss gnawed on her thumb, looked at her bracelet, and gnawed some more.

Gently Rory took her hand between his own. "I know it's hard, but look at it this way," he said to Bliss. "No one benefited from her death. There weren't any jealous lovers who'd want to kill her, because they'd all been paid off and were happy to take the money. As for a jealous husband——"

Ward gave a crack of sardonic laughter. "I didn't care who she screwed, as long as she didn't fuck with the ranch."

"Maybe she was just trying to get your attention with all her lovers and drinking," Savoy said bitterly.

Ward gave him a hard glance. "Then she didn't know me very well, did she?"

"Does anyone?" Savoy asked.

"The point," Rory said before an argument could explode, "is that there wasn't any motive for murdering her. No one was better off because Gem was dead.

Not you, not Savvy, not even Ward. He already voted her shares in the business, because Gem just didn't give a damn as long as there was plenty of money for expensive clothes, booze, pills, and younger men."

Bliss winced. Her stomach clenched as she wondered if her mother had looked in the mirror one day, seen the ruins of beauty, and decided that living was more trouble than it was worth. Or maybe she'd simply killed herself a little at a time until there wasn't anything left.

And the daughter couldn't help wondering if she'd been on the way to doing the same.

"It's so ugly," Bliss said hoarsely.

"It's over, sugar," Rory said, kissing her hair.

"But why would anyone paint such a cruel image?" she asked.

"Ask your father," Savoy said. "He collects the damn things."

Bliss looked shocked. "What are you talking about?"

"The family's private collection," Savoy said. "We have a lot of death paintings by this artist."

"You bet we do," Ward said. "And that collection is the best proof of all that your mother wasn't murdered."

Bliss turned toward him. "I don't understand."

"Simple," Ward said. "Your mother died nine years ago. The artist who painted the drowning woman has been dead for almost fifty years."

55

Lacey looked up from the stack of old photo albums. There were pictures of Grandpa Rainbow's wedding and the baby boy who grew up to be her father. She'd seen the first five or six Christmases and birthdays, and then the album photos gave way to people that Brody identified as his maternal grandparents or distant cousins. The rest of the stacked albums featured Dottie's family and, after he moved in with his son, an older David Quinn.

Set to one side was a huge envelope of faded, brittle newspaper and magazine clippings going back fifty years or more. Each clipping dealt with the scandals and sorrows of the Savoy and Forrest families. None of the clippings pictured or mentioned anyone called David Quinn.

Quietly Lacey flipped the last page of the only album that had pictures of David Quinn. "Didn't he have any photos of his own childhood and parents, like Mom's parents did?"

Brody frowned. "I never thought about it, but . . . no."

"Where was he born?" Ian asked.

"Weed."

Ian didn't even blink. "Northern California?"

Brody smiled. "Yes. Didn't think you'd know it."

"I'm a Central Valley boy. Did he travel a lot as a young man?"

There was a long pause while Brody searched his memories. "If he did, he didn't talk about it. Just California. He often said, 'Why go anywhere else? It's all here, all the landscapes anyone needs.' "

"Did he ever talk about college?" Ian asked.

Brody shook his head.

Ian looked at Lacey.

"Not to me," she said, "except to say it was a waste of time for anyone with talent."

Dottie made a sound like a terrier sinking its teeth into a rat's neck. Some of their worst battles had been over Lacey's schooling.

"He had the typical contempt of the undereducated for higher education," Brody said evenly. "To my knowledge, he never went beyond high school."

"How about high school yearbooks, or even earlier school photos?" Ian asked.

Brody shook his head. "I have some of my mother's, if that would help."

"Only if they went to the same schools," Ian said. "Did they?"

"No. They didn't meet until he was forty."

Lacey gave Ian an unhappy look, wondering if he

was thinking what she was thinking. She didn't ask. Her parents were upset enough as it was.

"So the oldest photo you have of your father," Ian said to Brody, "is his wedding?"

Brody looked at his wife, who was the official keeper of the family history. She nodded.

"Okay," Ian said. "Would you mind if I borrowed some pictures of him long enough to scan them into my computer?"

"Why?" Dottie asked bluntly.

"Lacey's going to give me a list of plein air galleries that her grandfather might have visited," Ian said. "Then I'm going to take a drive and see if any of them recognize his photos," *after I doctor them a bit*, "or his paintings."

Dottie looked at Ian's computer. "I have a scanner, but it would be faster to use my computer setup and simply print out the photos here."

"You can do that?" Ian asked.

"Yes."

Lacey took a deep breath. "Do you still have that personal-style program?"

Her mother turned hopefully. "Of course. I'll just take a photo of you and—"

"No, not me. Granddad."

Ian gave her a startled look, then a slow, approving smile. Without a word he went back to creaming the family photos for the clearest ones of David Quinn.

"Why?" Brody asked his daughter.

"Because he might have looked different in his other life," Lacey said, and waited for the explosion. She didn't have to wait long.

"Other life!" Brody and Dottie said simultaneously. "What are you talking about?" Brody demanded.

"The life your father lived before he married Sara-Beth Courtney," Ian said without looking up from the albums.

"Just because he doesn't have pictures of his childhood doesn't mean he led some sort of double life," Brody said. "He wasn't a sentimental man. He could have just thrown the pictures away."

"There are other things," Lacey said reluctantly.

"Such as?" Brody challenged.

"Such as," Ian said, "the fact that there's no official record of anyone called David No-Middle-Name Quinn before the marriage certificate he signed when he married SaraBeth Courtney. No driver's license in California, no birth certificate, no voting record, no property, no taxes, nothing."

Brody opened his mouth. Then he closed it and pinched the bridge of his nose. It didn't take a lawyer to figure out the most likely reason a man might take the trouble to switch to a new identity.

"So you think he was a felon," Brody said.

"I think we need to know who and what he was before he became David Quinn," Ian said carefully.

Brody grunted. "How many reasons can you think of for changing your identity?"

"Quite a few."

"Any of them legal?" Brody retorted.

"One or two."

His face paled except for twin slashes of red over his cheekbones. "You really think he was a murderer?"

Ian spoke before Lacey could. "I really don't know. It could have been some scam related to art that caused him to change his name. Did your father always paint, or was that new along with his new life?"

"He painted," Dottie said, frowning. "I can't remember why, but I'm sure of it."

"Even before he was David Quinn?" Ian asked.

Dottie looked at Brody.

"Yes . . ." he said slowly.

"You sure?" Ian asked.

"One of my earliest memories is of him saying variations on the theme of 'When I was your age, I could paint trees that looked like trees. A chicken could crap a better painting than this. What's wrong with you? Didn't you get any of me except a pecker?'"

"Wretched, *wretched* creature," Dottie muttered under her breath.

Brody shrugged. "I got used to it after a while. The point is that my father always painted."

"Landscapes?" Ian asked.

"As far as I know."

"What about fires?" Lacey asked. "Did you ever see him paint them?"

Brody gave his daughter a puzzled look. "Fires? Like fireplaces or campfires or candles?"

"Like burning cars or houses," she said.

"Not that I remember. But keep in mind that you knew the artistic part of my father better than anyone else. After I was eight, he gave up on me. He never painted around me and never let me be around him when he painted. He never showed me his paintings. Never showed my mother. He completely locked us out of that part of his life."

"The biggest part," Lacey said, finally understanding why her father found the whole subject of art distasteful.

"You were the only one," Brody said simply. "He took one look at the painting you did of the Christmas tree when you were three years old and fell in love. He let you into places and showed you pieces of himself that he didn't share with anyone else."

"Not all of it, apparently," Ian said. *Thank God.* "Mrs. Quinn, I'll take you up on the offer of your scanner."

"Call me Dottie," she said. Then added casually, "Everyone else in the family does."

Lacey groaned. *"Mom."*

Ian gave Lacey a quick, one-arm hug. "Bet your mother plans a mean wedding."

"I sure do," Dottie said. "And you're about to see how I do it." She took the photos from his hand, picked up her computer, and headed for her office, talking all the way. "First I photograph all the important participants and scan them into the style program. Then I decide clothing, hair, makeup, and shoe styles based on body type and coloring."

"Yeah?" Ian asked intrigued. He picked up the fat envelope of clippings and followed her. "Sounds like a program I once used to predict how people would look younger or older or with different noses, ears, hair, teeth, that sort of thing."

"My program will do that. It's a big hit when our hospital volunteers work with the antismoking clinic, showing people how smoking accelerates the aging process." Dottie gave him a look over her shoulder that reminded Ian of Lacey. "Should I ask what you were doing with the program?"

"Think of it as international planning."

Brody watched the two of them vanish down the hall. "You know that you're doomed."

"Huh?" Lacey said.

"She's already planning your wedding. Even before you got here, she asked me if I still could get into the tux I wore for—"

"No!" Lacey held up her hand. "Don't go there."

She stalked off after Ian and her mother, afraid to leave the two of them alone.

56

"It's awfully nice of you to see us after-hours," Lacey said, smiling her best Pasadena socialite smile. *Why not?* she thought. *It goes with everything I'm wearing, including my mother's carnivorous shoes.*

The tanned, trim, middle-aged man smiled, showing teeth as white as his silk shirt and slacks. "Any friend of Mrs. Roberts-Worthington is a friend of ours. She's done an absolutely fabulous job of raising AIDS awareness."

Mrs. Roberts-Worthington was a friend of Dottie's sorority sister, not of Lacey's, but she didn't feel any need to clarify the relationship. It was enough that they'd found an entrée into the Palm Springs plein air art circuit.

"This is my client, Ian Lapstrake," Lacey said. "Ian, Chad Oliver."

Oliver waited for Ian to show the veiled hostility or

contempt of the frankly heterosexual male for a frankly homosexual male.

"A pleasure, Mr. Oliver," Ian said, holding out his hand.

Oliver relaxed and shook Ian's hand. "Come in. My partner isn't here right now, but he should be back soon. Until then, perhaps I can help you."

Ian followed Lacey into the home that was also a gallery. Furniture, sculpture, paintings, everything was artfully coordinated in feel if not in era or medium. The fact that, like their host, the color scheme consisted of shades of white took a few moments to get used to. Even the art was executed in shades of pale, no matter what the subject.

"Coffee, wine, beer, a cocktail?" Oliver asked.

"Nothing, thanks," Lacey said. "It's enough that you've agreed to talk to us. We don't expect to be entertained."

"I insist," Oliver said. "I've been experimenting with canapé recipes. Anthony will be so pleased not to be the only beta tester."

Ian laughed. "In that case, make mine coffee."

The kitchen was the open sort, so Oliver could cook and entertain guests at the same time. Ian, who could always eat, set aside his computer case, sat on a bar stool overlooking the kitchen, and watched Oliver gather food and plates. He moved with the efficiency and grace of someone doing a familiar, enjoyable job.

Lacey, whose interest in the kitchen was minimal, wandered off to look at the landscapes. She recognized a name here and there, but mostly she recognized money. This wasn't decorator art. All the paintings were technically superior, a few were excellent, and one she would have loved for her own collection.

None of them were remotely like her grandfather's work.

She went back and sat by Ian. In answer to his raised eyebrow, she shook her head slightly.

Oliver pulled a plate of warm canapés from the microwave, set it on the counter near Ian, and handed over a cup of coffee. The plates were white except for a pale, ghostly ribbon of blue just off-center.

Ian popped in a miniature quiche, closed his eyes, and chewed with obvious pleasure. When he swallowed, he said, "Wow," and reached for more.

Oliver grinned, poured himself a glass of wine, and went to nuke another plate of canapés.

"Better dive in," Ian said to Lacey, "or all that's left will be a well-licked plate." Then Ian asked Oliver, "Don't suppose you'd want to share this recipe?"

"You cook?" he replied, startled.

"A man who lives alone and likes good food learns to cook real quick," Ian said. "And a man who's going to marry an artist who's mostly thumbs in the kitchen knows he'll be doing the cooking."

"I'm not mostly thumbs," Lacey said.

"Yeah?" Ian said hopefully.

"I'm *all* thumbs."

Oliver was still laughing when the front door opened.

Anthony Milhaven was twenty years older and six inches taller than his partner, and had the bearing of a man who had spent a lot of time in the military. Though surprised to find guests, he was as gracious as Oliver had been. Soon everyone was sitting on one side or another of the bar, eating and talking.

"You've been in the gallery business thirty years?" Ian asked Milhaven.

"Thirty-three, but who's counting?" He picked up his scotch and took a healthy swallow. "Damn, I needed that. Been a bitch of a day. Hate inventory. Hate taxes. Love these egg-thingies." He popped three into his mouth at once and looked at Ian. "What can I do for you?"

"We're trying to trace an artist," Lacey said before Ian could answer. "He might have been buying or selling paintings."

"When?" Milhaven asked, reaching for more canapés.

"On and off for the last thirty years, at least," she said.

"How old is he?"

"In his eighties. He's been dead for two years." As always, Lacey had to swallow hard. The image of the empty truck, the easel set up a hundred yards away, and desert silence made her want to cry. He'd been so alone when he died.

Milhaven saw the sadness in her eyes and wondered, but he didn't say anything.

Ian reached into his breast pocket and pulled out photos. With the Quinns' help, he had "aged" the best photos to represent ten-year spans of David Quinn's life. If these didn't ring any bells, he had a backup set with different hair, beard, and mustache styles to aid in jogging someone's memory.

"He was about five feet ten inches," Ian said, handing over the photos, "lean body, brown eyes, brown hair and beard that went gray from the chin up. Probably had paint-stained hands. Eyeteeth partially overlapped his front two teeth. No accent. No limp. No missing digits. No obvious scars. Somewhat stooped bearing."

"Were you a cop before or after you were a soldier?" Milhaven asked without looking up from the photos.

"After," Ian said without missing a beat.

Milhaven nodded. "Military shows in the posture. Cop in the eye and the gun under your jacket."

"Did you get your twenty years before you got out of the military?" Ian asked.

Milhaven nodded. "Retirement kept me alive until the gallery began to pay its way," he said, but his attention was on the third photo. It showed the face of a man who could have been between fifty and seventy years old. "I might have seen him, but it was at least ten years ago. Hard to say. I've got a head full of faces. Part of the business."

"Was he buying paintings?" Lacey asked.

With a frown, Milhaven stared at the photo. "He didn't buy any from me. I remember people who buy."

"How about selling?" Ian asked.

"You have any idea how many times a day someone comes in and tries to sell me something?" Milhaven asked.

Ian opened his computer, booted up, and opened a file of landscape paintings. "How about this?" he asked, turning the computer screen toward Milhaven.

"Fabulous," Oliver said, staring at stark desert mountains blushing pink with dawn and a foreground of skeletal shrubs as dark as fear.

Milhaven pinched his lips together and studied the image. Even when translated into pixels and put on a computer screen, the quality came through. "Hell of a painting. Is it for sale?"

"Not at this time," Lacey said.

"When it is, give me a call."

"I will."

He looked up, measuring her.

"I mean it," she said. "You remember faces and I remember people who help me."

With a brief nod, he went back to looking at the screen. The landscapes clicked by. Then came a painting from each aspect of the Death Suite.

Milhaven grunted. "Good, but hard to sell. Landscapes are much easier."

"Have you ever seen any like these before?" Lacey asked.

He shrugged. "I keep thinking I've seen this artist before. The landscapes, not the violence. What's his name?"

"David Quinn," Lacey said.

Silence, pursed lips, and finally a shake of his head. "Never heard of him."

"You ever heard of Lewis Marten?" Ian asked casually.

"Marten, Marten. Wait." He held up a hand to keep anyone from prompting him. "It's coming back. Painted fifty-sixty years ago, ran with Savoy Ranch artists. Died young. Of course, they all seem young when you're almost seventy." Milhaven looked closely at the computer screen, which had cycled back to the first landscape. "You thinking about selling these Martens?"

"The paintings aren't signed," she said carefully. "All I really want is—"

"Unsigned?" Milhaven sighed. "Too bad. Takes a real hit in value that way. You get a confident collector, though, and you've got a sale. Maybe ten, twenty thousand. Maybe more, depending on how in love with the painting the client is."

"I've had offers a lot bigger than twenty thousand," she said, remembering Savoy Forrest.

"Must have been a client. A gallery can't afford to go any higher and still turn a profit on resale."

"Do you own any Martens?" Ian asked.

"Personally or professionally?"

"I'm not fussy."

Milhaven looked at the computer screen. "You want to tell me what this is really about?"

"It's about finding out if you've been offered similar art by the man in the photo," Ian said.

For a long time Milhaven was silent. "I'll have to think about it. Check my records. I've got a hot list of clients who are interested in various styles of art or individual artists. So does every other gallery worthy of the name. It's called taking care of business. You have a card?"

Ian knew a here's-your-hat-what's-your-hurry when it was shoved in his face. He stood, took a business card from his wallet, and handed it to Milhaven.

"Rarities Unlimited," Milhaven said, reading the card. He gave Ian a look from shrewd gray eyes. "They have quite a reputation."

Ian's smile was all teeth. "Lacey remembers people who help her. I remember people who don't. Check your records and call us."

57

The weather had turned around again, back to brisk winds off the sea and a layer of clouds piling up against the inland mountains. Ian and Lacey pulled their jackets close as they ran from the upscale gallery to his truck. Shivering, Lacey leaped inside and slammed the door.

"Well, that was another waste of time," she said. "Everybody coos over the landscapes and recoils at the Death Suite, hasn't seen anything like any of it before, and would I like to sell?"

"Welcome to the wonderful world of investigation," Ian said. "I offered to take you home."

"My home is a sooty, soggy mess," she said. "I can't paint at the hotel and—"

"Why not? Susa left you enough paraphernalia for a whole platoon of—"

"I'd rather be with you," Lacey cut in. "Are you saying you'd rather be alone?"

He leaned over and hauled her close for a slow, steamy kiss.

"I'm not complaining about having you close enough to taste from time to time," he said when he finally lifted his head. "I'm just feeling guilty about keeping you from your work. Susa wasn't fooling when she said she was a picky bitch. She'll run you ragged." He bent down to kiss her again.

His cell phone rang. He wanted to ignore it.

So did Lacey, but . . . "It might be Milhaven," she said reluctantly.

"You're reading my mind again."

He pulled out his cell phone, didn't recognize the caller ID number, and took the call anyway.

"Ian Lapstrake," he said curtly.

The person on the other end of the line spoke with the muffled intonations of a disguised voice. "Tell her to stop asking questions about David Quinn or she'll die."

"The connection is bad," Ian said, automatically hitting the record button. "Could you repeat that?"

The sound changed. The man—or possibly woman—had hung up. He hit two buttons and the phone connected with the last call made. It rang twelve times. Someone picked it up and confirmed what Ian had already guessed. "This is a public phone, asshole." The line went dead.

Lacey saw the stillness in Ian's body, the coldness in the line of his mouth, the intensity in his eyes.

"What is it?" she asked.

"Somebody doesn't like you asking questions about your grandfather." Ian thought quickly. "I think it's time for you to meet the folks at Rarities. Dana loves to have smart women around and you'll be able to paint until your eyes cross." *And there are plenty of guards to keep Lacey safe while I find out what the hell is going on.* "You two will have a great time."

Lacey just stared at him.

"Okay," he said, switching gears, "how about catching up with Susa and talking about your upcoming show?" *From what I know about that outfit, the Donovans can take care of any little thing that comes up.*

"What's wrong?" she asked.

"The game just changed. You're out."

She ignored him. "Who called?"

"Public phone." Automatically Ian checked the gun in the harness. Secure, loaded, ready to go.

The reflexive gesture told Lacey more than words, but she wanted the words, too. "And?"

Ian started the truck without answering.

"Ignorance isn't bliss," she said. "Especially if there's something dangerous. That's why they post road signs. It keeps the ignorant from driving off cliffs."

He muttered something under his breath.

Lacey kept watching his profile, waiting.

Ian wove through San Diego traffic to the freeway and headed north.

"Let me help you with your short-term planning," she said tightly. "I'm not going to see Susa, I'm not going to visit Rarities, and the only 'home' I have is a hotel where a thief has a security passkey. Next suggestion?"

Ian had already arrived at the same conclusion about the hotel. He just didn't like it.

"Shit," he said under his breath.

"As a suggestion, it lacks detail."

Against his will, Ian smiled. "Okay. The guy said you should stop looking for David Quinn and that this was the only warning you'd get."

A combination of fear and fury swept through her. She let the rage burn away the cold fear. "That's it? Just a 'get out of Dodge' edict?"

"Yeah."

"Fuck him."

He glanced sideways for an instant, then back to the brawling steel race of the freeway. He'd expected the fear he saw in her, but the anger surprised him. It shouldn't have. Right now he was mad enough to kill, and it came from fear of her getting hurt.

"I'd rather bury him," Ian said.

"That, too." She blew out a hard breath, trying to think through the wild turmoil of her emotions. "Was he serious?"

"Public phone, disguised voice, untraceable. Yeah, I'd have to think he meant it. Or she. Couldn't tell."

"Why is he or she so worried about me asking questions?"

"If we knew that, we'd have a handle on who."

"Is paranoia catching?" she asked after a moment.

"I don't know. What are your symptoms?"

"Maybe I'm just having a string of bad luck—fire, theft, death threat—but I'm beginning to feel hunted."

"The fire was an accident," Ian said neutrally. "It said so in the report."

"Uh-huh."

"The theft was aimed at Susa. Common sense says so."

"Uh-huh."

Silence grew. And grew.

"It's catching," Ian said reluctantly. "I have it, too."

"You don't think I'm being crazy?"

"Before that telephone call I was paranoid. Now I'm certain."

Her mouth went suddenly dry. She'd really hoped she was weaving smoke. "Of what?"

"Correct me if I'm wrong on this, but up until the charity benefit, your grandfather's art was out of public sight."

"Yes."

"The art goes public, everyone goes nuts, someone tries to buy it and someone else tries to burn it. When that doesn't work, it's stolen. Then a whole new stash of the art is found. I'll bet that put somebody's gonads in a twist."

"Who?" she asked.

"Whoever doesn't want David Quinn's history or his art out in public."

Too many deaths. Not enough police work. Ain't nothing changed. Stay away from it, boy.

He should have taken his great-uncle's advice, but he hadn't. Now the woman he loved was in danger.

Too many deaths.

58

Usually Lacey thrived on art galleries, but at the moment she was suffering overload. She and Ian had both agreed that it would be smart to plow through as many galleries as possible before the caller had a chance to track her down.

Anybody who wanted to find her would have to move fast. Eleven galleries so far today, starting with two in Palm Desert, followed by four in San Diego, two in La Jolla, and three in Laguna Beach. In the past twenty-four hours, she'd seen a mind-boggling amount of pretty good art, some very good art, and a few paintings that made her realize all over again just how far she had to go as an artist. One of the latter had been Susa's.

They had discovered that four of the galleries were too new to have been used by David Quinn. Another three of them had only been in business for eight to fifteen years. The rest were old enough, but had changed management and/or ownership too many times for anyone to remember anything useful.

No one had seen anything like the Death Suite before, or if they had, they weren't talking about it. Everybody wanted to buy the landscapes.

The twelfth gallery on their list was also in Laguna. The business was crammed into an old, much-remodeled Victorian on the inland side of Pacific Coast Highway. Just enough had been spent on ambiance that the walk-in customers knew they weren't in a frame shop; the rest of the overhead was in location and stock. Franz Bischoff, Sam Hyde Harris, Paul Lauritz, Granville Redmond, Hanson Puthuff, Guy Rose, George Brandhoff, Edgar Payne, William Wendt, Maurice Braun—Lacey read the signatures aloud in a kind of a daze.

"You okay?" Ian asked, wondering if the pressure of the death threat had finally gotten to her.

"Yes. No. This is incredible. Museum-quality southern California plein air artists all over the place. Only a few of the paintings are major, of course, but all of the artists are."

"Whatever you say," Ian muttered. "They're all beginning to look alike to me."

"Then you need a break."

"We'll get something to eat as soon as we're through here."

"More hamburgers," Lacey said.

"Afraid so. They're easier to eat on the road than fancy food, and we've got a couple more galleries in Newport Beach to hit before they close."

Lacey stifled a groan. She was used to fast food, but she was also used to having some green stuff from time to time.

"I'll buy you a big salad before we go to bed," Ian said.

"Are you a mind reader?"

"Nope. Just a guy who's tired of so-so beef, bad cheese, and worse fries. We haven't had anything decent to eat since Oliver's quiches."

"Did Milhaven ever call?"

"Not since I last checked."

"When was that?" she asked.

"While you were asleep in my truck."

"Don't give me that long-suffering voice," she said, determined to act like everything was normal. "Whose fault is it that I haven't been getting my full eight hours of sleep at night?"

He gave her a dark, sideways look. "I wasn't complaining."

She licked her lips. "Neither was I."

"Feeling real frisky after that nap, aren't you?"

"Yeah. Wanna fight?"

"I'd rather f—" Ian cut off the rest of the word and smiled over Lacey's head at the clerk, an under-thirty woman with a power suit, one-of-a-kind jewelry, and expensive red-gold hair. "Hi," he said, "are you Mrs. Katz?"

"No, I'm Julia York. May I help you?"

Ian smiled. "We talked to Mrs. Katz earlier today. We're a little late for our appointment, but we're hoping not too late."

Julia took in the smile and the rest of the package, and loosened up considerably. "Mr. Lapstrake?"

"That's me. This is Lacey Quinn."

Julia nodded but didn't look away from Ian. "Mrs. Katz told me to expect you. She's up in the storage room."

Lacey wondered if she suddenly had gone invisible. Then she felt Ian's hand tucking loose curls behind her ears before settling on her nape in a gesture of intimacy that was as telling as it was casual.

"Lead the way," Ian said, caressing Lacey's nape.

Julia got the message. She smiled at Lacey. "Ms. Quinn, Mrs. Katz is looking forward to meeting you. Follow me."

The assistant had a nice pair of hips and she used them to advantage climbing the stairway to what had once been an attic and now was a storage room for art. She passed Ian and Lacey over to Katz by calling out brief introductions into the interior of the attic.

"Be out in a minute," Katz called from behind a rack of paintings.

Julia nodded to Lacey, gave Ian a predatory smile, and left without a word.

"Whew," Lacey said under her breath, watching Julia descend the stairs. "I was wondering if you were going to have to pull your gun to defend your honor."

"Guns probably turn her on."

"Scary thought."

"*You* think it's scary—what about *me*?"

"I think you're scary, too."

Ian smiled despite the gnawing tension in his shoulders and the echo of that voice in his mind.

Stop asking questions.

Or she'll die.

Stop asking.

She'll die.

Die.

59

It was five minutes later when Mrs. Katz finally bustled out from behind a screen and into the small cleared area of the attic. Her hair was short and improbably dark, framing a face that looked every bit of seven decades old. She reminded Lacey of a sparrow at nesting time—small, dark-eyed, nondescript, energetic, bristling with purpose.

"Hello excuse the mess I'm getting ready for a new show and what is this about some mysterious man?" Katz said.

Lacey sorted out the flood of words and said, "We understand you've owned this gallery for forty years."

"And worked in it for twenty more," Katz agreed. "My parents owned it and my grandmother was a painter back when women artists were rare enough to stop traffic. None of it came down to me but an eye for good art, which made me crazy because I can't paint worth spit. What can I do for you?"

Ian handed the photos over to Lacey and set his computer on a worktable.

"I was wondering if this man ever came to your gallery to buy or sell art," Lacey said, laying out a series of enhanced photos of her grandfather.

Katz picked up the photos and held them about two inches from her nose, peering at them. Ian saw the cataracts clouding her left eye and didn't have much hope for the outcome.

"Clean shaven, middle-aged or older, not handsome, not ugly, wallpaper clothes." Katz shrugged and handed back the photos. "It could be any one of a hundred men."

" 'Wallpaper clothes?' " Ian asked.

"Ordinary," Lacey guessed. "Unremarkable."

"Wallpaper," Katz agreed.

"Gotcha." Ian reached into his computer case and pulled out the backup photos, the ones where Quinn had more or less hair, a hat or no hat, glasses or no glasses. "What about these?"

Katz went through the first three without a pause, then stopped on the fourth.

Lacey looked over the woman's shoulder. The photo was a reworked wedding picture. It showed her grandfather with a short beard and mustache, glasses, and a leather cap with a bill. The facial hair was dark, making him look younger than the forty years he'd been when the picture was taken. The digital trickery still intrigued Lacey because she'd never seen her grandfather with anything on his face but his skin. Neither had her father.

"I recognize him. I know I've seen him." Katz frowned. "But I can't remember if it was here or somewhere else."

"Do you remember when?" Ian asked.

"Oh, years and years ago, forty, maybe even fifty, maybe even more. Never was much good at dates and numbers and things, but I know I've seen him."

Ian reined in his impatience and fired up the computer.

"Was he buying paintings?" Lacey asked.

Silence, then a sigh. "Too long ago for me to remember."

"How about this?" Ian said, pointing to the computer screen.

Katz bent over and got close enough to the screen for her eyes to cross. She backed up an inch or two and looked at six landscapes as Ian clicked through the file. When the Death Suite appeared, she blinked, tilted her head, and said what everyone else had. "Good but tough to sell. The landscapes, now . . ." She clicked back to them.

"Lewis Marten," she said. There wasn't any doubt in her voice. She might have trouble with time, but she'd worked in the plein air art business since she was ten years old, dusting and cleaning the gallery for her parents. "My father collected him, or tried to. My, that was a terrible thing losing all that art in the fire, just terrible."

"Hard on the artist, too," Ian said dryly. "He lost his life."

"We all die sooner or later, but we don't expect everything we did to die with us," Katz said. "If it weren't for collectors like my father no one would even know about Marten."

"You have some of his paintings?" Lacey asked eagerly. "Signed paintings?"

Katz's expression became cautious. "My father did."

"You don't have them still?" Lacey asked.

"My insurers don't like me talking about what I do or don't own."

"We understand," Ian said. He handed her a Rarities card. "We're not thieves sizing you up for a contract robbery, Mrs. Katz."

Katz read the card very carefully, then nodded her head once. "I had to sell five of my father's six signed Martens in order to keep the gallery after my parents died. Since then, I've bought two Martens. Neither of them is signed."

"When did you buy the unsigned ones?" Lacey asked.

"One was about thirty years ago and one was about ten, eleven years ago. I've heard of others coming on the market, but I've never seen them."

Lacey looked at Ian and wondered if he was thinking what she was about the timing. Thirty years ago Lacey's parents were buying a new home. About ten years ago Lacey had been trying to get enough money to study overseas. And her grandfather, despite his contempt for higher education, had given her the money to go.

"Now that you mention it," Katz said thoughtfully, "the men who sold them to me could have been in those photos you showed me, but I couldn't swear to it, wallpaper being pretty much wallpaper and all. Thirty years is a long time and I'd just had my first cataract surgery ten years ago so my right eye wasn't what you'd call real sharp."

"If Rarities contacts you directly," Ian said, "would you be willing to let them examine your three paintings?"

"I wouldn't have to pay anything?"

"We'll even pick them up and deliver them back to you," Ian said, *especially as I'll be doing it on my vacation time*. "Rarities' insurance carrier would cover you door to door. Plus we'd give you a hard copy file of our research and our conclusions as to the authenticity of the unsigned paintings."

"Why?" Katz asked baldly. "Normally Rarities charges thousands and has a waiting list as long as this century."

"We have other clients who are interested in unsigned Lewis Marten paintings. Having access to your signed painting would be worth a great deal." Ian smiled gently at her. "As you know, museums have all kinds of internal constraints on where and why and how long they can let out their collections. Paintings by Marten—signed paintings—are real rare. We'd appreciate a chance to look at yours."

"Young man, you've got a real nice smile," Katz said.

Lacey choked back a laugh.

"Thank you, ma'am. I have to give my grandmother credit for it. I got it from her."

"How about this?" Katz said, settling in to bargain with the relish of a person whose life's work consisted in working on a profit margin that changed from customer to customer. "You can take those three paintings and I'll take Rarities' opinion as to the art."

"And?" Ian asked warily.

"And you'll agree to sell the six landscapes through my gallery," she said, pointing a bony finger at the computer.

"They aren't signed," Lacey said, "and they're not for sale."

"Sooner or later everything's for sale," Katz said.

"Trust me. I've been to enough estate auctions to know. Do we have a deal?"

"*If* those five paintings come on the market, it will be through your gallery," Lacey said.

"Five? What about the sixth?"

"The desert landscape is promised to someone else."

"Good enough." Mrs. Katz's grin showed teeth that were as improbably light as her hair was dark.

"How many clients do you have waiting for them?" Ian asked.

"Enough for a lot more paintings."

Ian wasn't surprised. Seven of the eleven galleries they'd visited had said the same thing. Apparently selling fake Martens was a thriving underground business on the collector circuit.

And somebody was willing to kill to keep it that way.

60

Is Mr. Milford available?" asked a woman's faintly
raspy voice.

His hand tightened on the phone. Very few people
knew that name. Four of them had called him in the
past twenty-four hours. He'd hoped that his own call
would put an end to it.

Obviously it hadn't.

"Speaking," he said.

"This is Mrs. Katz from Seaside Gallery. I have a
line on five paintings by Lewis Marten."

"Signed?"

"Unfortunately, no. I've only seen digital represen-
tations, but the paintings look excellent. Definitely
some of his best work."

"All landscapes?"

"Two coastal mountains, three coastlines."

He didn't know whether to be relieved or irritated
that none of the crucial paintings were being offered

by any of the callers. *Why in the name of Christ doesn't the bitch just gouge me like her grandfather did? Why is she dragging it all out?*

"Are the landscapes for sale?" he asked, wondering if the answer would be different from the other galleries that had called.

"Not at this point, but that could change at any moment," Mrs. Katz said. "The owner has guaranteed that the instant the paintings are available, my gallery will represent them."

"I'll wait for your call," he said, and hung up.

He didn't expect to be waiting long. Estate sales happened quickly after death. The tax collector saw to it. As for the death, he would see to it, personally.

Maybe that will be the end of it. Finally.

But just in case it wasn't, he had some paintings to burn.

61

You're looking at that door like you've never seen one," Lacey said. She took off her coat and shook off raindrops as she ran her fingers through her wildly curling hair. "Is something wrong with it?"

"I was thinking about leaving it untouched except for the automatic electronic lock. Make it easy on the bastard if he tries to break in again." But even as Ian said it, he was throwing the bolt and jamming in his own handy little wedge.

"Why would you want to make it easy for anyone to break in?" she asked, startled.

Ian shrugged out of his wet denim jacket. Water stood in his short hair, making it spiky. "Because I'd like to have a little chat with him."

"If he's the one that made the telephone call," she said, rubbing her arms uneasily, "I don't have anything to say to him."

"I do. And then he'll have a lot to say to me."

The thin curve of Ian's lips had nothing in common with the smile that put children and bankers at ease. This smile was frankly predatory, as hard as the gun waiting beneath his jacket.

"You don't look very friendly," she said.

"I'm not feeling very friendly." Then he turned toward her and held out his arms. Bags of deli food dangled from one big hand. "Present company excepted."

She stepped close to him and let herself be wrapped up and hugged. Beneath the smiles and light conversation she'd been keeping up all afternoon, she was scared and off-balance, wondering where her secure world had gone.

"I'm still trying to understand . . ." Her voice died.

"What?"

"Everything. So much has happened, it's like a wave that keeps breaking, tumbling me around. Granddad, Susa, you, me." She took a swift breath that tasted of Ian. "The threat. Why would anyone want to kill me? What have I done to deserve it?"

He tilted her chin up with his free hand and kissed her tenderly. "Some people don't need a reason."

"But most people do."

"Sex. Money. Power. Secrets. Insanity."

"Well, that really narrows the field." She rubbed her forehead against his neck and fought the chill that kept taking her by surprise. "Nobody's going to kill for sex with me."

"Wanna bet?" he asked.

"I'm trying to be serious here."

He nuzzled her ear. "I'm serious."

Despite her uneasiness, she smiled. "You're not the one threatening me."

"Dang. I'm going to have to work on my technique. Puppy dogs don't get as far as wolves."

She went nose to nose and eye to eye with him. "You're trying to distract me."

"Yeah."

"This time are you going to tell me why you insisted we move my grandfather's paintings?"

"I was bored."

"Damn it, Ian—"

"Okay, okay," he said quickly. "I'm paranoid, remember?"

"So am I, remember?" she retorted. "You tell me your paranoid fantasy and I'll tell you mine."

"I don't think telling you will make you feel any better or help you dodge trouble down the road, so what's the point?"

"All right." She stepped away. "How about I tell you *my* paranoid fantasy?"

He thought of going to her, holding her again, reassuring both of them that she was safe and everything was all right. But she wasn't and everything wasn't, and fuzzy thinking like that could get her killed.

"Are you telling me before or after we open this deli stuff and get greasy?" Ian asked.

"During."

He gave up trying to distract her. "I'm listening. But only if you sit down and eat instead of picking at food the way you've done since the call."

She didn't have to ask which call. She just watched him unwrap a turkey club sandwich that had to be six inches thick and was held together with a toothpick as long as a dagger. She'd thought when she ordered it that something bland like turkey would be easier to eat, but it was the greasy, garlicky sausage sandwich that smelled good to her now.

"*If* my grandfather's forgeries are a common thread," she said after a moment, "and *if* my shop was deliberately burned to destroy them, and *if* it was my grandfather's paintings rather than Susa's that were the target of the hotel theft, then whoever did it might try to burn or steal the other paintings."

I would have to pick a smart woman, Ian thought as he put out another thick sandwich.

She waited until he reached for one of the three big boxes of salad. "Well?" she asked.

"It's your paranoid fantasy, not mine," he said.

"Then why did you move the paintings?"

He opened the salad box. "Same fantasy. Sit down and eat."

"Well, that was like pulling teeth." She sat cross-legged next to him on the floor by the coffee table and reached for a section of sandwich. "The only problem with that fantasy is—"

"If selling fake Martens is profitable, who benefits from burning them?" he interrupted.

Her lower lip pushed out. "I was going to ask you first."

"Beat you to it. Pass one of those forks, would you?"

She gave him a plastic fork. "So my shop was just one of those things—cold hands, hot fire, ocean wind?"

"That's what the preliminary investigation concluded."

"Even after you talked about paraffin and gasoline?"

"How'd you find out about that?" he asked.

"I heard some of the cops talking to the firemen after they talked to you."

"Worst gossips in the world." Ian bit into a spicy Italian sausage sub.

"But it's just a preliminary investigation," she said. "Surely after more work—"

"Don't count on it," he cut in. "While you and your mother were bonding over virtual hairstyles on the computer, I called the Newport PD on my cell phone for an update."

"Mmph?" she asked, chewing and swallowing frantically so she could ask questions.

"The short version is that they're understaffed and overwhelmed by the Birthday Candle Arsonist. Unless they hear on the streets that Cosmic Energy was a professional burn, they're going to chalk it up to homeless people starting a trash can fire that got away from them. That's where the evidence points."

She reached for the bottle of soda that had been part of the deli package meal and washed down the turkey.

"Sure you don't want some of the champagne that's in the fridge?" he asked.

"Are you drinking any?"

He thought of the phone call. *Stop asking questions or she'll die.* "Champagne doesn't sound good to me."

"Neither did beer," she said, sucking a slice of tomato off her thumb.

"Don't feel like bubbles." He took a swallow from her bottle.

"You're drinking Coke."

"Different bubbles."

She tossed her head in an attempt to keep her hair out of her sandwich. "You're on vacation."

"Sure am."

"But you're still wearing a gun."

"Yeah." He took another garlic-laden bite from his sub and then held it out to her. "Better eat some in self-defense."

As she took the sub, he tucked her damp curly hair out of the way and ran the pad of his thumb over her cheekbone with a gentleness that made her heart turn over.

"Let me help you, Lacey."

Her eyes searched his intently. "I don't want you getting hurt because of me," she said. "Can't you understand that?"

"I understand." He kissed her fast and hard, then smiled slowly. "I just don't agree. Unhand my sandwich, woman, or prepare to defend yourself."

Smiling, shaking her head, not knowing how he got around her so easily, she took a big bite and returned the garlicky mess to him. Then she waited until he sank his teeth into the soggy bread before she reached out and tugged lightly at the shoulder harness he wore over his T-shirt.

"Teach me how to shoot your gun," she said.

He grinned slowly. "You shoot my gun just fine."

"Ian, I mean it."

"I know you do." He sighed, set down the sandwich, licked his thumb, and said, "Have you ever shot a gun? Any kind of gun?"

"No."

"Held one?"

"No."

Bloody hell, as Niall always says. Annie Oakley would have been easier.

Ian wiped his hands on several napkins before he

drew his gun from its holster with a speed that startled Lacey.

"This is the safety," he said.

She looked where he pointed. "Safety."

"In this position it's on. The gun can't fire. In this"—his finger flicked—"it's off. See the red dot?"

"Yes."

"That's how you know you're in trouble."

He put the safety back on and tapped the muzzle with a fingertip. "This end shoots bullets."

"Ya think?" she said sarcastically.

"So don't point it at anything you don't want to kill."

She took a quick breath. "Got it."

He put the butt of the gun in her hands, automatically making sure that the muzzle didn't point anywhere important. The weight made her hands sag for a second before she recovered.

"Heavy," she said.

"Yeah. I keep thinking about a Glock, but I'm used to this one."

"A Glock?"

"A kind of gun. Real light compared to this. Plastic instead of metal."

"You're kidding."

"No. Point my gun at that window."

She lifted the weapon so that the muzzle was centered on a window about eight feet away. Rain lashed across the glass in the kind of sudden winter downpour that always took southern Californians by surprise.

"Put your finger over the trigger and pull back," he said.

It took a moment, but she managed.

"Bang bang, he's dead," Ian said, plucking the gun

from her hands and returning it to the holster. "Lesson over."

Lacey's cheeks flushed. She opened her mouth to give him hell, but he was already talking.

"If you have to use this gun it will be because I'm dead and a man is coming at you," Ian said, meeting her anger with dark eyes, watching her go pale at his words. "Point and shoot and keep shooting until you're out of bullets or you're dead. Nothing fancy about it. Just killing, pure and simple, because the second choice is to be killed. No training on earth can prepare you for it, and thinking a short lesson in a hotel room is going to make any difference is a good way to end up stone-cold fucking dead."

"You're trying to scare me."

"The phone caller was trying to scare you. I'm trying to educate you."

"By telling me I'm helpless?" She dropped the tasteless turkey sandwich on the table. "Gee, thanks, I feel ever so much better informed."

Ian quit pretending to eat and dumped his own sandwich on top of the salad. "You think you're the only one who's scared? I'm spending a lot of the time in a cold sweat, thinking of all the ways someone can kill and get away with it. I want to haul you to Rarities and leave you there until I catch this bastard."

"Without me, how are you going to catch anything but a cold from all that sweat?" she asked sweetly. "You can't offer anything to make gallery owners prick up their ears and dig in their memories. You don't have personal memories and questions that threaten someone enough to make him—or her—commit arson and murder. You don't have anything but a gun, and that won't make this cockroach come crawling up out of the bathroom drain to tell you his life story."

She was right, so Ian stuck with the part of the argument he had a chance of winning. "I never said you were defenseless. You're better armed than ninety-nine percent of the population."

"You just pointed out that I can't shoot a gun so I—"

"I'm not talking about guns," he cut in.

"Then what *are* you talking about?"

"Brains. I'll bet brains against bullets anytime, anywhere but a turkey shoot. This isn't a turkey shoot." *Please, God, keep it that way. It's always been staged in the past, wrecks and fires and drowning. No bullets.* "You're smart."

"I'm scared."

"That's smart. So let's put our smarts together and see if we can come up with this killer before he comes down on us."

Corona del Mar
Monday night

62

The raincoat-shrouded man moved quickly toward the electrical wires. No matter how many urban or suburban codes were written to keep things pretty, buried wires had to emerge somewhere in order to connect buildings to the basic necessity of the twenty-first century: electricity. The deserted storage yard was in an area zoned for light industry, so various wires were allowed to climb in unsightly tubes right up the outside of the buildings—and the gatepost.

Bolt cutters sliced through tube and wires with gratifying ease. As required of all public areas, electronic locks opened the instant the power went out. It was a simple safety measure to ensure that people caught behind gates or doors by a fire weren't trapped by the very security devices that had been intended to keep them safe.

The gate opened. No alarm bells went off. No backup lights came on. He hadn't expected any. People who had real valuables kept them in safes, not storage units made of heavy tinfoil and light security.

The same bolt cutters and a lot more effort got him through the padlock on the outside of unit 120. He pulled up slowly, expecting a squeal of metal on metal. Nothing but a rumble of oiled wheels. He rolled up the door just enough to get under and pull it down behind him so no light would show. It was utterly dark inside.

He reached inside his coat. The cold and damp made his fingers clumsy. It took a few moments before he got the big flashlight on. Eagerly he swept the cone of light around the room.

Empty racks. A lot of them. Three—no, four—fire extinguishers. Some freestanding shelves that still held goods. He raked the light over lamp bases and vases and Depression glass, South American weavings based on Escher's skewed fantasies, flutes made of exotic woods and decorated with magic symbols, costume jewelry shaped like Egyptian gods, old photo frames of silver and gilt, and dolls with smiles painted on their precious faces.

The flashlight picked up the gleam of hinges across the room. He went quickly to the closed cabinets. Fingers trembling, he yanked the first one open. Then the next. And the next and the next until every door was agape.

There wasn't anything inside.

Not one painting.

Not *one*.

"Nothing but fucking junk!"

With a guttural noise he spun around and shoved the nearest rack over, sending it crashing into another rack and then another, huge metal dominoes falling and scattering everything on their shelves in a raucous cascade of breakage and ruin. What didn't break in the fall he stamped on until it lay in pieces and he was panting hard and fast, a runner who hadn't meant to race at all.

He forced his breath to steady and deepen until his heart was no longer a savage fist beating against his chest. Losing his temper didn't make him any safer.

Killing her would.

He could hardly wait. This was one death he would enjoy.

Smiling, thinking about her fear, he smashed several of the empty wooden racks, scattered chunks of paraffin and sawdust over them, and reached into his coat for a glass bottle of kerosene. He emptied most of it on the ragged pile of wood. He pulled a colorful pack of birthday candles from his pocket, arranged them, and made a trail of oily liquid between candles and the pile of kerosene-soaked wood. Folding a matchbook open, he tore off one match, propped the matchbook against the candles, and lit the single match. A tiny, bright flame bit into the cardboard matchbook.

By the time the flame reached the rest of the matches, touched off the candles, and snaked over to the pile of wood, the man had already vanished into the rain.

63

Ian licked garlicky grease off Lacey's fingers until she giggled in spite of the shadows in her eyes. So did he.

"That's better," he said.

"Clean fingers? I could have used my napkin."

"Your smile. Did you know you think better when you're smiling? True medical fact."

She started to question the origin of that "true medical fact" when she saw the gentleness in his eyes and in the curve of his lips. She liked seeing him relax too much to poke holes in the moment. And then she realized that he felt the same way about her. Even as they sat there trying to figure out who might benefit from murdering her, he was trying to make it easier on her by teasing out smiles.

"You really are good for me," she said.

"Works both ways."

Her smile wasn't big, but it was real. She let out a long breath. "Okay, I'm ready to tackle it again."

"This time let's keep track. Find a pencil and paper while I do dishes."

"Dishes?" she asked.

He swept up trash and food debris and crammed it into the sitting room wastebasket. "See? Dishes done."

Lacey went to the supplies Susa had left her, pulled out a sketch pad and pencil, and returned to the sitting room. Ian had moved to the sofa. He patted the cushion beside him and kept his hands to himself. Much as he wanted to take off her clothes and sink into her until they were both breathless and blind with pleasure, he didn't. Right now she needed to make lists more than she needed to get laid.

And so did he.

She sat down, flipped open the sketchbook, and printed: NEW PEOPLE SINCE THE PAINTINGS APPEARED.

Ian looked at it, blinked, and said, "Since you brought the paintings to Susa?"

Lacey nodded. "Even if it's someone from Grandfather's past, whoever it is never said 'Boo' to me until the paintings went public."

"Like I said, brains will beat bullets every time."

I hope.

But neither of them said it aloud.

"Okay, the first person is Susa," Ian said.

Lacey's pencil hesitated. "You said it was a man's voice on the phone."

Ian shrugged. "There are a lot of Donovan men."

"Do you really think—never mind, I withdraw the objection, the point is to make a list with everyone on it no matter how nutty."

She printed Susa's name.

"Then there's Mr. Goodman," Lacey said. Mentally she played back the first night she'd met Susa. "I can't think of anyone else I saw for the first time that night who showed any interest in the paintings. Can you?"

"A couple of Goodman's assistants were old enough to set fires. I'll check them out. Leave some blank lines." Ian shifted against his harness until nothing dug into his ribs. "The next new person you met was Savoy Forrest, right?"

"Right." Lacey wrote down the name as she flipped through hours in her mind. "I didn't meet the gate guard at Savoy Ranch when Susa and I went painting, so does he count?"

"Put him down."

She did. "New people were kind of slow until the auction. Then there's a raft of them. Bliss, and Ward Forrest. Angelique White. Savoy's son, who said about three words to me."

"Don't forget the silk suit who tried to pick you up."

Lacey blinked. "I missed him."

"I didn't, but we won't count him since Pickford never got close enough to you for an introduction."

"Pickford? The accountant?"

"No, the son and lawyer, not the father."

"Whatever. I'll write 'em both down."

Ian watched Lacey's swift, stylish printing.

"Did I meet the sheriff that night?" she asked, frowning.

"Probably. He was with Bliss."

"Would I be unbearably naïve if I pointed out that he's the *sheriff*, for God's sake?"

"Hotel theft was an inside job, and he owns part of the security company." Ian took the pencil from her and wrote Rory Turner in dark, slashing letters. "He also has my cell-phone number."

"Then we have to include the deputies who followed us," she said, reclaiming the pencil, "even if I didn't meet them. Did you get their names?"

"Just write down deputy A and B." He twisted the top off another soda. "I'll name them if they look good for it."

"Gallery owners," Lacey said, and wrote the names down.

Then they looked at the names.

"Okay, let's take the incidents in order," Ian said. "Who knew you had the paintings?"

"Everyone on this list," she said dryly.

"*Before* the fire."

"Susa, and she didn't know my real name."

"Who did?" he asked.

"Besides you and me? No one. When I took the paintings back, everyone thought I was January Marsh. That's what doesn't make any sense. In order for the fire to have been aimed at destroying the paintings, someone would have to have known where I took them and who I was. You were the only one."

"You don't look worried," he said.

"If you wanted me dead, I'd be dead."

He smoothed the renegade curl away from her eyes.

"Since I'm alive," she said, "I'm concluding that you're not the one trying to kill me."

"I could be really sneaky and just stringing you along."

"I could be channeling the Queen of Atlantis."

He smiled. "Okay, we're innocent. How long did it take you to get your paintings back from Mr. Goodman?"

"Almost an hour."

"We know Goodman called Savoy, who could have arranged for his good friend the sheriff to have you followed to your shop. Or Goodman could have called the sheriff directly. Either way," Ian said, "you're tagged. All anyone had to do was show your picture up and down the blocks to get an ID—Lacey Quinn, not January Marsh."

"Where would they get a picture?" Then, before he could answer, she said, "The security cameras. I must have been all over them. Can you print photos from them?"

"In a heartbeat."

"Who has the authority to do it?" she asked. "Goodman?"

"Maybe. The sheriff, certainly. Or anyone on the security staff could do it on the sly for his or her own purposes and follow you the same way. The most direct route would be through the sheriff. Plus whoever the sheriff talked to—the Forrests, for instance."

He made quick notes and put a check next to the names that could have known where Lacey and the paintings went.

"You forgot Susa."

Ian blinked.

"Susa was alone the night the fire started and she knew where the paintings were." Lacey made a disgusted sound. "But she was no more likely to burn down my shop than I was. She's connected to those paintings as deeply as most people connect to a lover."

"But I like the way you're thinking," Ian said.

"Huh?"

"Mean. Low. Sneaky. Cold. Like a cop." He kissed

the corner of her mouth. "No-holds-barred. It's how you survive."

He put a check next to Susa's name.

And his own.

"Okay," she said. "Everyone with the check knew who I was and where the paintings were, and therefore could have set a fire to destroy the paintings. But why?"

"Let's stay with the 'who' for a while longer. Who knew the paintings survived the fire and were taken to the Savoy Hotel? Remember, the theft occurred barely twelve hours after the fire."

"You, me, Susa, the Newport Beach Fire and Police Departments—"

"Which means Rory Turner could have found out real fast," Ian interrupted. "If he knew, then we're back to the same group we had before the fire."

"How do we find out if he knew?"

"Savoy Forrest wants your paintings. The Forrests got Turner elected. Take it as a given that the sheriff quizzed the NBPD. What they know, he knows. What he knows, the Forrests know."

More check marks went on the list of names.

"Who besides the sheriff and the employees had access to the hotel security system?" Lacey asked.

Ian didn't answer. He just put check marks next to the sheriff and the security employees.

"What about the Forrests?" she asked. "If Rory Turner is in bed with the Forrests, then they could have access, couldn't they?"

"Maybe, but whoever the thief was had more than access. He also knew the security system inside and out. Remember, the fake bellman never showed anything useful to the cameras."

Lacey looked at all the marks and names. If they were making any progress, she didn't see it, and they hadn't even gotten to motive. "How come whoever it was—or they were—didn't just clean out my storage unit after I brought three more pictures out?"

"Because I dumped the tail before we got to the storage unit, so no one but us knew where it was. But I didn't dump the deputies when we went back the second time."

She shivered. "You really think it's the sheriff, don't you?"

"You have a better suspect?"

"But why? If it's the money, then burning the paintings isn't going to make the sheriff any richer. If it isn't the money, what is it? Even if you assume that the paintings portrayed real murders, I don't think the sheriff was out of grammar school when the first two took place, so why would he care?"

"Damned if I know. But I plan on asking him."

Lacey raked her fingers through her loose curls. "This is crazy. How would the sheriff know we've been going to galleries? We weren't followed, were we?"

"Not as far as I could tell."

"Then how would he know to call you and leave his cheerful little threat?"

"That's the second question I'm going to ask him."

Lacey stared at the sketch pad, then threw it on the floor in disgust. "We don't have shit and you know it."

"We don't have roses," he corrected. "Shit we've got plenty of."

"What we've got are paintings some people want enough to steal, some want enough to buy in the open, some want to sell on the quiet, and some want to destroy outright." She threw up her hands. "Maybe my shop was really an accident, just one of those coincidences. Then the motive for the rest of it is simple. Good old greed."

"That would make it easier."

"So you think I'm right?"

"I think there are enough hanging threads on that theory to knit a whole new sweater."

"So do I." She leaned back against the couch and swiped hair out of her eyes. "Now what? And don't say we go over the names again. Each time we do, we end up knowing less. Pretty soon we're going to be suspecting ourselves."

Ian slid one arm around Lacey's shoulders and the other under her knees. Before she could blink she was in his lap. "I've got a better idea," he said.

Smiling, she nuzzled against his neck. "Yeah? I want to hear about it in breathless detail. Really breathless."

"I checked my e-mail while you were driving."

She rolled her eyes. "Be still my beating heart."

"You'd be excited if you knew how rarely I check it," he said.

"Okay. I'm excited." She nibbled.

So did he.

"Susa has been on the phone with Savoy Forrest," he said. "You now have unlimited access to the ranch to paint for your show in November. So if it's not raining, we'll paint for a while and wait to see what Rarities and Susa have come up with in the way of gallery owners in L.A. and San Francisco to talk to."

"Unlimited access," she murmured, running her finger inside the collar of his T-shirt. "Now there's a thought to raise my heart rate."

"Tomorrow we see if the Savoy Museum will lend

us one or more of their original Martens so that Rarities can compare them to your inheritance. It will help if you're suitably impressed by how well they're displaying the three paintings from the auction."

"That sounds like Susa."

"Direct quote."

"Then we'll put together a list of—"

Lacey's cell phone rang, cutting Ian off. He hooked his hand under the strap of the big sack that passed for her purse and dumped it in her lap. She pulled out her phone.

"Hello?"

"Hi, Lacey. It's Tom, Shayla's brother."

"Did Shayla finally surface? She hasn't called me yet."

"No. I don't expect to hear from her for at least three more days." He hesitated. "I'm afraid I've got more bad news for you. The fire department just called. There's been a fire at the storage yard. We lost four units, including yours. Would have lost more if it wasn't for the rain and the fact that the fire station is only a half mile away."

"Please, tell me no one was hurt," she said starkly.

Ian watched her with night-dark eyes.

"Not even a scratch," Tom said. "I just wanted to alert you so that you can prepare a list for my insurer. No rush. Some time in the next few days is fine."

"Was 408 burned?" she asked.

"Nope. Way down at the other end and across the yard. We just lost the units above and next to yours."

She breathed out raggedly. "All right. Thank God no one was hurt. I'll get the list to you."

Ian waited until she ended the call. "What?"

"You remember all those hanging threads you talked about?"

"Yeah."

"One of them set fire to the storage unit."

64

It had been as bad a night's sleep as Lacey could ever remember having. Fires, wrecks, drownings, and a feeling of being hunted through each of the ways to die. Dreams as dark as her grandfather's paintings. Fear as real as her own racing heart.

The cynical suspicion in the eyes of the cops who had questioned her repeatedly concerning her whereabouts during the time preceding the fire in Tom's storage yard hadn't helped. The reasonable part of her didn't blame the police for asking. Two fires in such a short time stretched belief. The emotional part of her wanted to scream at them to quit wasting time with her and find the real arsonist.

She poured herself some more coffee. She didn't need it, didn't want it, and couldn't think of anything else to do. The breakfast she hadn't eaten sure didn't appeal to her. She could barely stand to sit near the cold scrambled eggs and toast.

Ian looked at Lacey's hollow eyes and pale lips and wanted nothing more than to get his hands on whoever was making her life hell.

"It's supposed to clear up later," he said. "Want to go paint something wonderful after we go to the Savoy Museum?"

Automatically Lacey looked at her watch. Even its outrageous chartreuse dinosaur didn't make her smile. "I've got to get that list of the unit's contents to Tom."

"Put the paintings on it," Ian said.

Her head snapped up. "What?"

"Tell them you lost several hundred unsigned and therefore uninsurable, valueless paintings in addition to the list of goods for Lost Treasures Found."

Lacey drew a deep, slow breath. "This pretty well puts the shop under. No stock. No insurance money because no insurer is going to pay off after two fires in a row. And do you really think the arsonist didn't get inside and see the empty racks?"

"I don't know." The cops sure hadn't been any help with details. "But we don't have anything to lose either way. If the guy got inside, he might say something to give himself away to us. If he didn't get inside, he might just get the hell out of your life. Since you're not claiming a penny for the paintings, the insurer won't care what really burned and what didn't."

She shrugged. "I guess. I just don't like lying."

"Not even to trip up a murderer?"

Her laugh was as painful as the shadows in her eyes. "I'm still having a hard time believing it. It would help if it made sense, but it doesn't."

"Murder isn't always rational. In fact, it rarely is."

"This comforts me how?"

Ian mentally kicked himself. "Guess I'm not the

comforting sort." Since he'd already stuck his size thirteen foot in his mouth, he might as well keep going. He knew from past experience that there was room for two feet, even as big as his were. "Savoy Forrest called while you were asleep."

"Wonderful." She rubbed her forehead. "What did he want?"

"Guess?"

"To buy the paintings?"

"Yeah."

"How did he find out about the fire?" she asked.

"He didn't say anything about the second fire. Just told me that the paintings from the charity auction are being proudly displayed in the museum and you were welcome any old time at all, and after you saw them maybe you'd feel so good about how they're being treated that you'd consider selling one or two, seeing as how you don't have any safe place to put them and all." Ian's drawling summary of the conversation was at odds with his hard eyes and harder smile.

"Does this move him to the top of our suspect list?" she asked rather bitterly.

"Right up with good old Sheriff Turner."

"Why would Savoy want to kill me?"

"I'll ask him right after I talk to the sheriff."

"Should I take him up on the museum offer?" Lacey asked.

"Have to, sooner or later. Rarities wants a look at the Martens the old man collected. As for selling them a painting, it's up to you."

Lacey started to dismiss the idea as she had every time the subject came up. Then she thought of all the bills that would have to be paid even though the shop was a write-off. Shayla would need money, too. Selling a painting would keep both of them afloat while they found new work or put the pieces of their old work back together.

"I'll think about it." Lacey raked fingers through her hair. "Did Mrs. Katz call back about her Marten?"

"No."

"*Damn.* How are we supposed to find any true Martens hidden in Grandfather's forgeries unless we have some real Martens to work with?"

Ian didn't answer, because she'd asked the question of the ceiling, not him. "We've still got private collectors," he said.

"The Forrests. It always goes back to them, doesn't it?"

"And your grandfather. And you. And the sheriff."

Lacey raked her hair again and tried to think of something more effective than *what a mess.* Then she brought herself up short. *No pity party. Doesn't do any good. Take one thing at a time and go through the list until something makes sense.* "All right. To hell with what we don't know. Let's go with what we know."

"Which is?"

"We need some real Martens for Rarities to work with. The Savoy Museum has them." She grabbed her big ratty purse and expensive cashmere coat. "Let's go get our wonderful guided tour."

"Unguided," Ian said.

"What?"

"The museum isn't open to the public today."

"Good. I'm not feeling very public."

Ian hesitated, then said bluntly, "You'd be safer here in the hotel room."

She stopped with her hand on the hallway door. Her chin came up. "For how long?"

"Until I find out who's threatening to kill you."

"How long?" she repeated. "A day or two? A week? Two weeks? Several months? *Years?*"

"Lacey—"

He was talking to her back going through the door. *"Shit."*

He shot through the door and caught up with her before she'd taken two steps.

"In the future," he said tightly, "I go first through the doors. That isn't negotiable. Got it?"

She started to argue, looked at the cold line of his mouth, and said, "Got it."

65

"Odd place for a museum," Lacey said, looking around the posh interior of the Savoy Tower lobby.

"Thirty years ago, yeah," Ian said, "One thing I learned working for Rarities is that institutions have become some of the biggest collectors around. It's a variation of the my-cock-is-longer-than-your-cock game."

She gave him a dark sideways glance. "Just little boys in thousand-dollar suits and million-dollar expense accounts, huh?"

"Pretty much."

The receptionist was a guard dressed in a uniform suit that might have cost a few hundred bucks. Her hair was short, her makeup minimal, and she must have been a cop in her previous life. It took her less than five seconds to spot the harness under Ian's dark denim jacket. Behind the chest-high desk, her foot moved just enough to hit a button.

"Give her the card, Lacey," Ian said. "I don't want the boys who are going to show up real quick to be nervous."

Lacey handed the guard Savoy Forrest's card.

"Mr. Forrest invited us to tour the museum anytime," Lacey said. "His private number is on the back. You can check with him."

As the woman called the number, two men came out of a side hall and walked quickly to the desk. The first guard held up a cautionary hand. The two men flanked Ian and Lacey and waited.

"Mr. Forrest? Sorry to bother you, sir. A man and a woman—"

"Lacey Quinn and Ian Lapstrake," Ian cut in loudly enough to be heard on the other end of the line.

"—say that you've invited them to view the museum after-hours." She relaxed visibly as she listened to Savoy Forrest. "Thank you, sir. I'll tell them." The guard hung up and smiled. "Sorry about that. We've had so many threats from eco-terrorists that we have to treat everyone as an enemy." She looked at one of the guards. "Show them up to the museum, would you? Mr. Savoy will join them up there if his meeting ends before they leave."

Lacey retrieved the business card that was the key to the kingdom and followed the guard into a nearby elevator. Ian was with her every step of the way. His jacket was open and his eyes never stopped moving and never truly looked away from the guard. She supposed that trick was part of the Advanced Paranoia training he'd talked about with Susa.

"You don't think," she said in an undertone, "that we'll have a problem here?"

"I think there's only one of me, and one is never enough to do a decent job of guarding anything."

"I'm here, too."

The line of his mouth softened. "You going to guard me, darling?"

"Yes."

The elevator door opened. Ian held Lacey back and gestured for the guard to go first. He led them down an office corridor with doors opening off both sides. Other than a hall carpet and a sign on the wall that simply said MUSEUM, the place obviously had been constructed originally with private business rather than public art in mind.

The guard unlocked a door that had the museum hours painted in discreet black on frosted white glass. Inside, the feel of the room changed dramatically. Business was just a memory; art ruled here. An oriental carpet in rich, age-muted colors warmed the room. To one side was a modest museum gift shop with art books, videos, and posters from previous shows prominently displayed. The rest of the space was given over to white walls holding plein air art painted by southern California Impressionists. The lights were turned off, leaving the exhibition room in a gloomy kind of twilight.

"Hello?" said a voice from the back of the museum shop. "I'm sorry, we aren't open today."

"Mr. Jordon?" the guard asked. "That you? I thought you weren't in today."

"I'm not," Jordon said, walking into view. He was middle-aged, with a graying, thin ponytail going down the back of his old sweatshirt halfway to his equally old jeans. "I'm doing inventory."

"Mr. Forrest told these folks that the museum was open anytime they wanted to visit and that we'd help them any way we could."

"Mr. Forrest," Jordon repeated.

"Yes, sir. Savoy Forrest."

Jordon looked at his grubby hands, sighed, and put a good face on it. "Of course. Welcome to the museum." He stepped over to a master switch and threw it. Light flooded the room. "If you have any questions, you'll find me in the shop counting books. Enjoy."

With that, Jordon vanished back into his inventory.

"Will you lock up after they leave?" the guard called out.

"Yes!" Jordon called back impatiently.

The guard went out the hall door, leaving Ian and Lacey alone. She looked at him, shrugged, and walked toward the paintings. The lighting was excellent and cleverly positioned to bring life to even the darkest painting. Under other circumstances she would have been intrigued by most of the paintings and enthralled by a few. Today she was simply fast. She went from painting to painting with a speed that suggested someone looking for something and not finding it.

Ian followed her, grateful that the display was one of the open kinds, rather than the maze that had made him nervous at the auction.

There were only fifteen paintings. Less than three minutes after Lacey had been given the run of the museum, she looked at him and shook her head.

"Nothing." Then she heard herself and cringed. "Nothing that we're looking for," she added quickly. "Some nice paintings, some good ones, one excellent piece of art. In all, a thin and reasonably academic cross section of southern California plein air artists. No Marten, signed or otherwise."

"Interesting," Ian said. "Any obvious blank spots or cards indicating that paintings are on loan somewhere?"

"Not that I saw."

"Neither did I."

"Let's look at the gift shop."

"What for?" he asked.

"Books that have Marten in the index. Posters of old shows by this museum. Catalogues listing the contents of old shows."

"Good idea."

Making enough noise that Jordon would know what they were doing, Ian and Lacey went through the contents of the gift store. It didn't take very long. Like the museum, the shop was small and focused in its content.

Ian watched Lacey go through the last oversized art book.

"Nope," she said, replacing the book. "He's mentioned, but not pictured. Not him personally, not his art."

"Is he mentioned as part of the museum collection?" Ian asked.

"No. Simply a talented artist who died tragically, et cetera, and very little of his oeuvre survived him." Without saying anything else, she tilted her head questioningly toward the small storage area where Jordon was rustling among the stock.

Ian nodded.

"Mr. Jordon," Lacey said, walking behind the small desk that served as a checkout counter for patrons wishing to buy books. "Sorry to interrupt, but we have a problem."

Jordon was on his hands and knees, counting books. His gray ponytail bobbed as he shoved himself to his feet. "What is it?"

"We were told that at least three of the paintings from the auction were hanging in this museum."

"They will be."

"When?"

"As soon as they're framed or cleaned or both. Let me check." He went past them to the small desk. His fingers moved over the computer keyboard like hurried mice. "Auction, auction . . . ah, here we are. Two are being framed and one is being cleaned."

"Cleaned?" Lacey said sharply. "I didn't give permission for any cleaning."

"Really?" He frowned. "Maybe there's a mistake." He checked the records again. "Two landscapes and a domestic scene. All untitled. All unsigned. All unframed."

"Domestic scene," Ian repeated.

"Yes. A woman in a spa."

Ian thought that was a rather precious description of murder, but he kept it to himself.

"Where, *exactly,* are the paintings now?" Lacey asked.

"The basement, I imagine. We have a modest frame shop there."

"Before you take us down to the basement," Ian said, "can you tell us where the rest of the paintings by Lewis Marten are?"

"Lewis Marten." Jordon frowned irritably, remembered that his unwanted visitors came from Mr. Forrest himself, and keyed in the name. "We don't list any Martens in the active file."

"Meaning?" Ian asked.

"No paintings by Lewis Marten are part of our present collection on display in this museum. They're either in rotation with other collections or in storage."

"What about in the past?" Lacey asked.

"Those records are kept at Savoy Ranch, along with any paintings that aren't being actively displayed at this time."

"How many paintings does the museum own?" Ian asked.

"Several hundred."

"With only fifteen on display. Hell of a way to run a museum," Ian muttered.

Jordon straightened and looked down his nose at Ian. "You're here for the Pickfords, aren't you? This was all litigated years ago. This is a bona fide museum open to the public, and all their caviling won't change anything."

"Pickfords?" Lacey asked.

"Jason and Stephen," Jordon said. His tone of voice said they already knew who he was talking about. "Do you really want to see the basement storage room?"

"More than ever," Lacey said.

In silence they followed Jordon into an elevator and down to the basement. He unlocked a room, turned on the lights, and gestured impatiently for them to come inside.

The two unsigned landscapes were on separate easels next to rows of framing samples. For each landscape a frame sample had been pulled out and rested on the corner of the canvas, giving an idea of the final effect. The drowning pool was on a third easel, its bleakly radiant canvas screaming of the dark side of humanity. Several frame samples were stacked near the painting, as though the framer hadn't decided which worked best.

Lacey glanced at the landscapes, checked the frames that had been chosen, and said, "Very nice."

She looked at the samples near the drowning pool, held up several in turn against the canvas, and then went completely still. She picked up the canvas, ignoring Jordon's instinctive protest. Silently she turned it into the light and studied the painting, flipped it over to see the back, and turned it right side up again before she set it back on the easel.

"Thank you, Mr. Jordon," she said. Then she turned to Ian. "Time to go."

Ian waited until they had left the Savoy Tower and were walking across the parking lot before he said, "What's wrong?"

"The drowning painting."

"What about it?"

"It's the first one. The one that was stolen from the hotel."

Ian stared at her. "Are you sure?"

"The bracelet isn't nearly as clear as it was in the second one. And the number on the back is twenty-seven, not thirty-six."

"Can you prove they were switched?" he asked.

"I didn't think to photograph the back of either painting while it was in my hands. Did you?"

A low curse was Ian's only answer.

66

The offices of Pickford and Pickford weren't as fancy as Savoy Tower, but they were big and had a peekaboo view of the marina through sheets of wind-driven rain. The weather clearing promised by the forecasters hadn't come about. A big storm had. Stephen Pickford was sitting behind a desk the size of an aircraft carrier. If he was happy to see the two people dripping on his thick rug, it didn't show.

"I'd like to say that any friend of Savoy Forrest is a friend of mine," Pickford said, "but I'd be lying."

Ian had picked up enough reading David Quinn's fat envelope of clippings to know what Pickford meant. "We understand that you and your son sued Savoy Enterprises over the funding of the Savoy Museum."

"Yes. We lost, but not on the merits of the case. What of it?"

"We're looking for some paintings we thought were

part of the Savoy Museum collection," Lacey said, "but can't be accounted for now."

Pickford shrugged. "They shift paintings in and out of that museum all the time. If they're not there, they're stored at the ranch house."

"Interesting," Ian said.

"Legal, too," Pickford said sarcastically. "We've got the legal judgment that says so."

"Was part of that suit a complete accounting of all museum acquisitions, past and present, active and inactive, in or out of storage, at the ranch or anywhere else?" Lacey asked.

Pickford's gray eyebrows lifted. "Yes."

"Could we see it?" Lacey asked.

"Why?"

"Not to do the Forrests any favors, that's for sure," Ian said calmly.

Pickford thought about it for five seconds. "On the condition that you tell me anything you find that we overlooked, yes."

"Done," Ian said.

Pickford smiled rather grimly and gestured to the door that joined his father's office with his own. "South wall, blue binding, volumes one through nineteen. The paintings are listed in an appendix. The records you're after should be in volume nineteen."

"Thank you," Lacey said.

"Have you ever looked through court records, Miss?" Pickford asked.

"No."

"Thought so. If you had, you'd be cursing me rather than thanking me."

After fifteen minutes Lacey understood what Pickford meant.

After an hour she was cross-eyed.

After two hours she and Ian were baffled. No paintings by Lewis Marten, signed or unsigned, were now or had ever been part of the Savoy Museum collection.

They caught Pickford just as he was coming back from lunch.

"We're confused," Lacey said.

"I sometimes believe that's the whole point of the law," Pickford said. "That's why I became an accountant. Numbers are more reliable."

"I was told by Savoy Forrest that his father collected a certain painter, yet not one of that artist's paintings is listed in the records of the suit," Lacey said.

"Doesn't surprise me. Slippery bastard."

"Savoy Forrest?" Ian asked.

"All of them." A red flush stained Pickford's cheeks. "Not an honest man in the family, by birth or by marriage. Crooks. Not that you'll ever prove it. They own the law in Moreno County and most of the goddamned state."

"Frustrating," Ian said.

"As hell." Pickford blew out a breath. "As for your paintings, they probably were acquired by Savoy Enterprises for the family gallery with the stipulation that the paintings pass to the museum as soon as the old bastard dies. Technically, though paid for with corporate funds, they're not part of the museum collection at all."

"Is this, um, family collection on view anywhere?" Lacey asked.

"Technically, yes."

"Meaning?" Ian asked.

"The paintings are at the ranch. You have to be invited to see them. I've never met anyone who was."

Lacey's smile was all teeth. "You just have."

67

The guard at the south gate had seen Ian and Lacey before. He checked off their names and opened the guardhouse window. Rain lashed in.

" 'Evening," he said. "Mr. Forrest isn't back from the club yet, but the housekeeper is expecting you."

"Which Mr. Forrest?" Ian asked, ignoring the rain coming in through his own open window.

"Ward. He left here about an hour ago. Were you expecting his son?"

"That's who we talked to."

"Then I'm sure he'll be along soon."

Lacey leaned across Ian to look at the guard. She didn't have to lean far. Though there were only two people in the front seat, she'd slid over to sit thigh to thigh with Ian.

"We didn't drive all the way out here because we like sight-seeing in the rain," she said to the guard. "We were told that we would be able to see the Forrest family art collection. Did either Mr. Forrest say when he'd be back?"

"No, but I'm sure the housekeeper knows."

Lacey started to object.

The guard kept talking. "Drive slow and watch the road where it climbs up the side of the canyon onto the bluff top. Ward told me the bluff was losing some stones with all the rain."

Ian ran up the window and drove onto ranch land. The windshield wipers worked hard to keep up with the rain. Muddy water washed from the high side of the asphalt to the low and gathered in puddles everywhere. Though sealed, it still wasn't much of a road.

Lacey grabbed the dashboard. "The guard isn't really needed. These bumps could knock you cold. How far is the house?"

"Couple miles."

She looked at the water-slicked, storm-stripped sycamores growing up from the dry riverbed to their left. "No wonder the road's coming apart. Rain like this sent Noah running to his workshop. Wonder if the riverbed will stay dry."

"It's a long way from the mountains."

"And that matters how?"

"Runoff."

Lacey glanced at Ian. She didn't need his terse conversation to tell her that he was in a bad mood. "Is this a general or a specific mad?"

He cut a sideways look at her, downshifted, and gave his attention back to the road. "General."

In the heavy rain, the truck's headlights made little more than a vague blur on the dark pavement. The tires bit through the water and occasional skim of mud without slipping. Even so, Ian stopped, put the truck in neutral, and switched into four-wheel drive. Better to do it now than stall out in mud on the side of a hill later.

"You want to talk about your general mad?" she asked.

Ian reached for the four-wheel drive gearshift on the floor and let out the clutch. The old truck groaned and took the road like a great turtle—slow but sure.

"We've talked about it," he said.

"And our conclusion was . . . ?"

"We're fucked."

"Did we enjoy it?" she shot back.

Despite his mood, Ian smiled. "We sure did."

The road narrowed to one lane with occasional turnouts so two vehicles could get past each other. It didn't follow the dry streambed. Instead, the road snaked alongside the bluff that rose on the north side. The rain lifted for a moment, then poured down with renewed enthusiasm. Somewhere to the west there must have been an opening in the clouds, because sun stabbed through the rain in rich flashes of gold. It made driving a misery.

The sun sank beneath rain as the road started upward in a series of twisting, tight turns that reflected its origins in horse-and-buggy days. Instead of gutters, water was hustled off the road by giving the pavement a slant up on the bluff side and down over the growing dropoff on the driver's side. Sheets of dirty water sluiced across the road, shot through with occasional tongues of mud. The higher they climbed, the more muddy the road got.

"You'd think they'd maintain it better," Lacey said, bracing herself on the dashboard again.

Ian didn't answer.

The downhill side of the road was scalloped from old slides where chunks of the shoulder had slid off into the riverbed. The uphill side had mounds of mud and pebbles that had drooled down the bluff and piled up at the pavement, making the road even narrower. As soon as someone dropped a 'dozer blade across the road next spring, it would be fine. Until then it would be lousy.

Remembering the guard's warning, Ian kicked on the high beams. They didn't do much. It was the time of day that wasn't light or dark, when distances were tricky to judge even when it wasn't raining.

"If you see any rocks—" Ian began.

The windshield exploded.

Lacey's scream drowned out the flat *crack* of a gun.

A rifle, Ian thought as he fought the waves of darkness sweeping over him. *A fucking turkey shoot.*

Even as his vision went black, he tried to yank the steering wheel so that the truck would turn away from the dropoff, but it was too late. Everything was slipping through his hands.

Lacey grabbed the wheel and tried to keep the truck on the road. There was a sharp *crack!* The truck jerked and bucked and sagged down on her side and began crabbing, tires fighting for traction. The rear wheels were already off the road, dragging everything down with them as they sank. Tires spun independently, spraying water and mud in rooster tails toward the riverbed a hundred feet below. It wasn't a straight drop, but it was a steep one.

The truck shuddered backward toward the void.

The left front tire caught traction. The truck stopped sliding and started vibrating with a horrible grinding sound. For an instant Lacey thought it would hold in place, but the downhill weight was too much. The truck quivered backward. She yanked open her seat belt and Ian's.

And then she felt it all sliding away.

"Ian!" She dragged him toward the passenger door, taking advantage of the angle of the seat. "We've got to get out before the truck goes over!"

He might have groaned. She couldn't hear much above the sound of the engine. Then his head rolled and she saw his face.

That's not blood on him. It can't be. I won't let it be.

She kicked open the door and half fell out onto the road, pulling Ian after her. She didn't feel the slam of the hard surface on her shoulder or the drenching chill of the rainwater sluicing over her. All she felt was the shudder and wrench of her breathing.

And Ian's.

He's alive. Oh, God, he's alive.

Behind her, the truck groaned and jerked and then simply disappeared. The crash and bang of metal told her that the truck was tumbling faster and faster, gaining velocity with every second.

From the corner of her eye she saw movement. A man was sliding down the bluff toward them. Relief swept through her—help was on the way. Then she saw the outline of the rifle and knew that it wasn't a rock that had broken the windshield or the sound of a tire exploding that she had heard. Someone had tried to kill them.

Now he was coming down to finish the job.

Hide. We have to hide.

There was no cover on the road. No way to haul Ian up the bluff. Nowhere to go but down.

She took it.

Ian shook his head and began struggling against the hands pulling at him. With the strength of pure adrenaline overdrive, Lacey shoved against him, taking both of them into the only safety she could find. When he felt the ground give way, he knew what was coming. He grabbed her and wrapped her close, trying to protect her as they went rolling and tumbling and sliding down the bluff into the darkness below until they slammed up against something bigger than they were and stopped moving.

Ian groaned. The first wave of dizziness had passed, leaving in its wake the nausea and blurred vision of a concussion. He'd had worse ones before. He could function if he had to. And his instincts were screaming at him that he had to. He tried to remember how he'd ended up in the rain with Lacey underneath him, but he couldn't.

Then he did.

"Lacey," he said in a low, urgent rasp against her ear. "Are you hurt?"

"Breath—knocked—out. That's—all."

"Did you see who was shooting at us?"

"A man."

"Only one?"

"Don't—know."

The agony that knifed through Ian's right arm when he shifted to draw his gun told him he had at least a sprained wrist and more likely a fracture. Either way, his right hand wasn't any good. He flexed his feet. Everything moved. The pins in his old ankle injury had held.

From above them came the sound of rolling dirt and pebbles, a curse, and then silence except for the rain.

The light was fading, but it was still good enough for the man to see them.

Lacey wondered if she would feel the bullet that killed her.

"If I move, he'll see it," Ian said against her ear. "Can you get my gun out of the holster?"

Hidden from the killer by Ian's wide shoulders, Lacey reached inside his ripped, muddy jacket and fumbled with the harness. Her fingers were cold, scraped, numb, and shaking. "Why doesn't he just shoot us?"

"Bullet holes are hard to explain. A wreck on a dark rainy afternoon isn't."

Earth and pebbles and water rolled down the hill to them.

"Hurry if you can," he breathed.

"I've got it, but I can't see the safety," she whispered raggedly. "Can't feel it. Too cold."

"Put the butt in my left hand."

She pushed the cold metal against his palm, waited for him to take off the safety for her, and tried not to think about the sounds coming down the hill.

"Can you see him without moving?" Ian asked against her ear.

She didn't want to look. She looked anyway, careful to move barely at all. "He's about a third of the way down the hill, angling toward us from my left."

Too far to risk it. Ian breathed warmth over her ear as he put his lips against it. "Lie still. No matter what."

Rain poured down in cold, relentless sheets.

The man came closer, slipped, and cursed. "Hey, you two all right?"

Lacey didn't move. Neither did Ian.

Soft, sucking sounds came, boots slogging and sliding through mud.

She locked her teeth against the scream clawing at her throat. Everything in her rebelled at lying motionless, helpless, while a killer approached to make sure they were dead.

A rock thumped into Ian's back. Another one clipped his ear. He felt the tension in Lacey's body and wanted to reassure her, but it was too late. The killer was too close, all options closed except one.

He rolled over firing and kept on firing until the gun was empty.

At first nothing happened. Then the man spun, jerked like a marionette, and flopped facedown in the dirt, all strings cut.

Without taking his eyes off the fallen man, Ian released the empty magazine, braced his gun upside down between his knees, and yanked a fresh magazine from the holder on his belt. Ignoring the rain and his dirty fingers, he reloaded with his left hand.

"Stay here," he said.

"You need more than one hand."

Numbly she followed him across forty feet of slippery hillside to the place where a man lay facedown, his arms flung limply above his head as though he'd grabbed at something that gave way, letting him fall. The hands were empty.

Ian crouched and jammed the muzzle of his gun behind the man's ear.

A groan answered, and an instinctive jerk away from whatever was causing pain.

"He's still alive," Ian said, disgusted. "I never could shoot worth a damn left-handed."

Lacey let out a breath that she hadn't been aware of holding. "He's got a rifle somewhere."

"It's off to the left. Don't touch it. Bastard probably has a shell in the chamber."

With a careless yank, Ian rolled the man over and shoved the gun muzzle hard under his chin. Beneath a coating of mud, blood, and rain, Ward Forrest stared up at the man he'd tried to kill.

68

With an unconscious sigh of relief that she was finally going to get a long, hot shower, Lacey unlocked the hotel room. Ian beat her to the door handle.

"After me, remember?" he said.

She just stared at him. Like her, he had disinfected scrapes and clean bandages wherever the doctors had found blood. He had dried mud just about everywhere else. If she hadn't been so tired that she was light-headed, she might have found his looks amusing. But she was that tired and she wasn't laughing.

"It's over," she said raggedly. "Ward Forrest is out cold in the hospital with a deputy baby-sitting him. You've got a broken wrist, and the sheriff has your gun and it's over."

Ian smiled at her. He could have pointed out the reasons that he felt like the other shoe hadn't dropped, but all he said was "Humor me."

"Ha, ha. You're humored."

But she let him go in first.

When he got back, she was leaning against the door frame, her eyes closed. Smiling, he tucked a wild, muddy curl behind her ear. Her eyes flew open.

"You want to shower before bed?" he asked.

"I'd take a bath, but I'm afraid I'd slide under and drown." Then she remembered the brutal painting and grimaced.

"Don't think about it," he said, kissing the corner of her mouth.

She nuzzled against him for a moment. "I feel like I dropped through reality into an alternate universe and I'm still trying to find my balance. Things look the same but they aren't. People try to kill you and your grandfather is a forger and maybe a murderer who appeared full grown at forty with no childhood and the cops look at you like you're a nutcase because you defended yourself against a nutcase and then they all but arrest you because you didn't get yourself killed and—"

He kissed her until she stopped thinking about it. "Go take that shower, darling."

"Alone?"

He held up his right arm. "The cast might be advertised as waterproof, but it isn't proof against what we'd do together in that shower."

"If you shower after me, I can't guarantee I'll be awake when you're finished."

"I love a challenge."

Ian watched her walk to the bathroom and told himself he was doing the right thing. She looked pale, fragile, with dark rings of exhaustion around her beautiful brown eyes. The last thing she needed was a romp in the sheets. And when he caught a look at himself in the sitting room mirror, he was surprised she'd even suggested it. His beard-shadowed, dirty, scraped, and bruised face would have made a great poster for a movie called *He Came from the Dead*.

The phone rang. He gave it the kind of look reserved for things that stick to your shoe, but answered it. Maybe Ward had come to after the surgery and was feeling chatty.

"Yeah?" he answered, not caring if he sounded rough. It was how he felt.

"This is the front desk. Sorry for bothering you so late, but a Mr. Quinn urgently wants to see Ms. Quinn."

Ian heard the shower running full force, looked at the time, and wondered how Lacey's dad had found out about the wreck.

"Send him up."

Ian was just drying his face when he heard the knock on the door. He went, checked out the spy hole, and then checked it out again.

The other shoe had just dropped. Hard.

With a soundless whistle, he opened the door. "Come on in, Mr. Quinn. I've got a lot of questions for you."

69

Lacey looked at the three examples of the Death Suite propped against the wall. Then she looked at her watch. "They should be here."

"They will be," Ian said.

"Think they'll bring Bliss?"

"After last night, I doubt it. The sheriff had to hold her to keep her from swinging at me."

Somebody knocked on the hall door.

Lacey walked to answer it with the quick, snapping steps of someone who is furious. "I still can't believe that Ward Forrest isn't under arrest."

"Even after last night?" Ian asked.

Lacey's mouth flattened. Her sketchbook was filled with notes from last night's staggering conversation.

"It's still wrong," she said.

"Amen. Now let's see if we can start making it right."

Left-handed, he opened the door. Rory Turner and

Savoy Forrest walked in. Both men looked grim and frustrated. Rory gave Ian a hard look and didn't offer to shake hands. He dumped the files he'd brought onto the wide coffee table.

"This better be good, Lapstrake," Rory said.

Ian smiled. "Oh, yeah. It's good."

Savoy started to say something, but a motion from Rory cut him off.

Ian closed the door and looked at the two men. They watched him with naked hostility in their eyes.

"I'm thinking good old Ward finally woke up and started talking," Ian said.

"Yes," Savoy said.

Ian waited.

"If he dies," Savoy said thinly, "you'll be arrested for murder."

"That's bullshit!" Lacey said, striding right up to Savoy and putting her face in his. "Your father tried to kill us!"

"So you say. He says differently."

"When did he wake up?" Ian asked.

"Early this morning," Rory said. "You got any coffee?"

Ian gestured with his cast to the telephone. "Call room service. Shouldn't take more than an hour."

Rory sat down on the couch and rubbed his face with a weariness he couldn't hide. "Okay. Here's how it is. Ward says he saw a truck go over the edge of the road, went down to help, and was shot for his trouble."

"You believe that?" Ian asked mildly, nudging Lacey into a chair. He didn't blame her for wanting to rip out a few smug throats, but it wouldn't do any good right now and might land them in jail.

"I think mistakes were made," Rory said carefully.

"Yeah, they sure as hell were," Ian said. "Let me list them for you. The first one is that Ward was checked out of the ranch by the south gate guard, wasn't checked back in at all, yet somehow he turned up on the main road anyway."

"There are more ways in and out of the ranch than the guarded gates," Savoy said.

"How many of them would you take when it was raining like a bitch?" Ian asked.

Savoy didn't answer. There was only one paved road in and out of the ranch and everyone at the table knew it.

"Did you call your father to tell him we were coming to see the paintings?" Lacey demanded.

"Of course. Why wouldn't I?"

"He must have left the house as soon as he hung up," Ian said. "Odd, don't you think?"

"He went target shooting at the club," Savoy said. "He does it all the time, including when the club is closed. He owns the place, so he has his own key, and comes and goes as he pleases."

"Does he usually run out to pop off a few right after he's got people lined up for a visit?"

Savoy shrugged. "He knew I'd come and take care of whatever the two of you wanted. He didn't have to wait around."

Ian looked at Rory.

The sheriff looked at his hands on the table.

"The third mistake was shooting out the windshield on my truck," Ian said. "There's a slug buried somewhere in the upholstery. Of course, you have to be looking for it to find anything."

Rory braced his elbows on the table. "You shot at him. He shot back. There might be a slug somewhere in your truck. So what?"

"I don't believe this," Lacey said, watching the sheriff with dark, furious eyes. "Did you *look* at the place we went over? Did you *look* at the truck? Did you do any damned thing except rush to cover up for your boss?"

"The road is always a mess after a good rain, the truck is upside down at the bottom of the bluff with the roof crushed into the frame, and what's left is pretty much buried in mud," the sheriff said.

"Convenient," Ian said. "Now I know what my great-uncle meant about nothing changing in Moreno County. No police work then and none now."

Rory shot to his feet. "Listen, you—"

"No, *you* listen," Ian cut in. "Ward avoided any manned gatehouses going back to the ranch. Why? He saw our 'accident.' How? From the top of the bluff? Okay, then what was he doing there standing in the rain with a rifle in his hands? He shot out the windshield and blew off the right front tire. You look, you'll find proof."

"My father had no reason to shoot you," Savoy said. "You're crazy."

Ian ignored him and concentrated on the sheriff. "If Ward saw us go over the edge and was just trying to help, why did he circle in from the side instead of hurrying straight down to see if we were hurt? Why didn't he call for help the instant we went over? And then," Ian said sardonically, "to really put the cherry on top of your fantasy sundae, you say I had a wild hair and unloaded my gun at the Good Samaritan who was coming to help us."

Rory started to speak, closed his eyes, and put his head in his hands. Ward could and had explained away each point Ian brought up, but listening to them all

laid out at once made the explanations less . . . believ-
able. He shook his head, baffled.

"Speaking of fantasies," Rory said, his voice rough,
"why would Ward want to kill you two?"

"We went over that last night," Lacey said. "Over
and over and *over.*"

Ian was more patient. If the sheriff wanted to rehash
last night, then that's what they'd do. At least Bliss
wasn't here, interrupting every other word.

"The instant Lacey showed up with those paintings," Ian said, "she was a target. Her place was
torched as soon as the deputies managed to follow her
home. Her storage unit was torched as soon as the
deputies followed her there. Her paintings were stolen
from a hotel owned by Ward, a hotel you admit that he
had access to and whose setup he'd overseen from security to employee uniforms. If you looked for a missing van from the fleet of white ranch vehicles, you'd
find one. If you searched the ranch you'd find the stolen
paintings, including the one he swapped out because it
showed Bliss's bracelet too clear for his comfort. Have
you looked for any of those things, Sheriff?"

"Talk about bullshit," Savoy said impatiently.
"Have you given Rory one credible reason why my father would do any of the things you describe? If he
wanted the paintings bad enough to steal them, he
wouldn't be burning them, would he?"

"Did you bring the records I requested?" Ian asked
Rory.

The sheriff gestured at the table.

"And?" Ian asked.

"I agree," Rory said. "I can't say much for the police work on any of the deaths except Gem Forrest's.
That one is clean. I headed the investigation myself."

"So did previous captive sheriffs on other Forrest or Savoy investigations," Lacey said.

Rory's face hardened. "What are you saying?"

"The truth," Ian said. "As far back as you go in the records, if there's a sheriff called Forrest investigating a Savoy death, a blind two-year-old could have done it better. It gives a whole new angle on how to get away with murder."

Savoy snorted. "You were right to leave Bliss out of this," he said to Rory. "She'd be screaming by now."

Rory didn't argue. Her father's near death had hit Bliss hard. She might fight Ward tooth and nail, but she loved him anyway.

"It all started when Benford Savoy the Second was killed on the ranch," Ian said, "and his great and good friend Sheriff Morley Forrest conducted the investigation and discovered that it was a tragic accident."

"That sort of accident happens every year, somewhere," Rory said. "Some fool mixes alcohol and hunting. The fact that this fool was a rich man over sixty doesn't make it any different than some poor slob from the sticks who drinks too many beers, trips over his own feet, and blows his stupid head off."

"Who benefited from his death?" Lacey asked.

"Savoy's? His wife inherited, if that's what you mean," Rory said, shrugging. "She wasn't even in the county when it happened."

Lacey pulled out her sketchbook and flipped it to the page where she'd made notes last night. "She inherited, but her adult son was supposed to be running the business. Except he was too busy drinking and raving over the countryside to care about the ranch, so Sheriff Morley Forrest kept on being the power behind the throne. He ran the Savoy businesses and everyone knew it. Correct?"

"Yes, but—" Savoy began.

Lacey kept talking. "Then you could say Morley Forrest benefited from his friend's death. His power became more direct. The widow depended on him to keep her wild son in line and out of jail. As sheriff of Moreno County, Morley Forrest was in a position to keep the family's dirty laundry out of sight."

"Are you really saying that my grandfather's death wasn't an accident?" Savoy asked in disbelief.

Ignoring him, Lacey flipped a page and continued. "About twelve years after his father's 'accidental' death, Three Savoy died in a car accident on the ranch. The cause? A mysterious 'mechanical failure' that somehow managed to dump his car into a ravine and him with it, and then burn so that nothing much was left but twisted metal. Rather spectacular results for an unexplained mechanical failure, but no one seemed curious. Just as no one would have been curious if Ian and I had ended up dead in a wreck that would no doubt have been written off as caused by 'mechanical failure.'"

"My grandfather was a drunk," Savoy said, ignoring the reference to yesterday's accident. "He didn't need mechanical failure to explain what happened to him."

"Somebody needed it," Ian said. "It's right there in the report."

"It was kinder on the widow than saying her husband was drunk, I'd guess," Rory said. "No harm done."

"Two days later," Lacey continued, "an artist

named Lewis Marten burned to death in his studio on Savoy Ranch. Like Morley, Marten had been a close friend of the family for years, since before Three married Sandra Wheaten. There were rumors that Marten was Sandra's lover before and after the marriage."

"There are always rumors," Savoy muttered. "Jesus, you should hear some of the ones about Blissy."

Rory slid two folders toward Ian. "Reports on the unattended deaths of Benford Savoy the Third and Lewis Marten."

Ian flipped through. It didn't take long. "The same blind two-year-old did the investigation on both of these. Not even dental records on the artist. Just 'It was his house so it must be his charred bones inside it.'"

"Nobody ever heard from Lewis Marten again," Rory said dryly. "Adds some weight to the assumption, don't you think?"

Lacey kept reading from her notes. "Though still in her thirties, and fertile, his widow Sandra Wheaten Savoy never remarries. As before, Morley Forrest remains the faithful factotum in public and power behind the throne in private."

"Hard on the pride," Ian said.

"I'd imagine," Lacey said. "But Morley had a plan. He was grooming his son, Ward, to marry the princess, Gem Savoy, despite the fact that the matriarch of the family was dead-set against it. Forrests were peasant stock, don't you know. Fortunately, the old lady died just in time for the engagement to be announced. Another accident on the ranch did her in. Another Forrest investigated. Another Forrest benefited. *Quelle* shock."

Savoy looked at his watch. "I've got to get back to the hospital."

"Go whenever you like," Ian said. "We'll just keep talking to the sheriff, unless he's going back to watch over the old man, too."

"I'm staying. I'd advise Savoy to sit down and stay."

Savoy gave him a hard look and sat down. Rory began searching through the files.

"Here," Rory said, handing another file to Ian. "Read it."

Ian looked at the sheriff/coroner's report on the Forrest matriarch's unattended death. "Broken neck. Odd."

"What's odd?" Rory asked impatiently. "She was in her seventies and fell off her horse at a dead run."

"My great-uncle was the first deputy at the scene," Ian said.

Rory stopped rubbing his face and focused on Ian.

"Carl says the tracks showed that after being thrown, Mrs. Forrest got to her hands and knees, and then stood and walked ten feet," Ian said. "Tough to do with a broken neck. He also told me that it looked like the horse had been scared right out of its steel shoes by something jumping out of a bush."

"No tracks were mentioned in the report," Rory said.

"My great-uncle said the ground had been swept before anybody got there."

Rory's eyes narrowed. "What did the sheriff say?"

"Sheriff Forrest wasn't impressed with the idea of someone spooking the horse and then finishing the job when the fall didn't kill her."

"What?" Savoy jumped to his feet. "Are you suggesting that she was *murdered*?"

"The ranch worker who found her was so upset, according to the report," Lacey continued, "that he went back to Mexico as soon as he talked to the sheriff about how he found the old lady with a broken neck. He didn't talk to anybody else, apparently, not even his buddies. Just took his family and left. The sheriff didn't see anything odd about that, either."

Rory sat still, listening. And thinking. "Is that all?"

"A few days later," Ian said, "Gem duly married Ward Forrest. A handful of timely deaths through the years had transformed Morley Forrest from factotum to father-in-law of the first family, and Ward Forrest from county sheriff to king of Moreno County."

"That's absurd," Savoy said curtly.

"No," Ian said, "what passed for police work in this county is absurd. Which brings us to Gem Savoy Forrest."

Another much thicker folder landed in front of Ian. He didn't pick it up. He just looked at the sheriff. "Did you check the corpse for broken fingernails, flesh under the nails, bruise marks?"

"Yes," Rory said curtly. "We didn't find anything except a suicide."

"She leave a note?"

"No."

"Unusual."

Rory sighed and rubbed his face. "Ward probably found it and burned it before I got there. Look, Gem had just been dumped by her latest too-young lover. She put her hair up fancy, made up her face, turned on the outdoor spa to a hundred and four, and swallowed enough vodka and prescription painkillers to make sure she never woke up again."

Lacey went to the first of three canvases leaning

against the wall. "This painting depicts Cross Country Canyon and Three Savoy's murder. If you look closely, you can see two figures watching the fire. The trail of flames point directly to the man holding what is probably the match used to start the blaze. So does the unnaturally bent tree."

Savoy grimaced. "You've got a good imagination."

"So did the sheriff who wrote up the report on Three's death," Ian said.

"The next painting depicts the murder of Lewis Marten," Lacey said. "Note the figure running away, literally stepping off the canvas and—"

"Ms. Quinn," Savoy interrupted savagely, "I know where this is going. But the artist who painted these died decades before my mother did. These canvases are the result of a sick imagination, not fact."

The bedroom door opened, revealing a thin, energetic old man. "Oh, I wouldn't go that far."

Savoy stared. "Who the hell are you?"

"David Quinn, now. Back then I was Lewis Marten. You can call me Grandfather, if you like. Gem was my daughter."

70

Sunlight was a golden glory over the land. There was just enough wind to make the tall grass ripple and shimmer like a second, greener sea. Lacey stood behind her Grandpa Rainbow, oblivious to anything but his painting. Ian stood to one side, watching.

A Savoy Ranch vehicle pulled up beside Ian's rented SUV and parked. Rory Turner got out and walked to Ian. Rory looked older than his age, like a man who hadn't been sleeping well.

" 'Afternoon," Ian said.

Lacey heard and walked quickly over to the men. "I hope you're not planning to talk to him until the light goes."

Rory looked from the gray-haired man to the dark-haired young woman who had ripped his life apart and given his wife a wounded, haunted look. *I'm not a Savoy. I never was. How can that be? How could Grandmother do that to her family? It can't be true!*

Yet it was. Sometimes Rory still had a hard time believing it, but each time he dug harder into the recent past or farther into the deeper past, it was easier to believe. Finding the stolen paintings at the ranch house, along with a safe full of the paintings depicting three ways to die had gone a long way toward making everything real.

"I thought you should know that Ward died a few hours ago," Rory said. "He never admitted calling you, but . . ." Rory shrugged. "It doesn't matter now."

Ian didn't offer any polite social lies about too bad, how sad. He simply nodded.

Lacey didn't even do that much.

"We thought he was going to make it," Rory said. "Then Savoy told him that Angelique White had pulled out of the merger. He just turned his face to the wall. I'd say it broke his heart, but he didn't have one, not the kind we'd understand, anyway. He talked to me before he died." Rory rubbed the back of his hand over his forehead. "You know what a strangler fig is?"

"No," Lacey said.

"It's a jungle plant that starts out as a seed that lodges in the crotch of a big, thriving tree," Rory said. "The seed puts out some leaves, sends down a root or two dangling toward the ground. Then, as the years go by, the roots finally reach the earth and the fig really starts growing. It's a vine, not a tree, so it can't support itself. It wraps around and around the big tree until it finally strangles its host. It's a slow death. Years and years and years. Its leaves take the sun the big tree once lived on, the vines wrapped around the trunk get stronger and stronger. When the tree dies and its trunk rots away, the fig vine lives on supported by its own lethal coils. That's what Morley Forrest was, a strangler fig who got started by cleaning up after Benford the Second and then by blackmailing Sandra Wheaton over the true identity of her daughter's father. Then he married his son into the family."

"Ward wasn't any angel," Lacey said.

Rory shook his head. "No, no he wasn't. He helped his daddy kill Three. He torched Lewis Marten's studio, not knowing that the man sleeping inside was one of Marten's rootless artist friends, not Marten himself. Then the Forrests settled in to take over everything the Savoys owned."

"Must have been real interesting when the first painting turned up with a blackmail demand," Ian said, looking at the gray-haired artist who wasn't any man's idea of an angel.

Rory laughed without humor. "Yeah. They weren't happy to know that not only had Marten escaped, he'd followed the sheriff when he drove Three home from a party and seen them push Three's car into the ravine, then set fire to everything. They paid for the painting of Three's death, of course. Numbered overseas account."

"And they sweated," Lacey said, smiling narrowly, "each time a new painting came with another demand. Grandfather liked that better than the money he got, though he liked the money well enough."

"Don't expect me to admire the bastard," Rory said.

"I don't."

"Talk about chutzpah," Rory said. "Selling his own unsigned paintings to greedy gallery owners."

"It almost got him killed," Ian pointed out.

"That's how Ward managed to track him down a

few years ago," Lacey said, "through the galleries the Forrests patronized. Each time a Marten turned up, Ward got the first call. When Ward got too close, Granddad decided it was time to get out."

"How did Quinn walk away from his truck in the desert and survive without the searchers finding him?" Rory asked. "Or did he tell you?"

Lacey's eyes closed. She didn't like remembering how hollow she'd felt when she was told her grandfather was dead.

"He staged the scene near a dirt bike trail," Ian said. "Then he took a bike out of his truck and rode off. It was a tough five miles to the next road, but he made it."

"Chutzpah." Rory shook his head and looked at Lacey. "Savoy wants to know if you're going to make any claim on the ranch."

"All I want from Savoy Enterprises is freedom for me, my grandfather, and Susa Donovan to paint here before it's all paved over."

"You've got it. And it won't all be paved over."

"You sound certain," she said.

"I am," Rory said. "Bliss and Savoy both decided that they couldn't change the past, but they could take a stab at the future. They'll be negotiating with a nature conservancy as soon as the estate is settled. They decided to turn over all the ranch land from the ocean to the ridgeline." Rory gestured toward the steep hills rising behind them. "The land on the far side will be sold off as quickly as buyers are found. Savoy Ranch is as dead as Ward Forrest."

Rory gave the blackmailing artist a long, hard look before he turned and went back to his vehicle. A door opened, closed, and the white SUV drove off, leaving

Lacey and Ian standing on the bluff where history, beauty, and murder tangled as deeply as light and shadow.

Silently she put her right arm around Ian and leaned against him. He slid his left arm around her and pulled her even closer. They watched as light changed from rich gold to glowing orange. Shadows slid out of the ravines and licked over the rumpled land that fell away to the sea. Eucalyptus trees whispered darkly as fragments of light tangled within their leaves.

When the last burning ember of sun slipped beneath the indigo sea, Ian tipped up Lacey's chin with his cast and kissed her softly. "We better get your grandpa packed up. Your parents are waiting."

"I still can't believe you agreed to drive all the way to Pasadena for dinner."

"It beats having a dead artist staying with us at a killer's hotel." Ian still hadn't forgiven her grandfather for the pain he'd caused by not telling her that he was alive. And for leaving her the paintings that had almost gotten her killed. "I'm figuring on parking the old reprobate with your parents, grabbing you, and beating feet for the foothills of Upland."

"You're kidnapping me?"

"Now you're talking. I'm keeping you, too. But don't worry. My future mother-in-law promised that she'd take care of every detail of the wedding all by herself."

Lacey's breath broke. "Wedding? When did I agree to that?"

"When I agreed to let you paint me any old way you wanted to, any old time you wanted."

"Oh. Then." She looked him up and down and her smile flashed in the twilight. "Yeah, that'll work."

"What are you thinking?" he asked warily.

"Racing stripes."

"Green?"

"Peppermint."

"The color or a flavor?"

She licked her lips. "Good idea."

"I've got lots of good ideas."

"I've got lots of paint."

He gave her a slow, I-can't-wait smile. "I'm frightened."

"Yeah. Right. And I'm still channeling the Queen of Atlantis."

"I've been meaning to talk to you about that, darling. Did their snakes really have racing stripes?"

"Some of them," she said. "Some of them had checks."

"Checks? Bet that tickles."

"Bet you'll find out."

From multi-*New York Times* bestseller
Elizabeth Lowell
comes another glittering novel of nail-biting suspense
The Color of Death

Katherine Jessica Chandler, an up-and-coming jewel cutter, had been handed the opportunity of a lifetime. One of the foremost collectors of gemstones in the world commissioned her to cut the Seven Sins—seven extraordinarily rare sapphires worth millions. Kate was sure this job would do wonders for her reputation in the gem world, until a murderer struck and the Seven Sins disappeared. Whoever was behind the murder and theft would stop at nothing to make his escape, and unless Kate could discover the killer's identity, she would lose not only her career, but her life as well.

Read on for a sneak preview of Elizabeth Lowell's *The Color of Death*.

Kate was so relieved to find Mike Purcell alone in the booth that she gave him a radiant smile. He responded with a leer. When his wife Lois wasn't around, Purcell had the reputation of being a real hound. Until yesterday, Kate hadn't thought much about the gossip. Then she'd learned at first hand just how true the gossip was, and she'd chosen her outfit for today accordingly.

She braced her smile to keep it from slipping, eased her right hand down her blouse to undo a few buttons, and told herself that it was all in a good cause. Apparently unaware of the gap in her clothing, she stepped closer to the case and bent over it.

"Come back to look at the blue sapphire?" Purcell asked slyly, leaning forward over the display case, close enough to sense her body heat. "Or maybe you have something else in mind."

Her smile stiffened, but he didn't notice. His eyes were on the cleavage she'd so generously displayed.

She swallowed hard and settled into the odious business of flirting with a man she'd rather have scraped off her shoes.

"Well, you never know." Kate stroked the hollow of her throat lightly, hoping to distract him from her breasts. It worked for about two seconds. "That is one mighty fine gemstone," she said in a carefully breathless voice.

The sapphire was indeed unusual, but not quite to the point of being a showstopper. At least, good old Purcell must have thought so or he wouldn't have displayed it so openly.

Kate thought Purcell was wrong. That was a gem guaranteed to raise the heart rate of any dealer who saw it.

Maybe Purcell just couldn't resist strutting the stone in front of the other second-tier dealers, she thought, gritting her teeth against her sudden distaste for the man who was older than her father. *Or maybe he knows that McCloud wasn't supposed to tell anyone about the Seven Sins, so he thinks it's safe. Either way, Purcell is slime.*

But all she said aloud was, "Emerald-cut sapphires of that size and quality don't come on the market every day."

"Day?" Purcell straightened and reached into the case without looking away from the smooth, firm tits he'd love to squeeze. "Honeypot, sapphires like this are rarer than a faithful woman. I ought to know. I've helped more than one of the little darlings do the adultery dance. And unlike this sapphire, I gave those gals a real thorough deep-heat treatment, if you get my meaning."

Kate's smile became all teeth. She made a sound like

a terrier sinking canines into a rat. "I still can't believe that the gem hasn't ever been heated. May I look at it again?"

"What are you offering?"

Same as last time, you jackal. A cheap peep show. "I won't be able to say until I look at it again. Reassurance, you know?" Kate said. "I just can't believe it's worth more than twenty-five thousand a carat. Before my client starts rounding up that kind of money, I have to be sure. I mean, this is only the preshow, after all. Lots of world-class gems haven't even been put out yet. Surely you understand?"

The husky hesitation in her voice made Purcell's palms hot. He'd seen bigger tits, but hers were here, now, and he wanted to see more of them.

"Oh, what the hell," he said, pulling out the small box that held the sapphire. "You handled those tweezers real well yesterday, just like a pro. Need a loupe?"

"No, thanks. I brought my own this time. I didn't want to take a chance on dropping yours again."

Besides, only an idiot used the same distraction twice, but pointing that out wasn't any part of Kate's agenda.

He grinned. "You didn't do any harm. You can go looking for a loupe in my lap any old time you want to."

Kate didn't think her acting skills were up to answering. Then she thought of Lee, missing for five months, almost certainly dead and—*Don't go there,* she told herself roughly. *Crying doesn't do a damn bit of good, especially now. Suck it up. You have a job to do.*

"You're way too kind, Mr. Purcell," she said hoarsely. "I felt like such a fool."

"You felt just fine from where I was sitting."

She swallowed hard and fished in the pocket of her jacket. When her fingers wrapped around the cool curve of the loupe, it steadied her. She opened the small 10x magnifying glass and looked at Purcell expectantly.

He waited, hoping that she would come around the glass like she had yesterday. He'd really liked squeezing that firm ass between his thighs and the heavy display case.

She didn't move.

"View's better from here," he said.

She shook her head. "No, you'll just get me all flustered again. I have to keep my mind on my business."

"You sure, honeypot?"

"That you'd get me flustered? I sure am." *And this time I might not be able to stop myself from parking my foot in your crotch.* "You have a way of making a woman forget what she's doing."

He laughed. "So they tell me."

He took the clear top off the box, nudged it toward her, and handed her a pair of jeweler's tweezers.

Ignoring the slick feel of his fingers rubbing over her palm, she positioned the tweezers and picked up the thirty-carat stone. Holding the loupe to one eye, she brought the sapphire closer until it was in focus.

The color was everything a blue sapphire should be. The inclusions didn't detract from the brilliance. The cut was superb.

Show time.

She set the gem back in its box and simultaneously fumbled with the loupe. It smacked against her collarbone and slid down between her breasts. She gave a stifled little shriek and went after the loupe with her right hand. As she fished around in her bra, she flashed more skin at Purcell.

She needn't have worried about holding his attention. He was staring at her breasts so hard he was sweating.

"You turn me into all thumbs," Kate said, smiling at Purcell, "but—"

The rest of her words were lost in a gasp as large, masculine fingers closed over her left hand, all but crushing it.

"C'mon, get a move on it," said a rough, impatient voice. "We're late. I've been looking all over hell for you."

Kate went cold as she glanced up into a stranger's hard, gem-blue eyes.

Scottsdale
Tuesday morning
9:40 A.M.

Sam Groves dragged his prey away from Purcell's booth and out into the hotel lobby.

"Let go of me," Kate said in a low, furious voice.

"Or you'll scream?" he asked without interest.

She said something under her breath.

"Yeah, that's what I thought," he said. "Don't want to call attention to yourself, do you?"

"Mr.—"

"Groves. Sam Groves." He crowded her against a potted plant the size of a delivery truck and took a credential holder out of his hip pocket. A badge flashed gold. "Special Agent, FBI. Any questions?"

"What the hell do you think you're doing?"

"That's my question." He turned over her hand, the hand that he hadn't released from his grip. One blunt finger traced the delicate bump of wax or glue or whatever had held the stone out of sight in her sleeve until it was time to make the switch. "A quick scrape, the stone drops, and it's switched before the mark knows what happened."

She gave him a look that said his deodorant had failed her sniff test.

"Open up," he said, "or I'll have to hurt your fingers."

"You already have."

"You're making me cry." He squeezed harder. "Open up."

"How can I?" she retorted, struggling quietly, uselessly against his grip.

Her dark brown eyes glared up at her captor. If he was bothered by her, attracted to her, or repelled by her, he didn't show it. His attitude made it real clear that he wasn't going to be distracted by a little skin. If anything, he looked bored.

But not careless. Her fingers were white and the hidden stone bit into her flesh from the force of his grip.

He replaced his credentials and moved his hand to her wrist without giving her a chance to escape. "Open up."

With an odd smile, she uncurled her fingers. A forty-carat, emerald-cut blue sapphire gleamed on her palm.

"Surprise, surprise," he said. "Something stuck to your delicate little fingers. Who are you going to sell this to?"

"No one."

"Yeah? You're just switching stones for the hell of it?"

"Something like that."

"You must think I'm as stupid as Purcell."

Kate met Sam's cool blue eyes straight on. The man might be a lot of things, but stupid wasn't one of them. Normally she would have been attracted to his intelligence and old-fashioned male strength. Not today. Today she wished she'd never met the son of a bitch.

"I'm sure you're very bright for a federal robot," she said. "But that doesn't mean you're right. I'm not a thief."

Sam's dark eyebrows rose. He'd met some confident con men in his time, but she was something else.

Federal robot.

He almost laughed. If she only knew how wide of the mark that shot was.

"Not a thief, huh?" he asked lazily. "That blue stone in your hand says you're a liar."

"You're assuming that the stone is valuable enough to be worth stealing."

"I sure am."

"The stone's only real value lies in the time a cutter spent on it."

"Oh, yeah, right," he said, not bothering to hide his impatience.

Kate's chin tilted up. The more her heartbeat settled down from being caught, the madder she got. "I can prove it."

"How?"

"Pick a dealer. Any dealer. Show them the stone and see what they say."

For a long moment, Sam simply looked at his unexpected captive. She had the kind of classy face that made a man want to please her, dark eyes that looked earnest, fine bones, rich black hair, and an unmistakably female shape that the loose clothing couldn't hide. Overall impression was of fresh, businesslike femininity. Intelligent, too. Quick in more than one sense of the word.

If he hadn't seen her pull the switch himself, he would have believed her innocent act.

But he'd seen the switch.

Then he remembered just how much eyewitness testimony was really worth—slightly less than a handful of warm spit. Three eyewitnesses would earnestly tell you that the guy was tall, short, average, thin, fat, average, hairy, bald, average, and looked just like you.

He glanced at his watch. The strike force meeting wouldn't start for another twenty minutes. Whatever else the woman might or might not be, she was more interesting than the pages of the catalogue he'd been thumbing through since the booths opened at nine. She smelled better, too.

And there was always the chance if he crowded her hard enough, she might volunteer some interesting leads into the gem-fencing community. So far the strike force hadn't done much but spend public funds following leads that didn't pan out.

"Okay, Ms. . . ."

"Natalie," Kate said quickly, hoping her mother wouldn't care if her name was borrowed.

"You have a middle and a last name?"

She'd already decided that Smith or Jones was a nonstarter. So she grabbed the first words she thought of: her profession and her mother's maiden name. "Cutter. Middle name Harrison."

"All right, Ms. Natalie Harrison Cutter. You have any ID?"

She was ready for that, too. "Up in my room. You aren't going there."

Sam decided to let it go for now. Without releasing his grip on her, he plucked the stone from her palm. "We'll just walk back to the conference room and see what some dealers think of this stone."

"Let go of me," she said, tugging against his grip.

"Not unless you'd rather wear handcuffs. I've seen you move, sweetheart. Quick and slick."

Kate locked her teeth together against the anger and adrenaline that wanted to spill out in a rush of scathing words. "Typical condescending FBI," she said distinctly. "*Sweetheart.*"

The left corner of Sam's mouth tilted up. "You know a lot of us federal robots, do you?"

"Let's say I'm familiar with the breed."

"The kind of familiarity that leads to contempt?"

Kate's sideways look said it all.

He grinned. "I like your style."

"I'll change it."

"Come with me, Ms. No-ID Natalie. We'll see how wide your sassy streak is."

"If I were a man, you wouldn't call it sassy."

"If you were a man, Purcell wouldn't have been so busy looking at your tits that he took his eyes off the main point—gems. What goes around, comes around. Sweetheart."

She shot him a dark glance, saw that she was being baited, and gritted her teeth.

Then she followed him because there was no other choice except to be dragged behind like a sulky child.

Sam selected the second booth on the left, well away from Purcell. The woman behind the counter was neatly turned out in a southwest-style jacket and black slacks. Her gray hair was cut close, as were her nails. Gems were arranged in the case like a rainbow. While not a very original design, the multicolored arc of gems was striking.

"Good morning, ma'am," Sam said. "Beautiful display you have."

The woman smiled, responding to the approval and warmth in his voice. The fact that the rest of the package was male and easy moving didn't hurt. She might have been old enough to be his mother, but her eyesight was just fine.

"Thank you," she said. "We try to please."

Kate bit the inside of her cheek to keep from screaming—or laughing. Sam was reeling the woman in the same way Kate had reeled in Purcell.

Only Sam didn't have to undo a single button.

Life really isn't fair, Kate thought angrily. *Why couldn't he have been as sleazy as Purcell? But, no. He's a one hundred percent pure FBI male. Clean shaven. Confident. Condescending.*

Oh, lucky me.

"I'm sure you do just that," Sam said, smiling at the dealer. "If you're not too busy, I need your opinion on something."

The woman waved one hand. "If a line forms behind you, I'll kick you out. Until then, how can I help you?"

Sam held out his hand, palm up. The sapphire glowed like a huge blue eye stolen from an alien idol.

The woman's breath came in with an audible sound.

"I say this is worth a lot of money." Sam tilted his head toward his captive. "My sweetheart here doesn't think so. Can you settle the argument for us?"

"That looks like the stone Mike Purcell was bragging on."

"Purcell?" Kate said quickly. "We didn't get it from him. My, uh, sweetie won it in a poker game last night."

"Yeah, she gave me hell on the half shell when I got in late," Sam said.

"If you'd come home a winner," Kate said with lethal sincerity, "I wouldn't have cared when you got in."

"Hey, fifty-eight big ones for a stone like this is winning in any man's book."

"May I examine it?" the dealer asked, pulling a black velvet pad closer and reaching for loupe and tweezers.

"Sure."

The dealer put the loupe to her eye with one hand. With the other, she used the tweezers to pick up the stone and bring it into focus in front of the loupe. She studied it intently for a long moment, shifted a tiny gooseneck light to a better angle, and looked again.

"What are you looking for?" Sam asked.

"Pear-shaped bubbles or curved growth lines," she said absently. "They're sure signs of a synthetic."

"See any?" he pressed.

"Not yet."

Sam gave his captive a sideways look that was just short of predatory.

The dealer set aside the loupe. "I have a spectroscope on the counter behind me . . . ?"

"Sure, use it," Sam said. "I want to be real certain. Unless it will harm the stone."

"None of the tests I use are destructive to the gem."

"You have a microscope, too?" Kate asked.

"Of course."

"Then just cut to the chase," Kate said. "If the stone

is a Chatham synthetic, you'll still get the black bar at 450 on the spectroscope, just like a natural."

The dealer gave Kate a speculative look and passed up the spectroscope for the binocular microscope. She set it on the countertop, put the sapphire in the stone holder, and bent over the eyepieces.

"What will that tell you?" Sam asked his captive.

"If she uses that microscope very carefully—"

"I'm GIA certified," the dealer interrupted mildly. "I know how to use a microscope." She glanced up at Kate. "What am I going to see?"

"Hexagonal or triangular platinum platelets," Kate said succinctly.

The dealer looked at Sam. "Why are you wasting my time? Your girlfriend knows more about sapphires than most of the people in this room."

"He doesn't trust me," Kate said. "That's why we're not married. Just sweethearts."

Sam buried a laugh. Damned if the quick-tongued little con didn't appeal to him.

The dealer turned back to the microscope. She gave the stone a good look before she finally straightened. "I'm afraid your, um, sweetheart is correct. The stone isn't worth what you paid for it."

"Yeah? How come?" Sam said, disappointed. "Sure looks good to me."

"Do you know much about colored gems?" the dealer asked.

"Nope."

"Like I told you, sweetheart," Kate said. "It's pretty, but it's not worth breaking a sweat over."

"No problem," he said easily. "I'm always willing to learn. And sweat."

Kate rolled her eyes.

The dealer smiled. "The stone is a Chatham synthetic. Uncommon, yes, thank God. All the other synthetics fail the spectroscope test."

"You mean that stone isn't a sapphire?" Sam pressed.

"Oh, it's blue sapphire, no question." The dealer looked at Sam's expression and sighed. "Obviously you have trouble believing in the expertise of a woman. There are a lot of male specialists who could do a formal appraisal of this stone, but it will take several days to several weeks and cost you hundreds of dollars."

"Help me out here," Sam said, frowning. "It's really sapphire?"

Subtly Kate tested his hold on her wrist. No change. No discreet escape possible.

Hell.

"Blue sapphire, yes," the dealer said. "Sapphires come in all colors except red."

Sam made an encouraging sound.

"When sapphires are red," the dealer said, "they're called rubies. Both sapphire and ruby have essentially the same specific gravity and—barring the impurities that give color—the same chemical composition."

He managed to look intelligent and confused at the same time. It was one of his best faces for questioning people. "So why isn't this, uh, blue sapphire worth anything?"

"It's synthetic," the dealer said patiently. "Manmade. When you buy gems, you're buying color, rarity, and clarity. The synthetics only have two out of three."

"Not enough to be in the money," Sam said.

"No. Although this is quite well done," she added,

handing back the stone. "The cut is exquisite. Unusual to see that kind of exacting work in synthetic goods. Most of them are machine cut and polished according to a bean counter's formula for maximum return."

Damn right it's exquisite, Kate thought. *I cut it myself.*

And that was one bit of news she wasn't sharing unless she had to.

Sam made a rumbling, grumbling kind of sound that managed to be cuddly rather than fierce. He shoved the stone deep into his jeans pocket. "Why would anyone put all that effort into a fake?"

"Synthetic," the woman corrected instantly.

"Whatever."

"There are several possibilities."

"Such as?"

"Well," the dealer said, "the most likely explanation is that the owner of a natural blue sapphire of that size might have an identically cut synthetic and wear it instead of the more costly stone. It's a way of keeping down insurance rates."

Sam nodded.

"It's also a way of protecting valuable stones from thieves," the dealer continued. "Most gem thieves, particularly the South American gangs, couldn't tell glass from synthetic from natural."

Sam managed not to grimace over the mention of South American gangs. He heard enough of that song from his supervisory special agent and from Ted Sizemore.

You'd think that there was only one nationality of gang on the whole frigging planet.

"Really?" Sam asked. "I wouldn't have thought gem thieves were that stupid."

"There are one or two real smart ones out there," the dealer said unhappily. "I've heard rumors that some dealers were making decoy shipments to thwart those hijackers when there were some particularly fine gems to protect. Perhaps your well-cut stone came from one of those decoys."

"Thanks for your time," Sam said, turning away.

Kate followed because she didn't have a choice. She looked narrowly at him as she lengthened her stride to keep pace.

"Well, sweetheart, what next?" she asked.

His smile was a lot less easygoing than the one he'd given to the dealer. "We go somewhere quiet and talk."

"No."

He raised his left eyebrow. "Why?"

"I don't want to and you don't want to force me."

"What makes you think that?"

"Because you're undercover and don't want to be burned over something that's going nowhere in terms of a bust." She smiled a razor kind of smile. "Right?"

He thought about it. "Close enough. For now."

"Now is all there is."

She jerked her wrist.

He held on just long enough to let her know that she wasn't escaping, he was letting her go. Then he watched her retreat with the lazy interest of a predator that wasn't particularly hungry at the moment. Whatever her game was, it wasn't part of the reason he was in Scottsdale. Until that changed, she was off his menu.

He had bigger fish to catch, gut, and fry.

Carnival Elation

7 Day Exotic Western Caribbean Itinerary

DAY	PORT	ARRIVE	DEPART
Sun	Galveston		4:00 P.M.
Mon	"Fun Day" at Sea		
Tue	Progreso/Merida	8:00 A.M.	4:00 P.M.
Wed	Cozumel	9:00 A.M.	5:00 P.M.
Thu	Belize	8:00 A.M.	6:00 P.M.
Fri	"Fun Day" at Sea		
Sat	"Fun Day" at Sea		
Sun	Galveston	8:00 A.M.	

TERMS AND CONDITIONS

PAYMENT SCHEDULE:
50% due upon booking
Full and final payment due by July 26, 2004

Acceptable forms of payment are Visa, MasterCard, American Express, Discover and checks. The card-holder must be one of the passengers traveling. A fee of $25 will apply for all returned checks. Check payments must be made payable to **Advantage International, LLC and sent to: Advantage International, LLC, 195 North Harbor Drive, Suite 4206, Chicago, IL 60601**

CHANGE/CANCELLATION:
Notice of change/cancellation must be made in writing to Advantage International, LLC.

Change:
Changes in cabin category may be requested and can result in increased rate and penalties. A name change is permitted 60 days or more prior to departure and will incur a penalty of $50 per name change. Deviation from the group schedule and package is a cancellation.

Cancellation:

181 days or more prior to departure	$250 per person
121 - 180 days or more prior to departure	50% of the package price
120 - 61 days prior to departure	75% of the package price
60 days or less prior to departure	100% of the package price (nonrefundable)

US and Canadian citizens are required to present a valid passport or the original birth certificate and state issued photo ID (drivers license). All other nationalities must contact the consulate of the various ports that are visited for verification of documentation.

<u>We strongly recommend trip cancellation insurance!</u>

For further details call 1-877-ADV-NTGE or visit www.GetCaughtReadingatSea.com

---

For booking form and complete information
go to <u>**www.getcaughtreadingatsea.com**</u> or call **1-877-ADV-NTG**

Complete coupon and booking form and mail both to:
**Advantage International, LLC,
195 North Harbor Drive, Suite 4206, Chicago, IL 60601**